FOUR DAYS
TO
TRINITY

Willow River Press is an imprint of Between the Lines Publishing. The Willow River Press name and logo are trademarks of Between the Lines Publishing.

Copyright © 2023 by Bill Mesce, Jr.

Cover design by Suzanne Johnson

Between the Lines Publishing
1769 Lexington Ave N, Ste 286
Roseville MN 55113
btwnthelines.com

First Published: July 2023

ISBN: (Paperback) 978-1-958901-39-7

ISBN: (Ebook) 978-1-958901-40-3

FOUR DAYS TO TRINITY

Bill Mesce, Jr.

preach there are all kinds of truth, your truth and somebody else's,
but behind all of them, there's only one truth,
and that is that there's no truth...
No truth behind all truths is what and this church preach!
Where you come from is gone, where you thought you were going to
never was there,
and where you are is no good unless you can get away from it.
Where is there a place to be?
No place.

Flannery O'Connor,
<u>The Violent Bear It Away</u>

THE FIRST DAY: Boone

Monday morning...

In especially grimly reflective moments, it would occur to Henry Gilmore that the Grapeland Assisted Living Community seemed to be getting more vibrant while Henry Gilmore was growing more dilapidated. He could remember his earliest days as a junior administrator when the place was a plain-faced white clapboard building called the Grapeland Retirement Home, and then it had been the Grapeland Rest Home, the Grapeland Senior Center, and now the Grapeland Assisted etc. Each time the name had changed, the institution had grown a little bigger, gotten a little nicer, the white clapboard front building taking on a colonnaded façade and ultimately reduced solely to reception and administration while the clientele resided in low, sleek dormitories. With each new addition to the institution came an expanded roster of residents. More residents meant a longer list of relatives who tried to assuage their guilt of boarding Maw-Maw and Paw-Paw at Grapeland. This was done by bothering, badgering, and nit-picking Henry Gilmore to distraction. Consequently, Henry Gilmore's hair receded further, the knot in his stomach grew more painful, and the droop to his shoulders became more pronounced.

Henry Gilmore turned off the ignition of his frightfully old Lincoln, but the engine did not cease immediately. It clunked and coughed in a manner quite undignified for a Lincoln, even an aged one, and continued running in a limping, pained fashion until with a final wheeze and sigh it died.

The Lincoln's epileptic spasms brought a similar wheeze and sigh from Henry Gilmore. Taking the bag from Mix Emma's Breakfast Shack with him, Mr. Gilmore carefully locked the Lincoln's door, wondering – as he did every morning – what threat he could possibly be protecting the rusting lump from that wouldn't actually be a mercy in disguise. The engine palpitations were only one of the betrayals of the Lincoln's luxury pedigree, joining the body rot around the wheel wells, and the splits in the vinyl upholstery. Just like the shiny spots on his outdated sky-blue three-piece suit, and the loose screw giving his wire-rimmed glasses a headache-inducing wobble, the Lincoln was just another worry for which he had neither the patience nor financial resources to address.

He stopped at the base of the stairs leading up to the clapboard administration building and gave up another wheeze and sigh because it was looking like the day's headaches were not going to wait until after his morning biscuit. Mrs. White, the head nurse, was waiting at the door. Her quivering, melting face looked even more downturned than usual.

"Yes, Mrs. White?"

"Jess Smith."

"Oh, my…" Which was all the unfulfilling catharsis a non-swearing man like Henry Gilmore allowed himself. He passed Mrs. White in the door and headed down the hall for his office, Mrs. White clopping alongside in her white Crocs. He steeled himself and asked, "What about Jess Smith?"

"There is no Jess Smith."

"Excuse me?"

"Gone."

"Oh, my my *my*…" Mr. Gilmore pushed open the door to his outer office. "'Morning, Miss Frye."

"Good morning, Mr. Gilmore," said the birdish little thing with straying gray hair behind the secretary's desk. "Did Mrs. White -- . Oh, well, there she is."

"Yes, Miss Frye, here she is."

"I suppose she told you about Jess -- "

"She is telling me now, Miss Frye, thank you. No calls, please." Mr. Gilmore went into his office with Mrs. White close behind. He signaled her to close the door and dropped behind his cluttered desk. He pushed mounds of Medicaid and Medicare and prescription drug reimbursement and Social Security paperwork aside and made way for Miz Emma's bag. Grease stains were starting to show through the paper. In a few minutes, the biscuit would have gone from a lovely, squishy softness to a disintegrating sogginess. "Do you have any details, Mrs. White?"

"Jess didn't come down to breakfast. I sent Benjamin to check and he came back and..." She shrugged. "We searched the grounds but haven't found any sign."

Mr. Gilmore pulled open a desk drawer and reached for a Costco-sized bottle of generic aspirin. "What about bed check last night?"

"I asked Vern, but Vern doesn't know."

"Why doesn't Vern know?"

"Because Vern didn't do the bed check."

"And why, God help us, didn't Vern do the bed check?"

"For the same reason Vern doesn't do most of the other things Vern doesn't do – for no particularly good reason. That means Jess might have as much as ten, eleven hours head start."

Oh, *my!* thought Henry Gilmore as he used Miz Emma's coffee to wash down three of the aspirin.

"Should I notify the police?"

Mr. Gilmore shook his head resignedly. "I'll make a call."

"What about Jess's nieces?"

Mr. Gilmore coughed on his coffee. "God, no! This is hardly the first time. Somebody always shows up soon enough with a smiling Jess Smith on their arm. Give me a few minutes and we'll search the grounds, again. Just to be sure."

"We won't have to look hard."

"No?"

"We'll just look for smoke."

"That's not funny, Mrs. White."

He waved her out and waited for the door to close behind her. He reached into Miz Emma's bag for his biscuit, precisely unfolded the waxed paper wrapping and stared sadly at the blob of sodden bread dripping off a gray disc of cold sausage.

Henry Gilmore wrapped the mess back up in its wax paper and dropped it in his wastebasket.

"Shit!"

Spook stirred in the bed, his nose wrinkling at the same smells he'd gone to sleep to, the same smells it seemed he *always* went to sleep to: gasoline, oil, sweat. Stale booze, dead cigarettes, farts. Dope smoke and sex. He looked over at the motel room's other twin bed.

Lenny and his slack-jawed whore were still asleep. One of Lenny's thick biceps – the one carrying a tattoo of a broken heart – was thrown across the whore's ample jellyfish breasts. His bearded face was buried in her tousled mop of bleached blonde hair and dark roots.

Spook swung his legs over the side of the bed. He yawned and stretched, then sat for a moment rubbing the sleep out of his eyes. Beer keg-esque Porky was still asleep on the floor between the beds, wearing nothing but a ragged, long-unlaundered pair of BVDs and – for God knows what reason – his heavy motorcycle boots. Shorty was also asleep on the floor, down by the foot of their beds. With his squat, naked form coated with a mat of hair, he looked like a tatty, garage sale-quality teddy bear.

None of them stirred as Spook stepped over their bodies toward the bathroom. The dozens of empty beer bottles and a drained bottle of tequila huddled on the dresser went a long way toward explaining their unresponsiveness.

Spook did not bother to close the bathroom door while he pissed. He could see himself in the mirror behind the sink as he stood over the toilet. The night clerk had looked apprehensively at Lenny and Shorty and Porky and their long, greasy hair and unkempt ZZ Top beards and thought, Jesus, these three are bad enough… And then he'd looked over to chocolate dark Spook.

Wouldn't he like a room all to himself? the squeaky-voiced clerk had asked. The other three had laughed and stood back to see how Spook would deal with the clerk. Spook had leaned over the counter and tipped his mirrored shades down to the tip of his nose, looking over the tops of the lenses at the little clerk. "I think I'd like to stay with my friends here," his voice deep and raspy, like two sheets of slate grinding against each other.

And that had been the last word out of the clerk. He didn't say anything about the four of them sharing a room for two, or sharing it with the drunken, giggling whore hanging on Lenny's arm, nor did he later say anything about the blaring radio and howling sing-a-longs that went on half the night. In a choice between house policy and survival, the clerk had prosaically opted for keeping his mouth shut.

Spook flushed the toilet then climbed into the shower, taking his time, luxuriating in the hot water and soap washing off the grime that always accumulated on the road. When he stepped out the others were still asleep. They wouldn't shower when they woke up. That smell of sweat and gas and oil, the slick tendrils of their uncombed hair, their sleeveless denim jackets…that was all their flag, their way of letting the straights know the rules and regulations didn't apply to them; that they were one percenters as in the one percent of bikers who weren't respectable, law-abiding, tax-paying gents.

Spook went back to the bedroom, pulled on his jeans and black T-shirt, and slid on his sleeveless denim jacket. On the back of the jacket, in red letters: "Lucifer's Children." Beneath was a picture of a diapered baby devil sitting astride a monster chopper, laughing maniacally, his pointed tail flapping in the breeze.

Spook stamped into his boots with no appreciable stirring effect on the others and went outside. After the dark, air-conditioned room, the heat and brightness of the sun hit him like a wall. The tequila had taken a bigger toll than he'd thought, and he slid on his mirrored shades.

A few rooms down, the Chicano maid had parked her housekeeping cart. She gave him a quick look, then turned away in a poor pretense that his presence didn't unnerve her as she fumbled with her keys and quickly ducked inside a room.

Spook hopped over the locked gate that led to the fenced-off motel pool. The pool was empty; the summer had been brutal, and water too valuable for that kind of indulgence. He draped himself on a lounge chair, fished around in a jacket pocket for the nub of a joint. He lit up and took a deep drag to clear the beer and tequila cobwebs out of his head. He took a second toke, dabbed the joint out on his tongue, and dropped it back into his pocket, then put his head back and closed his eyes.

He slipped in and out of a sunbaked semi-doze for a while. Something between a yawn and a growl from behind stirred him. He turned, saw Lenny standing outside their room door, scratching his paunch, adjusting the crotch of his faded denims. Spook guessed from the high sun it must have been close to noon. He hopped back over the pool fence, followed Lenny as he shuffle-clumped to the office in his heavy black Fryes.

The day clerk was a weedy, pimpled kid looking barely out of high school. Lenny threw a crumpled, grease-spotted fifty-dollar bill on the desk. "Keep the change, friend," he said in a lazy, gravelly drawl.

The clerk didn't take the money, ahemmed and shuffled a bit.

"You got somethin' you wanna say, friend?"

"Well, uh, it's actually *past* check-out time."

To which Lenny responded with a burp, the stale-beer-and-tequila quality of which showed on the flinching clerk's face.

Spook sat in a chair by an end table. Spook threw an ankle across his knee so that the toe of his boot rested an inch or so from a blue ashtray.

The clerk cleared his throat, blinking against Lenny's vapors. "Well, uh, past check-out time y'all gotta get charged for another day."

Lenny's broad, wind-burned face turned into a smile, and he chuckled way down in his throat. "Now, friend, you tellin' me I gotta pay for another day jus' 'cause I overslept a li'l?"

"Check-out time's ten a.m., sir. There's a card says so in every room. It's almost noon."

Lenny turned his smile toward Spook. "You believe this, Randolph? A guy oversleeps a li'l..." Lenny nodded his head, incredulous. "A guy oversleeps a li'l... Look, friend, you got somebody waitin' on this room?"

"Well, no – "

Lenny leaned over the counter. The clerk took a step back. "'N' 'at beaner you got workin' a rooms, she ain't even close to ourn yet, so what a fuck is a difference? I mean, am I right, friend, or am I right?"

Spook gave the ashtray a nudge with his toe, toppling it off the end table, coming apart in a blue spray on the linoleum floor. The clerk winced.

Lenny clapped one of his bear paw-sized hands on the clerk's neck and pulled him toward the counter, walking the line between a friendly gesture and the possibility of slamming his face into the countertop. "This your place, friend?" Lenny asked.

"N-n-no, sir."

"Guy owns it, he your daddy or your uncle or somethin'?"

"No, sir."

"Then fuck it, right friend?"

"Uh -- "

And that big hand with its hard, calloused fingers closed on the clerk's neck, producing discomfort just short of pain with a precise calibration of pressure. "I mean, am I right or am I right?"

A squeeked, "I guess."

"I thought you was a smart boy, friend." Lenny released the clerk's neck, patted him on the cheek. "Polite, too. I like 'at. You'll go far in this business, friend."

Spook followed Lenny outside. Shorty and Porky were already perched on their bikes where the four Harleys were nuzzled together in a fire zone by the office.

"Where's Sleepin' Beauty?" Lenny asked, climbing on his own bike.

"Still sleepin'," Porky said.

"'N' still a beauty," Shorty said. Shorty and Porky both laughed at that, their laughter grating with morning phlegminess. "She's so outta it, I think I coulda slipped it to 'er 'n' 'at bitch'd *still* be snorin'!"

"Well, if I had 'at toot'-pick *you* got, I'm *sure* she woulda slept through it!" Porky laughed.

Shorty didn't laugh. He tried to figure out how he'd let himself open for the cut, but that being too taxing an exercise, he resorted to a desperate, "Fuck you!" and punched Porky painfully in the arm.

Lenny jumped down on his kickstarter. "Well, if 'at pencil-neck in the office gives her any shit, she's always got somethin' she could trade for it."

"Yeah, 'n' 'at kid'll *still* get change back from his dollar!" said Shorty, and he and Porky laughed, friends again.

Spook rolled up next to Lenny and set a gloved index finger firmly on his shoulder.

Lenny looked down at the gloved hand, smiled an I-better-not-be-seeing-what-I'm-seeing smile.

"I told you not to call me that," Spook said.

"Call you what?"

"In the office. You know...*Leonard.*"

Lenny smiled a little wider and Spook let his hand drop.

"Whatever makes you happy, friend. But, um..." And he looked at where Spook's finger had sat on his shoulder, "don't do that again. Ok...friend?" Then Lenny fishtailed his bike through the parking lot gravel and out onto Route 87 heading east. Porky and Shorty followed.

Spook came out of the lot last. As their little squad rumbled down the highway, he laid back a little so Porky and Shorty trading bad jokes and cackles and fuck yous were all lost, and all he could hear was the wind rushing past his ears and the yammering roar of his bike.

Monday afternoon…

The Horseshoe Bar was one of those places that looked like it had seen better days the first day it opened. The bar itself – which was in the shape of a horseshoe, thus the "Horseshoe" moniker – was nicked and notched with use, and the abuse of years of restless pocketknives. The jukebox still played ancient vinyl 45s that had just about worn out their grooves. There were corners in the barroom that had never been dusted. Mouse traps sat behind the toilets in poorly ventilated bathrooms. Garland from God knows how many Christmases ago still hung dull and limp in the front window next to a faded Lone Star beer sign.

But these were little things. By and large, the Horseshoe managed not to be too dingy, too rundown of a watering hole. Walton Dieter Davis (prop.) worked hard to see it remained a more or less respectable neighborhood tavern.

He could keep the floors swept, the pretzels on the bar fresh. There were booths along the back wall with partitions of amber plastic where somebody could have a little something to eat with some semblance of privacy. When the lights were low enough and the jukebox records didn't skip too much, a little romance could be had without having to truck all the way out of town to the Candlelight Inn and their ten-dollar cover charge. Unfortunately, W.D. reflected, while he could throw faux mahogany paneling over the Horseshoe's cinderblock walls to spruce the place up (which he had), there wasn't a hell of a lot he could do to panel over some of his less auspicious clientele.

Like Hank Fletcher. Nearly every weekday on the dot of noon, Hank Fletcher's bulk came rumbling across the street from his realty office for a lunch running more liquid than solid. While W.D. set up Hank's first boilermaker, Hank stood by the bar, slipped his suit jacket off and laid it neatly across a neighboring bar stool. He'd loosen his tie and collar, climb up on a stool and set his splayed fingers down on the bar, making a frame in which W.D. was supposed to center his shot and frosted mug of Coors. "Center target," Hank called it.

The first boilermaker usually carried Hank through a discussion of the day's realty business, the weather, and the Houston Astros. Toward the end of his second shot, he'd start getting political and loud. He was now making a frame on the bar and nodding at W.D. to put his third one "center target."

"What they oughta should do is jus' *nuke* 'em sumbitches. Nuke 'em *all!*"

Cecil Tredway's head bobbed up and down like a dashboard dog doll. "Fuckin' A. Nuke 'em till they fuckin' *glow!* Hey-hey, W.D., I think I'm due here."

Cecil Tredway was another somebody W.D. felt he could do without; sitting at the bar off-putting respectable-type patrons, giving them the idea the place was a hang-out for retards. Cecil would truck on over at lunchtime straight from his Texaco station and plop at the bar not caring there was as much grease on his coveralls as in his stratospherically pompadoured hair.

W.D. reached into the cooler under the bar and fished a chilled can of Pearl up from the bottom. He flipped the can open and set it down next to the mug Cecil hadn't bothered to use with his first two beers.

"None a this woulda happened iffen ol' George a First had done it right," Hank Fletcher continued with impolitic volume. "Tweren't nothin' 'tween us 'n' Bag-gawddam-dad but some towel-head inna toll booth. Shoulda jus' bulldozed 'at li'l fucker 'n' gone up there 'n' run ol' Say-dam to ground. Iffen we'd a done it right back *then*, wouldna been no call ta hafta go back 'n' do it all *over* again, 'n' all these other crazy fuckers woulda been too scared to come outta their damn holes!"

"Fuckin' A," said Cecil.

""N' then we finally *do* get rid a ol' Say-dam for 'em 'n' how do they say, 'Thanks'? Damn, iffen they's supposed to be our friends, gimme some enemies why dontcha! To my mind, we should drop some nukes onna whole mess of 'em! All 'em damn A-rabs! Nuke a whole gawddamn buncha ragheads from those gawddamn Eye-ran people to them crazy fuckers choppin' peoples's heads off! Supposed to be our friends, huh? Friends my ass! Drop one square center target on 'at Khomeni feller, too!" He pronounced it Ko-meanie.

"I think Khomeni's already dead, Hank," Cecil said.

W.D. gave himself a break from the harangue to check and see if his other customers needed any freshening. There was old Buford Welmont, sitting off by himself at one end of the bar. W.D. could always tell how far Buford had gone through his Social Security check by how slowly he nursed his beers. Buford must've been down to his last few dollars; he'd been milking his Coors so long, W.D. figured he couldn't've gotten a head on it with a box of bubble bath.

Smitty McKee was sitting by himself at the other end of the bar. Smitty hadn't been too talkative since the housing downturn had made his one-man carpentry business more a hobby than a source of income.

Hank hadn't heard Cecil's Khomeni comment. Or didn't care. "We-all ain't got *no* friends over there. I'm not one to talk down George a First, but all these shit-for-brainses we got in there now, I gotta say I don't know what the hell goes through their heads makes 'em think anybody over there wants to hold hands with us. You ever see them big long curved swords them fellers got? Like on Sinbad or somethin'? They got 'at curve on 'em so they can stab ya inna back while they're still smilin' in your face! Nuke a whole gawddamn bunch, I say, 'n' just *take* the gawddamn oil like ol' Trump said!"

W.D. finished pouring a newly beckoned-for shot in Hank's center target. "I hope you're countin' on a slow afternoon at the office," he said.

Hank still wasn't listening which was what usually happened by his third round. "Hell, *we* found it! Dumbass sumbitches think oil is somethin' to keep the curl outta your hair! Who do y'all think runs all 'em gawddamn drillin' machines? A-rabs? Hah! It's *us, our* people! *They* ain't got no brains for that!

Shee-yet, an A-rab ain't nothin' more 'n' a nigger with a little sunblock! When's a last time any y'all seen a nigger on an oil rig? 'Member that nigger W.D. had inna kitchen for a while las' year? He was an o.k. boy, but gawd*damn*! Ya had to show 'im which way to put bread inna toaster! Any machine ain't a Cadillac goes right over them nappy li'l heads."

"Fuckin' A," Cecil said, nodding.

W.D. rolled his eyes. After three or four beers, Cecil would nod at the weather report.

W.D. started to put the whiskey bottle back, but Thelma Plover gave him a whistle from over by the jukebox. She held out her glass.

"Why'ntcha bring me over some change, hon?" she said. She thought she was sounding sultry, but the day's liquor had already produced an unattractive slur, and years of it had given her a doughy, blotchy face and a midriff bulge not served well by her too-snug jeans or lace-trimmed crop top. "If we gotta hear noise in this place, it should leastways have a melody."

W.D. came out from behind the bar, handed her some quarters and poured her a short one.

"Don't be so stingy," she said, nodding at her glass.

"One at a time, 'kay, Thelma?"

She patted his cheek. "You're a good fella, hon."

"Sure I am." If I was *really* a good fella, W.D. thought on his way back to the bar, I'd've cut you off three shots ago and thrown you out on your ass for your own good.

Change clinked into the jukebox and some sad George Jones thing crackled out of the speakers. W.D. hoped Thelma wouldn't start crying. She was close to the stage where she usually parked in a far booth and started crying when the booze mixed with sad songs.

Sunlight flashed through the bar as the front door opened and swung shut.

"Hey, Jed!" W.D. called out.

"Hey, Dub. Jee-*sus*, 's hot 'nough to boil spit onna sidewalk out there." A young fellow in work clothes climbed up on a stool and thunked his hard hat on to the bar. He ran a thick forearm across his forehead, wiping at the sweat.

"Hey there, Hank, how many mansions you sold today? Betcha they'd move a hell of a lot faster iffen you spent more time over *there* 'n' less time in *here*."

Hank humphed. "The way things are today I couldn't move a house with dynamite. Ask Smitty over there. I don't think he's worked on so much a doghouse this month, eh, Smitty?"

"I woulda been lucky to get the doghouse," Smitty said.

"Gimme anything cold 'n' I got some food to go here," Jed said waving a scribble-covered piece of paper.

"Hey, Sanchez!" W.D. called.

A small, burned-brown Chicano with a thick mustache peeked out the kitchen door.

"Ah!" Hank declared. "The loyal San-cho Pan-za!"

Sanchez smiled in well-practiced subservience.

"Here." Jed pushed the paper at Sanchez. "I ain't gonna read all this shit."

Sanchez squinted at the paper and went into his "angry Mex" routine, grumbling in machine gun-fast Spanish. W.D. knew Sanchez did it because it always amused the customers which was good for tips. "I no can' read dees! He wri' like doctor!"

"Whatever they get they get," Jed said.

W.D. set a mug down in front of Jed and they both laughed. "Hell, yeah!"

Sanchez, still squinting at the paper, went back into the kitchen.

The door flashed again. W.D. saw a couple hurry for the back booths. He picked up his order pad and started for the table but before he could even get out from behind the bar, the man had come over.

"You don't have to wait on us, W.D."

"'S o.k., Charlie."

Charlie Jeter gently took W.D. and steered him along the bar away from the booth. "Just a couple brews and maybe a couple chili dogs, W.D."

"Fine."

"'N' look … when they come up? Just give a yell, I'll come get 'em."

"Whatever you say, Charlie."

W.D. stuck his head in the kitchen door, passed the order to Sanchez, who, out of sight of the people at the bar, had dropped the angry Mex thing and was slapping meat on the crackling flattop with a casino dealer's efficiency. W.D. took his place back at the bar.

"Hey, Dub," Jed waved W.D. over. Quietly: "Ain't 'at Jeter from down to the furniture rental place?"

"Yeah, why?"

"You know who he's got with him?"

"Didn't really see."

"You know Ida Sue Reilly?"

Cecil perked up. "That checker from the Piggly Wiggly?"

Hank was listening, too. He'd finally heard something of more interest to him than himself. "That li'l bitty blonde with 'em grade A jumbo chabobs?"

"The one 'n' only," Jed said.

"Damn, 'at girl don't need to use her hands to run up the register," Cecil said. "She jus' gotta lean forward," and he offered a demonstration.

"She's only 'bout six damn years old," Jed tsk-tsked.

"Well, if Missus Jeter catches those two, neither of 'em is gonna get any older," W.D. said.

Jed abruptly stopped his share of the chortling and his head went up like a spooked goose: "Hey!" All heads at the bar turned to where he was looking.

"I didn't even see him come in," W.D. said.

"What a hell's *he* doin' here?" Hank asked.

"Hey, Reverend!" W.D. called.

Owen Dawson waved back. He had unfolded a metal tripod and was now fixing a camcorder on top.

"Not used to seein' you 'round here, Reverend," W.D. said.

Dawson shrugged and smiled meaninglessly.

"I almos' didn't reckanize you in your civies there, Reverend," Cecil Tredway said.

Instead of his usual clerical garb, Dawson was wearing boots and jeans and a khaki work shirt.

"Maybe he's goin' undercover," Hank chuckled. "Maybe he's doin' an expo-*zay* on the evils a drink or somethin'. Speakin' a which, how 'bout pourin' me a little more evil in ol' center target there, W.D."

W.D. wasn't paying attention. He was watching Dawson. As the reverend fiddled with his video hardware, W.D. was struck at how he looked -- ...well, just *not right* being there. It wasn't just about Dawson being a churchman and this being a saloon, although that was part of it. It was more like Dawson was a kid going where kids didn't belong.

Whether Dawson was wearing his reverend's duds or his civvies, like now, they hung loose on his small, bony frame like a kid wearing his big brother's hand-me-downs. He had a small-featured face, smooth and white, almost girly, and a head of girly limp, yellow hair. He had to be in his 20s, W.D. figured, him having had to graduate seminary school and whatever else church people had to do to become church people, but damned if he didn't look, especially from a distance, like he wasn't old enough to drive.

Dawson now had the camera running on automatic and came around to stand in front of the lens. He cleared his throat. "This here is The Horseshoe Bar and Grille in beautiful downtown Boone, Texas," he announced to the little microphone atop the camera. "These are some of the noonday regulars you see seated behind me. These *are* the regulars, aren't they, Mr. Davis? Come in like clockwork every afternoon, don't they?"

W.D. blinked, confused. "Hey, uh, Reverend, what-all's goin' on -- "

"For a start, let me introduce W.D. Davis, bartender and owner," Dawson said. He stood by the bar, put an arm around W.D.'s thick neck, and smiled at the camera. "Haven't seen you in church lately, Mr. Davis."

"Well, I -- "

"In fact, I don't know that I've *ever* seen you in church, Mr. Davis."

"Uh -- "

"Come on and show the viewers those pearly whites, Mr. Davis."

W.D. smiled politely at the camera then delicately slipped out from under Dawson's arm. "Look, Reverend -- "

But Dawson was already off, moving down the bar. "Over here: Cecil Tredway, auto mechanic extraordinaire, somebody else that prefers sleeping late on Sunday morning to keeping company with the Lord."

Cecil blushed. "Ain't 'at, Preacher, it's jus' -- "

"And here's Hank Fletcher, one of our prosperous local businessmen who -- . Oh!" Dawson had caught sight of Charlie Jeter and Ida Sue in their corner booth. His smile grew wider.

"Oh-oh," W.D. moaned.

Dawson went back to his camera and swiveled it around toward Charlie and Ida Sue.

"Hey, Reverend," W.D. cautioned, "I don't think you -- "

"And here I think we have a couple of the local inhabitants engaged in what I believe is referred to as a *flagrante delecto.*"

Charlie Jeter was already on his feet. "Time to go, Ida Sue."

It was all going a little fast for Ida Sue. She was still sitting in the booth, eyes wide and puzzled as they looked back at the wider and colder eye of the camera while she rambled on about how she hadn't gotten her chili dog yet.

Charlie Jeter went up to Dawson. "Ya know, Preacher, anybody else I'd pop one."

Dawson didn't look up from the camera's viewfinder. "I wouldn't blame you, either Mr. Jeter. Hey, there, Ida Sue! Let's have a smile!"

"Ida Sue!" Charlie Jeter barked. "C'mon! Put it in gear!"

Which was enough to snap Ida Sue out of her trance and forget about her chili dog. As Ida Sue's firm little tush disappeared out the door, ushered out by a shoving Charlie Jeter, Dawson turned the camera back around to the bar. He made sure it was running on its own before taking a stool at the head of the curved bar.

Jed slid off his stool and headed for the door.

"Hey, Jed! Where ya goin'?" W.D. called. "What about those lunches?"

"Catch ya some other time, Dub," and Jed was gone.

Smitty was slipping off his stool, too.

"Smitty -- "

"Gettin' a little strange in here, W.D. Even for me."

Red and angry, W.D. turned to Dawson. "Reverend, meanin' no disrespect or nothin', but you're the worst thing for this business since Prohibition. Mind me askin' jus' what in hell you're up to?"

"Making a movie, Mr. Davis. Hey, what're these folks here drinking? What's in that little glass, Mr. Fletcher?"

"Hm?" Hank had been so fascinated by the goings-on it took him a moment to realize Dawson was speaking to him. "*This* glass?"

"Yes, that little one there."

"Whiskey. Wild Turkey. The good stuff."

"Tell you what, Mr. Davis, why don't you pour me one of those little glasses of that 'good stuff'."

W.D. wasn't angry anymore. Too puzzled for that. "You want a shot...?"

"Of that good stuff. Wild Turkey you said, right, Mr. Fletcher? Some Wild Turkey, Mr. Davis."

W.D. leaned close to Dawson. "Reverend, you sure you know what you're doing?"

"Do you treat every customer that asks you for a drink this way? Would you like to see my I.D.?"

"Oh, no, Reverend," W.D. apologized. "It's jus' this ain't zackly a little sherry at the parsonage. But, you want a drink, you'll get a drink. Though I, uh, I'd appreciate it if you'd turn off that damn camera first."

"Not until I toast my movie," Dawson said.

Cecil Tredway leaned toward Dawson. "We was all sayin' how we hardly reckanized you outta your uniform so to speak, Preacher."

"It's a new day, Mr. Tredway. Turning over a new leaf. Saw myself in the mirror this morning and hardly recognized myself. Is that Buford Welmont over there?"

Buford held up his flat beer in salute.

"Mr. Welmont has a tough row to hoe, Mr. Davis," Dawson said. "Why don't you give him a fresh one and put it on my tab. Isn't that what they say: 'on my tab'?"

"You have to run a tab first, Reverend," W.D. said. He set a glass on the bar in front of Dawson and poured a light shot. "But whatever you say."

Dawson took the glass and held it up in the air. He turned toward the camera and raised his glass. "Ladies and gentlemen -- "

"We're a little shy on ladies here, Reverend, thanks to you."

"What do you mean by that, W.D.?" came Thelma's slurred voice from one of the back booths.

"Sorry, Thelm," W.D. said. "Forgot you were there."

Dawson stood up on the foot rungs of his stool. "Unaccustomed as I am to public speaking without the sheltering benefit of the pulpit, I'd nevertheless like to toast my film project." He tossed the drink down. His eyes screwed closed, and his mouth dropped open as he gasped for air.

Hank and Cecil laughed.

"Now that you practically managed to empty my place out, Reverend, you want to turn off 'at fu-, uh, the damn camera? Please?"

"My toast now done; I shall abide by our agreement."

While Dawson bent over his camera, light from the doorway flashed in the bar, again, and in came Bob Wheeler and Elwood Poteet. Elwood was plucking at his white shirt where it was sweat-stuck under his arms and complaining about the worst thing in the world was bleacher seats during an 11-inning one-hit loss for the Astros in 90 percent humidity. He stopped mid-sentence and Bob Wheeler froze right along with him at the sight of Owen Dawson and his camcorder.

"Owen!" Bob said.

"Afternoon, Robert," Dawson said. "I didn't know you were one of the habitués here."

"One of the *what?*"

"And I see that our esteemed editor of the local municipal journal is with you. As I recall, there *is* something of a tradition of libation in the literary professions, is there not, Elwood?"

Elwood Poteet leaned forward, squinting through his wire-rimmed glasses. "You look a little lit there yourself, Owen."

"Perceptive as a journalist should be, Elwood! Bravo!" Dawson headed back for the bar. "Mr. Davis, drinks for everybody including my good *compadres*, Mr. Wheeler and Mr. Poteet."

W.D. looked around to where Jed, Smitty, Charlie Jeter and Ida Sue had been sitting. "For everybody. Wow. Sure you can cover that, Reverend?"

Bob Wheeler stood next to Dawson at the bar. "Owen, what in a name of sweet Jesus are you doing?"

"Whatever it is, take some comfort that it is *not* in the name of sweet Jesus, Robert. Of that I can assure you."

W.D. had a bottle poised over Dawson's glass. "You goin' for another one there, Reverend?"

"Sure he is, W.D.!" said Cecil Tredway, enjoying the show. He reached into his pocket for some bills. "I'll pop for the preacher."

"You want to tell me what's going on, Owen?" Bob asked.

"The preacher there is makin' hisself a movie," Hank said. "Ain't 'at right, Preacher? Ain't 'at whatcha said?"

"Please, my friends," Dawson said, "the name is Owen. *Owen.*"

"What movie?" Bob asked.

"Yeah, uh, *Owen,*" Cecil said. "What's the name a your movie?"

Dawson's Wild Turkey-glazed eyes blinked. "Name? Name? It doesn't really have a name come to think of it."

By now Thelma Plover had come over to the bar for her Dawson-sponsored refill. "What's this here movie of yours about?" she asked.

"Ah, dear lady, that I can't quite tell you," Dawson grinned mischievously. "You'll just have to wait until it comes out."

"'S'got a love story in it?" Thelma asked hopefully. "All good movies got love stories."

"Oh, it's a love story all right," Dawson said. "Indeed! But all I can tell you is it'll be an X-rated movie. Oh, wait, they don't have the X anymore, do they?"

"NC-17," said Cecil Tredway. "That must be some love story."

"It's a movie about life, gentlemen," Dawson said, "and lady. And life, I'm afraid, is X-rated."

"NC-17," said Cecil Tredway.

"Come over here with me, Owen," and Bob Wheeler took Dawson by the elbow, pulling him over to the empty end of the bar. "What the hell're you doing here? What the hell're you doing *period*?"

Dawson leaned back against one of the bar stools. His liquor-stoked grin faded. He suddenly looked tired, sounded it, too. "You heard me, Robert. I'm making a movie."

Bob Wheeler shook his head. "You come in here, get yourself three sheets to the wind and start babbling about making dirty movies... You know how fast something like *that* gets around in a town like *this?*"

"Oh, *yes!*" Dawson said with glum relish. "I *do* know how stories get around a town like this!"

At which Bob Wheeler fidgeted. "Owen, if you're not careful you're liable a get your tail run out a town on a rail."

"Tail on a rail?" The crazed grin was back. "Robert, I had no idea you were such a poet!"

Bob Wheeler sighed with exasperation. "Owen, you look like you're going through a bad time -- "

"Oh, no, Robert, I'm having a *fine* time! Just fine! Robert – do you mind if I call you Bob? I've always been so formal with you, Bob. Bob, old friend, dear friend, I appreciate your concern, your obvious deep, deep concern, but as far as getting run out of town goes…ask me if I care."

"Owen, I'm your friend. Leastways, I consider myself your friend. There's a whole big part of this you're not telling me. What is it?"

A smirking Owen Dawson waved a tut-tutting finger in front of Bob Wheeler's nose. "I can't do that, Bob. It'd spoil the movie for you."

Dawson started to turn away, but Bob Wheeler grabbed him – gently – by the arm. "Does Sarah know about this?"

Dawson's grin turned dark. "No, Bob. But she will." He pushed himself off his stool. "I'd love to stay and chat, Bob, but…" He went to the camera and started to fold up the tripod. "My friends," he announced to the bar, "I'm off! I've got business to tend to."

"What kind a business?" Bob Wheeler asked.

"Now, Bob, do I ever ask you about selling insurance? Moviemaking business! Mr. Davis, what's the damage here?" Dawson slapped two twenties down on the bar. "Will this cover it?"

"If you don't figure in the loss of business."

"Great sense of humor, Mr. Davis. Wished I caught that on camera." Dawson stood in the doorway, gave the group at the bar a grand wave. "See you in the movies!" A flash of light from the doorway and he was gone.

It was quiet in the bar for a moment, except for the twanging jukebox.

"World can always use another love story," Thelma Plover finally said.

"'Specially a dirty one," Cecil Tredway said.

Bob Wheeler turned to Elwood Poteet. "You know what goes on here, Elwood? Some kinda prayer fatigue or something?"

"I have no idea, Bob."

"He said he was turnin' over a new leaf," W.D. said.

Bob Wheeler pulled his cell phone from its belt holster and headed for a remote corner of the barroom as he began punching in numbers.

"Who you calling?" Elwood Poteet asked.

"I'm gonna see if his wife knows what a hell's going on."

Around the corner from the Horseshoe, the neighborhood was one of elm-lined streets, and small, neat postwar houses with tidy lawns. Windcatchers hung from porch awnings and twirled in the hot breeze, wind chimes chimed. There were garden gnomes and plastic flamingos and plaster fawns, borders of white gravel and cedar chips, sprinklers uselessly spraying sun-withered lawns. The heat-cracked sidewalk was adorned with chalked hopscotch grids and adolescent testimonials of love usually in the shape of badly drawn hearts. Tennis shoes thundered up and down porch stairs, bicycles rattled along the uneven squares of the walk.

In the air, the hay-like smell of dried-out lawns, chicken deep-frying, the piquant aroma of lit charcoal heating up old grease on a barbecue grill, the flap and ripple of fresh laundry hanging in backyards.

"Hey, Preacher! Ya look a little lost."

Ten-year-old Ricky Joe Dunlap was tethered to a golden retriever slavering at the end of her leash. The heat had the dog gasping, but she still wouldn't let go of the dirty tennis ball in her mouth.

"Maybe a little," said Owen Dawson.

Ricky Joe had found the preacher standing frozen on the sidewalk, his head up a little like he was listening for something. He was thrown seeing the preacher without his collar and dark suit, looking like anybody else. Ricky Joe didn't know preachers were allowed to do like that.

"You take it easy in this heat, Ricky Joe," the preacher said.

"How 'bout some tricks, Preacher? You got any new tricks today? You comin' back to school with your magic show this Christmas?"

"They're not *tricks*, Ricky Joe. They're *illusions*. An illusion is when you fool somebody into seeing something that's not really there. And I don't have any new ones. All used up."

Ricky Joe felt his face pucker up in an unhappy way. He didn't know what all this stuff about loozens was, but he did like when the preacher did his tricks. He reached a pudgy little hand down to scratch the top of the retriever's head, but that didn't make him feel better.

But then the preacher set down all this hardware he was toting around on his shoulder and held up his left hand. "All right. One last illusion. Making you think something *is* that *isn't*." The preacher's hand came down in a graceful wave that held Ricky Joe's eyes, so the boy didn't see the preacher's right hand dip into his trouser pocket. He only saw the preacher's right hand come from behind his ear brandishing a quarter. Ricky Joe's mouth dropped, and a chuckle coughed in the back of his throat.

"It's not that hard, Ricky Joe," and the preacher handed the quarter to him. "We see what we want to see." He closed the boy's hands in his (Ricky Joe was surprised the preacher's hands didn't look much bigger than his own), and when he took them away, Ricky Joe's hand was empty. The preacher held up his own hands and showed them to be empty, too. "It's just as easy to make things disappear, too, Ricky Joe. Poof." The preacher took the boy's small, soft hand in his, again, and when he released it, the quarter was back in the boy's palm. "Poof."

The dog gave a muffled bark behind the tennis ball and dropped it at the preacher's feet.

"All right, Mollie. One last one for you, too." The preacher picked up the ball and tossed it on one of the lawns so it wouldn't bounce into the street.

Mollie took off barking after the ball pulling Ricky Joe, flush with his twenty-five-cent fortune, along after her at the other end of her leash.

Ricky Joe turned to wave goodbye to the preacher, saw him picking up his gear and setting it back on his shoulder.

"Bye, Preacher." He held up the quarter. "Thanks!"

"Be good, son," the preacher said, so quiet Ricky Joe almost didn't hear it, then he turned and headed on down the street.

"Afternoon, Reverend Dawson!"

"Hey, Reverend Dawson!"

"Howdy, Preacher!"

Dawson touched a finger to his forehead. "Good day, ladies," he said and continued on down the walk.

The town wags called it Widow's Row. There were three of them: Mrs. Dailey, Mrs. Hanratty, and Mrs. Ledbetter. They were cookie cutter copies of each other: each with a similar cheap, floral print housecoat over a cheap, floral print dress, cat's eye spectacles, a thin, piping voice. They alternated lunches on the porches of their three houses, breaking up the routine only to celebrate delivery of their Social Security checks with a trip to the S & S Cafeteria downtown and its "Early Bird Seniors Buffet."

This being Monday made it Mrs. Dailey's day. The three of them sat on Mrs. Dailey's porch, wobbling metal folding tables next to each seat carrying flowered Dixie plates of quarter-sandwiches and cookies. Mrs. Dailey, Mrs. Hanratty, and Mrs. Ledbetter each held a little sandwich gingerly between two fingers in one hand, and a fan or an iced tea in the other. Their blue-tinged heads nodded toward each other as they waved their sandwiches at Owen Dawson in greeting.

"I didn't know they could dress like 'at," Mrs. Dailey said once she was sure Owen Dawson had passed out of earshot.

"Modern times," Mrs. Hanratty said with a slight unhappiness. "They can do all these...*different* things now."

"Remember how Pastor Fritts was?" Mrs. Ledbetter said. "It'd be ninety-eight in a shade, and he wouldn't even take his jacket off in public."

"I suppose this is better," Mrs. Hanratty said. "At least he won't fall over from a stroke like Pastor Fritts."

"Pastor Fritts fell over from a stroke 'cause once he was inside that parsonage he drank like a fish," Mrs. Dailey said.

"Where'd you hear that?" Mrs. Hanratty asked.

Mrs. Daily shook her head signifying it was confidential, but she knew it to be true. "At least he's not one a those Catholic priests. Some a the things *they* get up to..."

"Did you see him just now with that Dunlap boy?" Mrs. Ledbetter asked. "He's always so good with the children. Remembers all their names."

"He remembers *everyone's* name," Mrs. Hanratty said. "I remember when he spoke over Marshall's grave -- "

"That was a beautiful service," Mrs. Ledbetter said.

"Yes," said Mrs. Hanratty, "I would've cried even if it hadn't been my husband's service. But, as I was saying, he remembered everyone's name who was there. You would've thought he'd been the family preacher for years."

"I can't say I care much for that wife a his," Mrs. Dailey said. "She puts on airs."

"It's not airs," Mrs. Hanratty said. "I think she's just shy."

"I don't care what you call it," Mrs. Dailey said. "I remember at the Christmas show over to the grade school last year -- "

"When the reverend did that lovely magic show?" Mrs. Hanratty asked. "Do you remember the magic show?"

"Lovely," Mrs. Ledbetter said.

"Well, that wife a his just wouldn't mix. Sat there all by herself -- "

"Maybe because she's so young," Mrs. Hanratty said.

"They're *both* too darn young," said Mrs. Daily. "Maybe you didn't like it Pastor Fritts didn't have enough sense to take off his jacket in the heat -- "

Mrs. Ledbetter frowned. "I didn't say I didn't *like* -- "

" – and maybe he was a bit of a boozer, but you knew he'd been walkin' the earth long enough to see some a life."

"Maybe that's why he drank," said Mrs. Hanratty.

Mrs. Ledbetter shrugged. "Some people aren't mixers. It's just not their way."

"Then they shouldn't marry preachers," said Mrs. Dailey.

Horace Luce saw Dawson coming and steered his power mower toward the sidewalk. "Hey, there, Reverend!"

Dawson held up a hand to his ear.

Horace throttled the mower back to a loud, uneven idle. "Can't turn 'er off or I might never get this relic started again. Say, Reverend, you comin' by the '42' tournament tomorrow night over to the County Barn?"

"My luck's running a little cold lately, Horace. And I'm not a very good domino player to begin with."

Horace grinned. He tried to whisper something conspiratorially to Dawson but the noise of the mower blocked it out. "Lemme tell you a secret, Reverend," he had to say in a shout when he repeated himself, "the women folk are bakin' pies. I hear one a those pies got your name on it."

"You're putting temptation in the way of the devil," Dawson said.

"We shake the bones 'bout seven," Horace said.

"And the pies?"

"Don't your wife ever feed you, Reverend?" Horace laughed but the hard stare he got back from Dawson turned his laughter nervous. "Well, uh, you got a whole one with your name on it, like I says, whenever you show up."

"We'll see, Horace."

Horace nodded at the camera on Owen's shoulder. "You fixin' to take some home movies or somethin', Reverend? Ya know, my son-in-law got this new one uses one a those disc things 'n' he -- "

"Aft'noon, Mr. Owen. How you? Hot 'un, i'n it?" The old black man had come up from the side of Horace's house. His work twills were soaked with sweat, and he carried a large pair of garden shears over his shoulder. He took off the bandana tied around his forehead and swabbed the sheen of sweat from his face. "Ah finished 'em hedges over 'roun' t'other side a the house, Mr. Horace. Ya got sumpin' else need doin'?

"Just a second, George. Hey, Reverend, you 'member ol' George here -- " Horace turned back to Dawson but the reverend was already gone, walking briskly away, across the street.

Every Monday-through-Friday around noon, Schuyler Kirkland would lock up his hardware store and pop down to the S & S Cafeteria for a quick lunch. He wasn't worried about losing business during his lunch break: everybody else in town was usually having lunch about the same time, too. Truth be told, Schuyler Kirkland didn't get much business on weekdays anyway. Most customers came his way on weekends when the do-it-yourselfers and home-fix-it types came in, sometimes more than once in a day as one of their do-it-yourself projects needed more doing and re-doing and eventually home-fixing. Otherwise, it was just occasional visits from the pros: the Smitty McKees and the like, although the housing business being what it was at the moment, even those gents weren't showing up that much these days.

So, when Mr. Kirkland, key in hand and ready to lock up, heard Owen Dawson calling him from down the block, saw him waving to hold on, to wait a second, he waved Dawson on. His daddy had told him when he used to run the store, "This town ain't so big you can ever afford to walk away from a customer." And with rumors about a Home Depot maybe going up at the Routes 7/75 crossroads, which wouldn't be all that much of a ride from Boone, Mr. Kirkland felt dedicated to cultivating as much goodwill and friendly connection as possible. "They don't buy from no store," his daddy used to tell him. "They buy from *you!*"

"Were you heading out to lunch, Mr. Kirkland?" Dawson asked. "Sorry, didn't mean to hold you up."

Mr. Kirkland smiled as he ushered Dawson inside ahead of him then took his place behind the counter. "Not a problem, Reverend. Hot as it is out there, I'd just a soon stay here in the air conditioning 'n' take care a you."

"Thank you, Mr. Kirkland." Dawson set his camcorder down on the countertop.

"Too hot for the collar today?" Mr. Kirkland asked, pointing at Dawson's neck.

"Too hot for the collar."

Mr. Kirkland touched the camcorder. "My, that's a nice lookin' piece of equipment there. I was thinkin' a gettin' myself one, you know, get movies a the grandkids 'n' 'at kinda thing. I guess you wouldn't call 'em movies with this, huh? Can't get myself to go ahead with it, though. Figure it took me 35 years to figure out my daddy's Bell & Howell 8 'n' I'm not sure I got another 35 in me to fool with this kinda thing. You takin' home movies, Reverend? I guess you'd call 'em home *videos* or somethin' like 'at, hm?"

"Actually, Mr. Kirkland, I've decided to make a movie. Not a home movie. A *real* movie."

"You mean a movie like in-the-movies movie?"

"Something like that."

Mr. Kirkland had been doing business across his countertop since he could see over it. In that time, he'd come to hold as gospel the first lesson his daddy had taught him about doing business across a counter: "The customer is always right." No matter how odd a request or statement, Mr. Kirkland had trained himself to show no more acknowledgment of its oddness than a slight raising of his gray-tufted eyebrows.

Which now rose slightly. "Well, that's an innerestin' thing to be doin'. My daughter's boy's talkin' 'bout goin' to school out to California for that kinda thing. Well, now, what can I do for you, Reverend? I don't sell much for these things, I'm afraid. Probly got some batteries'll fit all right, but that's 'bout all - - "

"Actually, Mr. Kirkland, I'd like to buy a gun."

At which Mr. Kirkland's eyebrows crept upward another degree or two. "A gun?"

"Yes."

"I didn't know you liked huntin'."

"Some kinds of hunting."

"What kind a lines you thinkin' on?"

"I'd like an elephant gun."

At this, Mr. Kirkland's eyebrows lost their sense of restraint and climbed as far as his facial muscles would allow. But 40 years of customer service discipline and his daddy's voice still echoing in his ear nevertheless managed to keep his tone conversational. "An elephant gun? Is that right? Funny thing, when my daddy had this store – I'm goin' back a good long time, now – he had one. Eight gauge shotgun. That thing'd get meat on both ends. I shot it once. Damn near broke my shoulder. Oh, scuse my French, Reverend."

"Consider yourself absolved, Mr. Kirkland."

"Now me, I don't stock those, Reverend. Don't have much call for 'em owin' to us not havin' all that many elephants in these parts."

"Well, those *are* the lines I'm thinking along, Mr. Kirkland."

"Hm." Mr. Kirkland turned and studied the padlocked rack of rifles and shotguns on the wall behind the counter. "Well, I got this." He used his keys to unlock the restraining bar on the rack and took down a shotgun. "Next best thing. Twelve gauge Winchester Super X pump. Be honest, this isn't much of a huntin' gun. Mostly they're for the po-lice, security folks 'n' like 'at, but I knew this feller was sellin' it, 'n' I know some folks like 'at kinda thing, so here we are. Thing is, it's also on the compact side, and since you're a little, oh, well, you're kinda compact yourself, seems like it might fit you better 'n' some a these other ones. "

The shotgun was sleek, the walnut stock was nicked and scratched but still held a bright shine. Mr. Kirkland handed it over and hid a grin when he saw how the weight of the gun pulled on Dawson's twiggy arms. "Heavy, hm?"

"I don't know why, but I didn't think it would be that, well..."

"It may not be an elephant gun, but you miss with the first one 'n' you can just keep pumpin' away. I don't know 'bout an elephant, but if you know what you're doin', you could knock down a house with this thing. Other good thing is, it's an easy shoot. Blind man could use it. Look." Mr. Kirkland took the weapon back. He showed Dawson where the shells slid into the receiver. "Just throw it up, squeeze it off, rack in the next one." He demonstrated, then handed the shotgun back to Dawson and talked him through the steps. "See?" Mr. Kirkland smiled, "awready you look like you been doin' 'at all your life."

Dawson nodded approvingly and set the shotgun down on the counter next to his camera. "You take credit cards?"

"All a big ones. How 'bout some ammo?"

"What's the largest I can get?"

Mr. Kirkland fished around under the counter and came up with a 25-count box. "Magnum double ought buckshot. If you're lookin' to bag somethin' smaller than a big buck... Reverend, you shoot a coon or a weasel with this load 'n' there won't be nothin' left but hair 'n' teeth. You got a deer lease 'round here?"

"I just have a pest problem."

Mr. Kirkland started to slide the box off the counter. "Then you won't be needing -- "

"It's a *big* pest problem."

Mr. Kirkland sighed his customer-is-always-right sigh. "Whatever you say."

"In fact, you better let me have six boxes."

"*Six* boxes?"

"I'll need the practice. You know; until I get the hang of it."

Mr. Kirkland started piling the boxes on the counter.

"And would you do me a favor, Mr. Kirkland?"

"If I can."

"For my movie. It's kind of an adventure movie. Do you mind if I record you handing me the gun as I hand you the credit card?"

Mr. Kirkland's eyebrows started another trip north. "Well, anything for a sale, Reverend. Uh, let me get you to sign the registration form first, ok?"

"Sure."

"It's no big deal," Mr. Kirkland said apologetically.

"I didn't think it was."

Mr. Kirkland set the form down on the counter with a pen. "You know, there's a wait, couple days for the background check."

Dawson frowned. "Couple of days?"

"I don't hear anything 'fore three days, 'n' you can just c'mon down 'n' pick 'er up."

"Three days."

"It's not me, Reverend. That's Federal. If it was up to Texas, I could wrap 'er up right now and send you home together."

"I don't think my problem's going to wait three days." Dawson started to reach for the Visa card he'd laid down on the counter.

"Well, hold on there, Reverend." Mr. Kirkland paused, considered, decided. "It's not like I don't know you. Don't tell nobody I did this, but I'll wrap 'er up for you, you go on 'n' take 'er. I'll send in the paperwork 'n' all, and we-all'll just pretend you came in three days from now."

"I appreciate that, Mr. Kirkland, thank you."

"I mean, you bein' clergy 'n' all. I'll wrap 'er up, I got this booklet I'm puttin' in with it. You know; how to keep 'er clean 'n' the like."

Mr. Kirkland wrapped the Winchester in brown paper and tied it up with string, then did the same for the shells. He set the two packages down on the counter as Dawson finished his part of the form. Mr. Kirkland scanned it to make sure Dawson had filled it out correctly. "Ok, now I got to ask you a couple questions. It's just a formality. You know."

"Sure."

"Have you ever been convicted of a felony?" Mr. Kirkland read from the form.

"Not yet," and they shared a laugh.

Mr. Kirkland checked off the appropriate box on the form and moved to the next question. "Have you ever been committed to a mental institution? Is that another 'not yet'?"

They laughed, again.

"And last but not least, do you use drugs or have you ever been addicted to drugs?"

"Nope."

Mr. Kirkland set the form back down on the counter. "'At 'bout does it, Reverend. Just sign right on 'at line there. Good. Now what was it you wanted me to do for this movie a yours?"

Dawson began to set up his tripod and mount the camera. "I'll hand you the credit card, you hand me the gun."

"That's all?"

"That's all."

"And, uh, Reverend, I don't mean to beat it to death, but this business 'bout me lettin' you take the gun without the wait period -- "

"Mr. Kirkland, I promise you: I won't tell a living soul."

Dawson was only a few steps out of Kirkland's when Elwood Poteet's Explorer pulled up, its tires chirping as Elwood pulled too close to the curb. Elwood leaned over and popped the passenger door open. "Hey, Owen! I've been looking for you!"

"Here I am."

"You got quite a load there, Owen. Why don't you throw all that stuff in the back and I'll give you a lift." Elwood noted the brown paper oblong as Dawson set it down on the rear seat. "You taking up hunting, Owen?"

"It's a prop for the movie I'm making," Dawson said as he slid into the front seat.

"Where you heading? The parsonage?"

Dawson nodded and Elwood pulled away from the curb. Elwood shifted in his seat and fidgeted with the air conditioning control. "No matter how cold I get this thing, never seems cold enough when it gets this hot."

"You have something on your mind, Elwood? Besides the heat?"

Elwood smiled embarrassedly. "Well..."

"Yes?"

"I just want to get it clear on what you were saying back there at the Horseshoe."

"That doesn't speak at all well of you as a reporter, Elwood. I thought a good reporter was supposed to be observant, have an eye for detail -- "

"Owen, let's just say I'm not used to seeing reputable ministers red in the face with good whiskey talking about making dirty movies."

"I didn't say a dirty movie, Elwood. I said an X-rated movie. Or whatever they call them these days."

"Whatever. Owen, I consider myself a good newspaperman and a good Christian. Church ministers making adults-only movies are newsworthy, but the Christian in me says before I go putting something like that in the paper, I'm going to talk to you first."

"*After* which you *will* put it in the paper."

It wasn't a question or a condemnation. The most unsettling thing for Elwood Poteet was that it sounded like Dawson was *telling* him to put it in the paper.

"Owen, you and me, besides being friends, we've got one thing in common: our business is the truth."

"Ahhh," Dawson said, and he turned to look at the well-kept houses and bleached lawns gliding by. "The truth."

"So, I'm asking you what the righteous truth to this matter is?"

"The righteous truth, Elwood, is that I *am* making an adults-only movie, and I hope you'll feel free to print that. As a matter of fact, why don't you take a picture of me with my camera for the story? If you don't have your camera with you, I have one at the parsonage. I can just run in -- "

"Owen!" Elwood cut in, exasperated. "Can I speak honestly?"

"Please."

"Without getting into whether or not it's an honest fact, the people around here fancy themselves good Christians."

"Just like you, right, Elwood?"

Elwood flushed. He flicked his eyes from the road to Dawson and caught a flash of a wide grin.

"Owen, if I print this story, they will tar and feather you. I mean that literally: tar and feather you. You are not some fuzzy head from north a the Mason Dixon who doesn't know how things work down here. This is meat and potatoes country, and the preacher eats chicken on Sunday. This is *not* San Francisco where some fag priest crusader gets into the *avant garde* theater to open men's minds to the inequities of western civilization. Down here, 'politically correct' means having the stars 'n' bars hanging next to your stars 'n' stripes on holidays." Elwood took another glance over at Dawson.

The preacher's eyes were aimed back out the window. He wasn't smiling now. "Print the story, Elwood."

Elwood ran a hand over his mouth. It came away damp. He wiped the sweat on his pants leg. "Just so I understand, Owen; you *want* to commit suicide?"

"Elwood, I don't know how you can be as good a newspaperman as you keep telling me you are if you're having such a problem with the English language. Print the story. Tell *other* people to print it. Do what newspapermen do, Elwood: print the truth."

Elwood was still shaking his head when he drew up in front of the parsonage. Dawson climbed out, reached for his camera and tripod, the wrapped shotgun and shells. "Owen, what does Sarah think about all this? Have you talked about this with her?"

"Not yet, Elwood, but don't worry; I will."

"Why don't I come in and the three of us sit down -- "

"She's not home just now, Elwood. Thank you for the ride…"

Elwood sensed a heaviness pass over Dawson for a moment, the way a cloud's shadow slides across pastureland.

"…and for your concern. I do appreciate it. You're a good friend, Elwood." Then Dawson's face broke into that annoyingly blithe grin. "Now; what about that picture of me?"

<h1 style="text-align:center">Monday evening...</h1>

"Now pitcher this," said Patrolman Billy Ray Barnes. He slid out from behind his scuffed desk and stood in the middle of the small office. He put his booted feet apart, leaned his slim frame back on his heels, cocked his head and stuck his thumbs in his gun belt. He was sure he looked like a gunfighter.

"I'm pitcherin', Billy Ray," said an enthusiastically engaged Arva May Arlin. She didn't look much out of high school and she wasn't. Her dimpled face was still round with baby fat, and it was a trait carried on through her entire chassis producing a not unattractive squeezability at the proper places under her short, print dress.

"Ok, now, pitcher this," Billy Ray said, again, seeing no reason not to enjoy the same dramatic moment twice. "I'm standin' there face to face 'n' toe to toe with two a the meanest, orneriest hombres you ever did see! Bad ugly 'n' bad mean, awright? 'N' these two ol' boys got them cold eyes, ya know? Killer's eyes? Colder 'n' a brass toilet seat on the shady side of an iceberg, know what I mean?"

Arva May's wide, blue eyes got wider and bluer (so it seemed to Billy Ray) as she nodded in understanding. "And then, Billy? Sweet Billy? Did they hurt my sweet Billy?"

"Well, Sweet Billy? Did they hurtcha? Huh? Did they?" The deep, raspy voice came from the front door. Billy Ray turned and saw the beer-bellied bulk of Boone Police Chief Clyde Thomas in the doorway. Billy Ray was still trying to figure out why he hadn't heard the door open when Clyde said, "'Cause if *they* didn't, *I* just might if you didn't do all what you were supposed to do today."

Clyde Thomas was in his blue seersucker suit which made for an awful lot of blue seersucker. It was his courthouse suit, and any given wearing might signify a bad day of testifying, or a bad day of budget wrangling, or maybe a bad day of politicking, but never anything good, and never anything likely to put the chief in a good mood. This time, it signaled an expedition to the county seat to plead for funding to replace one of the police department's three decrepit marked patrol cars.

"Hey, Chief," Billy Ray said, trying to regain his professional composure. "So, we get the new unit? I still like the idea a one a them SUVs. Half them new see-dans look like a big ol' sex organ on wheels, 'n' you need somethin' with a little more *hmmph* than 'at if y'all're gonna get some respect out there."

Arva May marveled at the wit and worldliness in Billy Ray's observations. Billy Ray saw her adoration and gave her a bit of a smiled Thank you, li'l lady, we do aim to impress.

"Arva May," Clyde said politely, "would you mind toddlin' on home? Sweet Billy here has po-lice work to tend to. You know; roundin' up mean, ornery types 'n' such."

"I understand, Chief. Sweet Billy, I'll be dyin' to hear the end a your story. Call me later?"

Billy Ray escorted her to the door. "Arva May, I wisht you wouldn't call me that in front a people," he whispered in her ear.

"I'm sorry, Billy Ray. It just slipped out. Still takin' me to the '42' tournament?"

"Don't you know it, girl! I'll see you at seven." He gave her a little peck on the cheek and held the door for her. "Lessen, a course, we got some sort a law enforcement emergency."

Clyde heard all this and shook his head. The most imminent law enforcement emergency he knew of facing Billy Ray Barnes was Billy Ray Barnes' possible strangulation death at the hands of Chief Clyde Thomas.

"Of course, Sweet -- . I mean, Billy Ray," Arva May said. "See ya tonight. B'-bye, Chief." She waved from the door as Billy Ray shooed her out.

"She's a cute one, ain't she, Clyde?"

"Adorable." Clyde was leaning over the window air conditioner. The unit had sprouted several unnerving noises in recent days. One sounded like a baseball card in bicycle spokes. Another sounded like a loose screw rattling around inside a snare drum. Another went tick-tick-tick-tick-tick... "You call that fella 'bout lookin' at this thing?"

"Well, uh, actually -- "

"Well, uh, actually *no.*" Clyde straightened up, frowning under the wide brim of his Stetson. He shook his head, tossed his hat on his desk, and peeled off his suit jacket. His white short-sleeved shirt was sweat-matted unattractively under his arms and across the equator of his bulging stomach. "Didja 'member to stop by my place 'n' pick up my uniform?"

"Right there under your desk."

"Under my -- ?" Clyde found his uniform jammed into a small paper bag. He pulled out an indelibly wrinkled khaki shirt and pants. "You couldn't leave it on a hanger?"

"Well, Jeez, Clyde, I didn't know you was goin' on a parade or I'da -- "

Clyde waved at Billy Ray to shut up. He took his uniform under his arm and stepped into the small bathroom at the back of the office. "By the way," he called through the open bathroom door, "what're you doin' here? Where's Waylon?"

"Well, we all kinda jiggered with the rotation. Waylon's got the midnight, 'n' Tobe took the day. We all thought, you bein' out a couple days -- "

"Tomorrow, y'all can just 'jigger' it back the way it was."

"Whatever you say. You're the chief, Chief."

"'Sides 'jiggerin'' the rotation, didja manage to accomplish anything resemblin' your actual damn *job* while I was away?"

"Wilbur McCoy was in yesterday bellyachin' kids comin' outta Abner Birney's store been cuttin' crosst his north pasture, makin' campfires 'n' such, leavin' a mess. Wants us to do somethin' 'bout it."

"Like what?"

Billy Ray shrugged. "Jus' somethin'. 'N' I guess you oughta know it looks like that minister over to St. Luke's Methodist, Dawson, he bought hisself a shotgun today. I got the paper on your desk."

"Billy Ray, considerin' 'at most everyone in these parts has at least *one* shotgun, and white wing season opens day after tomorrow, I'm hard put to consider 'at some kinda hot news."

Billy Ray saw one of Clyde's thick, hairy arms reach across the bathroom doorway to drape his sweat-mottled shirt over the sink. The arm reached up and pulled a dozen paper towels from the wall dispenser. He could hear Clyde using them to wipe the sweat off his body. Billy Ray turned away. He didn't want to see an exposed Clyde Thomas even accidentally.

"I don't think it's white wing, Clyde," Billy Ray said. "I called up ol' man Kirkland -- "

"That was awful officious of you," Clyde said, honestly impressed.

"Thanks," Billy Ray said, although he didn't know what "officious" meant. "Anyway, ol' man Kirkland says a preacher bought hisself six boxes a magnum double ought buck to go with that shotgun. You shoot down B-52s with that, Clyde, not white wing."

"You tryin' to say somethin', Billy Ray?"

"I'm jus' sayin' sounds awful heavy duty for white wing is all."

Clyde came out of the bathroom. He looked unhappily down at his uniform. "Damn, everybody's gonna think I slept in this thing." He hovered over an open box of doughnuts on Billy Ray's desk. "What's this?"

"From Arva May. For both of us, she says. She's a good girl, ain't she, Clyde?"

"I'm sure it's her moral character interests you most."

"What?"

"Got any jelly in here, Sweet Billy?" Clyde picked one out and took a bite, enjoying it almost as much as watching Billy Ray go through the fidgets every time he called him, "Sweet Billy." Clyde arranged his suit jacket and slacks over the desk chairs to let them air out. "What else?"

"Got a call from that Gilmore fella runs Grapeland. Looks like Jess White done got out again."

"Aw, hell," Clyde groaned through a mouthful of doughnut. "Start lookin' for smoke." He pointed Billy Ray toward the coffee machine against the wall.

Billy Ray poured them each a cup. "I said the same thing to him but he didn't think it was too funny."

"Must be the way you tell 'em."

"Anyways, he wants us to keep an eye 'n' ear out, but he don't want nothin' official. On the q.t., he said."

"That's 'cause if June Louise Smith Noonan 'n' her sisters find out Jess got out again, them 'n' their attorneys-at-law'll be all over ol' Gilmore like flies on a turd. They go after him 'n' they'll strip that ol' boy down to his damn bones. You see how much time you get to canoodle with li'l Arva May if Miz June Louise and Co. get wind Jess's off on the fly somewheres. She'll have us beatin' the bushes twenty-four-sevum." Clyde Thomas froze with an even more unhappy thought. "Hey, you didn't say nothin' to Arva May 'bout Jess gettin' loose, didja?"

"Hell, Clyde, she part-times up there to Grapeland. She's gonna find out soon's she shows up for -- "

"Let Gilmore worry 'bout that. My question is did *you* say anything?"

"Damn, Clyde, whaddya think I am?"

"That's why I'm askin'," Clyde said. He slumped behind his desk studying the gun registration form on his blotter. "Hm. Gotta say, the good Reverend Dawson don't zackly seem like the huntin' type to me."

"That's what I'm sayin'," Billy Ray said.

Clyde looked at his watch. "Six o'clock rounds, Billy Ray." He dug a set of car keys out of his suit pants pocket and tossed them to Billy Ray. "You can take the good car."

"Now, Clyde, when we jiggered the rotation, we figgered -- "

Clyde put his face in his hands. "Billy Ray, you are not the chief a po-lice, Tobe is not the chief a po-lice, Wesley is not the chief a po-lice, so I don't give all that much a frog fart in a gale wind what *y'all* figgered, awright? *I* am the damn chief a po-lice, 'n' *I* say go make rounds! I spent two gawddamn days chasin' Leroy Dobson 'roun' the courthouse tryin' to squeeze a squad car outta the county's Homeland Security money 'n' 'at's 'bout all the aggervation I got stomach for right now, so if you don't mind too much *get in the damn car 'n' make your damn rounds!*"

Billy Ray winced at the blast, made soothing motions with his hands. "Awright, awright, calm down, Clyde, 'fore you give yourself some kinda thrombosis or somethin'." He remembered to get himself a last doughnut from the box, then, as he swung the door open, 12-year-old Bobby Soffel came in, only his little tow-head and spindly legs visible from behind the huge canvas shoulder bag he carried stenciled with the banner of *The Boone Courier*.

"Hey, Chief," Bobby said. "Hey, Mr. Barnes."

Billy Ray held his hand out for the paper but Bobby walked straight to Clyde and put it on the chief's desk. Clyde fished in his suit pockets and gave Bobby two crumpled dollar bills. "You're a might late today."

"Mr. Poteet held it up," Bobby said. "Special front page story he put in at the last minute," and the boy scooted out the front door.

A curious Billy Ray leaned over a curious Clyde's shoulder as Clyde opened the paper on his desk and pulled his reading glasses from his breast pocket. "Damn..." Billy Ray said in an awed hush as he read the front page, oblivious to the fact that when he spoke with a mouthful of doughnut, he dribbled crumbs on Clyde's shoulder.

"Gawd*dammit*, Billy Ray!" Clyde snarled. "You learn your manners in a barn? Scat! You got rounds!"

"Yessir," Billy Ray said and scooped his Stetson up from the hat rack by the door.

Clyde turned back to the paper. There was a special box in the top right-hand corner of the front page. In the box along with a column of copy was a picture of Owen Dawson standing by his tripod-mounted video camera in front of the parsonage, like some proud high schooler standing by the vintage Camaro Daddy had bought him for graduation. The box carried the bold-faced headline, "Local Minister to Produce Adult Movie." Clyde's eyes moved from the newspaper to the gun registration form still on his desk. "Billy Ray? Sweet Billy?"

Red-faced, Billy Ray stopped in the open door. "Yeah, Clyde?"

"On your rounds, do a drive-by over to the parsonage. Make sure everything's quiet."

"Don't answer that," Elwood Poteet told his wife.

"It's driving me crazy, Elwood."

"That's what the machine is for, Miriam. Now, sit down and finish your dinner."

Miriam Poteet lowered herself back into her chair at the dining table. She had been married for almost thirty years to the publisher, editor, and chief correspondent of the weekly *Boone Courier*. And, for all those thirty years, aside from the occasional squabble about local taxes and elections, the chief items of her husband's professional concern was to make sure the "Around Town" column (which took up an entire page) didn't miss a birthday, bridge party, meeting of the Boone Floral Society, or some other such local social event. Miriam Poteet, therefore, was not prepared to have her phone ring off the hook all evening because people were angry over something in her husband's newspaper. Damned angry.

By the same token, Elwood Poteet was also ill-prepared to receive such criticism. Once, in writing an editorial supporting a move to install a new sewer pipe in Maine Street, the Main Street Merchants' Association had gotten up a head of steam over what was, essentially, a call for an open, stinking trench along the front of their shops until the new pipe was in. They had not been shy about sharing their sentiments with Elwood Poteet, and one of them (at least Elwood suspected it was one of them) had creatively expressed his dissatisfaction with the *Courier*'s editorial position by leaving a canvas sack of cow manure on his front porch along with the scrawled note, "How do *you* like it?"

This was different. During that last ruckus, none of the Main Street merchants had called him up to call him a liar, or to say he *must* be a liar because the story couldn't *possibly* be true, or to call him a dupe and a sucker for giving a "pervert" front page space in his newspaper, or to say, true or not, this kind of filth had no place in *The Boone Courier*.

And then there were calls from *other* reporters. Some were calling from quite far away. Austin, say. How they'd gotten wind of the story so fast was beyond Elwood. Sharks and blood in the water came to mind.

The phone kept ringing until the answering machine went to work. Elwood pretended to ignore the incoming message, pretending, instead, that his interest was in the plate of pot roast before him he kept picking at but had barely tasted.

"Elwood? You there?"

Elwood winced at recognizing the booming voice but he continued to pretend to concentrate on the dinner he wasn't eating. "Pass me a biscuit, dear?"

"Elwood, you better pick up your damn phone!" the machine roared, "'fore I come over there and have this out with you face to face! *Elwood!*"

"I think you better take that one, dear," Miriam said gingerly.

Elwood dropped his fork in his plate with a clink and took the call in the living room. "Hello, Fred."

"Don't you 'Fred' me! Right now, I'm talkin' as the gawddamn mayor, Elwood! The gawddamn *mayor!*"

"All right, Fred, I mean, Mr. Mayor -- "

"I just got back from Austin an hour ago -- "

"Another convention at the taxpayer's expense, Fred?"

"Don't smart-mouth me, Elwood! Not *now!*"

"I'm guessing you're calling about the story today -- "

"You're damn straight! Page one, Elwood? Page damn *one?* What was goin' through your damn *head*, Elwood? What the hell's a matter with you printin' 'at kinda stuff -- "

Elwood was starting to bridle. "Listen, Fred, when something newsworthy happens in this town, it's my job -- "

"You ain't the damn *New York Times*, Elwood, so give it a rest! You give a whole column to Miz Purdy Gubbs havin' a lady's club meetin' to talk 'bout her big vacation to Disneyland, so don't give me no horseshit 'bout your journalistic obligations! I get off the bus from Austin 'n' I get home 'n' Bea's tellin' me she got half a dozen messages from papers far away as Houston!

Houston, Elwood! This is *not* the kinda thing I want people talkin' 'bout Boone for! Not all crosst the gawddamn state!"

"What do you want me to do?" Elwood snapped. "I can't take it back. It's already out!"

Which seemed to stump the mayor for a bit. For a moment, the only sound Elwood got over the phone was the mayor's heavy breathing whistling in and out of his nose. "You better start prayin', Elwood, you better start prayin' this don't get much further than that! Otherwise, I swear to Christ I'll see you wind up *deliverin'* papers 'stead a printin' 'em!"

The mayor slammed his phone down leaving Elwood with his indignant response hanging in his open mouth. Elwood lowered the receiver softly into its cradle, then lowered himself just as softly into one of the living room chairs. He leaned his head back and closed his eyes.

"Are you all right, dear?" he heard Miriam ask.

He nodded.

"Will you be wanting anything else to eat?"

"No thanks, hon, I think I'm done with dinner."

Monday night...

"You have reached the residence of the Reverend and Mrs. Dawson. We can't come to the phone right now, but if you'll leave a short message at the sound of the tone, one of us will get back to you as soon as possible."

BEEP!

"Owen? Owen, it's a little after eight and this is Reverend Harper. If you're there, pick up the phone. Owen! Owen, you call me as soon as you get in. Understand? As *soon* as you get in."

BEEP!

"Reverend Dawson? I just can't believe a man a the church would produce one a those filthy movies! I don't even go to the picture show anymore because of all that filth, the language 'n' all those sexual things. Even the people in the theater are getting so rude 'n' -- "

BEEP!

"Reverend? I'm sure this article in 'at rag a Poteet's is a terrible mistake 'n' you'll make 'em print a retraction."

BEEP!

"Owen, this is Reverend Harper, again. It's just about nine o'clock. My phone hasn't stopped ringing! I'm getting calls from newspapers from all over this part of the state, Owen. You better not be sitting there listening to this! If you're there, *answer*, Owen, because if I find out -- "

BEEP!

"Know sumpin', Preacher? I don't even go to your damn church, but I think I can safely say you'd better pack your bags 'fore we bag *you!* We don't need your kind -- "

BEEP!

"Reverend Dawson, this is Mrs. Pickett. I'm not saying I believe everything Mr. Poteet wrote, at least not until I hear it from your own lips, but until things are straightened out, Mr. Pickett's lawyer has advised that we should withhold our gift to the church for those new pews. I'm sure this is only a temporary thing, as I said, until -- "

BEEP!

"Owen, dammit! This is Reverend Harper! It's midnight and I know you're there! *Pick up the damn phone!*"

BEEP!

THE SECOND DAY: Los Angeles

Tuesday morning...

The cab sailed east along Sunset, and Rita Scott was chagrinned to see the oppressive summer heat and smog alert had done nothing to thin the morning crowd of latte sippers and *Variety* browsers at the sidewalk bistros sprinkled along the boulevard. That should be their bumper sticker, she thought:

I'LL GIVE UP MY *VENTE* AND MY *VARIETY*

WHEN THEY PRY THEM FROM MY COLD DEAD

MANICURED FINGERS.

Between gaps in the office buildings and hotels to her right she could look past West Hollywood and out into the Los Angeles basin, the morning sun an unpleasant amber behind the burnt-brown pall locked in place overhead, the stinging haze merging in a blur with the characterless skyline. Out the other window: the Hollywood hills, a study in beiges and browns, all withered grass and dusty soil, the strident green of palm fronds providing an occasional slash of color. Sam Kinison used to joke about African droughts, and why didn't the natives use some common sense and just *move?* He would pretend to scoop up sand, yelling at the imagined sub-Saharans, "You know what this is? *Sand!* You know what this is gonna be in a hundred years? *Sand!* We've got deserts in America – *we just don't live in 'em, moron! Aaaaagh! Aaaaagh!"*

You're wrong, Sam, Rita Scott thought, rubbing itchy eyes, We *do* live in 'em; in fact, we supposedly smarter Yankees/Gringos/sole-remaining-superpower-straddling-the-globe-like-a-Colossuses are dumb enough to build whole fucking cities in 'em. Now *that's* a funny joke!

She coughed and her throat burned.

"Are you all right, Miss?" The driver was a short, swarthy, balding man, with bad teeth and a sing-songy Middle Eastern accent. He offered her a box of cough drops through the open panel in the bulletproof plastic partition between them.

"Thanks, but it won't help. The smog."

"Ah, oh, yes. Me, too. See?" He held up a plastic squeeze bottle of Visine, a bottle of Benadryl, another squeeze bottle of Dristan. They both laughed. "And even so…" He coughed, then shrugged philosophically and popped a cough drop into his mouth.

She noted his name on the driver's I.D. tag. Ismail Mohamed. "Where are you from, Ismail?"

"Iraq. But I came over before 9/11." He added this last hurriedly, as if to come over after 9/11 was some sort of taint. You're ok if you came over before 9/11; a refugee from tyranny and oppression, a seeker of freedom and The Good Life. After 9/11, you're suspect, you're probably one of those sonsabitchin' Al Qaeda or ISIS suiciders who got tired of setting off roadside bombs in Baghdad, and walked through our limp-dick couldn't-catch-flies-with-a-wheelbarrow-full-of-cowpies TA cops to set off bombs in the good ol' U.S. of A. Bastard!

"I was there," Rita said. "For the invasion. For about a month. "

"You were a soldier?"

"A newspaper reporter."

He smiled appreciatively. "Ah, you went with the soldiers, yes? You write about the war, eh?"

"Actually, I never made it *into* Iraq. I was at an airbase near Riyadh. They wouldn't let me off the grounds. They said I wouldn't go over too well with the Saudis."

"Ah, yes, the Saudis. Very old-fashioned with the women." Another philosophical shrug. He glanced in the rearview to study her: not an ogle, but an earnest appraisal. He took in her smooth, light mocha skin, the wonderfully you-should've-been-a-model cheekbones, the round but delicately small nose, the almond-shaped, wide-set eyes. "Too pretty to be at the war."

"Thank you."

"Ach…"

"What?"

"I don't believe you. Is too long ago. You would be a child then!"

"Ismail, whoever taught you English did a good job."

"I learned the English in school. How to talk to a lady I learned from my mother."

"I like your mother."

They laughed, again.

On the left she could see the high white cupolas of the Chateau Marmont poking above the lush foliage of the hotel grounds. Here the grass was tidy and brilliantly green, the flower beds full of color. For what movie stars and rock idols paid to stay at the Marmont, the Marmont could find water for the lawn. Across from the Marmont: a huge statue of Bullwinkle the Moose in front of the Dudley Do-Right Emporium.

"I was first in my family to come to America," said Ismail. "At home, everybody thinks you come to America you come to New York, you see the big Liberty statue in the water, you know? Liberty?"

"The Statue of Liberty."

"Yes, the lady. I come the other way. I come to California. The picture I send home is not the Liberty statue -- "

"You sent Bullwinkle?"

Ismail laughed. The bad teeth made it not a pretty thing to watch, but the sound was pleasant and light. "I send moose! At home they don't even know what is a moose! I send a picture, I say, 'Here is Liberty Moose!'"

Not quite as dignified as Lady Liberty, thought Rita Scott, but maybe these days more appropriate.

"That's it, right up there," she said, pointing to a cylindrical tower of smoked glass.

"You write about Iraq today?"

"I don't do that kind of work anymore."

Ismail seemed surprised and a little disappointed. "No more news?"

"Oh, I still write for a paper. But we only cover the *important* news. The stuff people *really* care about."

Which, she could see in the rearview, only seemed to confuse Ismail.

He pulled up at the foot of the glass tower's wide, tiled plaza, leapt out to help Rita with her suitcase. He told her what the fare was, she asked for a receipt, then paid him and threw on a ten dollar tip partly because she liked Ismail Mohamed who'd been welcomed to America by Bullwinkle the Moose, and partly to make herself feel a little better about no longer covering wars, crime, starvation, earthquakes, crooked politicians and all that stuff which had never paid her enough to throw ten dollar tips to people like Ismail Mohamed.

Eight hours earlier, a 40ish (but don't ask for specifics) black woman had stepped out of a cab in front of one of the terminals at New Jersey's Newark International Airport. She had cut a quietly attractive figure, accenting her natural assets with make-up applied subtly and with taste, wardrobed in a tailored suit flattering her compact, trim figure, accessorized with Italian footwear and a restrained sprig of unostentatious jewelry. And from what Rita Scott could now see in the reflective glass across the plaza, three hours waiting to get through Security and six hours flying tourist (with a stopover in Chicago) was enough to completely undo the tastes and skills acquired and cultivated over twenty-odd years. The make-up was blotchy now, the suit rumpled and bunching. The Italian shoes were killing her. And she desperately, *desperately* needed a shower.

She extended the pull-handle on her suitcase, wheeled it along behind her across the plaza toward the bank of revolving doors and wrestled it through, took a step into the lobby and felt herself suddenly jerked back into the swishing door partitions.

"Hey -- !"

The belt of her suit jacket was snagged somewhere in the revolving door. She tugged at the belt and the belt tugged back.

"Maybe if you didn't fight it so hard." She felt a hand on her back to hold her still, heard someone play with the end of the belt caught in the door. Then she was free and the crushed buckle was being held out to her. "I think this belongs to you."

"Thanks, Roger," she said.

He smiled at her with beautifully capped teeth, unconsciously touched at his hair to make sure the lacquer was holding it perfect. "Anything else I should go back in for?"

"I think that does it."

"Just get in?"

"I'm in a rush, Roger," she said trying to step past.

"His nibs can wait. You look a little discombobulated. Take a minute. Tic-Tac? How's the two-headed baby?"

She pushed past him, careful to make sure the little trundle wheels of her suitcase trundled across his Guccied toes as she headed toward the elevator bank. "Don't fuck around with me today, Roger. I'm not really in the mood."

"Glad to have your sunshiny self back!" He called after her. "We missed you! What're you doing after work?"

Which she pretended not to hear as the elevator doors closed.

She got off at the top floor where the elevators opened on the wide curve of a receptionist's desk embossed with large, highly italicized gold letters, *The National Investigator*.

"You're late, Ms. Scott," the plasticky blonde receptionist said as soon as Rita stepped out of the elevator.

"Give me a break, Courtney. I came straight from the airport."

Courtney nodded sympathetically. "The Bird told me to send you in pronto as soon as you showed up."

Rita nodded and started for the smoked glass double doors leading off the reception area. "I know. I'll just put my bag -- "

Courtney smiled apologetically. "Actually, Ms. Scott, he specifically told me to emphasize the word, 'pronto.'"

Rita stopped with one hand on the doorknob, hung her head.

"Why don't you leave the bag with me," Courtney said. "I'll have somebody take it to your desk."

Rita smiled a thanks, headed down the opposite corridor to the double pine doors at the end gold-lettered with, "Eric Bird III," and below that, "Publisher & Editor-in-Chief.

She didn't knock, and, inside, Eric Bird's secretary nodded her on through a second set of double doors. Beyond was a massive office, one curved wall consisting of floor-to-ceiling windows offering what would have been a spectacular view of Los Angeles if the smog ever cleared. Toward one corner of the office was a minimalist-styled desk of black lacquer, and at the other a lounging area – Swedish-style easy chairs and sofas around a glass and chrome coffee table. Behind one of the sofas, pacing along the bank of windows, was Eric Bird III. Despite the gray at his temples and the lines in his tanned face, his body was athletic-club fit, his steps light and bouncy. He had one hand tucked, Napoleon-like, inside one of the red suspenders holding up his Armani suit pants, while the other held his cell phone to his ear.

Eric Bird turned at the sound of the door, smiled at the sight of Rita and nodded her to one of the chairs around the coffee table without breaking the rhythm of his conversation. There was a silver coffee service on the table, some china cups and saucers, and a plate of pastries, biscuits, spreads, and jams.

"She won't sue, Joseph," Eric Bird was saying into his phone. "Joseph, relax, please. You're acting like this has never happened before. I would think by now you'd've developed a sense of who is *really* going to sue, and who isn't. *I*, on the other hand, *do* have that sense, Joseph, and I'm telling you she won't sue."

Rita settled into a chair near the coffee table, poured herself a cup of coffee. In the deep cushion of the seat she felt her body go slack. She was tired, and the bottomless foam cushions were no place to try to stay awake.

"Why?" said Eric Bird. "Because she knows we can drag this thing out for years in court, that's why…Yes, I *know*, but this lady isn't Carol Burnett, and who's fought it out since?…Worst case scenario? She sues, we diddle around in court for a year or two, the judge says, "Pu-*leeze,* people, do the court a favor and settle this thing,' and we say, 'Ok, we'll print a retraction.' We bury the retraction on page 64 and by then it's been so long nobody even remembers what it is we're retracting. Now, let's get back to this television project we were talking about.

"Ecclesiastical scandals are a dime a dozen. People *expect* them. A priest gets caught buggering the choirboys? What else is new? Some televangelist Bible-beater gets caught in a No-Tell Motel with a transvestite hooker? Surprise! But *this* has the whiff of something different."

And at "different," a little alarm went off in Rita's head. She focused her stinging eyes on the table. If she'd been more awake she would've seen the airline ticket folder there when she'd sat down. She set her coffee on the table, started flashing looks at Bird that signaled, Talk to *me!* while waving her hand to get his attention.

But Eric Bird just gave her a casual wave hello, and turned back to look out at Los Angeles and its stained sky. "I'm not saying we won't take some heat over this thing, Joseph…Well, ok, maybe a *lot* of heat. That's what Rita's for; to find out how *much* heat."

Now she was flashing him angry no-way looks, swishing her hands back and forth like a cop signaling no-thoroughfare-you-have-to-go-around-buddy.

Eric Bird blew her a kiss. "She can find out if this is just smoke or if we've really got a fire here. I'll probably have something to tell you by tomorrow night…Ok, Joseph, love to the wife, the kids, the dog, and whatever." He disconnected and tossed the phone onto the sofa. He put his hands in his pockets, turned to face Rita and smiled a smile full of immaculately even bleached white teeth. "Welcome back, love."

"No! Whatever it is…*No!*"

He put on a look of confusion and umbrage of dinner theater performance quality. "Rita, love, I have no idea what -- "

She pointed at the ticket folder on the table, careful not to let her fingertip get too close to it. "Either *you* better be taking a vacation, or you're giving *me* one for working so goddamned *hard* and so goddamned *long* without a break! If the choice is none of the above, I don't want to know about it, Eric."

"Rita -- "

"*I don't want to know about it, Eric!*"

" – my champ -- "

"Oh-oh," she grumbled, gritting her teeth. "Here it comes."

" – you're the best I've got. You're the best there is!"

"Pile it any deeper and I'm going to need a snorkel! I just got *back,* Eric! You were texting me on the goddamned *plane!* I spent four days trying to get a glimpse of the remarkable two-headed baby of Lodi, New Jersey, then somebody – some incredibly cheap, tight-fisted, inconsiderate *prick* -- "

A who-me? look from Eric Bird.

" -- booked me tourist – *tourist* -- on the redeye back. No sooner do I step off that hellwagon than I am *accosted* by a messenger at the airport telling me not to bother going home, Mr. Bird wants to see me, there's already a cab for me at the curb thank-you-very-much-now-go!" Drained, Rita let herself sink deeper into the chair.

"I should've had de-caf for you."

"Eric, I don't expect anything remotely resembling compassion from you, but maybe just a little common sense. I'm *burnt,* understand? *Fried!* I-can-no-longer-function!"

"I don't know, Rita, you seem quite full of piss and vinegar now."

"Oh, *pissed* I am!" With a tired grunt, Rita pushed up out of the chair. "Let me put it to you another way: *fuck off, Eric!*"

"Wait a second, relax, Rita, love." His smile never faltered, and he rested his hands on her shoulders, gently nudging her back down into the chair. "That's my fiery Nubian she-warrior! My little Amazon! Now you rest your weary bones a minute. Have a scone. They're very good."

More from fatigue than acquiescence, Rita let herself drop back into the chair.

"So," Bird said, sitting down on the table in front of her, "how *was* the two-headed baby of Lodi, New Jersey? Alien offspring? Government experiment gone awry? Toxic dumping-induced mutant?"

"Well, for one thing, it doesn't have two heads."

"You don't say!"

"Your tipster, the utterly *un*charming and somewhat butchy Nurse Trudy, exaggerated somewhat."

"I'm shocked! Shocked and dismayed! Shocked and dismayed and -- "

"Well, I guess that happens when you offer $5,000 bounties for *National Investigator*-worthy hot tips."

"You said butchy?"

"She pinched my ass. Asked if I had to get back to L.A. right away."

"Mmmm. Deeee-lish! But no two heads? *Qu'elle domage.*"

"It's a massive but, thankfully, benign tumor on the baby's collar bone."

"I saw the art you e-mailed to the photo department. If we shade it right, it could *almost* look like it *could* be birthing another head. Shame you didn't take Nurse Trudy up on her invitation. Pictures of *that* -- "

"That may sound enticing to *you*, Eric, but then you didn't see Nurse Trudy."

Playfully leering. "So if she'd been prettier -- "

"Did I already tell you to fuck off? Because I do so hate repeating myself."

"How's the scone?"

"To hell with the scone."

Bird gave her a friendly pat on the knee, than rose and sat on the sofa -- a safe distance, she noted -- across the table from her. He leaned forward, his tanned face sharp and eager. "I was looking over your story about televangelists last night. Your usual punchy stuff, Rita. It was almost real journalism."

"Considering my usual beat is two-headed babies, that's almost a compliment."

Bird closed his eyes in relishing reminiscence. "I especially liked, 'God forgives the preachers, and their hooker girlfriends become talk show stars.' Nice, lyrical quality there, Rita. Poetic, almost." He opened his eyes and his face turned grandiloquently sad. "But as you might have heard me saying on the phone, I'm afraid this kind of thing – even for *our* market – is *une peu passé.*"

"*Passe.*"

"A little flat."

"Flat."

"It's old, Rita. Redundant. Stale."

"Eric, do I have to remind you that the piece was *your* idea? I didn't even want to -- "

"And the *idea* is basically sound."

"Well, yeah, of course, it would be, wouldn't it?"

"It just needs another hook."

"And you've got one."

Bird held up a finger for patience. He went over to his desk and fished out a fax from the piles of paper strategically arranged about the ebon top. He handed the fax to Rita. "This started showing up on the net last night. Was on the network news by this morning."

"I can barely *see* it," Rita said, rubbing her tired eyes.

"Nutshell: there's this small town minister out in the great American heartland who has decided to get into the movie business."

"Ok."

"This isn't another *Passion of the Christ*, Rita. He doesn't want to make Bible stories, he's not talking about *Highway to Heaven* or *Joan of Arcadia*, or something like *Left Behind* or even *The Omen*. The kicker is..." He paused knowing that inevitably – as much as she didn't want to – Rita would nod for him to continue. "...he wants to make adult movies."

Rita shook her head. "You mean porn?"

"Now that's the thing. What *exactly* he wants to do – what *he* means by adult movies – I don't know. All that's showing up is exactly what's in the original story which was evidently published by some small town rag; *his* small town. That's why I need somebody to go down there, get the details, suss out if there really *is* some kind of story there; *our* kind of story."

Rita's mental alarm went off again, louder this time. Her eyes narrowed suspiciously. "Eric..."

"Yes, Rita, love?"

"Just where *exactly* in the great American heartland are you sending me?"

"And *this* is what makes you an even *better* -- "

"*Where*, Eric?"

"Boone, Texas."

"*Texas?*"

He bubbled along, oblivious to her violently shaking head. "It's only a couple hours' drive from the Houston airport. A pleasant ride through the open country, get away from all this goop we Angelenos laughingly refer to as, 'air.' Get to feel a nice, fresh breeze in your face for a change. Chili cook-offs, rattlesnake wrangling, and are there people with bigger hearts than Texans? You'll be getting yourself a real slice of Americana, love, see the *real* America and *real* Americans! Be great background for the piece, and a nice change of pace for you. Especially after wherever-the-hell New Jersey."

"Lodi. Eric, I haven't even unpacked -- "

"Better still, you've already got everything you need, the plane reservation is all set -- "

"Tourist, no doubt."

"We'll see if we can't get you an upgrade. Maybe."

"Eric, I don't want to go to Texas."

"Rita, love, aren't you *from* Texas? That's why I thought you'd be perfect for this! You know the ground! You understand the psychological terrain! You grasp the *ethos* of the place."

"Yes, I am from Texas. And in all the time that you've known me, in those few instances when you've allowed me to take time off, have you ever known me to go *back* to Texas?"

"Then you're overdue."

"There's a reason I don't go back there, Eric."

"Face your demons, love. Confrontational therapy. Best thing you can do."

"Send Roger. Me, I operate strictly north of the Mason-Dixon."

"That's frightfully retrograde of you, love. Positively 19th Century. These are different times, love."

"Have you been on Mars the last ten years?"

"From now on, Roger gets the two-headed baby stories, the Kansas crop circles, the strange lights over Area 51. It was a gross misuse of your talents to send you to, um -- "

"Lodi. Eric, you wanted me to do a story on TV preachers, I *did* my story on TV preachers, I'm done. Some fire-and-brimstone type out in Zeroburg, Texas wants to make skinflicks, that's *another* story for *another* correspondent. *Mine's* finished."

Bird stood with a sigh, turned back to take in the murky skyline view. "'X-Rated Movie Preacher In a Special Prime Time Report.'"

"What special prime time report?"

"Actually, I suppose it should say, 'NC-17-Rated Movie Preacher...,' but nobody knows what that means. Doesn't really *sing*, either. You say, 'X-Rated' -- "

"*What* special prime time report."

He turned back, smiling. "We're close to finalizing a deal with one of the cable news networks. We're going to get a regular slot. At the start, just a daily five-minute module, supply our own content. We see how that goes over, then who knows? That's what they mean when they talk about media synergy: the paper will tease and promote our TV stories, the TV venue promotes the *Investigator*, the module gets repeated on the network's internet site. We need this, because that's where business is in the 21st century, and, for the same reason, *you* need this."

"*I* need this? Like a hole in the head."

"We need a multimedia presence. No big secret, love: print is dying. And you don't want to die with it. If there's something to this story, it would be a great piece to kick-off our TV and internet presence with. That would mean a TV credit for you, Rita, love. *Tee-vee!* And..." He let it hang a moment. "...we haven't settled on an on-air host yet."

She stood slowly, just as slowly walked to where she could stand in front of him, wary, as if there might be a Bengal tiger trap concealed beneath the office's deep pile carpeting. "What network?"

"Afraid I can't say. Very hush-hush until we're ready to go public."

"You're pulling my chain. And don't give me that offended who-me look."

"This one time, Rita, love, *believe* me." Bird raised his left hand and traced a cross on his chest with his right. "Cross my heart, hope to die."

"I should be so lucky."

"Good morning, Reverend Harper."

"Did I wake you, Owen?"

"The phone ringing -- "

"The phone's been ringing all damn *night*, Owen! I've been trying to *reach* you all damn *night! I* haven't been to *bed* yet!"

"I'm sorry -- "

"What's that noise, Owen?"

"It's just the television."

"Every damn phone in the hierarchy in *Houston* has been ringing since six a.m.! *My* damn phone has been ringing ever since that paper came out yesterday! That is, when *I* wasn't on the phone trying to reach *you!*"

"I'm sorry, I was busy."

"You won't be busy anymore! You're on leave of absence as of this very second! Indefinite! There's a Fed Ex-ed letter confirming your leave already on its way to you. God, I can't believe you did this!"

"Did what?"

"For the love of *God*, Owen, the newspaper article! Have you lost your mind?"

"The *Courier* ran the story?"

"You almost sound pleased! Maybe you *have* lost your mind! It's right on the front page! Haven't you seen it? You've embarrassed every one of our churches! Every *one!* Not to say what it's done for the entire denomination! I pray to God that St. Luke's – which I *personally* assigned you to – will survive this scandal.

"Now, you listen to me Owen: we've called a meeting at four this afternoon at the church. I want you there to *apologize* to the trustees, to your church board, to the elders, to say you've been under a lot of pressure, and, oh, and that you're suffering some type of, I don't know, some sort of temporary breakdown or something. *Anything!* Maybe we can salvage *some* of the congregation."

"I don't know, David. I just don't -- "

"You don't know? *Dammit, Owen!* You *be* there! I mean it! Four o'clock!"

The line went dead with a click. No sooner had Dawson set the phone down in its cradle when it began to ring again. He reached over and turned on the answering machine.

"You have reached the residence of the Reverend and Mrs. Dawson. We can't come to the phone right now…"

Clyde Thomas and Henry Gilmore had covered about a half-mile across the park-like grounds of the Grapeland Assisted Living Community. The heat had kept most of the patients and staff indoors, and Clyde, picking at the damp spots on his shirt, thought all those poor, senile old farts were showing a lot more sense than Clyde Thomas and Henry Gilmore. Mr. Gilmore kept swabbing at his face with a frayed-edged handkerchief, but he was sweating faster than he could swab. Clyde led them up a low knoll from which they could see most of the grounds. Beyond the scattered buildings, the nursing home property ran unmarked into plains of thin, dry grass and dust.

"Fence woulda been nice, Henry."

Mr. Gilmore looked pained. "If we put up high fences, they say we're treating their relatives like prisoners. Give them freedom to walk around and *this* is what happens, and then they say we don't keep a close enough eye on them!"

"What was Jess wearin'?"

Mr. Gilmore shrugged. "We looked through the room closet but I couldn't honestly tell you what had been taken…if anything."

Clyde took off his Stetson, swabbed out the sweatband with his kerchief, then parked it back on his head. "Jess coulda wound up findin' somethin' on a clothesline, I guess. I'll keep an eye out for a report of that kinda theft. But I gotta tell ya, Henry, short a kickin' up a big fuss 'n' bringin' Dan Pickett out here with his hounds, I don't knows there's much all else to do."

Mr. Gilmore was shaking his head vehemently. "A fuss is the last thing I want."

"Havin' had the mispleasure a meetin' Jess's nieces, I can believe that. But, like I said, I don't know what all else to tell you, Henry. Lessen you can think up some place we mighta missed, some li'l hidey-hole Jess could squirrel into."

Mr. Gilmore shrugged helplessly. Then, with forced optimism, "This isn't the longest Jess's been gone, you know."

"I know. But I'm not worryin' any less. 'N' I'm not just worried 'bout somethin' happenin' to *Jess*. I'm worried 'bout *Jess* happenin' to *somethin'*. Or some*body*, if you know what I mean. Jess 'n' a book a matches come together somewhere 'n' -- ...Well, you know."

From his unhappy face it was clear Mr. Gilmore knew exactly what Clyde Thomas meant, and kept gloomily mulling it over until they were crunching across the parking lot gravel. He held the door of the patrol car open for Clyde. "I'd like to give it a little more time. Just a little more. Maybe Jess'll show up somewhere come supper time."

Clyde shrugged resignedly and slid onto the upholstery, a little irked Mr. Gilmore had kept him busy long enough to let the vinyl seat covers grow roasting hot. "Ok, Henry," he said and started the engine. "Your place, your patient; you're the boss."

Tuesday afternoon…

Spook ran the tips of his thick fingers along the worn tread of his Harley's rear tire. He pursed his lips unhappily, came out of his squat and walked to the small creek wandering through the bottom of the little hollow. He knelt by the water and washed the tire grime from his hands.

After, he went to the lone isle of shade – a low cottonwood at the rim of the hollow – and sat, propped against the thin trunk. Lenny was nearby, sprawled out on his bedroll. He had watched Spook probing his tire. Looking only mildly interested, he rolled to where he could lean over for a look at his own tires, ran his fingers along the treads.

Spook sighed. "If I ain't got much road left on mine, 'n' you ain't got much on yours…The way those other two shitheads motor, you gotta figger *they* must be on their fuckin' rims by now."

Lenny gave an uninterested shrug. He plucked a joint from the pocket of his denim vest, lit it, went to stand by the creek. The joint still dangling from his lips, he took a stand by the water, unzipped his fly and began to piss. They hadn't camped far from the road, and any drive-by who bothered to turn could see them. That was of no concern to Lenny. When he heard a car whoosh by, he proudly arched his back giving a more pronounced trajectory to his outflow. A semi's air horn wailed and Lenny raised a hand in salute.

"Tires cost money," Spook said.

"That's your capitalist system for ya."

"What I'm sayin', Len, is well's close to runnin' dry."

Lenny came back under the tree, propped his haunches against the seat of his Harley. "I hear ya." The move was casual, but meant to be obvious; letting his right hand fall close to the metal saddlebag bolted to the side of his bike.

"I'm not tryin' to stir no shit. I'm jus' sayin' the needle's gettin' to E, unnerstand? I'm jus' wonderin' you got anything in mind? Soon would be good."

They locked eyes, one set as cold as the other. Spook knew Lenny had a .357 Cobra in that saddlebag, and at this range a .357 Cobra would leave a hole in Spook big enough for Lenny to ride his Harley through. Spook also knew Lenny was the kind of sick fuck who'd put that kind of hole in you if you called him on his leadership skills. A few years out among the outlaws was like a few years in a Mad Max movie. The outlaws didn't think the way other people did. Lenny didn't think the way other people did.

They heard Harley engines crackling and popping down the highway, nearing.

Lenny's face broke into a smile, his hand retreated from the saddlebag. Spook took a breath.

"I shall lead my people to the promised land," Lenny said. "But nothin' happens 'til after breakfast."

Spook looked toward the sky, measuring the sun's height. "Lunch," he corrected, but Lenny wasn't listening.

Porky and Shorty roared off the highway and hit the shoulder with their rear tires fishtailing and spitting dirt. They jounced across the bleached grass and down into the hollow in a cloud of dust.

Porky stood up on his pedals, holding up a McDonald's bag triumphantly in each hand. "Come 'n' get it, ya damn dildoes!" He got as far as "...dil-" when his front tire hit a dip in the ground. The bike started to wobble, Porky dropped the bags and grabbed desperately for the handlebars, but before he could steady the bike, it went over on his leg.

Lenny shook his head hopelessly. "Dumbass." He walked past Porky still lying under his bike, over to Shorty and took one of the bags Shorty was pulling out from the straps around the carry rack on his rear fender.

Porky kicked himself clear of his bike. "Motherfucker!" he steamed and threw a few more kicks at the Harley. "Mother*fucker!*"

"Picked yourself up a hefty case a road rash there, huh?" Shorty chortled. He stopped smirking when Spook took the other McDonald's bag from his rack. "Hey! That's mine!"

Spook nodded at the two bags lying in the path where Porky had dropped them. One of them was bleeding Coke into the dry ground. "*That's* yours."

"Fuck, no, man, no *way!* We went into *our* pockets, man! *We* make the call!" Shorty looked over to Lenny, hoping for some kind of referee's judgment.

Lenny was leaning against his bike, his face embedded in a Big Mac. He was going to leave it up to them and enjoy the show.

Spook reached into his pocket. He dug deep and pulled out what was there: a couple of faded dollar bills. He stuffed them into Shorty's vest pocket. "There. We're even."

"Fuck even, man, I ain't drivin' all a way back there -- "

"He *can't!*" Porky cackled. He had pulled up the grease-stained leg of his denims and was looking at where the gravel had scraped away a few inches of skin. There was also a bright red stripe looking like a burn. "We're at the pick-up window 'n' Shorty goes, 'Where's my Quarter Pounder?' 'N' this pencil dick goes, 'The ticket says a cheeseburger,' 'n' Shorty starts givin' 'em all kindsa shit 'bout how they fucked up the order? 'N' how they's *always* fuckin' up his order? 'N' how he's gonna come in there 'n' whup somebody's ass 'cause he's sick a always gettin' fucked over, 'n ' so the kid's shittin' his pants now, 'n' so he throws in somebody else's Quarter Pounder to get rid of us, 'n' then I think he knew we scammed 'em when we boomed off into a sunset flippin' 'em the bird!"

"It's *my* story!" Shorty snapped, kicking some dirt Porky's way. "Whyntcha let *me* tell my own fuckin' story? Dipshit."

Porky was still laughing, kept laughing all the way up to the time he tried to stand on his hurt leg. "Fuck!" he swore with each step. "The fuckin' exhaust got me! I burned myself."

"*Fuckin'* dipshit," Shorty emphasized. He was kneeling by the bags in the road. He fished out the Coke container suffering the least spillage, then a squashed Big Mac out of the other bag, and joined Spook and Lenny under the cottonwood tree.

Porky hobbled in "Fuck…fuck…fuck…" fashion to the bank of the creek. He pulled off his filthy neckerchief, dunked it in the water and dabbed at his wounds.

"Watch out down there!" Shorty called out. "I slept down by there 'n' a fuckin' skeeters done ate me up alive."

"Fuck the mosquitoes," Lenny said, "It's them *snakes!* Fuckin' water moccasins, man."

Porky bolted away from the creek. "You shittin' me, man? *Snakes?*"

Then he saw the other three laughing so hard they almost choked on their food. Porky picked up a stone and threw it at Shorty. If it had hit, there would've probably been a fight, but Spook understood Porky's calculation. If Porky had thrown his stone at Spook or Lenny, Porky would've had to figure on likely winding up dead.

"Hey, W.D.! Turn it up!" Hank Fletcher called out.

"If y'all'd shuddup, I wouldn't *hafta* turn it up!" W.D. poked around the shelves under the bar until he found the remote control for the television mounted on the wall behind the bar.

"I understand they-all get ESPN out there to the Candlelight," Cecil Tredway said. "'N' a passel of all 'em other channels, too. Title fights, Monday night football 'n' all like 'at. Whyntcha get yourself one a those satellite dishes, W.D.?"

"Cecil, you're free to tool all the way out to the Candlelight 'n' their five dollar beers every time you get the thirsties," W.D. said. "Now, you want another one without satellite service or what?"

Cecil nodded and a second can of Pearl took its place next to its empty brother on the bar in front of him.

"Hey, shhh! Here it comes!"

The commercial ended and the news came back on. On the chroma key field behind the gray-templed newscaster was a map of eastern Texas with Boone highlighted. The lunch crowd applauded, even Buford Welmont who was sitting with the crowd today for the viewing; everyone except for Smitty McKee who had his usual, lonely seat at the end of the bar and never looked up from his beer.

"And," the newscaster began, "what started as a little note in a local weekly newspaper -- "

"Little note my ass," commented Hank. "Front gawddam page!"

"C'mon, Hank," said W.D. "It's the *Courier*. Gettin' on the front page a the *Courier*'s like gettin' on the front page a *Manure Monthly*."

"Is that a real paper?" Cecil asked.

" – is quick becoming the talk of east Texas. In the town of Boone, the resident Methodist minister – 27-year-old Owen Dawson – told residents of the small community he has served for three years that he intended to make, quote, an 'X-rated movie.'"

"He meant NC-17," said Cecil.

The key of the map was replaced by a still of downtown Boone.

A bright flash of sunshine signaled the opening of the front door. "I miss it?" Jed shouted, running for the bar.

W.D. shushed him and set a beer at his place.

"Although Reverend Dawson has not explained in detail just what the contents of his adults-only film will be, residents of this close-knit town have reacted strongly as has the regional hierarchy of the Methodist church. Senior Methodist officials are meeting in Boone today to discuss the matter with the town's mayor, other local representatives, and church officers, and are promising an appropriate response to the concerns of their congregation. As for Reverend Dawson..." The commentator smiled. "Not surprisingly, he hasn't been answering his phone."

"You can turn that down now," Hank Fletcher said, "'n' then come on over here 'n' lay one onna ol' center target."

"Hey!" Cecil Tredway said. "Where'd they get 'at pitcher a downtown? I don't 'member seein' nobody 'roun' takin' pitchers."

"I think that was left over from when they come up to cover that mess 'bout the sewer pipe on Main," W.D. said.

"Hey, Smitty!" Jed called. "'Member that? Wasn't that the time somebody left a li'l present for ol' Poteet on his front porch?" Jed grinned knowingly. "Smitty knows a *lot* 'bout 'at gift for ol' Elwood, ain't 'at right, Smitty?"

Smitty looked down into his mug of beer. The corners of his mouth twitched. "Like I told Clyde Thomas at the time; man, I don't know nothin' 'bout it."

Thelma Plover had been keeping to herself in one of the back booths. She'd seemed oblivious to the news, and was now standing over the jukebox punching buttons for one of her sad love songs. Twanging guitars made a bad combination with the television. Nobody seemed to mind when W.D. switched off the T.V.

"Whaddya think, Smitty?" Jed called over. "You think maybe Preacher Dawson's gonna wind up with a gift on his porch, too?"

Smitty grinned into his beer and drained his glass. "I don't know nothin' 'bout it."

W.D. was shaking his head. "Damn if I know what y'all're gettin' so het up over. Hell, Smitty, you ain't been to church 'cept for your momma's funeral 'n' how long ago was that?"

Smitty wasn't smiling anymore. "That ain't the point. Point is ya gotta respect what a church is *suppose'* to be which is more 'n' 'at sumbitch preacher does. Ya know, a lotta li'l kids go to that church even if their parents don't."

Hank Fletcher spun around on his stool. "Smitty, you don't have no kids neither."

"That ain't the point," Smitty said. "Point is a fella gets up front a the church 'n' takes advantage a his position 'n' starts shovelin' out poison into minds don't know no better."

"Yeah!" Hank said, excited with understanding. "I know whatcha mean! It's like how I'm a registered Democrat -- "

"Hank," W.D. said, "you haven't voted Democrat since Clinton, 'n' you hated *him!*"

"That's what I'm sayin'!" Hank said. "Just 'cause I'm registered with the Dems don't mean I don't vote Republican when Dems wanna give the store away to all them street corner niggers 'n' every wetback Mex goes on the rolls!"

"I forgot what the point was," Cecil Tredway said.

"Point is," Smitty said, "don't matter what your church is. It's what ya believe in." He nodded at the TV. "Nobody's lookin' at the preacher 'n' laughin' at *him.* They all laughin' at *us.*"

Even Buford Welmont had an opinion, or at least as much of one as he ever had; he nodded emphatically along with Smitty.

And so did Cecil Tredway. "Ya know, W.D., I'm no Bible thumper, but I gotta say, what the hell kinda pitcher does it make with a local preacher in here swillin' liquor?"

"What're you talkin' 'bout?" W.D. exclaimed. "*You* were payin' for him!"

"Still," and Cecil shrugged W.D.'s objection into irrelevance.

Jed finished his beer with a burp. "Well, this is all gonna be old news by tomorrow. 'At Methodist honcho Harper is gonna shit-can Dawson for sure 'n' 'at'll be the end of it."

Smitty signaled for another beer. "Won't be the end of it long's he's still hangin' 'roun' town. Hey, Sanchez! Where the hell's my chili? You go all a way to Chihuahua for them beans?"

Tuesday evening...

Mrs. Hanratty was sitting down in front of her television, a bulky, cabinet affair dating back to the Reagan Administration. It was one of the younger artifacts in her home.

She had set up a TV table next to her easy chair. On the TV table was a paper plate of Mrs. Paul's fish sticks, a small plastic cup of ketchup, and a tall glass of sweet tea. There was also a pill prescribed for her blood pressure, another for her heart, one for joint pain, one for her low blood iron, one for her cholesterol, a threesome to do something about her disintegrating knee cartilage, and a pair of oat bran tablets. On the television, Vanna White was spinning consonants.

The phone rang once. A signal. Mrs. Hanratty sighed. Nearly everyone she knew knew better than to call during her dinnertime.

She went out on the porch. The day had cooled somewhat, but the sky was still bright with sunlight, the eastern horizon showing only the faintest traces of evening mauve. Mrs. Dailey was on her own porch, eagerly waving her over.

Mrs. Hanratty made her way carefully down the stairs. She was always worried that in the lowering light of late day, her eyes would betray her, sending her tumbling down the stairs and to a hospital and from there up to

Grapeland. She never saw one of her friends leave Grapeland except in an ambulance or a hearse.

She met Mrs. Dailey on Mrs. Dailey's lawn just as Mrs. Ledbetter, answering her own signal, came puttering across from the opposite side.

Mrs. Dailey was looking quite pleased with herself in that haughty way she had when she was sure she was first with the good gossip. "I just heard 'bout that meeting they were all having over to St. Mark's," she said. "You know; with that Reverend Harper? And Mayor Riley was there 'n' all? The one to discuss Reverend Dawson? And Reverend Dawson was supposed to be there?" Mrs. Dailey beamed, flush with breaking news. "Well, I just got off a phone with Bea Riley and she told me -- "

"I know," Mrs. Hanratty said blithely. "He didn't come."

Mrs. Dailey didn't bother to hide her disappointment at being preempted. "How did you know?"

"My cousin's boy is on the church board a trustees," Mrs. Hanratty said. "His wife called me just a little while ago -- "

"Would that be, oh, what's her name?" Mrs. Ledbetter's brow furrowed as she tried to remember. "That little red-headed girl."

"Lisolette."

Mrs. Ledbetter smiled. "Yes, that's right. I met her once, remember? When they were over here, her husband was looking at your septic tank for you? Nice girl, very pretty."

"Yes," Mrs. Hanratty said. "She *is* nice. Very good with her children, too. As respectful a group a little girls as you could want!"

Mrs. Dailey was still miffed at the grand theft of her thunder. The digression into the various nicenesses of the little red-headed bigmouth who was wife to the son of Mrs. Hanratty's cousin on the church board of trustees only compounded her irritation. "When were you going to tell *us* the news?" she interjected.

"After my shows," Mrs. Hanratty said. "You know if I'd come out here to tell you I'd be out here half the night."

Mrs. Dailey huffed and looked offended. "Not *half* -- "

"Well, I'd miss my shows, anyway. That's the point. I was *going* to tell you."

Mrs. Dailey made a humph-ing noise indicating sort of an acceptance of what wasn't quite an apology. "Well," she went on, "anyway, maybe your cousin's daughter-in-law *didn't* tell you they're going to let him go. I mean completely! Move him right out a the parsonage."

Actually, Mrs. Hanratty had been told as much, but she thought it wise to allow Mrs. Dailey her moment.

"Oh, my!" Mrs. Ledbetter said. "Where all are they going to live?"

"Not in Boone, I can tell you that!" Mrs. Dailey declared. "Who wants him here? He starts with this kind a thing, you don't know what all else he'll get into."

"I feel sorry for his wife, that's who I feel sorry for," Mrs. Hanratty said. "Such a pretty little girl."

"If you ask me," Mrs. Dailey said, "she brought it on herself. If she'd been more involved 'stead a always putting on airs, maybe she would've known what all her husband'd got up to 'n' this whole doodad would never a gotten started. It's all over the TV, you know."

"I saw," Mrs. Ledbetter said, clucking her tongue. "Could've knocked me over with a feather when it came up on the TV."

"Everybody in Texas is going to think we have loonies like that just running 'round loose!" Mrs. Dailey said. "Just *running* 'round *loose!*"

"I wish he'd a gone to the meeting," Mrs. Hanratty said. "Maybe they could a talked about it. Maybe he could a made a *nice* movie. That would a been all right, wouldn't it?"

Mrs. Dailey shook her head intolerantly. "No, that wouldn't a been all right!" Her eyes grew narrow and suspicious. "You know those stories 'bout those movie people? What if he started mixing with them? What if *they* started coming *here*? Those are the people who *make* all that filth! It just rots the whole country's mind, just *rots* it! Things people get up to today 'n' it's the movies and TV do it to them! You know, my grandson was going to get me that satellite television for my birthday but I told him, no, sir! I'd been over to their house, I'd seen the kind a things they have on, all that chopping people up 'n' sex things, 'n' the children are right there watching it! No! No kind a movie woulda been all right! He's a minister – or he *was* -- "

Mrs. Ledbetter's eyes went wide. "Oh, do you think they'll send him out a the ministry?" She started clucking again. "What would he do?"

Mrs. Dailey spoke with the conviction of knowing that everybody in the affair was going to get appropriate comeuppances. "I don't know, but if he'd done what he was *supposed* to do, he'd never have this problem, and what he's *supposed* to do is watch over peopleses souls; not make dirty movies. He's going to have his hands full looking after his *own* soul now."

After Rita Scott gave her name to the rental car clerk, the young woman with the piled high cotton candy hair checked her computer terminal and made sad, musing little noises with her tongue. "Seems you're late, Miz Scott."

"I know," Rita apologized.

Whatever customer service training Ms. Cotton Candy-Hair had gotten from the car rental agency had tempered her drawl down to something most out-of-staters could understand, but it was still there. And when she looked at Rita and smiled a cold, mechanically polite smile, Rita didn't hear, "Seems you're late," but instead heard, buried in that tempered drawl, "Well, it's time to give the nigger a hard time." In truth, if there *was* a subtext to Ms. Cotton Candy-Hair's drawl it was probably nothing more than, "It's the end of a long day and I could do without *this* headache," but that's not what Rita heard because some cuts run so deep they never heal. She believed that being coldly, obligatorily polite was just a more civil way for some people to say, "nigger."

"You were due in this afternoon," said Ms. Cotton Candy-Hair.

"I *know*," Rita said. "They rerouted us to Denver because of a security scare" (some poor Pakistani trying to make his prayers in the privacy of one of the lavatories had been taken for a Moslem praying in preparation for a kamikaze mission; a steward had kicked in the bathroom door, a punch had gotten thrown, and then it was off to Denver). "The only way for me to get here was to fly to Dallas/Ft. Worth and take some little puddle jumper here. I called my office from Denver to have them notify you I'd be delayed."

Ms. Cotton Candy-Hair continued to study her screen. "I don't see any note for a 'hold' here, ma'am."

"Then somebody must've messed up."

Beautifully non-committal and non-accusatory: "Somebody must have."

Rita was still wearing the same suit she'd slept in on the flight from New Jersey the night before. She hadn't gotten that much sleep on the plane out of L.A. before the fracas around the bathroom had brought her back to consciousness and the news that, for security reasons, her plane was now heading in the wrong direction. And then there had been a catnap in a rather abusive plastic chair at the airport in Denver. So, she was understandably tired and uncomfortable and cranky, and now Ms. Cotton Candy-Hair was, in equivalent terms, poking a stick through the bars of a lion cage. But Rita Scott had dealt with the public long enough to know that the surest way of guaranteeing inaction was to start screaming, so she simmered, she boiled, but she kept the cork in her temper until the immediate need to explode passed.

"Might I ask," she said, biting the words out with her own brand of cold politeness, "if there is *some* kind of vehicle I can rent?"

"We don't have much left, I'm afraid," Ms. Cotton Candy-Hair said in a wide-eyed apology which Rita was sure meant, "Time to put the nigger through the hoops." "We have a luxury sedan, and a Corvette. Either one might be a little pricey -- "

Rita smirked as she fished out her company credit card. "Which one costs the *most*? The Corvette? I'll take it!"

The clerk looked puzzled, unsure the black woman across from her had heard right. "Ma'am, that's three hundred dollars. Per *day*. Plus insurance. And mileage."

"Don't you worry about it, honey," Rita said. "Just start the paperwork rolling. Give me the works. Insurance, expanded driving radius, multiple drivers, anything else you can think of. Shoot the moon." Eric Bird III, she thought in a savory vindictiveness, you want to send me to Texas? Then you can pay for the privilege. Pay, pay, pay, and pay, then just pay, pay, and pay some more, and then pay, pay, pay, and *pay*...

Bob Wheeler ran his Monte Carlo slowly past the snug little cottage that was the parsonage.

"Is anybody even home?" Elwood Poteet wondered aloud in the passenger seat, squinting out into the night. There was no porch light on at the parsonage, and, at first glance, the windows all seemed dark.

"I see Owen's car in the driveway," said Bob Wheeler.

"I don't see Sarah's, though," said Elwood.

Bob leaned across Elwood's lap, thinking he'd caught a glimmer seeping out around a drawn curtain. "Is that a light?"

"I can't tell. Bob, if you don't watch where you're going…"

Bob frantically pulled on the wheel when he heard his hubcaps scrape along the curb. He pulled the car back out into the empty street and headed down the block and around the corner.

"What're you doing?" Elwood asked.

"I'm going 'round t'other side a the block. Maybe we can see lights on in the back a the house."

Elwood nodded approvingly.

"See anything?" Bob asked.

"Looks like Herman Iny's getting himself an in-ground pool. He must be doing pretty well."

"We're not here about Herman Iny's pool, Elwood. That's the parsonage back there. See anything? Any lights?"

"Nope."

"Ya know, Elwood…"

Elwood waited expectantly.

"I mean, I'm just thinking…"

"Yeah, Bob?"

"I mean, if he *is* home…"

"What is it, Bob?"

"I just thought, *if* he *is* there, maybe you should take the lead."

"*I* should take the lead?"

"That's my thinking."

"Why should *I* take the lead?"

"Well, Elwood, let's face it. You bein' a newspaper man 'n' all, buttin' in to people's private business is kinda your job, isn't it?"

Elwood Poteet shifted in his seat and frowned. "I don't know that's how I'd rightly put it, Bob; 'butting into -- '"

"I didn't mean anything bad by it, Elwood. I mean, well, you know what I mean."

"*You're* the one on St. Mark's board a trustees. Doesn't that make this 'kinda *your* job'?"

"Well…"

"I thought so."

They cruised by the parsonage a second time, squinted and peered at the dark cottage, and, again, Bob Wheeler cruised on by, turned the corner.

"You going 'round, again?"

"Guess I'm trying to work up to it."

Elwood sighed sympathetically. "It's not gonna be any easier tenth time around."

On the next lap, Bob Wheeler pulled his car up to the curb in front of the parsonage, killed his headlights, switched off his engine. He and Elwood Poteet sat for a long moment in the dark car, staring at the little house across the lawn, listening to the cooling engine tick.

"We sit here any longer, somebody's gonna think we're neckin'," Elwood Poteet said.

They both took a breath, and then climbed out of the car. They stood side by side on the walk, but they didn't move beyond that.

"I told Owen what to do about this crabgrass," Elwood Poteet said, tsk-tsking over the condition of the parsonage lawn. "You got to put down 'at Surflan in the spring. Too late, now. I tell him every year."

"Well, we're not all big newspaper magnates can afford ChemLawn, Elwood."

They stood for another moment quietly studying the parsonage.

"I think I see some lights on behind the curtains," Elwood said.

"Well, let's knock and see who's home."

"Yeah," Elwood sighed, not moving.

"Yeah," Bob sighed, not moving. "You didn't have to print the damn story, Elwood."

"I'd give you a lecture on journalistic responsibilities, Bob, but to tell you the truth, 'bout now I kinda wish I *hadn't*."

They walked slowly up the S-shaped flagstone walk to the front door.

"Definitely lights on inside," Elwood said as they got closer to the door and were better able to see the glow around the edges of the curtains.

Bob Wheeler stood at the door, started to ring the doorbell, changed his mind to reach for the brass knocker, changed his mind and rang the doorbell then rapped the knocker. "Owen? Owen! It's Bob and Elwood, Owen! C'mon, we see the lights! Open the door, Owen, please!"

They heard the lock chain rattle inside the door, then the dead bolt slide free, and the door swung open. Just inside was the foyer, and from there they could see down the hall that led to the back of the house. The hall and rooms were dark. They heard Dawson's voice call from the living room. "Evening, Bob, Elwood."

"Can we come in?"

"You know you're always welcome."

Inside, the air was stale and warm, smelling of sweat and old food, of piled, unwashed clothes and liquor. It was something of a shock in a house that had always smelled of Fabreze and aerosole-spray potpourri. Elwood closed the door behind them. They could see through the foyer archway into the living room, so brilliantly lit they both squinted.

"We missed you at the meeting this afternoon," Bob Wheeler said.

"Things to do, Bob. I've been busy here all day. See for yourself. Couldn't spare the time."

"Busy with…?" and Bob gestured around the living room.

Dawson was sitting in the middle of the living room floor, a saucepan of macaroni and cheese parked between his crisscrossed legs. He looked around the room with a proud, proprietary smile. "Busy with my movie."

Bob Wheeler looked over at Elwood Poteet hoping to see that somebody in the room knew what was going on and how to deal with it, but Elwood looked back at Bob with the same sense of being at a complete loss on both counts.

"I have to sit down," Elwood said.

The overheated, odious air had rolled over them like a wave, but then Bob and Elwood were hit a second time by what they saw. Sarah Dawson had kept the little cottage in the proud, tidy way of a young girl who'd never had much and now had her own first – if modest – home. Wood shined with polish, lamps and bowls sat perfectly centered on clean, ironed doilies. But now, unwashed clothes littered the floor, and two dress boxes of photographs had been upended, their contents spilled across the parquet and rifled through. On the sofas and chairs, more pictures: snapshots, framed photos, albums. Scattered among them: Dawson's diploma from divinity school; Sarah's from high school. The little wax bride and groom from their wedding cake. A childhood treasure of a doll, a miniature *faux* trophy cup with a plaque reading, "World's Best Boyfriend," a red pillow with a gold embroidered "The Gulf Coast" over a silk-screen picture of a beach and surf and sailboats and water skiers. As Bob pondered the litter splashed all about the room, he thought of a garage sale; all the family memorabilia, odds and ends, worthless yet emotionally-laden junk usually stashed in attics and cellar trunks, tucked in bins under beds and boxes piled atop closet shelves, now dumped in a pile to be poked, picked over, foraged through.

As for the brightness of the room, every light was on: every table lamp, the sconces over the fireplace, the overhead. Other lights had been pulled in: bedside lamps, desk lamps, even a pair of caged work lights. They were burning up the air in the room, percolating the stale smells, making the room closed in behind shut windows and drawn curtains hot and clammy and fetid. With the back of his hand, Bob Wheeler dabbed at the sweat breaking out across his upper lip and forehead. He looked over to where Elwood Poteet had gingerly insinuated himself among the Dawson family artifacts on the sofa and wondered if there was room to do likewise because he, too, felt the need to get off his feet.

"I was going to ask you if you were serious about this movie thing," Bob said, his voice feebly imitating the casual, "but I guess I don't have to. All a this…this is all part a your movie?"

Dawson, too, looked like something to unload at a garage sale. He was still wearing the clothes Bob had seen on him the day before at the Horseshoe. Now they had the rumpled, withered look of having been on a body too long, of having been slept in, sweated in. Dawson's hair was matted, his face had an unwashed, oily sheen. His eyes were red and bleary, their lids heavy, the skin around them puffy and blue. There was a spoon already sitting in the pot. Dawson scooped a hardened clot of macaroni and cheese out of the pot and shoved it in his mouth. He held the pot out in an offer to Bob and Elwood.

"We ate," Bob managed to say. "I tried to reach you all afternoon, Owen."

Dawson shrugged. "Problem with the phone."

Bob looked over to the phone table that sat along the foyer wall, saw the phone smashed against the floor.

"It's awfully stuffy in here, Owen," said Elwood, fanning himself. "It's a nice, cool evening outside. Well, cooler than it is in here. How 'bout we open a window?"

Dawson stiffly climbed to his feet and turned to a corner of the room where his camcorder sat on its tripod, aimed at some small object tacked to a corkboard propped on an easel. "I don't think so. This is what they call in the movies a, 'closed set.' It's all the lights. I wanted to make sure I had enough light. What about it, Elwood? You take pictures, you're the expert. Do you think I have enough light?"

"I guess, Owen. I don't rightly know for this kinda thing."

Dawson took another spoonful of macaroni and cheese, set the pot down on a chair where he found a nearly empty bottle of sherry, using its last few swigs to wash down the food. "I was going to offer you gentlemen a drink…" He apologetically gestured with the now empty bottle and tossed it on the chair.

"That's fine," Elwood Poteet said. "We didn't feel like having anything."

Bob Wheeler cast another look down the dark hallway. "Where's Sarah, Owen?"

Dawson bent over his camcorder, fiddling with the focus while he put his eye to the viewfinder. "Galveston, she said. That cousin of hers, again. Could you fellas just wait until I finish this shot? In fact, one of you could help. How about you, Bob?"

"I, uh…"

"I just need your hand, Bob." Dawson put a hand on Bob's shoulder and guided him to the easel. Bob looked over his shoulder at Elwood helplessly, and Elwood looked back just as helplessly. Close up to the easel Bob could see what had been tacked to the corkboard: a matchbook. "Just point your finger there. That's it; perfect!" Dawson returned to his camera. Bob looked down at the matchbook, a gaudy red and white thing promoting some placed called, "The Shady Tree Motel." Dawson recorded for a few seconds. "Ahh, that's good. You're done, Bob, thank you."

"Owen, I think we should get Sarah on a phone and ask her to come home," Bob said. "Maybe all of us can sit down and talk about what's going on. We'll get Lily over, Elwood can call Miriam, it'll be all of us. Like we always do, you know. Get a bucket a chicken or something. And just talk."

Dawson pushed the pot of macaroni and cheese and empty sherry bottle clear of the chair and they clattered on the floor. "Nothing to talk about, Bob," he said tiredly, dropping onto the cushions. "I'm going to make my movie."

"Then at least tell me how to get in touch with Sarah, let her know what's going on."

"Sarah's not coming back, Bob."

"Did she leave you, Owen?" Elwood Poteet asked. "Is 'at what this is all about?"

"What this is about, Elwood, is my *life!*" Dawson said. "That's what all this is. That's what my movie is. It's the story of my life. It's about how you think things are one thing, but they turn out to be something else. An illusion. Sleight of hand. Some people might use the word, 'lie.' You find out that what you've believed in all along…" Dawson winced suddenly, as from a sharp pain, but it passed quickly, seemed to have left him drained. "…turns out there's nothing there. Never was." Then the exhaustion was gone, and he was back into his disturbingly blithe, conversational mode. "Sarah's not coming back because that's the way the movie is supposed to go."

"This movie of your life," Elwood said.

"Yes."

"You think of your life as an X-rated movie, Owen?"

Dawson grinned mischievously. "Well, let's say the story takes a few unexpected turns in the last act, Elwood. Definitely *not* for the kiddies. Surprise twists."

From where he was still standing at the easel, Bob could see into the small, unlit dining room. Resting across the arms of one of the dining chairs was an oblong package of brown paper and string. Alarmed, Bob looked over to Elwood who came over, recognized the package he'd seen Dawson carrying from Kirkland's store.

"And what're you doing with this, Owen?" Elwood asked.

"Oh, don't worry about that, Elwood. That's just a prop for my movie."

"What kind a prop?"

Dawson shrugged. "You know. Just a prop."

"You don't look well, Owen," Bob said. "I think you should see somebody."

"Oh, I will, Bob. I do plan to see somebody. And it'll be part of my movie. That's what the movie's all about. I'm going to go see somebody and that'll be the big finish. The climax, as we movie people say."

Despite the burning lights and the suffocating air, Bob Wheeler felt a chill, a cold lump coalesce in his stomach. He could feel Elwood Poteet move closer to him, the way children in the dark draw together when they're afraid.

"Walk out of here with us, Owen," Bob Wheeler said, and he could hear the squeak in his voice as his throat tightened. "Come home with me. Lily and I'll put you up. She won't mind."

"Or us," Elwood offered. "Miriam'd be happy to have you."

Dawson turned away, lowered himself to the floor and began sifting through the splayed photographs there.

"Even just a motel," Bob pushed. "Just get outta here for a few days. We'll find somebody you can talk to, help you through this -- "

"I don't think so, Bob," Dawson said. "I'm going to help myself through this." He looked up, grinned, a sarcastic smirk. "If a minister can't minister to himself, who can he minister to?"

Bob got down on one knee by Dawson. "Owen, I'm your friend. You know that, don't you?"

The sarcastic twist faded, and Dawson's face turned sorrowful, but not for himself. "I know, Bob. I appreciate it. Both of you; I really do. You've always been good friends." Then his face went blank. "But I've got to finish my movie," he said the same way he might've said, "Excuse me, but I've got the lawn to mow."

And then Bob Wheeler grew frantic. Wherever his friend Owen Dawson was going, Bob saw him going beyond where he'd be able to pull him back. "For God's sake, Owen -- " and he reached out to put a hand on the younger man's shoulder.

But Dawson pushed it away, and now that acidic smirk was back. "For God's sake, Bob? For *God's* sake?" He got to his feet and looked up at the wooden cross mounted to the wall above the mantelpiece. "I wore out my knees praying for God's sake and it hasn't healed a goddamned thing. Not a goddamned thing! You just wear out your knees talking to yourself!" Then he reined his temper back in with a sigh, reached down his hands to help Bob Wheeler to his feet, patted his friend on the shoulder. "Sorry, Bob, Elwood. I didn't mean to lose my temper at you. I thank you for your concern. But I don't need it."

"Owen," Elwood said, "you're not thinking clearly."

Owen Dawson smiled…beatifically. In epiphany. So full of the rightness of his thinking he seemed to suddenly verge on tears. "You're wrong, Elwood. I am thinking more clearly than I ever have in my life. If you could see the world as clearly as I do right now your eyes would *bleed!*" The moment passed, he looked at his friends gently. "You two need to go home. To your wives. Everything'll be -- "

The sound of glass breaking off somewhere in the house. Then, again; a window breaking.

"What the -- " Bob turned for a window but Dawson held him tightly by the shoulder, directing he and Elwood into the foyer.

"You might want to wait here a minute," Dawson said. "I think the natives are a little restless tonight."

The three of them stood in the foyer listening to one window in the house after another shatter, a rock tumble along the floor, another rumble across the dining table, glass tinkle and break again on the hardwood. Through the foyer archway they could see flickering lights – firelight – around the edges of the closed curtains along the front of the house.

"Stay here," Dawson told them. He walked calmly across the living room, took the video camera from its tripod, poked the lens through the curtains and put his eye to the viewfinder.

"Owen!" Bob called. "C'mon away from there before you get yourself conked in the head!"

Dawson stayed at the window. Through the gap he'd made in the curtains, Bob and Elwood could see wavering orange and yellow light dance across his face.

Then there was a new light – striking flashes of blue and red – and the wail of a police siren. Bob and Elwood heard the screech of tires, the tinny voice of a bullhorn: "Awright now, y'all! This here's an unlawful assembly! If y'all don't wanna spend the night in the lockup, get on home! I'm not kiddin', now; scoot!"

Dawson came back to the foyer and reached for the door.

"Jesus, Owen, stay here!" Elwood cautioned.

But Dawson only gave them a delighted smile before swinging open the door and there, on the lawn, framed squarely by the doorway, stood an eight-foot-high flaming cross.

"Owen!"

He was out the door, his video camera at his eye as he slowly circled the burning cross.

Beyond the flames, Bob could see Clyde Thomas standing by his squad car, bullhorn in hand, while Billy Ray Barnes – riot gun in hand – pushed back at the small, solemn crowd standing at the curb.

"C'mon, folks!" Billy Ray chided, "Y'all ain't got no business here!"

"Butt out!" a voice from the crowd called. "This ain't got nothin' to do with the law!"

Clyde raised the bullhorn, again. "Wrong! This is *my* business! The fire department's on its way! Now, if y'all don't get on home, I swear I'll have 'em turn the hoses on *y'all!* I'm gonna say it one, last time: *Git!*"

Slowly, the crowd thinned, people drifted off into the shadows, left their front porches to peek out through their front window curtains. Doors along the street slammed closed, porch lights winked out, until there was only Dawson and his camera, Clyde Thomas and Billy Ray, and Bob Wheeler and Elwood Poteet standing in front of the parsonage. The sad rise and fall of a fire truck siren was out in the dark, drawing closer, but the fiery cross was already dying down.

A peeved Clyde Thomas turned to Dawson. "Ya know, preacher, you didn't help nothin' comin' out with 'at thing." He nodded at the video camera.

"Sorry to be a bother, Mr. Thomas. You can send the fire department home. Just let it burn out. There won't be any more trouble, Mr. Thomas. That's a promise."

Clyde slipped a hand under his Stetson, scratched his head thoughtfully and flapped his lips in an exasperated sigh. He looked to Bob Wheeler and Elwood Poteet for some kind of explanation on what the hell was going on, but they just fidgeted and shuffled their feet and looked over to Dawson who, if he had one, wasn't sharing.

"Go on home, fellas," Dawson said. "And…thank you."

The parsonage door closed behind Owen Dawson and a few moments later the lights behind the living room curtains started going out one by one until the cottage was black and empty-looking behind its broken windows.

Bob and Elwood looked to Clyde Thomas.

"You heard the man," Clyde said, "Go on home."

The fire truck was pulling up to the curb.

"You can tell them to go on home, too," Clyde said to Billy Ray, nodding at the truck. "And Billy Ray; put the shotgun away, first."

THE THIRD DAY: Lovelady

Wednesday morning...

The alarm clock didn't wake Billy Ray Barnes so much as antagonize him. He buried his head deeper into his pillow until the Big Ben ran down to silence. In a short, blessed moment of quiet, he almost drifted back off to sleep, but then just as quickly tensed at the sound of his bedroom door swinging violently open.

"Billy Ray! Le's go! God didn't intend me to be yer alarm clock! Boy, I said le's *go!*" His mother's voice had a pitch that *always* made her sound irritated and impatient, even when she *wasn't* being irritated and impatient, but when she *was* – like now -- she sounded *really* irritated and impatient. "Billy Ray, I said it's time a git up 'n' *don't* you be givin' me no 'five mo' minutes' back-sass! *Up!*" At that, the flat of her calloused hand cracked across his buttocks like a fly swatter.

At which Billy Ray flinched, spasmed, then went slack, again, his head sinking face down into his pillow into which he mumbled, "Fi' mo' minusss..."

"Ok, *fine!* Jus' go *on*, then! *Be* late! Clyde Thomas calls up 'n' wants a know where his deppity is, *don't* be askin' me to tell 'im no *fibs!*"

"I won'," Billy Ray said, sliding his head under the pillow.

"I don't believe in tellin' no *lies*, Billy Ray! You *know* that! Child a mine or no, *don't* be askin' me!"

"I won'."

"Clyde Thomas calls up 'n' wants a know where his deppity is, I'm gonna *tell* 'im! 'He's *layin'* in there like the Queen a Sheba -- '"

Billy Ray Barnes realized the only five more minutes he was likely to get was of a shrill earful by his mother which hardly seemed worthwhile. He slowly sat up in his bed. "Ok, Mama," he yawned, "I'm up, ok? See? I'm up."

"I ain't got no *time* to be messin' with ya like this ever' mornin', Billy Ray! I gotta git down to the shop for that early crowd." Standing in the doorway of his room in her pink "Pearl's Beauty Salon" smock, she was all spindly limbs, a well-defined potbelly, and a cigarette parked at the corner of her mouth so permanent-like Billy Ray figured she must've come out of her mama's womb sucking on it. She smiled proudly over her son's decision to join the new day, turning all cooing motherly love: "That's my boy, my big ol' po-lice man! Now, what does my big ol' po-lice man want for his breakfast? Whatcha want, hon, hm?"

Billy Ray had gotten his feet to the floor but had yet to muster the energy for standing. "Ain't got no time for breakfast, Mama." He cut off her protests with a martyr-like wave-off. "No, no, *you're* the one goin' on 'n' on 'bout me gettin' to work on time 'n' all. I'll just get me somethin' on the road."

She frowned in maternal concern. "Ya can't be *doin'* like this all a time, Billy Ray! It ain't *good* for ya! Ya gotta eat *right* in a mornin'! Maybe if you 'n' Arva May stop cattin' 'roun' ever' night where ya can get some decent sleep, ya'd git up early 'nough to have a *proper* breakfast!"

Billy Ray was fishing around under his bed with one of his feet. "You shine my boots, Mama? Where's my boots?"

"No, I did *not* shine yer boots! I am *not* yer slave, Billy Ray Barnes! Ya want a shine on 'em boots, I'll show ya where the Shinola 'n' rags is!"

Billy Ray had finally gotten to his feet. He gave his mother an autonomic peck amid her teased, bluish hair and a gentle shove out of the room. "I gotta change now, Mama. 'Scuse me." He closed the door behind her and let himself fall back on the bed.

"I *heard* that, Billy Ray! *Git up!*"

Fifteen minutes later, Billy Ray Barnes was clomping down the front porch stairs in his unshined boots to the dirt driveway, his mother right behind him still going on about how he *always* made her late for work and how he'd *better* be sure to get himself a decent breakfast and a lot of other lifestyle direction he didn't even bother to pretend to hear which didn't seem to dissuade his mama even the least little bit from continuing on. He gave his mother another kiss on her straw-stiff hair and guided her forcefully to her car, a little Chevy so old the paint and primer had flaked off in places revealing bare steel.

"'N' you drive *careful!*" she called out as – still deaf to her -- he climbed into his patrol car.

The first few days Billy Ray had parked the patrol car in his driveway, he'd felt the chest-busting pride of a hunter who'd nailed a henhouse-raiding puma's pelt to his door. It had certainly been the newest and fanciest thing on the block which, considering the general sense of neglect and disrepair in Billy Ray's neighborhood, wasn't saying all that much. The sad thing now was the unit was *still* the newest and fanciest thing parked on the block, despite the toll the years – and Billy Ray – had taken on the rusting, blue-smoking, black-and-white Ford.

He opened all the windows because if he used the air conditioning the car would overheat. He turned the key but it took more than one try for the starter to convince the engine to kick over. The patrol car started with a few coughs and a lot of rattling before it settled into a steady rumble. Billy Ray turned the car down the street leaving behind a wake of blue smoke. Boy, it would've been sweet if ol' Clyde could've talked the county into popping for a new patrol unit, he thought, especially if they got themselves an SUV. Clyde would probably have gotten to take it home but still, sometimes, maybe, he could've coaxed the chief into letting him take it out on rounds once in a while. Even that would be better than tooling around in this rust bucket all the time. "I see some kid come out the back a Kirkland's store at night 'n' he jackrabbits, only way I'm gonna catch 'im in this thing is to get out 'n' push!" he once told Clyde Thomas. "That's not zackly how you intimidate the criminal element."

To which Clyde, rubbing his head like he'd suddenly come down with a headache which he seemed to do a lot when he talked with Billy Ray, said that if Billy Ray had such a mad-on about his patrol unit maybe he should just leave it at the curb in front of the station and do his rounds on foot. Which pretty much ended the discussion.

Billy Ray pulled in at Abner Birney's convenience store on Groveton Highway and bought two packs of Sno-Balls and a root beer slushie. When he got home that evening his mama would ask if he'd gotten a decent breakfast and he'd say yes and she'd somehow know he was lying (as she somehow always did) and light into him again. But then his mama's breakfast repertoire was limited to cold cereal and Eggos, so he always figured despite all her yowling and yammering he really wasn't missing out on much.

Later, Billy Ray would credit his keen sense of observation for the discovery, but the fact was he only noticed the car because he was arranging his white and pink Sno-Balls on the seat next to him buffet-style so he could work his way through them on the drive to work. He was trying to figure out whether or not to eat the whites or the pinks first, or alternate them but if so which one to start with, and as he looked up to ponder the various possible configurations, he saw the boxy tail of an old Cavalier jutting out from behind the dumpster in back of the store. That alone didn't stir much curiosity in Billy Ray, but he noticed a sticker on the rear bumper and Billy Ray was always a sucker for a nifty bumper sticker. "If you can read this you're too damned close," was a favorite. He was also fond of, "Kill 'em all! Let God sort 'em out!" "I speed up for old people!", "Honk if you love beer!", "I brake for blondes!" and "My other car is a Rolls!" "Nuke the whales!" *always* made him laugh, and, "If you're not a hemorrhoid get off my ass!" was one he particularly treasured. Billy Ray would have wallpapered both bumpers of his patrol unit with them if Clyde Thomas would've let him, but Clyde said the only thing appropriate for a municipal vehicle was an American flag, "Support your local police," and a yellow ribbon decal which Billy Ray thought, well, ok, yeah, I support the troops 'n' all, but there wasn't much funny there. Hell, he couldn't even remember where he was supposed to be welcoming the troops home *from*.

So, having finally made his selection, Billy Ray climbed out of his patrol car with a pink Sno-Ball in one hand and his root beer slushie in the other. He moseyed over to the Cavalier, but all the Cav was wearing on its tail was a Jesus fish and a "Honk if you love Jesus!" sticker. He took a slurp of his slushie to wash down a wad of Sno-Ball and was about to turn back for his car, but stopped himself and, instead, walked closer to the Cavalier.

With the inexplicable exception of Arva May Arlin, there were few people in Boone who figured Billy Ray Barnes for much in the brain muscle department. To the unanimous agreement of the Horseshoe Grille congregation, Smitty McKee once assessed that, "Get that Billy Ray Barnes boy on *Jeopardy* 'n' he's gonna end up *owin'* money!" But Billy Ray was not without his talents.

From the time he'd been old enough to hold a .22 rifle without tipping over, Billy Ray's dad had taken him out into the public lands to teach him to track and shoot, and Billy Ray had spent the most memorable parts of his youngsterhood banging away at everything from squirrel and jack rabbit to white-tail and wild boar (Billy Ray had been 10 when his dad was lost during Operation Iraqi Freedom after his National Guard unit had been called up; Billy Ray always said his daddy had been "lost in the war" which had a more heroic ring to it than the more specific, "Daddy worked supply in Saudi Arabia and died when a water truck backed over him"). The upshot being that Billy Ray might not have been able to read the front page of any of the big state newspapers without somebody explaining some of the harder parts to him, but he had no trouble reading sign.

The Cavalier was spotted with what looked like a past rain but which Billy Ray recognized was pollen blown off the grassland alongside the highway and around the convenience store lot, and that had settled on the car overnight with the dew. From the looks of it, Billy Ray guessed the car had been sitting behind the dumpster at least two days, maybe three.

Billy Ray crammed the substantial remainder of the Sno-Ball into his mouth to free up one hand and walked around to try the driver's door. Locked. He looked through the dusty window and saw the passenger door was locked as well. Hanging from the rearview was a small, wooden cross.

He took a musing sip of his slushie, and as he stepped back from the car, he saw past the hood to a muddy depression taking up where the convenience store blacktop ended. And out on the mud he noticed a piece of white cloth.

There was something vaguely familiar about the shape of it, familiar enough for him not to think it was some stray bit of trash blown clear of the dumpster.

Billy Ray found a long piece of metal molding sticking out of the dumpster and used that to try to reach out from the edge of the blacktop and pick the bit of cloth from the mud. He reached too far, lost his balance, and slipped into the mud ankle deep. "Jee-*sus!*" he fulminated, though he was impressed with himself that he'd managed the slip and stumble without losing his slushie. No longer having to worry about keeping his boots clean, he sloshed his way over to the bit of cloth which turned out to be a pair of woman's panties. They were small in the waist, baggy in the seat, plain, white, stained a little yellow in the crotch. Leading up to where the panties had been laying and then across the remainder of the muddy depression and out into the grassland, were small, narrow footprints; no shoes, just bare feet.

And then the slushie and the Sno-Ball didn't feel so good in his stomach. He scooped up the panties between two fingers, keeping them at arm's length mindful of the yellow stain, then, back on the blacktop, tried kicking the large clumps of mud from his boots as he took down the tag number of the Cavalier. He went back to his patrol car, put the panties in the plastic bag that had held his packs of Sno-Balls, and tried the car's two-way radio. There was a loose wire somewhere and the sound kept dropping out, so he went back inside Abner Birney's store and used the store phone to call the Department of Public Safety.

Despite the hotel lying directly under one of the flight paths leading in and out of Houston International, Rita Scott had been so exhausted she'd slept eleven hours deeply and undisturbed by the regular engine roarings overhead. She awakened so refreshed she almost didn't hate Eric Bird III for being cunning enough to know which of her buttons to push to get her to Texas…almost. And she almost didn't hate herself for being the kind of person susceptible to such button-pushing…almost.

Thinking back to the rental car clerk, she decided to forgo having to deal with some cracker waitress in the hotel coffee shop, and so had breakfast sent to her room, being sure to order more on her company credit card than she intended to eat. After a shower and a change of clothes she finally felt up to dealing with the world outside the door of her hotel room.

At the front desk, the smiling clerk informed her she had missed checkout time by ten minutes. She contemplated making an issue of it, but then slapped her *Investigator* credit card on the counter gleefully, said, "Ok, fine," and barely resisted saying, "Ah, what the hell, why don't you throw an extra *two* days on the bill, and maybe a little something for yourself while you're at it!"

She dragged her luggage across the taffy-soft hot tar of the parking lot and jammed it into the passenger seat of her little cherry red Corvette. She started the car and got the air conditioning going full blast, then sat idling while she spread the rental agency-supplied map across her lap. Her fingers ran up and down the maze of lines radiating from Houston as she tried to find the quickest route to Boone.

Her searching finger began to drift. She ordered it to stop and get back to business, but the digit continued to roam until it came to rest on a small dot labeled, "Pennington." Her finger rested there a moment, and Rita felt her throat tighten. She pulled her hand away from the map and re-started the plotting process, this time finding what she'd been sent to find: Boone, Texas.

Twenty minutes later, she was heading north on U.S. 45. Houston fell behind and the open plains and low rolling hills of east Texas taking its place. She passed through the small dusty burgs of Westfield and Spring and Tamina, and with each of them the reassurance that had come with rest and a shower and a change of clothes began to flicker like a bad light.

You are a nigger heading into the Texas boonies, she said to herself in a drawl that had taken hours of diction classes and years of practice to remove. You are a nigger in the Texas boonies, and her foot pressed down on the gas pedal. The Corvette easily flexed its speedometer past 65, then 70. You are a nigger in the Texas boonies and it's harder to hit a moving target...

"So, I 'membered what you always say 'bout us havin' to be vigilantes," Billy Ray said.

"*Vigilant!*" Clyde Thomas corrected, rubbing his head. "*Vigilant.* Not *vigilantes.*"

"Well, so anyways that's how I spotted it."

Clyde Thomas was leaning back in his wooden desk chair, creaking slightly back and forth impatiently. Billy Ray's story – like most Billy Ray stories – was taking much too long to get to the point. "Spotted *what?*"

"So, I'm goin' down Groveton -- "

"You awreddy told me that part, Billy Ray."

" – 'n' I'm at Abner Birney's store – y'all know the one? Over to Groveton Highway by the McCoy place?"

"Yeah, Billy Ray," Clyde said, twirling his finger at Billy Ray to skip ahead.

"It's outta my way, tell ya the truth, but it's my preference since it's 'bout the only one a those places I know ain't run by some Hindoo or a Messican-- "

"*Billy Ray!*"

"So I see this car parked back a the dumpster. Looks to be there a coupla three days, maybe. 'N' just over on the ground I find this." Billy Ray held up the white plastic "Thank You!" bag from the convenience store.

"What's in the bag, Billy Ray? I left my see-through-plastic-bags glasses home today."

Billy Ray put his shoulders back proudly and emptied the bag out on Clyde's desk.

Clyde frowned at the panties. "Those brown spots better be mud, Billy Ray, or you're gonna get clonked inna head with my stapler, throwin' this on my desk like that."

"Yeah, Clyde, 's just mud."

Which didn't account for the yellow stain. Clyde picked the panties up with his letter opener, took the plastic bag from Billy Ray and set the bag down on his desk and the panties down on the bag. "Ya know I eat on this desk, Billy Ray."

Billy Ray missed the admonishment. "Exhibit A, Clyde. Ladies panties."

"I got it."

"White cotton, size six."

"Got that, too, Billy Ray."

"'N' you look close, you'll see the waist is all stretched out indicatin' they was removed by force."

Clyde picked the panties up again with his letter opener to study them more closely – but not too close. "Maybe they're stretched out 'cause whoever they belong to is overweight."

Billy Ray's proud smile faded. His face twisted in confusion. "Well, uh - -"

"Or 'cause they're old. They don't rightly look fresh outta the pack, Billy Ray."

"But it don't look like somethin' come outta the trash, neither!"

"No," Clyde said, trying not to give Billy Ray the satisfaction of seeing his own curiosity up, "No, they don't. Coulda just been a couple those kids Wilbur McCoy's complainin' 'bout tearin' off a hunk."

"I don't think so. The car, Clyde!" Billy Ray's smile was back, almost fevered now. "The *car!*"

"Ok, Billy Ray; the *car*. What about the *car?*"

"I called Public Safety 'n' ran a make. You never guess who it belongs to."

"You're right, Billy Ray. I'm not *gonna* guess. Would you just *tell* -- "

"Sarah Dawson. That's the preacher's wife, Clyde."

Clyde Thomas stopped rocking in his chair. "I know who it is, Billy Ray."

Billy Ray plucked the panties from Clyde's letter opener and held them up in display. "These'd fit her, dontcha think? 'N' last night, Clyde, we didn't see her car at the parsonage, right? Just the preacher's. Didn't see her stickin' her nose outside to see what all was goin' on on her own front lawn, right? Know what? I'm startin' to suspect -- "

"Don't say it, Billy Ray."

" – foul play."

Which was when Clyde Thomas started rubbing his head, again. He looked at Billy Ray with a frown partly because he didn't like the way all these little bits and pieces were shaping up either, and partly because Billy Ray was making a sort of sense which was so end-of-days-omen rare as to be worrisome in itself. "You ask Abner Birney 'bout this car behind his place?"

The displayed panties lowered like a flag saluting a death. "Um, well, no, I guess I didn't. I got kinda excited -- . I could go out there right now 'n' -- "

"Well, you could if you didn't have the mornin' rounds to do that you shoulda done an hour ago."

"Rounds?" Billy Ray stomped around in a child's circle of frustration. "Damn, Clyde, you're worryin' 'bout *rounds?* When we got -- "

"Nothin'. We got *nothin'*, Billy Ray. 'N' I don't want you mouthin' off none a these suspicions 'n' theories 'n' all, understand? Keep that loose lip a yours buttoned up."

"But what about -- "

"Billy Ray!"

Billy Ray sighed and set the panties back down on the desk. "Sure thing, Clyde. My lips are sealed." Billy Ray mimed padlocking his mouth.

Clyde wished he could do more than mime it. "I'm sure there's nothin' to all this. But I'll look into it."

"You gonna go talk to Dawson?"

"Not right away. If there's nothin' to this – 'n' 'at's probably how it is – I don't want 'im gettin' all lathered up for nothin'."

"'N' if there *is* -- "

Clyde Thomas silenced Billy Ray with a sharp look. "I just wanna get more a pitcher a what is or isn't goin' on 'fore I go pokin' into his private bidness. Seems he's got enough goin' on right now."

"Good thinkin', Clyde."

"Thank you. Means a lot to me you think so."

"What about -- " Billy Ray started to reach for the panties.

Clyde scooped them up, put them back in the plastic bag and locked the plastic bag in one of his desk drawers. "They stay here where nothin' can happen to 'em." He reached for his hat and his car keys. "Now go on 'bout your bidness, Billy Ray, 'n' if I hear you blabbed one word a this anywheres to anybody, *you're* gonna be lookin' at some foul play."

About a half-hour to an hour south of Boone – depending on how heavy your foot is on the gas pedal – going south on state 19, there's a little jig in the highway, and from around the bend, sticking up above a wall of post oaks, you can see a revolving sequined star. The star sits on a tall pole, and as you come around the bend, under the star, there's a twenty-foot sign in neon script reading, *"Bubba's RV's: Why Leave Home Behind?"* Under the sign is a neon illustration of a cartoonish little Cape Cod on wheels. Under the rolling neon Cape Cod is an office trailer with a sign over the door reading, "Office," and around that trailer, clustered like elephants at a water hole, are two dozen RVs and trailers in all shapes, all brands: motor homes, trailers, motor coaches; Heartlands, Itascas, Winnebagos, Jacos, Keystones...

In that trailer, behind a desk almost too big for its space, cluttered with registration and loan paperwork, family photos, and any little thing that had caught its occupant's fancy – a snow globe from Graceland, a Tom Landry bobblehead complete with narrow-brimmed fedora, and the like – sat Taylor "Bubba" Hopkins.

What made Bubba Hopkins a successful salesman was a sincere desire to make people happy, and an instinct for knowing what would put a smile on a face. That's why he'd hired Cissy Gubler, sitting at her little desk on the other side of the trailer, fussing with the lot accounts on her computer. She'd showed up in the doorway of Bubba's trailer/office last May, shaking with nervousness, clutching a resume shorter than the menu of a curbside taco cart. Bubba knew nothing would make her happier than getting a job straight out of Boone County Community College, the ink still wet on her bookkeeping certificate. (In his more honest moments, Bubba would admit that Cissy Gubler looking more naked dressed than most women looked naked might've had, well, maybe just a little influence on his decision.)

And when Mrs. Bubba got an eyeful of young Cissy with her breasts like two packed scoops of vanilla ice cream and an ass like a ripe, split honeydew melon, Bubba knew nothing would turn the missus' frown upside down like a new Lincoln, especially since Mrs. Bubba always got drooly over that good-looking Texas actor fella doing those Lincoln commercials Bubba didn't think made much sense.

When Bubba saw the boxy little Dodge hatchback pull on his lot, he knew right off there was a fella needing a smile. It was a car screaming "practical," and practical people were always short on something to smile about. When the young driver climbed out with his pinched, Sad Sack face and clothes hanging on him like limp sails on a small boat, Bubba knew his first instinct had been on target. Boy like that gets his ass kicked on a first day a school and it never stops, Bubba thought. Time to bring some sunshine in 'at boy's life.

"I'll be out on the lot, Cissy," Bubba said. He stood, hitched up his daisy yellow polyester slacks as far as his sagging belly would allow, shot the cuffs on his brilliantly blue cowboy-styled shirt with embroidered parrots on the breasts, made sure his pinky ring with a chick pea-sized diamond was face out to catch the sun, then he grabbed his Stetson, gave Cissy a here-I-go wink, and headed out onto the lot.

"Howdy, son!" Bubba hailed, clomping across the blacktop in his mirror-shined Tony Lamas. The little fella from the Dodge flinched and for a second Bubba thought he might run (Jesus, boy, you *did* get yer ass beat every day in school, didntcha?), but Bubba grabbed the young man's hand between his two paws and started pumping. "Mornin', son! You're my first customer a the day, 'n' 'at's a pretty lucky thing, ya know!" Bubba could feel the young man trying to pull his hand back.

"Lucky for who?"

Bubba laughed, not letting go of the hand. "For both us, son, for both us! But lemme let that set a bit. What's yer name, son? Conversatin' gets a might easier I got a name to call ya."

"Dawson."

"That's what everybody calls ya? Dawson?"

"Well, Owen -- "

"Owen, there we go, 'n' you just call me Bubba. Where ya from, Owen? I see ya comin' from up north-way."

"Up by Boone. Well, Boone."

"No kiddin'? Boone? Damn if I ain't got family up that way, 'roun' Grapeland. That pracally makes you 'n' me neighbors, Owen-boy! So, what kinda favor can I do for my neighbor? Obviously ya come on in to look at some a these jewels. Ya got anything paticalar in mind?"

Dawson kept tugging on his arm, trying to get his hand back from where Bubba was still holding it tight between his meaty palms. "Well, to tell you the truth, it was just one of my tires was low and I thought -- "

Bubba finally let go of Dawson's hand but threw an arm around his shoulders to keep him from straying. "Well, neighbor, we surely can help ya with that, but I'm gonna tell ya sumpin' 'n' ya g'ahead 'n' tell me it ain't for true. I'm doin' this a lotta years 'n' this is the only time I had somebody roll on the lot tellin' me all they come in for was they need air in their tires. Hell, son, there's gotta be at least three fillin' stations 'tween here 'n' Boone where ya coulda got yer tire situation took care of."

"I only just noticed -- "

"So what I'm thinkin', Owen-boy, I'm thinkin' maybe ya wanted to steal yerself a little peak at these jewels. Ya know; just curiosity-like."

"Well, I hadn't really -- "

"Owen-boy, like I said, I'm doin' this a looong time, 'n' I know a fella says he ain't here to buy nothin', just look, but what that tells me is 'at fella's got hisself some dreams. I'm not bein' all fancy, like I'm some kinda headshrinker, don't get me wrong, I'm just sayin' anybody who takes a second look at one a these beauts, even iffen he don't wanna buy, it's 'cause some li'l piece a him thinks, 'what if?' That make sense to ya, son? Ya gonna tell me y'ain't never drove by one a these jewels 'n' just once thought, 'what if'?"

"What if," he heard the boy say, quietly, maybe more to himself than Bubba.

Bubba felt Dawson relax under his arm. Bubba knew he'd gotten the boy – and it was hard to think of this weedy little Dawson fella as anything but a boy – percolating on that thought.

Bubba let his arm drop away from the boy's shoulders; he wouldn't leave now. "What's yer line a work, Owen-boy, ya don't mind me askin'?"

"Hm?"

Bubba smiled; Dawson seemed lost in what-ifs as he started to drift among the aluminum and fiberglass hulks warm and shining in the morning sun.

"What all do ya do, son?"

"Oh, well, I'm kind of between things right now. I'm taking a little trip to, um, work some things out."

"Getcher head clear 'n' all like 'at 'til the dust settles, so to speak."

The boy nodded, and Bubba gave him a fatherly I-understand-son smile.

"Ya know sumpin', Owen-boy, 'at's not a bad place to be."

"It's not?"

"I bet yer the kinda person everybody always thought was a serious fella, 'n' they were right. You always had sumpin' ya felt ya had to be doin', am I right? 'N' now, like ya said; ya *don't.* I'll bet ya the diamond in this here ring – 'n' trust me, son, this ain't no prize out a gumball machine – y'ain't never had a proper vacation. Am I right, Owen-boy?"

Dawson reached out to touch the flank of a bus-length Fleetwood. He pulled his hand back; the metal hull was hot under the sun. "Never did," he said in that same quiet voice.

There was something about the way he said it – sad, the way Bubba thought only old men looking back at all they hadn't done could be sad – that touched Bubba. I'll bet this boy ain't seen no more a the world than a goldfish in a bowl, Bubba thought, and that made him even more convinced it was his job – hell, his *mission* – to see this boy drove off his lot happier than when he'd rolled on it.

Bubba set his hand lightly on Dawson's shoulder. "Well, maybe it's time ya gave yerself one, don'tcha think, son? Don'tcha think ya deserve it? Fella bein' serious all a time, prolly always thinkin' he's got too much other stuff to tend to 'n' all like 'at. Am I callin' it for true, son?"

"Amen," the boy said.

"So ya say yer just kinda here 'n' there 'till ya figger some stuff out, right? So I'm thinkin' ya need sumpin' like a kinda headquarters, a safe base a operations, like the Army says, without havin' to truck with a lotta motels 'n' check-outs 'n' all like 'at."

"Yeah," the boy said, and Bubba could see his pale eyes start to fire up as they caught hold of the idea. "A headquarters."

Bubba gave Dawson an I-know-just-what-you-need nod and aimed him at an enormous hunk of sun-blessed silver and black aluminum. "This here's thirty-eight foot a Gulfstream Crescendo -- " (Bubba pronounced it Cree-send-o) " -- and this jewel's as much a home away from home as yer gonna find on this lot. She's even bigger 'n' she looks; got three slide-outs to open up yer livin' room, the dinin' area -- Hell, son, I seen *houses* ain't as nice as this!"

"It *is* big," Dawson said, but not in a good way.

"Don't let 'er scare ya, Owen-boy. Trust me, ya can drive 'at li'l bug-a-boo a yers, ya can handle this. Now, 'member what I said 'bout it bein' lucky you bein' my first customer 'n' all? See, ya come late in the day 'n' I'm havin' a bad day, maybe I try to make it up by stickin' ya, but, no, sir, Owen-boy, ya come on in first, I'm feelin' optimistic, so I give the first customer a the day a break. I won't lie, she's got some miles on 'er, but she feels like new, trust me, 'n' them miles bring the price down under a hunnert."

Bubba saw Dawson waver on his feet like the morning heat was getting to him. "A hundred...thousand...?"

Bubba was so impressed with his own generosity he assumed Dawson was reeling because he was similarly impressed. "Hell of a price, I know, 'n' a bargain. These jewels usually go twenny, thirty, forty more."

"...*dollars?*"

It was then Bubba noticed Dawson was sidling back in the direction of his car.

Bubba took Dawson lightly by the elbow, guiding him to another part of the lot. "Look, I'm just showin' ya the top a the line to get a conversation goin', son, let ya see what some a the possibilities is, 'at's all. Who-all's got that kinda money these days? I only keeps this monster on the lot 'cause people like to come in 'n' gawk at 'er." Bubba steered Dawson toward an Itasca 27-footer. There was a small Mexican boy, ten or twelve, dousing the fenders with a hose and scratching at tiny specks of dirt with a fingernail. "Yo, Es-tay-ban," Bubba called and waved the boy away from the coach. "Now, this here jewel is a bit older 'n' a might smaller, but she's still a Class A, got all them acooterments ya want, any single fella'd kill for an apartment this nice. 'N' she gets ya under forty."

"Thousand." Dawson didn't look any less pained than he had at a hundred thousand.

Gawd*damn*, Bubba, Bubba reprimanded himself, yer not only losin' the sale, yer depressin' the hell outta this boy, 'n' he was no Smilin' Sam when he got here.

"Now let's hold on a sec here, Owen-Boy," Bubba said, holding up a finger as if to say, Don't you move! Bubba patted the globe of his belly, walked around in a little circle which brought him back to Dawson. "Let's try this t'other way 'roun'. Ya don't mind me askin' straight out, son, how far can ya go?"

"You mean how much do I, um...?"

Bubba nodded.

Dawson pointed back toward his little Dodge.

"Hm," Bubba said, and Dawson nodded along with him.

And then it came to him. "Hey, Es-tay-ban! Where ya got 'at Winnebago come in yesterday?"

"'S out back, but we ain' done nothin' yet, Senor Bubba. She still look like shi-"

Bubba waved at Esteban to shut up and made a key-turning motion to send him off to the office for the keys. Bubba began leading Owen around the trailer/office toward the rear of the lot. "Now, see, normal I don't do no trade-ins on passenger vee-hicles 'cause I got no trade in 'em, but that relative I got up to Grapeland? That's my cousin, 'n' he's got hisself a car lot up there, so I'll give 'im a call and see maybe we can work us a three-way deal here, Owen-boy."

Bubba stopped them before they turned the corner of his trailer. "I'm gonna tell ya some stuff up front, Owen-boy, so when ya see 'er, ya can look at 'er in the right light. Now, she ain't no beauty queen. She's easy the oldest thing I got on the lot 'n' I'm not gonna lie to you; she's seen a *lotta* road. Fella owned her, he lived in 'er, I mean this was his *home*, unnerstand what I'm sayin'? His wife up 'n' died ten, twelve years ago, he sold his house, got hisself out on a road, 'n' man, he seen a lotta this country. But, see, then he got the phlebitis 'n' they hadda take his foot off 'n' he couldn't drive 'er no more, so his son down to Lovelady, he lets the ol' fella park it out back 'n' this fella was livin' in there 'til he up 'n' died couple weeks ago. The son ain't got no use for 'er so I took 'er off his hands. Now, here's the thing, Owen-boy. Ya gimme a couple weeks 'n' I could have 'er lookin' like all them other jewels on the lot, but then you 'n' me are back talkin' numbers 'at don't work for ya. But ya take 'er like she is, 'n' iffen my cousin says yeah, we'll call it an even swap, 'n' ya got yourself a steal, 'n' 'at's no lie."

Bubba gave Dawson an are-you-ready look, the boy nodded, and Bubba steered them around the corner.

The only chance Bubba figured he had to make Owen Dawson happy was that this Dawson boy could see past the dings, and the splotches and streaks of rust, and the body rot around the wheels, and the replacement entry door painted in mismatched maroon primer, past the low, thick skirt of caked-on dirt, an amber dusting of pollen, old rain streaks, and a list bad enough she looked like she'd tip over because of two flat tires on the right side. And she was old, *really* old, boxy and square-edged in a way they hadn't made RVs in years, a bread box on wheels.

If Dawson could see past all that, Bubba would have made himself happy, too, not just because he'd done right by Owen Dawson, but because he'd do it while saving himself a couple of weeks and a few thousand dollars getting this pile of tin in saleable shape, and even then, the chances of unloading a dinosaur like this one were, as his daddy used to say, Slim and none, and Slim done left town.

Lying in the shade under the high side of the Winnebago was a fuzzy, ragged-around-the-edges mutt; mostly yellow Lab with a few other breeds thrown in. When the dog saw Bubba and Owen, it crawled out from under the RV, its tail wagging lazily, its mouth – surrounded by a graying muzzle – gaping open in a yellow-toothed grin.

Bubba looked to see how Dawson was taking it all in. The expected possibilities were surprisingly absent: Dawson didn't look appalled or shocked, there was no dismay or disappointment. The boy's brows had come together, but not in anger. It looked to Bubba like he was studying. Thinking.

"Does it run?" Dawson asked after a bit.

"She may be a might banged up on the outside, but the engine's prolly the best thing on 'er, I guaran-damn-tee you! One a them dago car racers'd sell his mama to have an engine like this one in his ol' Formula One Lotus hemi under glass Indie 500 dual exhaust overdrive hot rod!"

Esteban was back with the keys, and Bubba sent him back for the air compressor and jump starter.

Dawson was walking slowly around the Winnebago, the dog sniffing around at his heels.

"He likes you," Bubba said, nodding at the dog. "Ya like dogs? I love 'em! Grew up on a farm with six of 'em, all different sizes 'n' shapes! I'd take this one home iffen I awready didn't have me a couple. They're all them bitty ones 'cause that's what the missus likes, I'd just as soon have a big ol' bowzer like this un, but still, nice to have 'roun'. Now this ol' mutt, he belonged to the fella what owned this vee-hicle. Name's Pooch. Not a lotta 'magination there, I grantcha, but for a dog's name, it don't get much more on a money then 'at."

"Pooch." Dawson stopped, turned that same studying look on the dog. The dog, still grinning, pushed the flat top of his head under Dawson's hand. Dawson's fingertips began to move slightly back and forth through the short, yellow hair, and the dog pushed up closer to him.

"Thing is, 'bout Pooch here, this vee-hicle is the only home this dog ever knowed. Fella's son told me 'at dog was even *born* in 'er!" Bubba pushed his Stetson back on his head, and he went gravely serious. Even if it was mostly an act, Bubba didn't think that made it any less honest since it was true to what he had to say. "See, here's the thing. Seems 'at ol' boy owned this, he made his son promise whatever happened to this vee-hicle, Pooch went with it. 'N' the son made *me* promise. Believe it or not, we even got it in the contract."

Owen pulled his hand away from the dog as if he'd been nipped, stepped back from the Winnebago. "I'm sorry, Mr. -- "

"Bubba."

" – Mr. Bubba, he seems like a nice dog and everything, but there's no way I can take it -- "

"Him."

" – him with me. Providing this thing actually moves."

"Now, now, le's not be too hasty here," Bubba said with a skillful blend of sympathy and calm. "Looky here. C'mon over here, Pooch. Watch this. Sit up, boy! C'mon, sit up! Looka that! My kids don't sit up 'at straight! Now, Pooch, lay down. Yeah, there's a good boy!" Bubba rewarded the dog with a ruffle of his half-erect ears. "'N' he's hell on playin' Frisbee. Goes hog-wild over it. He's got his own box a toys 'n' all inside. Ya don't have to do nothin' 'cept feed him 'n' let him out to do his bidness. 'N' Owen-boy, when you pull this jewel into some campsite at night, 'n' it gets a li'l chilly like it do, 'n' ya hear them coyotes cryin', he's plumb fine company. Help me pass many a night I gotta work late, ain't 'at right, Pooch? Listen, son, ya tell me things is all up in a air-like with ya? I'm gonna tell ya 'nother true thing; ya don't want to be on the road at night by yerself 'cause that's jus' as lonely as lonely gets."

Which seemed to register with the boy somewhere deep inside.

Esteban was back tugging a mechanic's dolly behind him. On the dolly was a battery charger and a small compressor trailing an extension cord running back to the trailer/office. Esteban attached the compressor to one of the flat tires and started it pumping, then set jumper cables from the charger to the Winnebago's battery. "Any time, Senor Bubba." Esteban held up crossed fingers and Bubba batted them away before Dawson could see them.

Bubba opened the entry door. Pooch, smelling home, scooted past him, bounding to the front of the RV to climb into the passenger seat. "Now tell me 'at don't bust yer pump!" he chuckled at Dawson who stood outside, still with that studying face.

The inside smelled of cigarette smoke and stale beer, bad cooking and dog. Some of the upholstery had been patched with duct tape. "Once you get 'er on the road, get some windows open to air 'er out, maybe give 'er a few shots a Febreze, she'll be all nice 'n' fresh for ya!"

Bubba slid behind the wheel. Outside, Dawson had moved around to watch him through the dusty window. Bubba smiled confidently, although inside his head he less confidently was saying, Oh, Gawd, please, do me this li'l favor...

Bubba turned the key. The engine coughed, spluttered, spat blue smoke, then fell into a rough rumble. "You just need to clear her throat out a bit!" Bubba called out the driver's side window. He fed the engine more gas, the smoke cleared (more or less), and the engine settled (more or less). Bubba waved at Dawson to come inside and sit behind the wheel.

"Just see how she feels, son," Bubba said, guiding him into the seat. "Ok, like I told you, she ain't no thing a beauty, but ya got you yer stove, a.c., yer own bathroom... I mean, listen, ya don't know where yer goin'? This is like havin' yer own li'l world, yer own li'l country, like it's the United States of Owen!"

For the first time, Bubba saw Dawson's lips start to flicker in what might've been the tiniest of smiles. "The United States of Owen," the boy said in that quiet, contemplative way of his.

Then Dawson looked over at Pooch in the passenger seat. Pooch looked back, his face still in a dopey, drooling grin.

"Well?" Bubba asked.

"I guess she's all right -- "

"All righty, then! Lemme get my cousin on the phone, I'll get out a set a papers, 'n' le's get you on yer adventure, son!"

That little smile again. "My adventure." But then Dawson frowned. "Yeah, well, but this business about the dog..."

"Hot one today, huh, Chief?" Abner Birney called across the store from the checkout station in the middle of the floor.

"This time a year they're *all* hot ones, Abner," Clyde Thomas said. He opened one of the glass doors to the refrigerator where the soft drinks were on display and flapped it a bit to fan the icy air against his face. "Day like today, even a cold drink don't seem cold enough." He plucked out a Dr. Pepper and walked over to the counter.

In a land of 7-11s and Quik Cheks, Abner and his non-franchise roadside pit stop were dinosaurs; last of the independents. There was no day man, no night man, no "Open 24 Hours," no movie cross promotion give-aways or flavored coffees or fresh-baked doughnuts delivered daily. There were just cold drinks and plain coffee and food that came in either boxes or cellophane, toilet paper and a few other sundries, and runty Abner Birney ruling his little convenience store domain from his command post, a circular checkout counter in the center of the store equipped with a closed circuit monitor for the store's security cameras, a six-inch TV always tuned to ESPN, and a spittoon to deal with the fallout from the chaw of Skoal permanently parked in Abner's veiny cheek. "That it?" Abner asked when Clyde planted the Dr. Pepper on the counter.

"How much you charge to let me roll 'roun' in your ice machine?"

Abner started to laugh as he rang up the soft drink, then stopped to consider. "Gets any hotter, maybe I'll climb in there with ya, Chief." Something on the TV below the counter caught Abner's eye and he made a pained face. "Man, that's gonna cost 'im."

"Whatcha got on there, Abner?"

"Putt-putt."

Clyde cocked his head like he wasn't hearing right. "They got miniature golf on TV?" He craned over the counter to peek at the television in time to see the picture zoom in on a little blue golf ball whizzing through a metal loop-de-loop then exiting out and passing cleanly through the slow-moving blades of a pint-sized windmill.

"Attaway!" Abner declared. "That gets it back! Them's the national finals," he explained nodding toward the TV.

"Finals?" Clyde shook his head. "I didn't even know they had tourneys. Jeez 'n' damn, Abner, is there any sport you *won't* watch?"

"Gotta keep yerself open to new experiences, Chief."

Clyde looked around the store whose layout and décor he couldn't remember having changed even the slightest bit in the 32 years he'd been a Boone law enforcement officer. "Yeah, new experiences, sure." He took a sip of his Dr. Pepper and poked at the rack of snack cakes. "Say, Abner, what's that car out back?"

Abner's beady eyes got a little beadier in a frown. "'S still out there?"

"Damn, Abner, don't you know what's sittin' just outside your store?"

Abner drew himself up in his seat to what little height he had, let out a haughty sniff through a fleshy nose shaped like a piece of rough-edged gravel. "I am management, Chief. I don't tend to the trash. That's what I got *him* for," and he nodded to the Mexican stocking the back shelves. "Why? There some kinda ordinance 'bout parkin' a car in a store parkin' lot?"

"It's your lot, Abner, you can park a damn Abrams tank out there you want to. I was just worried maybe it's an abandoned vee-hicle. Looks like it's been there a while. I could call Cecil Tredway 'n' have him tow it to the impound if you want."

"Naw, t'ain't abandoned." Abner heaved over, let go a stream of tobacco juice in the direction of the spittoon which missed and splatted against the linoleum floor. "Damn. My aim's really off today for some reason."

Which made Clyde grimace at what that might signify as to the environmental conditions inside Abner's command post.

"I got a boy works part-time," Abner said, "colored boy comes in couple hours at night, some weekends. Says he was gonna be outta town a couple days, would it be ok he leaves his car back there. Says he just got the car 'n' where he lives, they see nobody's home 'n' 'at car is *gone!* Y'all know how it is over in 'em colored neighborhoods. So I says yeah, sure, why not?"

Clyde tapped the rim of the Dr. Pepper bottle thoughtfully against his chin. "This boy said it was *his* car?"

Abner Birney's beady little eyes got beadier. "There a problem?"

Clyde shrugged. "He a good kid?"

"Never misses a day," Abner said. "Does his work with no pissin' 'n' moanin'."

"How long he been workin' for you?"

"Just a couple months. He in trouble?"

"Like I said, Abner, I was just worried about that car is all. Look, he shows up, you have him call me down to the station so I know everything is square on 'at car. You got an employment card on him?"

Abner took another shot at the spittoon. "Damn. Well, actually, Chief, I was kinda payin' 'im under the table-like."

Clyde rolled his eyes. "Don't tell me that, Abner! I'm an officer a the law! You don't tell me nothin' like *that!*"

An unimpressed shrug. "Well, then, ok, I musta misfiled his paperwork. How's 'at? Better? You could ask Miz Dawson. Or up there to the ree-form school."

"Sarah Dawson?"

"Yeah, her husband's the preacher over there to -- "

"Yeah, St. Mark's, I know. How do you know her? The parsonage is clear t'other side a Boone. 'S a long way to come for a snack cake."

"She does some kind a volunteerin' up there to the ree-form school. After doin' whatever it is she does up there, she comes in now 'n' again to get a cold drink or somethin', ya know, on 'er way home-like. So, we got to talkin', ya know, 'nough to say hey 'n' all, 'n' a couple months ago she says maybe I should talk to this boy 'bout maybe givin' 'im a job. Says he's a good kid, he awready got one job but he needs to make some extra money, is there somethin' I can do, ya know, talkin' nice 'bout it like you figger a church lady would, talkin' 'bout Christian charity 'n' all. Says 'at Miz Gorsham up to the ree-form school -- "

"Kay Gorsham?"

" – I guess, says I could check with her, like for a reference. That's where he's got his other job. So, I took 'im on. He's been doin' right well, too. Cleared out that whole back room one day, didn't even ask 'im, sweeps up out front with nobody tellin' 'im..."

Clyde took another sip of his Dr. Pepper, paced restlessly along one aisle. By the front door was a magazine rack. The magazines were shrink-wrapped, the plastic wrapping colored to obscure the cover photos but leave the banners clear: *Juggs, Voluptuous, Plumpers...* A hand-written sign hung on the rack: "Adults Only." "Abner, you been told 'bout keepin' these behind the counter."

"I keep the kids away. 'Sides, the pitchers is all covered -- "

"Behind the counter, Abner! 'N' you with a church lady comin' in here regular-like." Clyde took another sip of his soft drink and made a face; it was already not cold enough to suit him. "She been in lately? Sarah Dawson?"

"I guess maybe not since last week or so. Why?"

"Why you watch putt-putt on TV? I'm passin' time, Abner." Clyde drained his bottle and left it empty on the counter. "You have that boy call me he shows up," and he turned for the door.

"Chief, this colored boy, he done somethin', y'all can have 'im, but I don't wanna make no trouble for 'im for nothin'."

"Just have him call me when he shows up, Abner."

"You got it, Chief." Something on the TV screen caught Abner's eye and he made a pained face, again. "Man, that clown head gets 'em ever' time!"

"Damn, Abner, I almost forgot to ask; what's this boy's name?"

With the wind slipping by the Corvette, the steady thrumming of the engine, and the blasting air conditioner, Rita Scott never heard the police siren. In fact, if Rita hadn't caught the red and blue police flashers in her rearview, she would probably have blown past the speed trap and the cop and never have known it because the rattling, smoke-spitting cop car, falling ever more embarrassingly behind, had a better chance of shaking itself to pieces than of catching the fleet little red streak ahead.

Rita pulled over to the shoulder and the police car chugged up behind her. In her side view glass, she saw the driver's door swing open and a muddy, pointy-toed boot stamp down on the pavement. The driver pulled himself out and stood by his car for a moment while he hitched up his pants, adjusted his Stetson and mirrored shades. He hooked his thumbs in his belt, the palm of his right hand resting on the grip of his pistol. He walked slowly and deliberately in what she was sure was a practiced gunfighter's walk meant to intimidate.

She shook her head at the obviousness of it all, reminding herself to stay calm and relaxed even as it kept running through her head over and over: You are a nigger in the Texas boonies...

"Mornin'," the cop said. The Corvette was low, and it was hard for him to lean down to the window, so low he almost lost his hat getting down far enough. Rita turned away to hide her smile as the cop bobbled his hat back on to his head.

"Good morning -- " she caught his name plate " – Officer Barnes." She held up her license, but he didn't take it. She looked up and caught the shades pointed in the direction of her thighs. The interior of the Corvette seemed to have been designed, at least in part, for the purpose of rucking up skirt hems.

"We don't get many a these 'roun' here," he said.

She shifted her legs a bit to let him know she'd caught him in his non-law enforcement-related observations, and the cop flushed, stepped back and hastily ran his eyes up and down the sleek lines of the car. "Corvettes, I mean."

"That's what I thought you meant."

"Uh, yeah, well…" He cleared his throat a couple of times, pointed his head this way and that as if he now couldn't figure out where he was supposed to properly put his eyes, then safely buried himself in business by reaching for the citation book in his belt. "Ma'am, you were really hoofin' it back there. I'm 'fraid I got to cite you. May I see your driver's license, please?"

She waved it, reminding him she'd been holding it up all along. "Sure. Write 'em up, Officer."

He propped the license on his open citation book, but his pen didn't move. He lifted up his mirrored shades for a better look at the license. Rita saw soft, boyish eyes. "Hmmm," the cop said. "California, huh? Los Angeles?"

"Los Angeles."

"Mind me askin' what brings you way out here, ma'am?"

"That a police question?"

The cop looked up and down the empty stretch of highway, the dusty grasslands on either side with their few grazing head of cattle, and back to Rita. "No, ma'am. Just curious."

"I heard so much about Southern hospitality I thought I'd come out here and try it myself."

The cop's lips pursed, and Rita guessed he couldn't tell if she was joking with him or not. "This your car, Miz Scott?"

She passed the rental papers through the small window. "No, it's a rental."

He studied the papers and went, "Hmmm," again. "Well, the signature's yours, but this paper here don't say Rita Scott. It says Eric Bird III Publishing Company."

"I work for him. He's the man who publishes *The National Investigator*. You know that paper?" which, to Rita, was something of a litmus test. Most people who admitted to reading *The Investigator* (and most people didn't, including a lot of people who did) tended to be self-conscious in owning up to reading about two-headed babies, Elvis' ghost, and Big Foot stalking Colorado ski resorts. Officer Barnes, however, seemed absolutely thrilled.

"No lie?" he said brightly.

"No lie, Officer."

"They send somebody all the way from California out to this pile a dust?"

"Here I am."

"You doin' a story *here? In Boone?*"

"No lie."

He cocked his head back in grinning skepticism. "Aw, c'mon! What story we got they'd send you way out here?"

"I'm here to do a story on some minister in Boone who says he's making some kind of dirty movie."

Officer Barnes stopped grinning. His face went blank, his head tilted this way and that and it made Rita think the cop was shaking that information around in his noggin trying to find the right place to process it. Then his face wrinkled up in what she guessed was deep thought, he leaned back down and propped himself on Rita's windowsill, almost losing his hat again. He handed her license back and Rita didn't ask about the ticket the cop hadn't written. And then the corners of his mouth began to curl up ever so slightly. "Ya know," he said smugly, "I can give ya the whole deal on 'at story."

"Is that so?"

He pointed to the shoulder patch on his uniform. "Don't it say Boone P.D. right there? Now this," and he nodded at the car, "I'm gonna let ya go with a warnin' this time, but you be careful down here from now on."

"I will. I appreciate that, thank you, Officer -- . What's your first name?"

"Billy. Well, William, factually, but everybody calls me Billy. Well, Billy Ray, factually."

"Listen, Officer Barnes, is there some place we can talk? About this minister? I'd love some coffee. I've been driving all morning. How about me taking you to a late breakfast at Boone's finest coffee shop?"

Which flustered him. Rita couldn't tell if she was just being that much more forward than the local gals, or he was that uncomfortable having breakfast in a Boone public place with a black woman.

"Um, ah, well, no, thank you, Miz Scott, I'm 'fraid that won't be possible."

"That's a shame." She started the Corvette's engine. "I was looking forward to quoting you as 'Boone Police Spokesman Billy Ray Barnes -- '"

"Well, uh, look, ma'am, we got some coffee 'n' doughnuts over to Po-lice Headquarters. Would that do?"

"That'd do quite fine."

Billy Ray Barnes beamed and was so eager heading back to his car he almost tripped over his own muddy boots. "You just follow me on in, Miz Scott."

"Right behind you, Officer."

The Boone County Juvenile Reformatory didn't look too unlike any other modest-sized school serving a modest-sized community: a blocky, red brick building of a certain, unimpressive size, a colonnaded entrance. However, most modest-sized schools in modest-sized towns didn't usually put heavy steel caging over the windows, or an eight-foot-high chain link fence tipped with razor wire around the sunburnt grounds.

Clyde went past the columns of the main entrance and through a set of double fire doors into the lobby. The grounds outside had been park-like quiet. Inside, yells and shouts echoed like thunder off the bare wood floors and beige-painted plaster walls. The yells and shouts were coming from a little crowd shoving and tugging each other this way and that near a door off the lobby leading to the administrative suite. Kay Gorsham was there wearing one of her two fading career woman suits, and Ed Lewis, one of the school coordinators, was there as well. Ed's ruddy, veined face was even ruddier now, as he hung on to the arm of a writhing teenaged Black boy, maybe 15 (Clyde's rough guess; he could never tell ages on the colored). Holding on to the boy's other arm was a fellow younger and leaner than Ed in a blue security attendant's uniform.

"Fuck you!" the boy spat out. "Fuck all y'all white mothuhfuckas! Fuck all y'all!"

Ed Lewis, in a tactic frowned on in most penology administration training programs, responded by spitting back, "Fuck you, too, Junior, you low-life ball a shit!" and shook the boy violently by the arm. Lewis finally let go of the arm, flinging it away distastefully while pushing the boy into the arms of the security attendant. "Get 'im the hell outta here, Garrett! I want him in isolation! He gives you trouble, mace the little prick!"

"Yessir, Mr. Lewis," the security man said. He tried wrestling the boy down the corridor, but the boy fought, struggling to get in a few last verbal shots.

"You think you sumpin', bitch? I'm gonna tear yo crackuh ass up you gimme a chancet at you one on one! Don't you close yo eyes 'roun' me, you pussy-ass, no-dick white piece a shit! You jus' gimme a chancet 'n' *see* how'm I gonna fuck you up!"

Lewis paced after the boy, following him down the corridor. "*Fuck* you, Junior! Fuuuuck *you!*"

Clyde stepped up to Kay Gorsham. "Another one of our soon-to-be-rehabilitated future responsible citizens?"

"Sure," Kay said drolly. "He's almost old enough to vote."

"Da's right, all y'all muthuhfuckas!" the boy called down the corridor, still struggling with the security man. "We awready put one nigger inna White House! Next one not gonna be so nice, get us some *real* badass in there, get us dat Al Sharpton in there! Den *all* y'all honky muthuhfuckas gonna get yo ass tore up! Be *my* turn, then! 'Hey, crackuh, pull dat piece a shit over! You speedin', Pillsbury, outta the car! Whatchu *mean* you wasn't speedin'? *I* fuckin' say you was fuckin' *speedin'*, crackuh, 'n' you open yo muthuhfuckin' bitch-mouth one mo' time 'n' --. I *tol'* you to *shut-the-fuck-up!*'" and with his free arm the boy mimed bringing a billy club down on somebody's head. "'See? You didn' shut the fuck up? *Now* you gonna shut the fuck up, huh? You want some mo'? G'ahead 'n' say some mo' shit! *Yeah,* heah ya go, bitch, open yo mouth agin! *Yeah,* take another one on yo muthuhfuckin' dumb crackuh head! Now is *my* turn to go Ferguson on *y'all's* ass! Yeah, *my* turn, white milk, *my* turn now!'"

When the boy and his escort finally disappeared behind a bolted metal door down the corridor, Ed Lewis turned to Kay. "The day that nigger turns 18, he's gonna walk right from here into the state lock-up!"

Kay pushed her steel-rimmed glasses up into her silver-streaked hair and rubbed her eyes tiredly. "I'm not sure we're accomplishing as much as we might, Ed," she said icily. "Maybe if we hang a few as an example? String 'em up outside the windows so the other boys can watch the crows peck out their eyes?"

Lewis ignored the sarcasm. "There's no rehab for trash like that, Kay! I want him shipped *outta* here before he taints the other kids! He's a bad influence, Kay! *Bad!* Like a *plague!*"

Kay Gorsham and Ed Lewis were deep enough in argument to forget Clyde for the moment, so Clyde took a seat on one of the uncomfortable wooden benches in the lobby. He looked up at a mural across the lobby, a somewhat prettified view of the BCJR's grounds (no razor-wire topped chain link fence in sight and the grass looked *awfully* green and trim), with some kids playing baseball in the distance, and, in the foreground, a blonde, blue-eyed, fair-skinned grownup smiling down at a politically correct mix of black and brown and red and white boys all smiling back at him.

Clyde heard a rustle and looked over to a corner of the foyer where an elderly Black man moved a dust mop along the edges of the floor. The old swamper nodded and smiled deferentially at Clyde and Clyde nodded back.

"Ed," Kay was saying, trying to keep her own rising steam bottled, "you've got two choices with these kids: you can either break bones or try to turn them around."

"Guess which way I'm leanin' right now."

"You press on them like you do and they're only going to press back harder."

Lewis turned his back on her. "I don't feel like having a philosophical-moral-psychological-whatever discussion just now. I got problems up the kazoo. The main drain off B-wing is stopped up and all the toilets on the tier are backing up, and I've got three people waiting to be interviewed."

"How do they look?"

"They look fine," Ed Lewis said. "The *last* couple looked fine, too. Right up 'til I told them the pay, and then they just looked *gone!*"

"It might make a better impression if you calm down before you talk to them."

Lewis "humphed" and pulled a box of Marlboros from his breast pocket, then began patting his pockets for a light. Clyde whistled to get his attention and tossed him his lighter. "Hey, Clyde," Lewis said.

"Ed."

Lewis lit his cigarette, tossed the lighter back. "See y'all 'round," and he stalked off down one of the corridors.

Clyde pocketed his lighter, shrugged over the prominently placed if ignored sign warning against smoking in government buildings, then turned to where Kay Gorsham was leaning against the lobby wall, her face turned heavenward. "Bad day?" said Clyde.

She laughed tiredly.

"Need to talk to you, Kay. Your office?"

She shuddered. "Please. I've got so much work piled up in there I don't even want to *see* it." She crossed and dropped heavily on the other end of the bench where Clyde was slouched. "I thought you stopped smoking."

Clyde flicked his lighter absently. "I did. Lighter's a habit, I guess. Used to carryin' it 'roun'. Nice to be polite 'n' offer a light when the occasion arises."

"That sounds like you."

He shrugged self-consciously, dropped the lighter back in his pocket and pulled out a pack of Wrigley's. He offered her a piece and soon the two of them were working their jaws and snapping gum together on the bench.

She turned a tired smile to Clyde that was not purely politeness. "So. What's my favorite lawman up to these days?"

Clyde flicked a glance at the Black swamper still moving his dust mop in the same place. "Maybe your office is better. Get a cup of coffee there?"

Her reluctance to go back to her office was understandable. The windowsills were piled high with files, her desktop blanketed with paperwork. Clyde poked at a photo barely visible above the paper drifts: Kay, perhaps ten years ago, arm around what could've been a teen-aged version of herself.

"How's Li'l Lulu?"

"Well, first off, you have to call her Lorianne full out," she said as she poured them each a cup from a Mr. Coffee stationed on a chair in the corner. "My daughter feels that's more grown up and now she considers herself all grown up since her divorce. You take anything with your coffee?"

"Some sugar."

"She's living over your way with her boy, taking classes over to the community college which is nice, I guess." She set Clyde's coffee down on the desk in front of him then slid into her seat on the other side. "She doesn't speak much with her father or me. Another by-product of the divorce, it seems." She threw her glasses tiredly on the desk, then reclined in her chair and let her body go slack with an exhausted sigh.

"Think you might be overdue for a vacation, Kay," Clyde said.

"That an invitation?"

"An observation."

"I'd prefer an invitation."

Which made him fidget, which, in turn, made her chuckle.

"Ok, Clyde, down to business."

"That fella's the preacher over to St. Mark's; Dawson. His wife."

"Sarah Dawson?"

"Yeah. Heard she does volunteer work here."

"Yes, going on a couple of years now."

"What all's she do? She work with the kids?"

"Not anymore."

"So she used to?"

"The first few months, yes, but I pulled her off that. I don't think she knew what to do with them. She didn't have but a few years on the oldest ones and, age aside -- ... You ever meet her?"

"I know her to see her but that's 'bout it."

"She's pretty much still a kid herself. Where she grew up, I don't think she'd seen much of what we deal with in here."

"If she doesn't work with the kids, what all's she do?"

"Helps out around the office. She doesn't have much in the way of office skills, but, you know, helps with the filing, tidies up, that kind of thing. Mostly she does things like hosting fund-raising events, bake sales, meet-and-greets, things of that nature. You know; church-wifey kinds of things." She cocked her head reflectively. "I don't think she cares for it much, though."

"Why? She say something?"

Kay shook her head. "You can just tell. She's bored with it. It's gotten to where she shows up right when she has to but not a minute before, and leaves the minute she doesn't have to be here any longer. Oh, she smiles, she's always nice to everybody, but I think it's just something to do for her. Or..." and she considered a moment, "...maybe because she thinks this is the kind of thing a minister's wife is supposed to do."

Clyde did some considering himself. "Or maybe because it's what the *minister* thinks a minister's wife is supposed to do."

"Maybe. I don't want to be unfair, though, Clyde. Considering she isn't but a kid herself in a lot of ways, she's done fine by us, got us money for a literacy program, a computer skills training program... And she did take an interest – an honest interest – in some of the kids. Well, really, this *one* kid. He isn't actually a detainee. I guess you might call him an alumnus."

"An alumnus."

"Well, he'd been in and out of here more than a few times when he was younger."

"As a detainee."

She nodded. "But during his last term... I think he was really trying to turn himself around. Got his high school equivalency, took whatever programs we offered: job skills, literacy course, psych counseling... We had to turn him loose when he hit 18, but the poor kid didn't want to go home! He was sure if he did, he'd just get in trouble again and he didn't want that."

Evidently Clyde wasn't completely successful keeping the skepticism off his face because Kay Gorsham said, "You don't believe it," with a dry smile.

"If you say so. I don't know the boy, Kay. You're the pro."

At which she let out a rueful huff. "And it's not like I haven't been buffaloed before by more than a few of these stinkers. They get you thinking they have seen the error of their ways and almost as soon as they're out they're back in for something worse." Her face turned vaguely softer. "But this kid… I really believed this kid was trying. Well, we couldn't keep him here, but we did what we could; we gave him a job. Put him on the custodial staff. Take care of the grounds, handyman stuff, you know."

"'N' he was workin' out pretty ok?"

"He made me a believer, Clyde."

"'N' Sarah Dawson took an interest in this kid?"

"She seemed to, especially once he finished his last term. They spent a lot of time talking, and that seemed to help him stick with it. Let's face it; pushing a mop around this place and cutting the grass is hardly an incentive to go down the straight and narrow. She even got him a job off the grounds, kind of a way of helping him take a few first steps out of here. Just part-time work, but it was something, over at some convenience store over to the Groveton Highway."

"This boy's name wouldn't happen to be Leroi Jefferson, would it, Kay?"

Kay Gorsham sat up a little in her chair, her face grew very cautious. Clyde had seen that kind of look before, usually across a poker table when somebody started wondering why the quiet fella who'd done nothing but see or check suddenly started throwing in handfuls of blue chips. "That's his name."

"You still holdin' his juvie file?"

She didn't say anything, putting a fingertip thoughtfully to her lips while she studied Clyde Thomas a bit harder.

"What's the matter?" Clyde asked in a rather ham-handed display of false innocuousness. "His file sealed?"

"No, Clyde, his file isn't sealed." She leaned forward, clasped her hands before her on her paper-littered desk. "I believe in this kid, Clyde."

"I know you do."

"We don't get many of them that can turn it around, or who even *want* to, but I believe in *this* one."

"'N' here I was figgerin' after all this time you'd be all jaded 'n' everything."

She smiled. "I *am*. But still, every once in a while, one gets to you. He gets you thinking you really *can* do some good, maybe just this once."

"You think that's what hooked Sarah Dawson on 'im?"

She shrugged, not having considered it before. "Maybe. I think so. She didn't have much to do except be a preacher's wife, and from what I could see, that didn't seem to be much of a job. This could've made her feel like she was actually *doing* something."

"Y'all sure it wasn't somethin' else?"

This, too, was something Kay Gorsham hadn't considered before, but Clyde could see her realize she was obliged to weigh it now. She thought it over carefully, running it through, gauging what she remembered. "If it was," she said frankly, "nothing I saw."

"His file, Kay."

She hesitated.

"Look, if there's nothin' goin' on, it's no harm no foul. But if this boy *is* in trouble, you really want him out there diggin' himself a deeper hole?"

She took some keys from a desk drawer, unlocked one of the file cabinets, started to lay a manila folder on the desk in front of Clyde, but then held it close to her bosom. "Now, what'll I get from you in trade?"

Clyde cleared his throat. "C'mon, cut 'at out 'n' gimme."

"Why?"

"'Cause 'at was a damn long time ago."

"Not so long."

"'Bout six belt notches ago. 'Fore you got to be a happily married woman."

"Well, married, anyway."

"Kay, stop messin' 'roun' 'n' lemme see the damn file please?"

His fidgeting got a chuckle out of her. She dropped the file on the desk in front of him, touched him on the shoulder, left her fingers there long enough to bring some red up in Clyde's cheek, and went back to her seat.

"By the way, how is ol' Tad?" asked Clyde. He slipped on his reading glasses, keeping his eyes anchored on the file as he started paging through.

"Oh, he's fine," Kay said. "Happy as a clam. Why not? It works out fine for him. He's got a second income to spend on beer and that damn boat of his and somebody to iron his shirts. I don't remember seeing you with glasses last time I saw you."

Clyde grunted. "I probably didn't need 'em last time you saw me. Gettin' old, everythin's wearin' out."

"They say you're only as old as you feel."

"I feel like shit, Kay, pardon my French. This is the kid you're sure is a self-reformer? Hm, petty theft, petty theft, petty larceny, vandalism -- "

"It's a lot, Clyde, but it's a lot of little stuff."

"Grand theft auto isn't so little."

"They went joyriding. If they'd been four white kids from the Boone High School football team, it wouldn't've even gotten to court. It's all the kind of stuff a kid with too much time on his hands and hanging around with the wrong crowd -- "

"Possession of a controlled substance -- "

"Caught him with a joint in his pocket. *One* joint."

"Probation violation – well that goes without sayin' – but then you have this assaultin' a po-lice officer." He looked up at Kay over the tops of his glasses awaiting a response.

Kay shrugged, already aware of how lame it was going to sound. "That was the marijuana bust."

"The *one* joint in the pocket."

"The cop says the kid threw the first punch, Leroi says he socked the cop when the cop started getting physical for no reason. I couldn't honestly tell you which of them is telling it true, so I call it a wash. But he's been clean since he got out. No complaints, comes up clean every time he pees in the cup, and the fella at the convenience store is happy."

Clyde turned a page and frowned. "Statutory rape."

"It was dismissed."

"Over to Latexo. Seems that case *is* sealed." He looked back to Kay. "The boy ever say anything 'bout it?"

"No. Just that it wasn't what it looked like, but for the sake of the girl he wouldn't talk about it."

"Protecting the young lady's reputation," he said dubiously. "That's nice. Y'all don't see that kind a chivalry too much these days. 'Specially in rapists."

"I believe him, Clyde."

"So you keep sayin'."

"I don't remember you being this crotchety, either. You're going to wind up one of those old farts sitting on his porch with a yellow dog chasing kids off your lawn with a hose."

"Sounds like a good ol' time to me. Says here when he got released the last time, no permanent address."

"A sad, familiar story. Leroi was being raised by his grandmother over to Latexo."

"Parents?"

"The father skipped out when he was still a baby. The mother left him at Gramma's about five years ago, and now Mama's doing time in Arizona State on a distribution rap."

Clyde nodded. It *was* a sad, familiar story.

"Gramma died when Leroi was inside on his last term," Kay said. "I think that was one reason he didn't want to be released. These kids come off tough, but for the ones who aren't outright sociopaths, they still like to know there's someone home waiting on them. Chuck 'em out on their own and they go back to being little boys alone in bed scared of the dark."

"You got an employment record on him? Somethin' tells me where he's at?"

Kay didn't look any happier over this request than the one for Leroi Jefferson's juvenile file, but this time she didn't hesitate. She turned to another file cabinet and soon had Leroi Jefferson's employment card sitting on the desk in front of Clyde.

"Says here he's livin' with a Teneisha Gail Williams over to Latexo," Clyde read. "Who's she?"

"Well, if there'd been a preacher and a ring, it'd be his wife. But all they have is a baby."

"Gotcha."

"I don't think you do. He knocked her up before he went in for his last term. But since he got out, he's tried to do right by her. Stuck with her through the birth, is living with her, paying the bills, providing for her and the baby. That's why he wanted that second job at the convenience store; he needed the money for Teneisha and the baby."

"Well, he just done turned saint, didn't he? He hasn't been 'roun' a few days, has he?"

"Last week he asked for some time off; he and Teneisha were going out to Midland to see some folks of hers."

"Midland," Clyde mused. "Might as well say he was goin' t'other side a the moon. I don't suppose he left a number or any kind a contact information for this girl's folks?"

She shook her head helplessly.

"What 'bout Sarah Dawson? How often she put time in up here?"

"Sarah? She isn't on any kind of regular schedule. Two, three days a week usually, just for a couple of hours."

"When was the last time she was in?"

"Last Thursday, I think it was. Said she wasn't going to be by this week. She was taking a few days off, going to visit family out of town."

Clyde Thomas took a last look at the file, a last look at Leroi Jefferson's employment card. He took a pen and small pad from his breast pocket, copied down some information from the employment card, then pushed it and Jefferson's file back toward Kay. "Thanks," he said, slipping his glasses back into his pocket. "Listen, if either of 'em calls or shows up – Leroi Jefferson or Sarah Dawson – you tell 'em to get in touch with me double pronto, understand? 'N' let me know soon's you hear from 'em." He tiredly pulled his bulk to his feet.

"You're not going to tell me what this is about, are you?" Kay asked.

"Like you said, I'm just turnin' into a crotchety ol' fart, frettin' for no good reason. But I'd feel a sight better if I could talk to this boy for five minutes. Thanks, again, Kay." He turned for the door.

"Clyde?"

He turned and she was tugging at the collar of her blouse in a way that made him uncomfortable, more so when it worked with her slight smile that was both inviting…and sad.

"Those extra belt notches don't bother me, Clyde."

And for Clyde, it suddenly grew very hot in the office. He ahemmed and harrumphed and reached for the door.

The phone started ringing, Kay stared at it with a look of Death Row resignation.

"Say hello to your husband for me, Kay," Clyde said. "I always liked ol' Tad."

And as the door closed behind him, he heard her mutter, "Then *you* try living with him," before she took a deep breath and picked up the phone.

" – now *me*, I knew 'fore 'at story come out inna *Courier* there was somethin' mighty fishy goin' on with this Dawson fella 'cause he'd been in the Horseshoe Bar that very same day. 'N' well, he goes in there with his camera – he got this *video* camera, even though he says he's makin' a *movie* – 'n' he told all those boys he was gonna be makin' *porno*…"

Billy Ray Barnes was sitting at a desk that had a little desk plate reading, "Chief." He was leaning back with his muddy boots propped on the desk, a cup of coffee in one hand, and a *churro* in the other waving around like an orchestra leader's baton, stabbing at the air for emphasis: "…*video…movie…porno…*"

"Is that what he said?" asked the Black woman sitting across from him. "That he was going to make pornography?"

"Well, uh, factually, I don't recollect the *exack* words," Billy Ray said with an attempt at dismissiveness.

"The story off the internet said, 'adult movies.'"

Billy Ray dunked the end of his *churro* in his coffee and took a squishy bite. "Well, those sound like what he prolly said," Billy Ray said through a mouthful, "but *I* knew what he factually *meant*."

"Of course."

Billy Ray waved his *churro* at her. "You sure you don't want one a these?"

"Positive. So -- "

"They're really good."

"So," she tried, again, with the practiced patience of a watchmaker, "Reverend Dawson said he was going to make this movie -- "

"'N' then I *really* knew somethin' was up today when I found his car! I mean, his *wife's* car..."

And somewhere amidst Billy Ray's self-congratulatory tale recounting his discovery of Sarah Dawson's car behind Abner Birney's store, Billy Ray finally noticed Clyde Thomas propped in the doorway – *finally*, because, in point of fact, Clyde had been standing there for quite some time -- swabbing sweat out of his Stetson with his kerchief, fixing Billy Ray with a look that went back and forth between pained resignation (as in, "This is no more than I should come to expect on any given day") to downright pissed.

As soon as Billy Ray caught sight of Clyde Thomas and his alternating looks of pained resignation and being downright pissed, Billy Ray and his coffee and *churro* suddenly shot out of Clyde's chair, and Billy Ray stumbled around the office trying to pretend he was on his way somewhere...anywhere.

The Black woman turned in her chair. Clyde quickly caught her stylish, casual outfit, the easy way she wore it, the pen in one hand and scribble-jammed pad in the other, and his feeling of pained resignation began to expand geometrically.

"He's so vigilant," Clyde said, "I'm surprised we found 'at car 'fore they come up with flying cars. I was gonna ask who all owns 'at fancy set a wheels outside, but now I know."

"Hey, Clyde," Billy Ray said with a feeble smile, still bumping nervously around the office. "I wasn't spectin' you back so soon."

"So I see."

"Clyde, this is -- "

"Rita Scott." She walked over to Clyde with her hand out. "I'm a reporter with *The National Investigator*. You must be Chief Thomas."

Aw, shit, Clyde thought. He didn't take her hand, wearily brushed by her for his chair. "'Fraid I am."

She started fishing around in her shoulder bag. "I do have identification -- "

"Oh, I believe you – Miz Scott, is it? -- I believe you. Who-all'd lie about *that*? That *is* 'at paper I see by the checkout over to the Piggly Wiggly? Usually got some actress fresh outta dee-tox on the cover? Or Elvis on a flyin' saucer?"

"It's a big paper, Clyde," Billy Ray said as if that was some sort of defending credential. "National, right, Miz Scott?"

"I suppose that's why they call it *The <u>National Investigator</u>*, Billy Ray." Then Clyde turned that pissed look back on Billy Ray and it burned so hot Billy Ray backstepped until he bumped into a wall. "You been runnin' your gums, Billy Ray?"

"C'mon, Clyde, you know me."

"You're always sayin' 'at like I *don't* know you!"

Billy Ray slunk away behind his own desk, dropping his *churro* in his wastebasket on the way.

"Chief," the Scott woman said, "no sense getting angry with your man. My paper sent me out here to look into this business about the Reverend Dawson. It's no secret; it's all over the national press, the internet -- "

"I know," Clyde grumped.

"Your officer was kind enough to -- "

"Open his big damn mouth!" Clyde suddenly barked, then turned on Billy Ray with a roar: "Jesus H. Christ, Billy Ray, what I gotta do? Carve it in your head with a knife?"

Clyde stormed over to the coffee machine, picked up the pot, then looked angrily around the stand. "Where the hell's my cup?" He turned and saw an apologetically smiling Rita Scott holding up the cup she'd been using. Clyde slammed the pot down.

"I'm guessing," said the woman, "you'd be reluctant to answer a few questions?"

"Damn, nothin' gets by you, does it?" Clyde snapped. He dropped in his chair, made a face at the flakes of dried mud on his desk, and started rubbing his head which had begun to throb. Clyde took a moment, a deep breath, and tried to speak in a tone that seemed vaguely reasonable as he brushed his desktop clean.

"Look, Miz Scott, this is no Elvis story, or a Loch Ness Monster, or stuff like 'at. We're talkin' 'bout some *real* people here, some of 'em pretty nice people. This is a li'l thing got all blown up over nothin' 'n' some a these nice people been gettin' kinda beat up by it. I know you got pages to fill, but not with this, ok? Not makin' a mountain out a molehill? There's a fella in Lubbock says he's got Hitler's brain in a Mason jar in his garage. Whyntcha go talk to him?"

Rita Scott sat across from the chief. "Just a little thing blown out of proportion? That's what you're saying?"

"This preacher went a might off his head for some reason. Maybe it's the heat, I dunno. Maybe he's got personal problems which is nobody's bidness." Clyde turned a .50 caliber armor-piercing glare on Billy Ray: *"Nobody's!"* Then back to Rita Scott: "He said a few stupid things, but that was a couple days ago. Story's already dyin' down. Why stir it up again?"

"You're right," she said. "The story *is* dying down. Because there isn't much to it. But the *whole* story isn't out there. Like the part about the Reverend Dawson buying a shotgun, and about how nobody can find his wife, and how his wife's car turned up abandoned -- "

And with each item she ticked off, Clyde Thomas felt his face grow hotter and more twisted until he turned and exploded – again: "Gawd*dammit*, Billy Ray, you're lookin' to get yourself skinned down to the gawddamn bone! There anything you *didn't* tell 'er?"

Billy Ray had sunk down in his chair about as far as he could go and was holding his coffee cup out in front of him as if that would deflect some of the blast. "Jesus, Clyde, well, I mean nobody said this was some big secret or anything! I mean, well, 's all public information, ain't it? Ain't 'at what you said, Miz Scott?"

And now Clyde Thomas' red-faced stare turned on Rita Scott who only offered a blasé, barely apologetic grin.

"Like Miz Scott said, Clyde, the public's got a right to know!"

"That don't give *you* the right to be the one to tell 'em!" Clyde roared. He closed his eyes, took a deep breath, rubbed his head again, then opened his eyes and shook his head at Rita Scott. "Shame on you, ma'am, for exploitin' the feeble-minded. Ok, you think the public's got a right to know? Here's some fresh news for the public. Got your notebook ready? Here we go: Patrolman William Raymond Barnes is 27, still lives home with his mama, still wears the jockey shorts his mama buys him at the dollar store. 'N' here's your headline story: he thinks I don't see him, but when he picks his nose, he rubs it off under his desk."

"Clyde -- !"

"I'll bet it looks like a booger minefield under there!"

"Jeez, Clyde -- !"

Clyde turned to Billy Ray in wide-eyed innocence. "Whatsa matter, Billy Ray? Don't the public got a right to know no more?"

Rita grinned, nodded appreciatively, tucked her notebook and pen back in her shoulder bag. "A little disgusting, but a point deftly made."

"Thank you. You come out here from where?"

"Los Angeles."

"Then let's just say I hope you enjoyed your trip to Texas 'n' *adios.*"

"You can't make me leave, Chief."

"That's right, Miz Scott, so let's just say I'm strongly *advising* you to go on home."

Rita stood. "I'll take your advice under consideration. But since there's no law against me asking questions -- "

"'Ceptin' a law a common sense!" Clyde shook his head, frustrated. This was like telling someone to leave their burning house and having them tell you it was *their* house and you didn't have any right to tell them what to do in *their* house…even while they were choking on the smoke. "Look, Miz Scott, I don't know what people're like all them other places you go rootin' 'roun' for all this 'news' you think everybody's got a right to know, but 'roun' here? People don't cotton to gettin' their private bidness poked into. They don't like their neighbors doin' it, 'n' – meanin' no offense – they sure as hell won't like it from *you*, if you know what I mean?"

"I think I get the picture. But I'm still staying."

The chief threw up his hands in a small flutter of surrender. "Fine. I told you there's rattlesnakes out there, I did my good deed. You still wanna walk among 'em, it's on your own head. But listen up, Miz Scott," and here Clyde Thomas leaned forward, speaking with a tired have-it-your-way tone, "since I *did* warn you; you stick your nose where it don't belong 'n' it gets bit off? Don't come cryin' to me."

"I'm not much of a crier, Chief."

Clyde looked her over in quick appraisal. "I 'spect not."

She turned for the door, then stopped, turned back to the chief. "This Owen Dawson…is he a friend of yours?"

"Don't hardly know the man 'cept to see him on the street."

She cocked her head; an unspoken question: *Then why all* this*?*

Clyde shook his head as if he wasn't quite sure of the answer himself. "I'm a peace officer, lady. They pay me to keep the peace. 'N' it looks like you make your livin' disturbin' it."

Rita Scott pulled her Corvette into the No Parking or Standing zone in front of St. Mark's Methodist Church and killed the engine. The church was what she'd expected: a simple bit of whitewashed clapboard, and across the sun-bleached lawn, on the same lot, the homey little cottage that was the parsonage. The bulletin board in front of the church carried the message, "Services for this Sunday cancelled." In front of the parsonage, sitting in a circle of burnt grass, was an eight-foot-high fire-blackened wooden cross.

With the air conditioner off, the interior of the car almost immediately began growing stuffy, and by the time Rita had dug her Canon PowerShot out of her bag she was sweating. She climbed out of the Corvette and took a picture of the cancellation message against a background of the church; a nice up-angle, getting most of the steeple in. Very arty; Eric Bird would like that. She took another picture facing the other way, the bulletin board in the foreground and, looming up behind it, the remains of the fired cross. Not as artistic, but a nice, stark graphic. Front page material.

It was only then she noticed what she couldn't see from the car; that the door to the parsonage was slightly open, that some of the front windows were broken. She crossed the lawn and stood at the parsonage door. She pushed at the door gently and it swung further open. Behind drawn blinds and curtains the house inside was dark, but even in the shadows Rita could see papers scattered on the foyer floor, looking to be part of a spill through the archway that led to the living room. She knocked, she called out, she even rang the bell, only to hear each sound echo emptily inside the dark house. She pulled up the Canon's flash head, took a picture of the papers on the floor, then grasped the stem of the doorknob between her fingers, careful to touch nothing with the tips of her fingers, and pulled the door back to where she'd found it. She stepped back on the walk, took a picture of the exterior of the parsonage, then crossed to the house next door.

She rang the bell, and the door was answered by a harried-looking young woman with her arm around one toddler with a jam-smeared face, and a second similarly decorated toddler clutching the hem of her housedress. "Would y'all stop *hangin'* on Mama? It's too *hot* to be *hangin'* on Mama!" Then she turned to Rita and impatiently asked what she wanted.

Rita smiled her warmest smile, spoke in her most deferential tone: "Excuse me, ma'am, I hate to bother you, but I'm trying to find the minister from the church next door and he doesn't seem to be home. You wouldn't happen to know where I could find him, would you?"

When Clyde Thomas allowed himself a drink -- or three -- in his off hours and began to commiserate with whomsoever cared to listen about what he didn't like about being the Chief of Po-lice for Boone, Texas, days like this one came near the top of the list. Wilbur McCoy was standing in front of his desk beating his gums and no amount of hand-signaling or shushing could get him to stop, despite Clyde clearly being on the phone talking to someone other than Wilbur McCoy while Billy Ray Barnes was sitting just across the office not doing anything of particular importance and certainly available for badgering.

Wilbur McCoy poked Clyde in the shoulder trying to get him turned away from the phone. "Hey, Clyde, whatchall gonna do 'bout this sumbtich done burnt down my shack? Hey, *Clyde!*"

Clyde looked over to Billy Ray's desk for some help, but Billy Ray was still in a deep sulk over his scolding earlier. Clyde had assigned him the office equivalent of the rock pile, having him plow through the several coats of paper inundating the office bulletin board to weed out the outdated "Wanted" posters and state circulars, then organize the remainder by topic in several neat piles on his desk. When Billy Ray was done with that, Clyde intended to give him some other pointless, time-wasting thing to do with them.

"Hey, _Clyde!_"

Clyde buried the phone in his chest. "Gawddammit, Wilbur, hold your water a second!"

Wilbur harrumphed, stuck his calloused hands in the straps of his coveralls, made a lot of tantrum-type stomping across the floor, pulled a chair away from the wall and dropped into it making as much annoying noise in the process as he could.

Clyde turned back to the phone. "Yeah, hon, sorry, it's a bit busy here. As I was sayin', this is Clyde Thomas, Chief up here to the Boone P.D., 'n' I'm tryin' to reach Dennis Bemis in the County Prosecutor's office."

The lady on the other end of the phone asked him to hold on for a second.

Wilbur McCoy saw Clyde holding. "Now?"

No, mouthed Clyde. He peeled himself a stick of Wrigley's, balled up the foil wrapper and threw it at Billy Ray to get his attention. He missed.

"Mr. Bemis is in court just now," the phone lady said.

Clyde looked at his watch and thought, In court my ass. He pictured Denny Bemis having lunch on that fine, big mahogany desk of his watching the Astros on the digital TV mounted on his wall shelves, telling his secretary through a mouth full of barbecue that he was all busy on County Prosecutor business and not to be disturbed until, oh, say the seventh inning break. "Would you tell Mr. Bemis that when he gets a chance, to gimme a call soon's he can? It's pretty important. Thanks." Clyde hung up the phone, took a deep breath, rubbed his forehead. "Now, Wilbur."

Clyde hadn't even gotten it all out of his mouth before Wilbur was out of his chair and storming around Clyde's desk. "Some sumbitch done burnt down my shack where I store my feed 'n' all up to my north pasture! I been down here complainin' a million times 'bout those kids startin' fires in 'at field! A _million_ times! I knew sumpin like this was gonna happen, I _warned_ y'all, but didja come do anythin'? Naw, naw, y'all's too damn busy writin' parkin' tickets 'n' all like 'at -- "

The more Wilbur spoke, the more excited he got, and the more excited he got, the more he crowded Clyde's desk. Clyde kept waving him back. "Wilbur, you been down here a million times 'n' each a those million times I *told* you your place is over the town line! I got no jurisdiction! You need to be callin' the county sheriff -- "

"I don't know *him*, Clyde! I know *you!*"

Clyde wasn't sure what the reasoning was there. "Ok, fine. What happened?"

"I *told* you! Some sumbitch done burnt down my shack!"

"I was hopin' for a li'l more dee-tail then 'at, Wilbur."

"What dee-tails? I pulled up to the gate 'n' there it was! Burnt to the damn ground! 'N' then I come straight here for all the fat lot a good it's doin' me! Tellin' me to go to the sheriff 'cause you don't wanna be bothered -- "

Clyde briefly considered re-explaining the jurisdictional problems involved, then almost instantaneously realized what a useless exercise it would be. "'N' you want me to do what, Wilbur?"

"I want somebody in this here office to get off his damn ass 'n' get up there 'n' find some clues to who done it!"

Clyde pulled on his reading glasses, tugged a pad of foolscap in front of him and took a stub of a pencil from a broken-handled coffee mug he kept on his desk filled with leaking pens and pencil nubs. Go find some clues, the man says, like it was as easy as going over to the Piggly Wiggly for a case of Dr. Pepper "Ok, Wilbur, where's this shack at?"

"I *told* you, Clyde!" Wilbur said, practically screaming. "Jee-*sus*, don't nobody *listen* to me? My north field!"

"Which is where, Wilbur?" Clyde said, unperturbed.

"'Bout four miles up the Groveton Highway, 'n' a couple hunnert yards in. Ya can't miss the sumbitch! Still smokin'! Burnt *flat* to the ground, ya hear?"

"Flat to the ground. Got it."

"Hey, Wilbur," Billy Ray said. He'd stopped making his piles of paper and was standing by the wall where there was mounted a map of Boone and the surrounding areas, and another of all of Boone County. "You said up to Groveton Highway?"

"Yeah," Wilbur said. "You go on past 'at ol' Baptist church, then I got a access road first right after the cattle guard, just a li'l past -- "

"Abner Birney's store."

"Yeah! You can't miss it!"

"I know," Clyde said. "Burned flat to the ground. Still smokin'. Billy Ray, I needed your help 'bout a minute ago! For now, you can just go back to doin' what I *told* you to do."

"But Clyde," Billy Ray panted, fidgeting around the map, "'a''s right up where I found -- "

Clyde slammed his pencil down on the desk, spat his gum out like a rifle shot, and turned a mouth-sealing glare on Billy Ray. "Gawd*dammit*, Billy Ray, you just don't *learn!* How many times I gotta tell you to *shut that damn mouth a yours!*" Billy Ray turned back to his desk, his sulk deeper than before. Clyde re-composed himself and turned back to Wilbur McCoy. "Ok, Wilbur, we'll check it out, but don't hold your breath. Fires don't leave too many clues. I'll get back to you later."

After Wilbur left, Clyde pushed his wheeled chair across the office next to Billy Ray's desk, but Billy Ray didn't look up from making his paper piles.

"Don't know why you bite my damn head off all a time," Billy Ray pouted. "I was just sayin' this fire ain't but a coupla hunnert yards from where I found Sarah Dawson's car."

"'A's right," Clyde said, "'N' if you don't learn to watch 'at yap a yours, everybody else in town'll know it, too. Boy, you're gonna have to learn the meanin' a confidentiality, or you're gonna have to get yourself another job. Hear me?"

Billy Ray nodded.

"Now; put 'at stuff down, get your hat 'n' drive on out to Wilbur's shack 'n' see what there is to see."

Billy Ray smiled. "You bet, Clyde!" He almost knocked the hat rack over he was so eager about pulling his Stetson down. Then he froze. "But I ain't had lunch yet."

Clyde Thomas rubbed his head. "You can stop at Abner Birney's store 'n' take your meal break there. Watch putt-putt with Abner."

"What?"

"Never mind."

Billy Ray headed for the door.

"Hold on a second 'n' finish listenin' to me, Billy Ray. First, ya find anything, ya tell me 'n' *only* me, understand?"

"Yessir, Chief!" and Billy Ray headed for the door, again.

"Hold *on!* I'm not kiddin', Billy Ray. Ya let 'at mouth a yours slip one more time 'n' I swear to Christ -- "

"Y'ain't got nothin' to worry 'bout, Clyde! I learned my lesson -- " Billy Ray had a foot out the door already.

"I said hold *on,* for Chrissakes! Wouldja wait 'til I'm done? 'Fore you go, call Tobe 'n' Waylon, see which one wants to pick up some overtime 'n' have 'em come in here to watch the store while you're up there."

"Why? Where y'all gonna be?"

Clyde was reaching for his own hat. "Got to take a quick run up to Latexo."

"What for?"

"Chief a po-lice up there's a friend a mine. Told me he's got officers do what they're told with no back-sassin' or askin' damn fool questions. I told him I didn't believe there was any such thing lessen I saw 'em for myself."

It was a small park, no more than a cultivated traffic island, really, harboring a couple of small ash junipers and border beds of Indian Blankets, set off by two small streets angling into Boone's Main Street. Rita Scott sat on a bus stop bench in the shade of a juniper, holding a tall, take-out cup of sweet tea against her sweat-damp cheek.

From this little park she could see most of downtown Boone; a few sleepy, characterless blocks set off at one end by the squat brick cube of the police station, and at the other by the only slightly less blah town hall. There were no Starbucks or Wal-Marts here, no Price Clubs or Pizza Huts, no Subways or Targets. There was no place in those few, short blocks where she was going to be able to get an iced French vanilla latte or low-fat frozen yogurt or a Chicago pizza with pineapple topping or a fat free oat bran muffin. The only source of entertainment was a boxy little cinema with a 1928 cornerstone awkwardly carved up into a two-screener with a cramped marquee. Rita wagered people took their trade to the same butcher shop and grocery and corner drug store their parents had gone to, and were waited on by the children of the people who'd waited on their parents. When they walked through the shop doors and set little bells overhead jingling, they were usually greeted by name. Rita was sure if she'd seen a photo of Main Street Boone in 1955, it wouldn't look much different than what she was looking at now.

Except for the kids: addicted to the internet and cable TV which had penetrated Boone's time warp protective membrane, oblivious as to how uncool it looked trying to be cool in downtown Boone sweating bullets under the Texas summer sun inside black, saggy Goth wear, or zipping along the cracked sidewalks on skateboards with their hair moussed into blue-dyed spikes.

She appreciated Clyde Thomas' warning to take her nose-poking elsewhere, and, even more, that it hadn't been a threat; just a simple statement of fact. It was a lesson she'd learned back before her days with *The National Investigator*, back during her legit news days: nobody liked strangers poking into their private business, and some people liked it even less when the nose poker was Black. But Rita had also learned people had fewer qualms about strangers poking into somebody *else*'s business. A friend may not turn on a friend, but a neighbor might.

Out of greed. Just as often out of vanity. Or jealousy. Spite. Vindictiveness. Self-importance. Prejudice. Pettiness. Self-righteousness. Misplaced sense of duty. Sometimes even out of a malicious sense of sport. Whatever; you could get almost anyone to open up. You just had to suss out their particular key.

Somewhere nearby she heard a rattling jangle, like someone shaking a small cage. She turned and saw two elderly women trying to wrestle a metal shopping cart over the doorsill of Byrum's Groceries. The metal cart rattled and squeaked while one woman shoved and the other tugged while also holding the door open.

"Push!" the old woman holding the door urged.

"I am!" said the other. "Ferris!" she called to someone in the store. "Ferris! Come help me!"

"He's hidin' in the back room like he always do."

"Ferris! Please!"

"Might as well leave off, you'll be still calling him when the Second Coming comes. *Push* it!"

"I *am!*"

"May I?" Rita reached around the woman in the doorway, grabbed the rim of the cart and toggled its wheels free from where they'd wedged in some buckled floor tiles, then yanked the cart over the doorsill. She got a glimpse into the store, to the doorway at the far end leading to a backroom, and a sour-faced bull of a man peeking around the doorframe. "There you are, ladies!"

They didn't say thank you. They gave her a cold and polite smile that, Rita supposed, was as much of an acknowledgment of her assistance as she was likely to get. She saw their eyes giving her their once over and in her head she pictured one of them drawling, "Y'all ain't from 'roun' these parts, are ya, pardner?"

"How far do you have to go with this?" Rita asked. "Maybe I could help --"

"That's not necessary," said one, giving her another of those cold, dismissive smiles.

"I have to sit a minute," puffed the other, while her friend flashed an annoyed look to which the first lady responded with an I-can't-help-it-look.

"Then let me at least get you this far," Rita said and parked the cart by a bench in front of the grocery store.

While the one elderly woman sat to catch her breath, the other stood fidgeting by the cart, signaling to both her friend and to Rita they wouldn't be parked there very long and Rita's service would no longer be required, and hadn't really *ever* been required, and she could go now.

"I'm surprised the gentleman inside didn't come out to help," Rita said. "He must've heard you."

"Oh, he heard all right," said the woman standing by the cart. "That's just how Ferris Byrum is. The only effort that man ever puts out is punching the buttons on his register! Or putting higher prices on his canned goods!"

"That's a shame," said Rita.

"His father was never like that," the woman on the bench said. "Lovely man. If you didn't stop him he'd carry your bags all a way home for you, just leave the counter 'n' all!"

"Well, back in those days you *could* leave the counter," the other woman said. "You never had to count the cash in the till in those days if you had to run crosst the street!" She gave a sneery look at a young Goth rollerblading along the street, rapping the fenders of parked cars with his knuckles for no reason other than to hear the *thunk*. "Not now. Hooligans. If I had a business, I don't know I'd even let some a these loons in the door!"

Rita nodded sympathetically. "I know what you mean, Miss -- ."

"Mrs. Dailey." Mrs. Dailey seemed resigned to the fact that her friend on the bench – who introduced herself as a Mrs. Hanratty -- wasn't leaving any time soon. "Maybe I'll sit a minute, too."

"It's this ungodly heat," Mrs. Hanratty said. "I don't remember the last time we had a summer like this."

Mrs. Dailey cast a nasty look through the display window of the grocery behind them. "Look at him in there, pretending nothing happened! I see you, Ferris Byrum! If I could drive to the Piggly Wiggly, you'd starve! Yeah, pretending he doesn't see me! Only reason he has this place is his daddy built it up! Only reason Ferris's still here is he doesn't have the smarts to do much all else!"

"Oh, leave poor Ferris alone," said Mrs. Hanratty. "He can't help the way he is. And it's a hard job."

"I'm sure, very hard taking peoples's money all day."

"Ladies," Rita Scott said, "I was wondering if you could help me with something. You see, my name is Rita Scott and I'm with *The National Investigator*."

"Really?" said Mrs. Hanratty, impressed. Mrs. Dailey was impressed, too, but she made an effort to hide it.

"Oh, you read my paper?"

"Well," Mrs. Hanratty admitted with a self-conscious nod. "I mean, sometimes, you know…I'm just curious. I don't take it seriously, but, you know…"

Rita nodded non-judgmentally.

"I never buy that trash!" the other woman said haughtily. "I even tell Ferris he should just toss it in the street!"

"But you always read *mine*," Mrs. Hanratty said.

"I don't."

"You *do!* Whenever you come over -- "

"I may *leaf* through it, sometimes, just to see what kind a trash is in there, but I do *not* read it!"

"She does," Mrs. Hanratty said with a little wrinkle of a grin.

"You tell those stories that go on and on and in every direction, and I need *something* to pass a time 'til you come back to earth! That is not *reading* the paper!"

Behind Mrs. Dailey's back, Mrs. Hanratty gave Rita a yes-she-does nod.

"Well," said Rita, "My paper has sent me all the way from our headquarters in Los Angeles for a story."

"A story?" Mrs. Hanratty asked. "Here in Boone?"

Mrs. Dailey nodded, understanding. "You must be here about Reverend Dawson."

"That's very astute of you."

Mrs. Dailey seemed quite pleased with herself. "Why else?"

"This business with the reverend must be very embarrassing for you. I mean for the whole town."

"Not exactly what you want your place a residence known for," Mrs. Dailey judged. "Boone, loon capital of Texas."

"I see what you mean," Rita said. "It's a shame that's all people outside of Boone know about your town."

"It's sad," Mrs. Hanratty said, shaking her head.

"It's a disgrace!" Mrs. Dailey said.

"You know," Rita said, brightening as if suddenly struck by an idea, "you could do something about that."

"Who?" Mrs. Hanratty asked.

"*You!*" Rita said.

"Me?" Mrs. Hanratty said.

"Her?" said a doubtful Mrs. Dailey.

"I mean *both* of you ladies! In all these stories about Reverend Dawson and this movie of his -- "

"That *filth* of his!" Mrs. Dailey said.

" – yes, filth," Rita agreed emphatically, "nobody's ever spoken up for the town; for the kind of people – the *real* Boone people – who live here. Listen, I know you may not think much of my paper, but what *I* want is to see that somebody speaks up for this town! Somebody to let people know that whatever's going on with Reverend Dawson doesn't represent the good heart of Boone."

"Well," Mrs. Hanratty said pensively, "I *guess* that would be a good thing." She turned to Mrs. Dailey. "Wouldn't it?"

Rita could see Mrs. Dailey was already imagining how her name would look in print next to a quote about how good the God-fearing, church-going, decency-loving people of Boone really were, and how they weren't like this loon preacher at all. "I 'spect."

Rita smiled and reached into her shoulder bag for her pad and pen. "You don't mind if I take notes, do you? I want to make sure I get everything down correctly. You always hear how the press twists words around, and we don't want that to happen here, do we?"

The street was a curbless band of cracked and potholed blacktop wandering without much intelligent design through a neighborhood of not-quite-but-almost shacks; sagging, sad assemblages of unpainted, weather-beaten clapboard and peeling tarpaper. Each house was fronted by a square of bare, dusty earth littered with trash, broken toys and furniture, sometimes the rusted, rotting hulk of a car sitting on cinderblocks and stripped for parts.

There were old Black men and women sitting on porches because there wasn't much else for them to do, and young mothers – *too* young – yelling at babies sitting in the dirt, pawing holes in the ground, playing with sticks and headless dolls because there wasn't much else for them to do, either. Some older boys jostled each other under a makeshift basketball hoop – a fruit basket with the bottom punched out, nailed to a telephone pole – while others sat on front steps staring at nothing, trying to figure out a way to pass a day as empty and meaningless as the one that had come before, and the ones still to come.

Whatever little something or nothing was occupying their time and minds, they stopped and their eyes locked on Clyde Thomas' patrol car as it rolled slowly along the bad road, the uniformed man inside craning over to scout out house numbers, because this was a neighborhood where a cop car only meant bad news, and bad news was something the neighborhood already possessed in excess.

Clyde Thomas wasn't having too much luck with the house numbers. They were either lost, defensively removed, or maybe some of these almost-shacks had never had one. But then even without the number, he knew when he'd found the place he was looking for and pulled the car onto the dirt shoulder.

The house wasn't in any better shape than the others. Same beaten, drab look. But the trash was neatly stowed in rubber trash bins, their lids thoughtfully weighed down with stones to keep out the raccoons and coyotes which had left the piled trash bags by the other houses torn and spilling. The bare dirt in front was unlittered, and a low, cheap, slat-wood fence set it off from its neighbors. The windows were not dressed with yellowed and torn old shades or faded curtains or ragged towels, but bright-colored window dressing; K-Mart cheap, maybe, but a rare splash of color on the street.

On the front porch, a Black woman sat on a kitchen chair with her back to the street, bent over a small wooden table, while one hand rested on a cheap baby stroller, slowly rolling its pudgy little sleeping occupant back and forth.

Clyde took a moment working up his mental stamina, rubbed at a little ghost of an ache in his head, then climbed out of the car, plopped his Stetson on his head, and headed for the fence gate.

The woman turned at the sound of the squeaky hinge and Clyde saw she was only a young girl, probably still deep in her teens. She had a puffy, small-eyed face that wasn't particularly attractive, needed the kind of orthodonture she could never afford. She wore a drab housedress, squinted at Clyde through the kind of unattractive prescription glasses you bought cheap off a rack at the drug store.

Clyde Thomas tried a smile. "Teneisha Gail Williams?"

She did not smile back but squinted past him to the insignia on the door of his car. "Dat say Boone, dunnit? What all do a Boone po-lice want here?" She never stopped softly rocking the baby.

"I'd just like to ask a few questions 'bout Leroi Jefferson."

"Boone po-lice ain't got no right here."

Clyde stopped a few feet from the porch. "I don't have any jurisdiction, 'at's for true. I can't arrest nobody. But I can ask questions anywhere. 'A's the law." Clyde turned to the sleeping baby; a soft little ball of round cheeks and stuffed-sausage arms and legs topped with a puff of kinky hair to which was clipped a pink bow. "She's more 'n' a li'l cute," Clyde said.

The girl nodded; an acknowledgment, not really a thanks.

"I'm tryin' to find Leroi, Teneisha Gail."

"Leroi's a good man. He work two jobs to take care a his own. He don't run off like some a dese," and her head gestured at the houses around them. "He be tryin' to make us a home. He finish' his schoolin' so he can be better. He be helpin' me finish *my* schoolin'. 'N' 'a's all I gots to say 'bout Leroi to ya. Ya gots some other questions, ya bes' take 'em on back to Boone."

Clyde nodded sympathetically. He took off his Stetson, swabbed out the sweatband with his kerchief, then used it to dab at his forehead. "Hot out here. Mind if I come on up in the shade? I promise I won't wake the baby."

Clearly she did mind but she didn't say anything.

Clyde stepped softly on the stairs, then onto the porch, the old wood creaking and squeaking under him. There was a kitchen stool by the door and Clyde set it close to the girl and sat. He stole a quick look through the screened windows, saw a spare but neatly kept living room. He leaned over for a closer look at the baby. "She *is* a she, isn't she? Yeah, I thought so from the bow.

Really is a cute li'l thing." He sat up, trying to balance on the small platform of the stool. On the table was an open book, a textbook it seemed to Clyde, with large type and small words. "I could do with a cold drink, if you don't mind."

"'A's what dey got stores fo'."

Clyde nodded, an ok-that's-the-way-it's-going-to-be nod.   His tone became more business-like: "Miz Kay Gorsham – 'at's Leroi's boss up to the reformatory – she thinks mighty high a Leroi. 'N' I think mighty high a Miz Gorsham's opinion. But I don't know what to think, Teneisha Gail, when you start soundin' like Leroi did somethin' 'n' you're tryin' to protect him. Makes me think maybe he *did* do somethin'."

"Leroi didn't do nothin' wrong!" the girl said firmly. "But 'roun' here, when sumpin bad happens 'n' da po-lice needs a name to blame, it's easy to come 'roun' here."

Which Clyde was not prepared to dispute. "Ok, Teneisha Gail, let's try this another way. I didn't come here to talk to you. I came up here to talk to your neighbors…" -- which got her curiosity up -- "…'cause y'all weren't supposed to be here."

"Whatcha mean?"

"Few days ago, Leroi told his boss up to the reformatory he was gonna take a few days off. To visit y'all's family in Midland. With *y'all*. You don't believe me, call up his boss, Miz Kay Gorsham up to the reformatory, 'n' ask her." Clyde let a moment go by, let that bit of information percolate down into young Teneisha Gail Williams, saw her face fill with puzzlement…and a little concern. "But now here *you* are…but no Leroi. I'll bet you don't even have family in Midland, do you, Teneisha Gail?"

She shook her head, not so much in response but as if that might clear the confused picture in her head. "He say he was gonna see *his* family in Midland."

"I saw his file up to the reformatory, Teneisha Gail. Leroi doesn't have any family in Midland. Ok, you don't know where he is, either. Have you heard from him since he left?"

She shook her head, still trying to find a way to put everything together in a good way and not having any luck at it.

"You know Sarah Dawson?" Clyde asked.

"Lady from a church up to Boone. Leroi tol' me 'bout her. 'A's a lady help him get his GED. She give him this here book to help me," and she nodded at the book on the table.

"She ever come 'roun' here?"

"Lady like 'at don't come no places like this."

"Did you ever know her to lend her car to Leroi for anything? Help him out, maybe he's got errands to run or somethin'?"

"Iffen she did, he never said nothin'." She turned to Clyde and now she was a scared little girl in over her head. "Wazzit mean?" she asked weakly.

Clyde felt a pang. "Teneisha Gail, I believe you when you say Leroi's tryin' to do right by this here family. I believe Miz Gorsham when she says the same thing. Could be this is all nothin'. Sometimes a young man takes on so much he just needs some time to himself. The thing is I need to know where he is; I need to talk to him." He pulled a business card from his breast pocket, wrote a number on the back and set it on the open textbook. "If you hear from Leroi, you tell him to call me soon's possible. That there's my card. My office number's on the front. I got my personal number on a back. If he calls, you give him those numbers 'n' tell him to call. 'N' in case he doesn't call, *you* call me soon's you hear from him. Understand, Teneisha Gail?"

She picked up the business card, studied it unhappily, and nodded.

Clyde slid off the stool, careful not to disturb the baby, set his Stetson back on his head.

"I want it to be awright," the girl said, looking down at the sleeping baby.

"Believe me, Teneisha Gail, so do I," and Clyde started down the stairs and across the dusty front yard to his car.

Rita Scott caught Elwood Poteet as he was locking the doors of *The Boone Courier* on his way out to lunch. He jumped when she set her hand lightly on his shoulder.

"Mr. Poteet?"

"It was almost the *late* Mr. Poteet," he said, still gasping.

"Sorry about that."

"Back in Los Angeles, don't they know how to go, 'ahem,' and things of that nature?"

She smiled. "You know who I am?"

Elwood Poteet looked at his watch. "Miz Scott, it is almost one o'clock. You have been in town since this morning. I'm willing to bet there's few in town *don't* know who you are by now."

"I guess it's true what they say about how fast news travels in a small town."

He smiled with a certain grimness as he unlocked the door and beckoned her inside. "For speed, CNN's got nothing on the Boone Grapevine." Inside, he showed her to a bench in the waiting area by the front counter. He offered her coffee or a cold drink, she said no, watched him pull the blinds across the front windows.

"You're remarkably shy for a newspaper man," Rita observed.

"Shyness has nothing to do with it."

"The eyes of Texas are upon us?" she guessed.

"Something like that." Elwood drifted behind the front counter, made as if he was checking some front page proofs. "What can I do for you, Miz Scott?"

Rita rose from her seat, closed the distance, leaned against the counter across from him. She looked to the few desks beyond the counter, a few yellowed *Courier* front pages in glass-faced frames on the walls, a few more page proofs marked for correction. "Weekly or bi-weekly?" she asked.

"Used to be bi-weekly. Went weekly about six years ago."

"Press on the premises?"

"In the basement."

"Whole building must shake when you're running."

"It's a good feeling. You ever work a small paper like this? Maybe when you started?"

"I interned for a state daily, that got me a fulltime job at the same place right out of college. Most of the big papers don't have on-site presses anymore, but the old-timers used to tell me about those days, how you could feel it through the whole building when the presses were running. Sorry I missed that."

He made a few edit marks on the proof, set it down, and fixed Rita with a sad, resigned look. "You didn't come fifteen hundred miles to discuss the grand ol' days a journalism with the editor-in-chief a the weekly *Boone Courier*."

"It was your story brought me here, Mr. Poteet."

Which made Elwood Poteet wince. "I am painfully aware of that, Miz Scott. And so's just about everybody I pass on the street who now cusses me out instead of saying hey. You may have noticed 'at fresh coat a whitewash across the front a my building. That's the second coat in two days. I have to keep covering up some a the critiques the local readership has been leaving spray-painted out there. This is a family paper and some a the language they've been using isn't very family-friendly."

"Mr. Poteet, you help me out, provide some background information and whatever else you have on Owen Dawson, and I'll cite you and *The Courier* as a source. That's national recognition, your paper's name in my -- "

Elwood chuckled. "Ma'am, that and prostate cancer are about the last two things in the world I want."

"We're both newspaper people, Mr. Poteet. We both ask the same questions -- "

He held up a hand. "Hold on, Miz Scott. Meaning no disrespect, I don't consider us in the same business at all. I looked you up, you know."

"Googled me, did you?"

"We may be a bit out in the sticks, but not *that* far. I got a computer looks like something out a *The Flintstones*, but I can limp my way around the internet."

Rita retreated to her place on the bench, crossed her legs, crossed her arms. "And what did you find?"

She expected an attack, but that wasn't what she got. The only thing on Elwood Poteet's face, in his voice, was curiosity. "Not all that much. Your name came up in a story in *Time* from a few years back. Piece on tabloid journalism. It said how sometimes even straight news reporters couldn't say no to the money. You got mentioned as an example. Something about that didn't make sense to me."

"Making money didn't make sense to you?"

"I don't know anybody who ever got into this business for money. So, I have to think it's about something else."

"Like?"

He shrugged.

"I was happy for the money," Rita Scott said, "but you're right; it wasn't about the money. That just made it easier."

He waited. "I'm listening, Miz Scott."

"None of this has anything to do with Owen Dawson."

"In a kind a way, it does," Elwood Poteet said. "You want me to talk to you, and right now, I don't see any reason to."

She studied him carefully. "This is like that scene in *Silence of the Lambs:* '*Quid pro quo*, Clarice,'" she said, doing a fair imitation of Anthony Hopkins' Hannibal Lecter.

"Never saw it. Not my kind a thing."

"You won't tell me anything helpful unless I tell you something personal."

He came out from behind his counter, pulled a chair up near her at the bench and sat. "Miz Scott, I don't want a damn thing from you, *especially* something personal. I'd just as soon you upped and left out. But since I don't expect you're going to do that, I want to know how somebody good enough to cut it with the big dailies winds up doing what you're doing. And it's not just for the money."

"What's a nice girl like you etc.?"

"I guess."

"People didn't care."

"What people?"

She stood and gestured at the windows with their drawn blinds.

"Didn't care about what?"

"Much of anything. They still don't. You know what gets their attention, Mr. Poteet. Some Hollywood celebrity goes on trial for killing his wife, for doing nasty things with little kiddies, and you have the American public on the edge of its collective seat every day through the verdict. But do a story explaining how Federal budgetary economics really work? Try to explain Middle Eastern politics? Eyes glaze over, they're bored, and *that's* the cardinal sin. It doesn't matter if you inform them, but God help you if you *bore* them. Unless the head of the Federal Reserve bursts into flame during a hearing, nobody cares, even though *that's* the news they're going to wind up paying for, and their children, and their children's children. Every day they're shipping kids home from somewhere in the world in body bags, but what are people interested in? Whether or not some starlet has anorexia. What celeb is in rehab, or getting divorced, or getting back with their ex, or decided they're not the sex they were born with.

"And if you still insist on reporting 'real' news, tell one side facts they don't want to hear, then you're un-American; tell the other side what *they* don't want to hear and you're part of a cover-up conspiracy; you're the 'fake news.' Put up news that nobody reads, nobody watches, nobody listens to, nobody agrees with, and it doesn't matter how important it is, you're cancelled, you're bumped, back-paged, you're out of a job."

She picked up a current issue of *The Courier* from a stand by the door. "You think it's any different here, Mr. Poteet? You've got this story here on school budget hearings. How many people here in Boone cared about how your town finances the education of young minds? The resources you're putting into forming the next generation of citizens? 'A small but vocal crowd,'" she read and made a sour face. "The operative word, Mr. Poteet, is 'small.' Did you even have a hundred people there? Fifty? I didn't think so. The last time the school budget went up for a vote, what was the turnout? What was the percentage of eligible voters who actually showed up at the polls? I'll bet you a week of my considerable salary it was less than 10%."

"Six percent," Elwood said quietly.

She folded the paper and pointed to the front page box around the photo of Owen Dawson and his video camera. "But this poor guy cracks up, starts talking about making some kind of adult movie about his troubles, and *that* everybody is concerned about. And *you* put it at the top of page one." She put the paper down and turned to Elwood Poteet with a ruefully accusatory glare. "Without even looking, I can tell you that the biggest section in your paper is local sports. Right?"

At which all Elwood could do was study the toes of his wingtips.

"Don't lecture me, Mr. Poteet. The difference between us is degree: not pedigree."

It had come out angrily, and she hadn't meant it to be. She bobbed her head in a gesture of sheepish apology, but Elwood Poteet passed it off with a shrug, then he offered a comforting smile. He rose to his feet with a grunt, paced pensively around the waiting area. "I can't help you, Miz Scott. Owen Dawson is a friend a mine. A good friend. And you're right; I'm responsible for you being here, and for a lot of what's going on in this town right now, most of which I'm not all 'at happy about. And I'm worried, Miz Scott; that's the other thing.

"Owen's...Owen's not right. I don't know why, I don't know what's going on with him. Everything I know about this business – all the *little* I know – was in 'at one piece I ran. I look at the trouble 'at story caused, and I'm not about to open my mouth again and make things worse. It wouldn't matter if you were from *The New York Times*...I'm just not going to hurt him anymore. That may not exactly be the most professional journalistic attitude, but..." A so-be-it shrug.

She nodded understandingly. She picked up her bag and turned for the door.

"Miz Scott, I do wish you'd find another line a work. You seem too nice a lady for this business."

"I'm not that nice."

"You're angry about the way things are. You're angry because you wish it was different. You wouldn't feel like that if you weren't a nice lady."

She smiled a thanks, held out her hand which Elwood took for a moment before he held the door open for her.

Billy Ray Barnes pulled his patrol car off the Groveton Highway onto Wilbur McCoy's unpaved access road. With its shocks in no better condition than any other part of the car, the only thing keeping Billy Ray from bouncing out of his seat was his seat belt. "Yeeehah!" he yelled, holding on to the wheel with one hand like a rodeo bronc rider as the car hit a water cut in the road that damned near put his tail bone up into his hat.

When he'd gone about 200 yards up the road, he got out of the car, thoughtfully locked it behind him, and leaped the drainage ditch alongside the road, impressed with his own agility and grace. Those same abilities, however, failed him as he tried to negotiate the barbed wire fence bordering Wilbur McCoy's north pasture which put a tear in both his pants leg and his calf as he tried to slip between the strands.

Cursing the ruination of his uniform pants as well as the wire bite in his leg, Billy Ray limped to the top of a knoll just inside the fence. At the top of the knoll he paused, took off his Stetson to wipe at his sweaty forehead with his shirtsleeve. From this height he could easily see the quarter-mile down to Abner Birney's store, even make out the mud patch out back and Sarah Dawson's car still sitting by the dumpster. Looking at another angle, in a clearing amid a thin copse of dogwoods offering shade to a few lazing beeves, he could see what was left of Wilbur McCoy's shack. Wilbur may have been overacting some, Billy Ray, thought, but he had not exaggerated: there was nothing left of the shack except a black patch of ground and a pile of charred planks and corrugated roofing tin still throwing off wisps of smoke.

Billy Ray limped down the knoll to the ashes careful to step around the cow chips liberally strewn along the hillside. "Try usin' a outhouse some time," he said to the beeves as he passed where they sat under the dogwoods, sprinkled with a few fallen white blossoms. The beeves looked back at him with big, empty eyes and mooed. Billy Ray mooed back.

The air in the clearing where the shack had stood was still rich with the smell of burnt wood and scorched earth. But there was another smell, something sickeningly sweet, and it was heaviest hovering over the pile of charred lumber and ashes. Billy Ray found a long branch and started walking through the ashes. That sick smell was so strong he had to hold his nose. With his branch, he picked at the blackened pieces of wood, then got the tip under the scorched sheet of roofing but the tin was too heavy to flip. He dropped the stick and crouched down to grab the edge of the metal square, still warm, almost too hot for his hands, and down there by the ground the smell was chokingly thick. He held his breath and flipped the roofing away.

Free, now, the smell was suddenly overwhelming, billowing up and washing over him, but Billy Ray didn't notice the smell as he started running back towards his car, didn't notice the cow chips he slipped in, stopping only long enough to drop to his knees and vomit.

A few flagstones branched off from Bob Wheeler's driveway, past a signpost that read, "Bob Wheeler: Insurance," to the doorway of a small, square addition tacked to the side of Bob Wheeler's garage. Bob Wheeler stood in the open doorway. "You would be Miz Scott."

"My fame precedes me," Rita said.

"More like infamy."

"It's very hot out here, Mr. Wheeler."

Bob Wheeler considered a moment, then stepped aside and nodded at Rita to come in. The addition was just big enough for an old, scuffed desk, a few file cabinets, a few chairs. Bob beckoned her to a seat, waited until she sat before he took his place behind his desk. Behind him, the air conditioner hummed and flipped up a few hairs at the top of his head. "Elwood Poteet told me sooner or later you'd probably find your way here."

Rita had her notebook out, was referring to some of the jottings. "I thought he might. You and he are longtime friends after all, or so I'm told."

Bob made a face. "Have you been told a lot?"

"You'd be surprised."

"Not really. Small towns; gossip is practically a Number One sport."

"They gossip in big towns, too, Mr. Wheeler."

"But it gets lost in a big town. In a small town, it rattles 'round 'til it pokes someone in the eye."

She flipped to another page of her notes. "I'm also told that both you and Mr. Poteet are good friends with the Reverend and Mrs. Dawson."

"You *have* been busy. They're good people, Owen and Sarah. You should leave them alone. *Everybody* should leave them alone."

"I think you might get some argument about that."

"About leaving them alone?"

"About how good these good people really are."

Bob made a sour face. "Ever since 'at damn story broke, people been running for their pitchforks and torches. 'S all just a lot a people overreacting to something they really don't know a lot about. Last week, he was their beloved preacher, then something happens they don't understand, they don't ask what's wrong, they just…just…"

"Run for their pitchforks and torches."

"Anybody who knows Owen – I mean *really* knows him – knows he's a warm, kind, sensitive young man."

"His actions of the last few days hardly seem to be warm, kind, or sensitive."

Bob Wheeler's face clouded. "I know. And I don't know what 'at's about. It scares me for him." Then his face grew hard as he fixed his eyes on Rita. "I know this; you being here and doing what you're doing isn't going to help him or this whole situation."

"Maybe it could, Mr. Wheeler."

"How so?"

"If whatever is behind Reverend Dawson's…let's call it a breakdown…if that information were to get out, maybe people would stop thinking of him as some kind of blasphemer. Or nut. Actually, the word 'loon' is getting bandied around quite a bit."

Bob smiled bitterly. "That was pretty good. Almost had me thinking you're doing a public service, Miz Scott. Maybe you should try selling insurance some time." He pretended to look at his watch. "Well, I'm sorry, Miz Scott, but I've got -- "

"An innocent question."

An amused smile, now. "Is that possible?"

"It's a strain. When was the last time you saw Owen Dawson?"

"Last night."

"Not since then?"

"Elwood and I were thinking a going by tonight after we closed up, just to see how he was doing."

"You haven't called?"

"Owen disconnected his house phone last night. His cell goes to voice mail. He was getting a lot a pretty nasty calls."

Rita Scott flipped her notebook closed and slid it into her shoulder bag. "See? Perfectly innocent, perfectly painless."

Bob Wheeler rose, gestured toward the door. "Then if that's all, Miz Scott -- "

She made no move to leave. "How about Sarah Dawson?"

Bob frowned. "What about her?"

"When was the last time you saw her? I understand she wasn't at the parsonage when all the fireworks happened last night."

Bob lowered himself back into his seat. Rita could see his face grow more guarded. "I guess it would've been the week before last. We all had dinner together, Elwood and his wife, Owen and Sarah..."

"Is Sarah Dawson warm, kind, and sensitive?"

Bob Wheeler abruptly stood up, his mouth twitching angrily. "She's a nice girl, Miz Scott, and I think 'at's about all a time I'm going to give you."

Still making no move to leave: "There's stories about her, you know."

"Gossip, you mean. Rumors. Back fence talk."

Rita gave a rose-by-any-other-name shrug. "Mr. Wheeler, I admit my paper tends to put a certain spin on things -- "

"You're being awful kind to yourself."

"Yes, we play up the sensational -- "

"*Overplay* it."

"Fine," she said, unperturbed. "However you want to say it. But we don't lie. There's going to be a story whether you help me or not. But you can go on the record putting all this back fence talk, as you call it, to rest."

He stepped by her and opened the door to the outside. "Miz Scott, you want to print made-up stories about Sarah or Owen, 'at's your business; yours and your paper's lawyers'. *I* haven't heard any stories about them, but then I don't truck with gossip or gossipers. My mama always taught me to be polite, even to people I don't like. I let you in, I sat with you, we had a polite conversation. Now, I'm politely asking you to leave."

He remained in the doorway as she walked down the flagstones to the driveway to her car. "Hell of a job you have, Miz Scott," he called out to her.

She didn't turn, so he couldn't see her face or that she was agreeing with him.

Clyde Thomas spent the ride back to Boone from Latexo in a deep, dark brood. The high points of peace officer work in Boone rarely went beyond hauling in drunks on the weekend, poking into the occasional burglary or vandalism which, more often than not, traced back to the local kids, maybe stepping into a marital spat when boozed-up Hubby started throwing his fists and hot-tempered Honeybunch went for a steak knife. On a rare occasion, somebody got themselves run over by a car, or lost a duel with a semi on one of the highways that crossed just outside of town, but those were simple tragedies; things that might make you ruminate about the here-today-gone-tomorrow fragility of life over a few drinks at the Horseshoe, but nothing to *brood* about. And maybe you didn't always find out which one of these creepy little brats tricked out in droopy black drawers with a half-dozen metal studs in his ear spray-painted PRINCIPAL FRYE SUX DIX IN THE BOYZ ROOM across the front of the high school, or who broke into Boland's Pharmacy one night and made off with a hundred Vicodin and a gross of Trojans, but they weren't the kind of criminal acts that had you lying awake at night *brooding*. They were simple, routine. Understandable.

But Clyde was brooding now. What seemed to push him deeper into his brooding, ironically enough, was that he wasn't sure what he was brooding about. A cracked-up minister and his talk about making dirty movies, a missing Sarah Dawson, a missing Sarah Dawson's car abandoned behind Abner Birney's store, a missing Leroi Jefferson who, despite his recent ascension to near-sainthood, seemed to have been telling a lot of lies lately. Clyde didn't know what any of it meant or how any of it fit together, but it all seemed to be coalescing into a big, dark cloud over a brooding Clyde Thomas.

He stopped off on the way through town to pick up something to take back to the station for lunch, spent the rest of the ride enjoying the smell of nachos and hot cheese and chili filling up his patrol car. He had gotten just enough out from under his brooding cloud to look forward to a quiet meal at his desk, maybe plug in his portable to listen to some C & W, when he came through the station door and felt that little bit of forget-the-brooding-for-a-while mood drown under a wave of *Sheeeeeyet...*

Waylon Meeks had, apparently, been the off-duty officer to take up Billy Ray Barnes on the offer of overtime, and his usual, perky self was at his desk. A little younger than Billy Ray and a few points smarter – but not much – it wasn't moon-faced Waylon bothering Clyde. Unlike Billy Ray, Waylon usually had a good instinct for keeping his mouth shut and knowing when it was a good time to stay out of the chief's way. Waylon stood when he saw Clyde in the door, smiled his usual deferential smile, and gestured to the Black woman sitting at Billy Ray Barnes' desk. "Hey, Chief. Chief, this is -- "

"Miz Scott," Clyde moaned.

"You know her?"

"Don't remind me." Clyde walked past her, dropped his hat and his bag of lunch on his desk. "Miz Scott, how unhappy I am to see you again. I didn't see your car out front."

"Parked around the corner," she said cheerily. "I thought if you saw it you might not come in."

"Damn perceptive lady. You might not want to sit at Billy Ray's desk, Miz Scott. I'm of a mind it affects intelligence." As Rita pushed Billy Ray's wheeled desk chair over to Clyde's desk, Clyde reached into his lunch bag and pulled out an 18 oz cherry Coke, a cardboard cup of chili, a package of Saltines, and a Styrofoam tray of nachos swimming in melted cheese, salsa, and green chilis. "Hope you don't mind while I have my lunch."

"Please," Rita said.

Clyde crumbled the Saltines into his chili, turned squinting eyes at Rita.

"Do I need to blow my nose or something?" Rita asked.

"Just wanted to see if somebody took the tip of it off yet."

"Pardon?"

"'Member I said if you stuck 'at pretty li'l nose a yours somewhere it didn't belong -- "

"I remember. Except the part about you calling it pretty." She batted her eyelashes flamboyantly. "Do you really think my nose is pretty?"

"It'd look a lot prettier back in Los Angeles. Now; what can I not do for you this time?"

"Same thing you didn't want to do for me last time: provide information." She made a questionable face at the spread in front of Clyde. "Not that it's any of my business, but the cholesterol count there must measure into the thousands."

Clyde was fanning his mouth after downing some too hot chili. He soothed his singed tongue with a hefty slurp of cherry Coke. "Well, Miz Scott, you're right; it's *not* rightly any a your business. But 'at wouldn't stop *you*, would it?" He burped. The chili didn't taste as good on the return route. "Pardon. I may not be smart enough to watch my cholesterol, but I *am* smart enough to know when I'm not wanted."

"Everybody says that," Rita said. "And then they go ahead and talk to me anyway."

Clyde kept his attention on his nachos. "There's some like 'at everywhere. Mostly we got nice people here, Miz Scott."

"I'm sure you do. Like the nice people who burned a cross on Owen Dawson's lawn, for instance. And broke his windows."

Clyde grunted. "Like I said, there's some -- "

"I know, a few bad apples. You know, those look pretty good," she said, nodding at the nachos. "Do you mind if I...?" and she grabbed a chip.

"Help yourself," Clyde said. "What 'bout all 'at nasty cholesterol?"

"*My* cholesterol's fine," Rita said, chomping down on the cheese-salsa-green chili-drenched nacho. "I have an offer for you – OOF!" Her mouth dropped open, her eyes watered up, and Rita grabbed for Clyde's cherry coke, taking deep draws on the straw until her mouth cooled down, only to have the green chilis light up her stomach. "My *God...*"

"Them chilis take a might gettin' used to," Clyde said. "You were sayin'."

"'*Quid pro quo*, Clarice,'" she said, again in her not-bad Anthony Hopkins. Clyde Thomas frowned quizzically. "What a hell's 'at mean?"

"Didn't you see *Silence of the Lambs?*"

"I gotta deal with enough real-life nasty people. I don't need to see 'em at the pitcher show."

Rita questioningly looked over to Waylon Meeks who shrugged and said, "'Fore I was born."

Rita turned back to Clyde. "A trade. I'll give you something you don't know -- "

Clyde was already nodding as he stirred more Saltines into his chili. "'N' I give you somethin' *you* don't know."

"*Quid pro quo*," Rita said. "Deal?"

Clyde noisily sucked up some chili from his plastic spoon and shrugged.

Rita took out her notebook, began referring to this page and that. "I know the day the Reverend Dawson announced he was making his 'adult movie,' he'd been knocking back drinks at a local bar. I know you have paperwork for his purchase of a shotgun and enough ammunition to take on the Taliban. I know his wife's car's been sitting in back of some store just outside of town, and nobody's seen Sarah Dawson for about a week. I also know that maybe over the last year or so, Sarah Dawson may not have been too happy here in Boone."

Clyde made sure not to look or sound too interested. "She say somethin' to somebody?"

"No. She's just been spending a lot of time out of town. I also know she might have been having an affair with a Black kid in the county reformatory which may be why she's out of town so much."

Clyde set his chili down. There were a lot of people in Boone besides Rita Scott, he thought, who deserved to get the tip of their probing noses bitten off. "Who the hell told you that?"

She smiled apologetically; her way of saying, You know I can't tell you.

"They know that for a fact?"

"The story is -- "

"The *story*," Clyde said, disgustedly.

" -- she was spending a lot of time with this kid. But, no, I wouldn't say it's a proven fact."

"But that's good enough for you."

"My paper would consider it reportable."

"I'll bet they would." He pulled his cherry Coke back to his side of the desk, wiped off the end of the straw with a napkin.

"I don't have cooties, you know," Rita said snidely.

"Didn't think you did. But you do got lipstick." He held up the now streaked napkin and Rita nodded a humbled retraction. Clyde took a sip of his drink, stirred the ice around with his straw. "Got a name on this supposed kid she's havin' this supposed affair with?"

"Not yet."

He kept his eyes on the ice swirling and rattling in his cup, but he felt Rita Scott's eyes on him. Something in his face must have tipped her because she announced, with a delighted sense of discovery, "But *you* do!"

"Me? Naw. I'm just a hick cop in a hick town, Miz Scott. *You're* a big city sophisticated snoop. You're way 'head a me."

She smiled admiringly. "Boy, you must be a hell of a poker player, Chief. I almost believe you. Here's something I'll bet you *don't* have: Owen Dawson's gone."

Clyde stopped stirring his drink. "Whatcha mean gone?"

"I mean gone. Threw a few bags in his car early this morning along with that movie camera of his and took off. Didn't tell anybody, not even his closest friends in town."

Clyde set his drink down. "Who told you that?"

"His neighbors; more of those nice people you were telling me about."

Clyde's head started to hurt.

"I don't think he's coming back, either," Rita went on. "He didn't pack much, just a few small bags. But he left the door to his house open when he took off."

"I suppose you went inside, poked 'roun' 'n' such?"

"No."

"You're not tellin' me you got some scruples hid 'hind 'at pretty li'l nose, Miz Scott?"

"More like I don't want to get nailed for trespassing. Look, Chief, I haven't lied to anybody here. I may have finessed a few things, but people knew who they were talking to when they talked to me…and they talked anyway. I didn't go anywhere I wasn't let in. Everything legal, everything proper. You don't like what my paper prints? Tell all those nice people of yours to stop reading it and my paper'll be out of business tomorrow. Now: *quid pro quo.*"

Clyde Thomas shook his head and frowned, but not over Rita and her demand. He'd begun to brood, again, and told her truthfully, "You have me at a disadvantage, Miz Scott. You know most everything *I* know' 'n' it seems a sight more."

"I don't have this reformatory kid's name."

Which was an issue that Clyde Thomas did not get a chance to address because just as he opened his mouth to lie yet again about not knowing Leroi Jefferson, Billy Ray Barnes came crashing through the front door looking pale and sickly. Before anybody in the room could say anything, Billy Ray cannonballed through the office toward the bathroom, leaving the office door swinging open behind him.

"Jesus, Billy Ray!" Clyde snapped. "You're lettin' out the cool air! How many times I told you to keep them damn doors -- "

"ClydeJesusChristClyde…" Billy Ray gasped. He had left the bathroom door open and was bent over the sink throwing cold water on his face. "OhmiGodClyde…"

"He don't look so good, Chief," Waylon Meeks said and Clyde briefly wondered how much more the town would have to offer in police officer pay to do better than Billy Ray Barnes and Waylon Meeks.

"I went out there to Wilbur McCoy's place like you said," Billy Ray panted. "'N'…Jesus Christ…" Billy Ray closed his eyes and shuddered.

Clyde signaled Waylon to close the front doors. He flashed a look at Rita, saw her focused on Billy Ray the way he'd seen yard cats fix on a field mouse. "Billy Ray," he warned.

"I tried to get you on a radio, Clyde, I swear I tried, but a damn thing up 'n' quit on me. I been havin' problems all week with 'at damn thing -- "

"Billy Ray -- !"

"I found her, Clyde," Billy Ray said, stumbling into the bathroom doorway, almost sobbing. "I found Sarah Dawson's body up there, all burnt to a -- "

"*Billy Ray!*"

For the first time, Billy Ray noticed Rita. Rita waved a hello at him.

" – crisp."

Rita headed for the door. "*Quid pro quo,* Chief. Thanks much. I'll be sure to close the door behind me. Wouldn't want to let the cool air out. *Ciao.*" And she was gone.

The office was quiet for a moment, except for the rattling and clattering of the questionable air conditioner. Clyde kicked back from his desk, uninterested in lunch. He felt his face growing hot and red and the chili and salsa had nothing to do with it. He slowly got to his feet, stalked over to a rightfully fearful Billy Ray, grabbed Billy Ray by the front of his shirt and manhandled him across the office and shoved him into his desk chair. Somehow, Clyde managed to speak without shouting, keeping his tone icily even. "How do you know it's Sarah Dawson?"

Billy Ray touched his chest. "Wearin' a li'l gold cross. She always wore 'at li'l gold cross. Arva May's mama was on a church committee picked it out. It was a welcome gift when they first come to town. Arva May showed it to me when the committee bought it."

Clyde Thomas reached over and grabbed Billy Ray's Stetson by the brim, turned it upside down, and then finally letting his anger vent, smashed the crown down on the desk over and over in punctuation: "*I…GAWD…DAMN…WELL…TOLD…YOU…'BOUT…YOUR…GAWD…DA MN…MOUTH!*" Which left Clyde gasping and spent. He shoved the crumpled Stetson into Billy Ray's arms, Billy Ray's wide eyes looking ready to tear up, then grabbed him by the shirt, yanked him to his feet, and started pushing him toward the door. "Go…home…" Clyde rasped.

"Wha'?"

"Go home, Billy Ray! Go home 'n' stay home! Don't come in tomorra, don't come in a day after!"

"H-h-how long -- "

"'Til I decide if you still got a gawddamn job here!" Clyde exploded and shoved Billy Ray out the doorway. Sucking in air, Clyde staggered back to his desk, dropped in his chair, put his face in his hands. "Waylon?" he mumbled tiredly through his fingers. "You there, Waylon?"

Waylon Meeks had plastered himself against a wall clear of the Clyde vs. Billy Ray business. "Yeah, Chief?" he said timidly.

"Call Public Safety. Get a make, model, tag numbers on Owen Dawson's vee-hicle. Then I want you to call the fillin' stations on a roads outta town, see if maybe he stopped for gas on his way to wherever he's goin'. But 'fore you do any of that…"

"Yeah, Chief?"

"You wouldn't have any aspirin, wouldja? Big atomic bomb-sized ones?"

Tucked behind a column in a remote corner of the second-floor rec room, Henry Gilmore had an unobtrusive bird's eye view of the rear flagstone veranda which lay between the two residential wings of the Grapeland Assisted Living Community. Behind him he could hear the quiet clicks of domino games, the flutter of a deck of cards, the conversation of some of the less ambulatory "guests" parked in front of the TV.

"I miss when Kathy Lee was on in the mornin'," he heard one of the ladies say.

"'At was a hunnert years ago, Winnie, I don't know why you're still on 'bout it."

"I still miss her is all. I don't know why everybody was always on 'er for talkin' 'bout li'l Cody."

"'Cause people got tired a hearin' 'bout li'l Cody, Winnie."

"But it was her *son*! What mama don't always talk 'bout her children! I always talk 'bout *my* children!"

"I know, Winnie, 'n' we're all gettin' tired a hearin' 'bout *them*, too!"

Out on the veranda, several of the male attendants were setting up folding tables for Gypsy Spurlock. Her real name was Trudy Spurlock, but Mr. Gilmore had never heard her called anything but Gypsy, couldn't even remember how he knew her true name was Trudy it was so rarely used. Gypsy

Spurlock toodled around Boone and the surrounding counties in an ancient, tail-dragging Ranchero weighed down with banged-up boxes filled with knick-knacks, personal accessories, and junk jewelry, peddling her wares on a circuit of local fairs, church bazaars, community centers, and places like the Grapeland Assisted etc. She showed up at Grapeland every Wednesday afternoon, set up her stuff on tables on the veranda, put up hand-painted signs advertising, "Costume Jewelry and Personal Adornments," and hyped translucent scarves made of petrochemical synthetics which, she claimed, "perfectly imitate the original Indian silk."

Oddly, though, it was not her constant peregrinations which had earned her the name "Gypsy." Ask anybody about the name and the response was almost universally, "Well, don't she *look* like a Gypsy?"

Gypsy Spurlock was a short, bottom-heavy woman of indeterminate middle years, who often dressed in eye-searing colorful tops and bottoms sharing only the same sense of outlandishness and nothing else in terms of color or style coordination. Today she was wearing a red-yellow-orange-striped top with puffy short sleeves, under a purple velour vest, hot pink Capris, yellow ankle socks with puff balls, and silvery Nikes. Her badly bleached hair was teased into a kind of nest, she wore big-hoop earrings, a couple loops of gold chain around her neck, rings on every finger, and a half-dozen jangling bracelets on each arm.

But despite her cheapjack goods and outlandish wardrobe, it was not Gypsy Spurlock Henry Gilmore was watching with a frown from his second floor spy nest. Helping Gypsy lay out her displays was Arva May Arlin. Rather than being her usual chipper, always-smiling self, Arva May was also frowning, like there was something on her mind, and Arva May's frown made Henry Gilmore's frown deepen, and when he saw her conversing with Gypsy Spurlock – Gypsy no doubt asking why Arva May wasn't her usual chipper self and Arva May telling Gypsy *why* she wasn't her usual chipper self – Henry Gilmore's frown grew so deep and contorted the muscles in his face began to hurt.

Behind him he heard the clip-clop of Crocs on the linoleum floor, sensed Mrs. White at his shoulder.

"She ask about Jess?" Henry Gilmore asked, nodding down at the veranda.

"They're kin, Mr. Gilmore. Of course she asked. The first thing she does when she comes in is to go stick her head in Jess's room and say hey."

"What'd you tell her?"

"There'd been a small accident."

"Oh, my," Henry Gilmore groaned, not seeing where that was an improvement over the truth.

"A *small* accident," Mrs. White amplified. "*Very* small. I told her we were having X-rays taken at County General just as a precaution. I said it was entirely possible Jess'd be back before she finished up this afternoon."

"It would be nice if that was true," Henry Gilmore sighed.

"Yes, it would."

"Did she…believe you?"

"She stood there, nodded through the whole thing, then asked me flat out if the truth was we'd upped and lost Jess again."

"Oh, my."

"I told her don't be silly, then I sent her off to help Miz Gypsy. I'm hoping that'll take her mind off it a while."

Henry Gilmore massaged the taut muscles along his brow. "I don't think it's taking her mind off it."

"Well…," Mrs. White said quietly, her way of saying she couldn't think of anything else to do.

"If you don't mind, Mrs. White, could you ask Miss Frye to try to get Clyde Thomas on the phone for me?"

As Mrs. White clip-clopped off, Mr. Gilmore rubbed harder and more frantically at the aches around his eyes and thought, We're all going to hell.

"It's nice to see you out here like this," Gypsy Spurlock said. She was arranging her *faux* Indian ivory figurines next to her *faux* Hummel figurines. Gypsy Spurlock spent a lot of time alone on the road, and, as a consequence, had grown quite attached to the sound of her own voice. "I always enjoyed your company, baby, 'n' it always made me sad you could only squeeze out a few minutes for ol' Miz Gypsy. I never liked seein' no young person cooped up in a office like they do you. Ain't fittin' to see no young person all boxed up like 'at. Ya know, I went to college back when a lotta Texas ladies didn't. Coulda been workin' in business but after a few months boxed up in some office, I just couldn't do it no more. An office 'n' a jail cell got the same number a walls, hon, that's how I see it."

"I guess," Arva May said without much feeling as she set little jewelry boxes out on one of Miss Gypsy's display tables.

"Those little felt boxes, you can leave 'em open. Peoples gotta see the goods, baby. But those, they got those see-through plastic tops. Just set 'em out. Put the big boxes up to the top, 'n' the li'l ones down there along the bottom. 'A's good like 'at, baby, thanks. This is nice," Miss Gypsy prattled on. "You always been one a my favorite people, baby. Most young people wouldn't have much truck with ol' folks, but here you been, up here workin' with 'em."

"Like you said, Miz Gypsy, I'm in the office most a the time."

"Maybe, but I seen you with 'em, Arva May, always sweet with 'em, always givin' all 'em time for a nice word." Miss Gypsy was laying out her *faux* satin scarves and *faux* lace doilies next to a spread of *faux* silk hankies.

"Well, maybe it's 'cause I got kin here."

"Still, baby, like I said, you don't see much a that in young people these days."

"Well, we got this minister?" And Arva May momentarily brightened at the memory. "Over there up to Boone? 'N' he's always sayin' when y'all got through all thee'ses 'n' thou'ses in a Bible, all Christian charity is is just treatin' other people the way you want 'em to treat you. So, whenever I come up here, I just always think how some day it might be me in here 'n' how would I want people to treat me. Even if they're not kin." Then she looked up at the windows of the Grapeland Assisted Living Community and grew glum, again.

Miss Gypsy stopped fussing with her *faux* this and *faux* that and set a comforting hand on Arva May's shoulder. "What's a matter, baby?"

Arva May shrugged and shook her head uncertainly. "I think somethin's wrong 'n' 'at's why they put me out here. No 'fense, Miz Gypsy, I'd work with you every time you come by, you always been sweet 'n' all with me, but when I was up here Monday, they said when I come back there's gonna be this passel a billin' has to go out 'n' for me to be ready to have my butt in a chair all afternoon doin' data entry 'n' Excel sheets. I got this feelin' like they're just pushin' me out a the way."

Miss Gypsy gave Arla May's shoulder a squeeze and pinched her downy cheek. "Don't look a gift horse, baby. You're out here in a sun 'n' air 'stead a all boxed up; enjoy it. I don't like seein' a pretty girl like you with her smile all turned upside down 'n' all. Your face is too pretty for that."

Arva May blushed and smiled. "Thank you, Miz Gypsy." She went back to setting Miss Gypsy's goods on the tables, came across a dozen small boxes topped with see-through plastic. "Oh, you still have these?" she asked excitedly.

"What's 'at?" Arva May held up one of the boxes for her to see. "Oh, a's a whole *new* bunch! Last load went so fast! I recollect you awready bought one, didn'tcha?"

"Yeah, but 'at wasn't for me," Arva May said, still beaming down at the one display box she held in her hands..

"But *now* you want one for yourself?"

"Naw, I don't wear much 'roun' my neck. Boys just use it as an excuse to look at my boobs. They say, 'Aw, nice lookin' necklace you got there, Arva May,' but 'at necklace is dyin' a loneliness while they're practically down the front a my blouse. Even my boyfriend does it 'n' he's one a the nicer boys!"

Miss Gypsy nodded with sage understanding. Then she grinned mischieviously. "Maybe *I* should try wearin' one a those things. Been a long time since a man give *my* ta-tas the eye, 'n' I don't knows I'd mind so much!" Miss Gypsy guffawed, Arva May laughed behind her hand. "Oh, I'm just *nasty!*" Miss Gypsy playfully reprimanded herself.

"You *are*, Miz Gypsy!" Arva May laughed. "Shame on you!" She tapped the display box. "My mama was on a committee got one just like this for the minister's wife. But that one was solid gold. I could never afford to buy one like that."

"Getcher boyfriend to buy you one. 'A's what boyfriends are for, ain't they? That 'n' lookin' at your ta-tas!" Miss Gypsy guffawed again, a horse laugh echoing around the veranda. "Oh, I'm bein' bad today!"

"Aw, my boyfriend could never afford one neither."

"Well, them there is just as good 'n' just a fraction a the price. 'N' 'cause you're one a my favorite babies, I'm gonna take off 'nother ten percent just for you!"

"Oh, no, Miz Gypsy!" protested Arva May. "I know you pay good money for these fine things 'n' then truck 'em all over Texas… Naw, that wouldn't be right -- "

Miss Gypsy put her arm around Arva May, again. "Don't you naw-naw-Miz-Gypsy me, baby. Iffen it'll put a smile on 'at pretty li'l face a yours, it's worth it." She picked up another one of the boxes with its see-through plastic display cover. "Lookit, baby, 'n' tell me 'at's not even shinier 'n' the real thing!"

The filling station phone booth was stifling, and Rita had to keep swabbing her forehead with the sleeve of her blouse. She noticed the sweat stain on the sleeve and made a note to add the cleaning bill to her travel tab. The connection clicked and rattled and for a moment Rita thought she was picking up somebody else's line. "Eric? Eric, can you hear me?"

"Rita, is that you? I thought I lost you for a second. Rita, my dear, you sound like you're calling from the bottom of the Marianas Trench. Are you using your cell?"

"No. I can't get a signal anywhere in this dump. I'm on a pay phone."

"Good God, do they still have those?"

"Listen, Eric, I have a reservation on a flight home tonight. I need you to cancel it for me."

There was a pause, then Bird said, in a slightly reprimanding tone, "I don't think we can get a refund on such short notice, love."

"I made it because I didn't think we were going to have this much of a story… *love*." She could almost *hear* the interest ripple through Eric Bird III.

"The priest really *is* making porn?"

"He's not a priest, Eric. He's a minister."

"Pity. It's saucier if he's a priest."

She opened the phone booth door to let some air in. "Well, he's not, sorry. I still don't have the skinny on what he's intending with this movie of his, but it's starting to look like that's not the best part."

"Do tell, Rita, love."

"The minister's wife. She might've been having an affair -- ..." Rita noticed passersby stopping and turning. This is why news travels fast here, she thought, and closed the door, turned her back to the sidewalk. "She might've been having an affair with a Black kid who was locked up in a reformatory where she did volunteer work."

Eagerly: "Reformatory? As in juveniles?"

"Right."

"She was getting it on with a minor?"

"I don't have that solid, yet, but that seems to be the case. At least he was a minor when it started."

"Oh, yeeeessss..."

"Try not to drool into the phone. This connection's bad enough."

"This is better than Mary Jane Letourneau. Teacher/student, pretty hot. Church lady and young Black gangsta? *Muy calliente!*"

"It gets better."

"Oh, *yeeeeeessss!*"

"The wife is missing. They found her car abandoned this morning. And now the minister's gone missing, too. Two days ago, he filled out paperwork to buy a shotgun and ammunition."

"Tell me there's more, Rita, love."

"There's more. What's that noise, Eric?"

"I'm purring."

"Here's the punch line. The local P.D. found a burned body this afternoon they think might be Sarah Dawson's."

"I just creamed in my thong. Theories?"

"The cops aren't saying boo. My thinking if the d.b. is her, the minister found out about the affair, popped his cork, offed his wife, and now he's off gunning for the kid. Or, the minister found out about the affair, popped his cork, the *kid* panicked and offed the wife, and now the minister's gunning for the kid. Either way, the minister can't do much gunning without a gun, and there's still a day left before the gun buy clears the background check period. Eric, are you *singing?*"

"Forgive my exuberance, love, but this just turned into the absolutely best of days! All right. Stay put. See if Dawson shows up for his gun. What about this kid? What do you know about him?"

"I don't have him I.D.'d yet. I think the local cops know who he is but aren't talking."

"Milk it out of 'em, Rita!" Bird sounded like a cheerleader. "*Grrrrrind* 'em!"

"What about my plane reservation?"

"I'll have it taken care of."

"I'm not making a long-term camp here, Eric. I'm giving this until the wait for the gun is up and then I'm out of here. I don't think I could take much more of this place than that." She thought but didn't say, I don't think this place could take much more of *me* than that.

"You can be such a snob, Rita."

"Be that as it may, there's also a logistical issue."

Warily: "Yeeessss…?"

"I didn't plan for this long a stay, Eric. I don't even have fresh underwear."

"Don't they have laundromats down there, love?"

"Not funny, Eric," but she didn't think he'd been joking.

A pause, then a clearly audible sigh, even through all the static. "Buy what you need, Rita. But try to keep it simple, ok? Cotton undies are just as serviceable as silk, love."

Clyde Thomas stood atop the knoll in Wilbur McCoy's north pasture, saw the same view Billy Ray Barnes had seen that morning: Abner Birney's store with Sarah Dawson's car out back, and, closer by, the charred heap that had been Wilbur's storage shed down among the white blossomed dogwoods. Clyde twirled the long stem of a blue bonnet he'd picked down by Wilbur's fence, waved the petals under his nose, an aroma preferable to the one wafting up from the site below.

The cattle still parked under the dogwoods were getting more of a show than Billy Ray had given them. Poking through the debris was a group of men from the Boone Volunteer Fire Department led by their chief, Tim Elway. Barney White, the county medical examiner, was there with his assistant and a stretcher team from the ambulance parked behind Clyde's car on the access road. And, of course, there was Wilbur McCoy, pointing at this, yelling about that.

Barney White and his people were wearing air filter masks and rubber gloves, and they were wrestling a black lump out of the debris and into a rubber body bag. One of Barney's men suddenly turned away, ran off and grabbed onto one of the dogwoods, yanked his mask away and vomited. One of the beeves mooed at him.

Clyde looked away from the scene below, put his eyes on the petals twirling around in his fingers. That's a hell of a nice shade of blue, he thought.

He looked up at the sound of Wilbur coming closer, crabbing about something. Wilbur was hounding Tim Elway as Tim made his way up the knoll.

"Just leave off for a bit, will ya, Wilbur?" Tim snapped, then turned to Clyde. "Hey, Clyde."

"Hey, Tim. So?"

Tim's shoulders went up and down. "Well, he was storin' more 'n' feed 'n' tools in there. Gas for his tractor, kerosene for lamps, he even had some emergency flares. Once a fire got into that, whole thing went up like a Fourth a Joo-ly barbecue. Burned hot 'n' fast. Didn't leave much to make a guess 'bout how it started, or point a origin…" His shoulders moved again, helpless.

"So you couldn't tell me if we got us an arson or an accident?"

"Damn, Clyde, we're the Boone V.F.D. I don't know much 'bout 'at kinda thing. Somebody has a fire, we all go put it out."

"Not this time," Wilbur McCoy snarled from where he was standing a few steps down the slope.

"Well, we can't put 'em out if you don't call 'em in!" Tim snapped back.

"'N' then you *bill* me for puttin' it out? What kinda nonsense is 'at, the fire department *bills* you for puttin' out a damn fire?"

"You're over the town line," Tim said in the tired way of somebody who's already explained something more than he should have to. "I don't write the ordinances, Wilbur." Tim turned to Clyde for help.

"Don't look at me," Clyde said. "I awready been through this with 'im."

"I'd just as soon let my whole damn ranch burn *flat* to the damn ground 'fore I go callin' a damn fireman 's gonna *bill* me for doin' his damn job!"

"Well, then, you g'ahead 'n' burn it down, Wilbur," Tim Elway said. "Fine by me. Enjoy yaself." He turned back to Clyde. "With all those accelerants he had stored in there…" The shrug again. "I'm just not that smart. You want me to call in somebody from outside?"

Clyde shook his head. "Just write it up how you see it, Tim. How 'bout a time?"

Tim's face knotted in calculation. "Well, let's see, Wilbur says it was still smokin' when he found it this mornin'…structure that size wouldn't burn long…the accelerants woulda burned off pretty fast; 'a's why they call 'em accelerants…"

"After midnight?"

"Oh, easy. You could throw a coupla hours on 'at no problem."

Barney White was on his way up the slope, now, peeling off his mask, tucking his rubber gloves in his hip pocket. Beyond him, Clyde could see Barney's crew strapping the filled body bag to a stretcher.

"Hey, Barney."

"Hey, Clyde. Hey, Wilbur, there another way to the road 'sides this?"

"Wazzamatter, your boys too soft for a walk back up a hill?" Wilbur sneered.

"What it is, Wilbur, is there's no way to get that stretcher through your fence. They're gonna have to snip that wire."

"Oh no they *ain't!*" Wilbur declared and started running back down the hill.

A winded Barney took a stand by Clyde and Tim and the three shared a chuckle watching Wilbur run down the hill yelling and waving his arms.

"That was nice, Barney," Tim said.

"Thanks, Tim."

"You know there's a gate 'bout another hunnert yards up the road?"

"I know. I'll go move the ambulance up in a sec. I just wanted to see Wilbur go batshit."

"Whatcha got for me, Barn?" Clyde asked.

Barney reached into his breast pocket for a pack of cigarettes. He offered the pack around.

"Quit," Clyde said, offering Barney his lighter and pulling a stick of gum from his own breast pocket for himself.

"Smart move," Barney said, took a deep drag on the cigarette and coughed. He watched the stretcher team follow Wilbur across the field. "Nasty," he said. "I mean *nasty*. It's not just the fire, Clyde. Tim, you tell him how hot she burned?"

"I told him."

"As the fire weakened the walls, the whole shee-bang came down on the vic. That metal roof, burnin' timber, all 'at right down on the body. It's not just burned bad, Clyde, but it's pretty beat up. One a those roof beams come down right on the face. I'm gonna have to put the jaws back together like a jigsaw puzzle 'fore I can even try a dental I.D. I got my boys goin' through the ashes to make sure we got all the teeth."

"Nothin' personal might give an I.D.?"

"Clothes, personal items, 's all gone. 'Cept this." Barney held out a plastic evidence bag. Inside was a misshapen, inch-long fire-blackened metal cross, a few streaks of gold showing through the black, on an equally damaged, filigree chain.

Clyde took the bag, held it up for a close look. "Could be a woman's, dontcha think?"

"Maybe, but I couldn't tell you from the body. It's 'at bad. Soon's I get it on the table I can tell you somethin', but right now there's just nothin' a work with"

Clyde fluttered the evidence bag. "One a my boys thinks *this* means it's a woman."

"Pardon me sayin'," Tim said, "but 'at's not exactly no huge brain trust ya got workin' for ya."

"I know," Clyde said.

"Who's doin' the theorizin'?" Barney asked. Clyde Thomas' pained hesitation was answer enough. *"Barnes?"*

Clyde winced, and Tim and Barney put on a face like one of Wilbur McCoy's beeves had just dropped a fresh pile of cow chips right in front of them.

"Jee-*zus*," Tim said. "How'd 'at guy even get on a cops?"

"Passed the test," Clyde said.

"Musta cheated," Tim said.

"Ya gotta be clever to cheat on a civil service test," Barney said. "Barnes isn't 'at kinda clever."

"Musta been dumb luck, then," Tim said.

"'N' I do mean *dumb!*" Barney said and he and Tim laughed.

Which only made Clyde wince again since he didn't have the nerve to admit he'd only mentioned it because he, Clyde Thomas – God help him – actually had bouncing around in his head the same idea bouncing around inside the cocoanut of Billy Ray Barnes.

"You heard 'at thing Smitty McKee said about Billy Ray 'n' *Jeopardy?*" Tim asked.

"I heard it," Clyde said.

"'At boy's got less sense then a box a hammers," Barney White said.

"I know," Clyde said. "But I'm askin', Barney; *could* it be a woman?"

Barney pondered a bit. "Well, the vic went fetal,'n' now it's all rigid-like. All crumpled up-like, so it's hard to get a pitcher a the build. But, it does look a might on the slight side. Could be female. But I wouldn't bet money on it just yet."

"Awright, Barney," Clyde said. "Let me know soon's you got *anything*, ok?"

"Ok, Clyde."

"'N' double pronto."

Barney started down the hill toward the vehicles on the road.

Then another possibility came to Clyde. "Say, Barn?" Clyde called. "What about a kid?"

Barney stopped on the slope and turned. "Whaddaya mean a kid?"

"A teenager, say."

"Like maybe one a those teeny-bopping firebugs Wilbur's been yowlin' 'bout?"

"Maybe a little older. Say a male, 18, 19."

Barney shrugged. "Jeez, Clyde, I'm just a Podunk county M.E. I'm not some episode a *CSI Boone*." He weighed the proposition. "Depends on a build. Get a kid 18, 19, on a smallish side, maybe, yeah, 's possible."

"Some way to tell if the vic is colored?"

"I'll pull out all my morphology texts. There's markers to look for, but right now I couldn't say."

"You got somethin' in mind, Clyde?" Tim asked.

"Yup," Clyde said.

"Gonna tell us?" Barney asked.

"Nope," Clyde said. He took a last whiff of the blue bonnet then let it drop into the high grass of the pasture as he started down the hill toward his car.

A celebration of the completion of the educational cycle! A commemoration of a rite of passage! A mourning of the passing of youth, and a salute to the transition into the world of true adulthood! And a lot of other horseshit from fucking Red.

Fucking Red had a gift – a golden gift, Kelly had to admit – for lending an oratory majesty to the most mundane crap, and why she and the rest of their little troupe hadn't learned better by now than to buy into it every time he ladled it up was either a tribute to the quality of fucking Red's golden gift, or a sad indictment of what suckers the rest of them were. You would've thought after that time he'd talked them into going off the trail at Lake Huston. Red babbled something about how God had told the knights of the Round Table that they had to go to a place in the forest where there was no trail so they could each find their own way to the Holy Grail. They had gotten lost and were practically crawling – exhausted, thirsty, and bug-bit – when they got back to fucking Red's van, that that would've been lesson enough.

But then fucking Red would get all big-eyed and sad, talk about how he'd only been hoping to give them a last, grand adventure as the days of their youth came to a close. Kelly – who'd been the first to say, while they'd been floundering around out in the bush, that they should kill fucking Red and set fire to him as an SOS signal for the park rangers – would also be the first to melt and say something along the lines of, "Ok, let's forget it and don't do it again."

Knowing he would.

Maybe they'd just gotten used to it. Like a ritual. Maybe it had become "their thing."

Whatever. For sure what none of them had had in mind, and certainly Kelly hadn't had in mind – even making an allowance for the usual fucking Red b.s. factor – was her squatting over a toilet in a dim, grim roadside public women's room. Her legs were cramping painfully as she tried to keep her ass clear of the seat and whatever Ebola-quality microbes were no doubt swarming on it. No easy task while batting at the flies hovering around her head and trying not to gag on the stale atmosphere of disinfectant, damp cement, and whatever it was in the next stall that hadn't been – or couldn't be – flushed by a previous occupant.

Process completed, Kelly quickly yanked up her cut-off denim shorts, toggled the flush lever with her sandaled foot, unwilling to touch the clammy metal, then stood over one of the rust-stained sinks cursing fucking Red, again, as she tried each soap dispenser and found them either empty or clotted solid. She made do with fitful spits of cold water (there were no hot water knobs) in the sink, made a mental note to make sure she doused her hands with Purell as soon as she got back to the picnic site. Upon brief reflection, she made another mental note to submerge herself in a vat of Purell as soon as they got back to their shared house that night.

After the cellar-like dimness of the women's room, sunlight and clean air was such a shock (though a welcome one), she didn't notice the car horns blaring on the nearby highway, or locked tires screeching on pavement. She certainly didn't think they had anything to do with her which is why the Winnebago bearing down on her came as a bit of an unhappy surprise.

She shouted something obscene, probably several somethings blurring together, as she lunged back into the doorway of the women's room as the Winnebago jumped the gravel drive, stones spitting out from under its tires like machine gun bullets as it lurched awfully damned close to the bathroom. It then heeled violently back onto the gravel before skidding to a halt in the parking lot, just missing fucking Red's van and stopping dangerously near the rim of the embankment leading down to the picnic area.

Once Kelly passed through the adrenaline-fueled panic over the imminent fear of being ground into mush by the Winnebago, her panic switched into adrenaline-fueled pissed-offedness and she stormed toward the RV.

"Hey, fuckwad! What the hell's the matter with you? You get your license out of a gumball machine or something?"

As she came up on the driver's side, she saw through the film of dust and pollen on the window a figure hunched over the wheel, head in hands, back heaving as if sobbing. She couldn't make the driver out very well – the figure was no more than a shadow – but thought, for a moment, by the slight build, it might even be a woman. Sally had often accused her of being a bit of a sap ("There are worse things" she would say back, even though she secretly agreed it was an annoying flaw, even to herself), and she felt herself start to melt over the quivering driver. "You ok, miss?"

"Oh, God, oh, God, oh, God…," and now she could tell, by the babbling mumbling, it was a man…although a damned small man.

Kelly stepped closer, saw another figure – a dog – its forelegs on the driver's lap, licking at the driver's face.

"Hey," she called up quietly. "Mister?"

The shadow inside straightened, turned to her.

"Mister?"

"Did I…? Are you alright? Please tell me I didn't hurt you."

"I think I caught a few rocks in the shins -- "

"Oh, God!"

"Didn't even break the skin, I'm fine. Are *you* alright? You look a little shook up. Why don't you turn your engine off and come on out here. I won't hurt you; I promise."

His head turned this way and that, as if he was unsure of what to do.

"That was a joke; about hurting you."

Through the glass she could hear him sigh, and then, "Um, maybe, uh, yes, yes."

She walked around to the other side of the RV, waited while she heard him struggle with the door lock, then finally the door and the screen door swung open. He almost fell out of the doorway as the dog -- a thick-gutted mutt-- cannonballed past his legs, a Frisbee in its yellow teeth.

Kelly laughed as the dog lifted a leg and peed here, and again there, and again in another place, all while still grinning around the Frisbee. "Looks like somebody's been holding it a long time," she said, meaning the dog. It was impossible for her to stay pissed when there was a dog around...and where the object of her pissed-offedness looked as pathetic as this guy. Until she'd gotten a good look at him, she'd thought, by his build, maybe he was some kid who'd just gotten his license.

Still looking shaken, still standing in the doorway, he was almost fragile-looking; the kind of patchy beard she'd seen on many a freshman unsuccessfully trying to declare his imagined maturity and even more imagined independence; she figured maybe her own age, not much older. She instinctively looked for him to make the typical guy moves: a quick up-and-down look guys thought went unnoticed but always was, taking in her bare, tanned, legs, the equally tanned belly her crop top showed off. But he didn't do that. Shy? Gay? "How long have you been on the road?"

"Hm? Not that long, really. I just bought this...this *thing* this morning."

"Well, that explains a lot." It didn't explain anything, really; pale face, sunken, bleary eyes – he looked like he'd been driving for days. She took in the rust streaks on the R.V., the dings, the caked-on dirt. "If you just got this puppy today, I hope you got a hell of a deal on it."

"I'm starting to wonder if it wasn't a mistake. He – the salesman -- told me it wouldn't be any harder than driving a car."

"Now you learned something about salesmen. Call it a life lesson."

Something about the phrase seemed to resonate with him. "Life lesson."

The dog was dancing this way and that around his legs, batting at him with the Frisbee. The Winnebago driver looked at the dog, puzzled, took a step back every time the dog gave him a thump with the Frisbee.

"Looks like somebody wants to play," Kelly said.

It seemed a revelation to the man, and Kelly was wondering if he knew any more about dogs than he did about driving a Winnebago. "This might be a stupid question," she said, "but is this dog yours?"

She had to laugh when it looked like the man didn't know how to answer.

"He...came with this," and he pointed at the RV. It looked to Kelly like he was weighing a further explanation, then gave up with a sigh and shrugged helplessly, apologetically.

"Well, I can't help you with driving that tank, but this goes like this." She whistled at the dog who bounded anxiously her way. Kelly tugged at the Frisbee, the dog tugged back. "What's the dog's name?" She took a quick peek under the dog's belly. "What's *his* name?"

"Pooch." Was he blushing over her taking a gander at the dog's equipment?

"Original as hell." Kelly stopped tugging on the Frisbee, held up a finger. "Whoa, Pooch, sit!" Pooch sat. She pointed at the Frisbee and then at the ground. "You want to play? Put it down." Pooch set the Frisbee at Kelly's feet. Kelly quickly scooped it up, Pooch's forelegs began to fidget nervously, knowing what was coming, then Kelly whipped the Frisbee into a smooth glide past the edge of the parking lot embankment, out over the level ground toward the lazy gurgling stream bordering the picnic area.

Pooch took off after the whirling disk, his paws pounding the ground in a frantic tattoo. The Frisbee started to lose speed and altitude, Pooch expertly reined in, gauged the disk's gentle descent, put on a sudden burst of speed, leapt, and pulled it down out of the air. The dog trotted back to Kelly, head up and proud.

"Nice catch, mutt," Kelly said, ruffling the dog's ears as he pushed the Frisbee against her legs. He let her tug the Frisbee free. She held it out to the man. "Give it a shot."

He didn't look all that enthused at the idea, and it soon wasn't hard to see why. He flung the disk awkwardly, the Frisbee immediately hit the ground on its rim and rolled away. It seemed to make no difference to Pooch who was just as thrilled about chasing a badly thrown Frisbee as Kelly's graceful toss.

She had almost laughed, then saw the embarrassment on the guy's face and guiltily bit back the half-dozen acidic witticisms which had quickly bubbled up in her head i.e. "So how'd those pitching tryouts with the Astros go?" "Arm just come out of the cast?" "Ladies and gentlemen, give to Jerry's Kids!"

Pooch returned the Frisbee and dropped it at the guy's feet, but he didn't pick it up.

"I've never been good at this sort of thing," he said quietly, rubbing his throwing arm. Did this little fragile flower throw his arm out with one Frisbee toss?

"Not everybody is," she said, scooping up the Frisbee. "Ok, Pooch, we're going for the gold now! Go long!" She sent the Frisbee on a long, soaring arc out over the creek. The dog lit out, again, didn't think twice about splashing happily into the water –

"Oh-oh," from the Winnebago driver.

"He's fine," Kelly said. "It's a slow current. He lives for this."

--until his feet cleared the sandy bottom, then he paddled on, his flat, little head peeking above the water, his fur wet and slicked back like a seal's. Pooch picked off the floating platter and began paddling back to the bank.

"C'mon," Kelly said, starting down the embankment toward the stream. She introduced herself, but the man didn't say anything back. "Would you like me to call you, 'Hey, you'?"

"I'm sorry. Owen."

She turned, held out her hand. "Pleased to meet you, Owen."

He hesitated for a second before he took her hand. Lightly. As if afraid to let it sit there. "Miss Kelly."

"Just Kelly, Owen." Jesus, she thought, what an odd fucking bird. Maybe he was one of those weirdies with Asperger's or something. Like the guy on *The Big Bang Theory*. There was something about him – what exactly, she couldn't say, maybe that Asperger's thing, that he threw a Frisbee like a total dork, that everything seemed to embarrass him – that made her want to take his hand and lead him to some safe place. She could hear Sally now: "Oh, Kelly, another stray puppy?" That was, after all, how fucking Red and then Ben had wound up housemates, and so had that dude with the funny Polish name who'd lit out with their TV when the rest of them had been fighting for survival at Lake Huston.

A dripping Pooch came loping up to her, took a stance and violently shook the loose water out of his fur. Kelly and Owen stepped away from the scattershot spray.

"Damn!" Kelly laughed, "I swear they know what they're doing when they do that!" Pooch let her again pull the Frisbee out of his mouth and she threw it in a low skim toward a set of picnic tables a short way upstream.

Sally was there, flinging a plastic tablecloth over one of the tables, and, by the water's edge, a sun-burnished Ben and fucking Red in their baggy, paisley surfer shorts, were each sitting in front of a painter's easel. Metal painting kit boxes were at their feet, each held a palette in one hand, dabbed at the canvas with the brush in the other, occasionally exchanged the in-hand brush for one of several held in their teeth. You'd almost think they knew what they were doing, Kelly thought.

The Frisbee skidded to a halt at the feet of one of the men; unkempt sandy hair, wire-rimmed glasses, a patchy beard like the one on the weirdie from the Winnebago, a T-shirt with a picture of a sunglassed Jeff Bridges from *The Big Lebowski* under the caption, "The Dude Abides." Pooch almost bowled him over as he rooted around in the dirt trying to scoop up the Frisbee.

"Sorry!" Owen called out.

"Him you don't apologize to," Kelly said.

The young man looked up, saw Kelly, raised his middle finger in her direction, a salute she smilingly returned. The painter took the dog's jowls in both hands and gave them a rough rub. Pooch dropped the Frisbee and began licking the man's face. "Mmmmm!" the man called out. "I just *love* the smell of wet dog!" The man picked up the Frisbee, held it teasingly over Pooch. The dog leapt again and again at the out-of-reach saucer, barking happily, frantically, then the young man tossed it with the same ease and grace as Kelly in a straight, even flight along the bank. The dog rocketed after the saucer, his tongue trailing outside his mouth, his paws digging deep and kicking up little spurts of sand. The dog pulled the disk out of the air, paraded back triumphantly, then wandered off into the cool shade of one of the willows hanging over the water and plopped tiredly into the dirt, idly chewing on the Frisbee.

"And, evidently, that," announced the painter, "is that. Hey, Sally, how about drawing me a beer?"

Sally had turned from the table to tend something sizzling in one of the picnic area's cinderblock barbecue pits. "I'll draw you a beer when you finish your picture."

"Everybody likes a little ass, Sal, but nobody likes a smart-ass."

The second painter laughed. Fucking Red; the same unformed slimness as his painting partner, but his face was broad and elfin, framed by an uncombed tousle of red hair and a similarly ungroomed red beard. On his T-shirt, a print of Monet's "Water Lilies." "Caution, Benjamin," he said. "Otherwise, you'll find yourself exiled over there to the doghouse with your fragrant companion."

"As long as Kelly here has kidnapped you, mister, you up for a beer?" invited Ben. "We're having a little celebration here. Figure since your dog's already invited himself, don't see any reason you can't join him."

"Uh, thank you, but I don't want to impose. I didn't mean for the dog -- "

"No reservations required, Owen," Kelly said. "And around this bunch, you don't even need to be remotely polite."

Owen smiled shyly. "Thank you. I'm having a little celebration myself."

"Then let's celebrate together," Ben said. "Hey, Hon," he called to Sally, "Would you get this gentleman a beer? Our guest? Pretty please? Pretty pretty please, pretty pretty lady? I'm not asking for myself, mind you, but for the sake of our guest?"

"As long as you asked nicely."

Ben sat at the picnic table, pushing the stacks of paper plates and a cluster of condiments out of the way. Owen fidgeted as if unsure where to put himself until Kelly put a hand on his shoulder and gently shoved him toward the same table. "As ugly as he looks, Owen, he doesn't bite. I don't think."

Sally pumped beer from a pony keg sitting in a vat of ice into two party cups. She set one down in front of Owen. Kelly watched him closely. Sally had a bit more to show; she tended to spill out of her tops when she bent over, but this Owen guy didn't steal so much as a glance down her cleavage. Instead, he buried his eyes in the checked tablecloth.

Ok, that's not Asperger's, that's not even gay, Kelly thought, but she liked that Owen was trying hard not to be a typical male jackass.

"Ben's only behaving properly because we have company," Sally said. "Otherwise, he's not as well-behaved as your dog. And not nearly as cute."

Which set Ben to barking and panting in canine fashion.

"See?" the girl said. Ben reached for the other cup, but she held it out of reach. "When you finish the picture, I said."

Ben threw himself to the ground on one knee, hands clutched over his heart. "Yea, yea, yea, milady," he spoke in a Shakespearean boom. "I shall pour my life's blood upon yon canvas to slake thy thirst for art. This I do so swear! Now, please, noble lady, slake *my* thirst for yon cup of the golden nectar, the fruit of the gods, for a little *brewski!*"

Sally held a hand out over Ben's head, tossing her own head back regally. She spoke with her voice high and wobbling, an impression of doddering English royalty. "I bid ye rise, poor knave, poor peasant, poor slob. By the Order of the Garter -- "

"Black garter, I hope," Ben slavered, "with seamed fishnets."

" --I decree this goblet of the king's piss to be thine. But just this one for now."

Ben rose, she handed the cup to him, and he poured it into his mouth with excessive slobber. "*Ahhhh!*" he thundered, satisfied, and immediately thereafter burped with nearly equal volume. "So nice I had to taste it twice!"

Sally laughed and gave him a playful slap. "God, you are *so* grotesque!"

It was standard stuff, Kelly knew, almost a bore it was such a familiar, look-how-clever-we-are performance, but they were showboating for the new guy. For his part, Owen seemed mystified, amused, even a little afraid, all at the same time.

It wasn't Asperger's, and he wasn't gay, or a dork. My, God, he's *that* innocent. Like he was born yesterday.

Ben sat down next to Owen while Sally went back to the grill. Pooch trotted over and parked himself close by Ben, panting heavily around the Frisbee.

"I don't think he ever gets bored," Owen said.

"You just have to know how to talk to him," Ben said. He turned to Pooch, put on a dopey, wide-eyed face. "Rat's renough," he said in a goofy, throaty sing-song. "Ro rore playin'!" Ben turned back to Owen expecting applause, seemed puzzled by the blank face on his seatmate. "Scooby-Doo," he explained.

"Excuse me?"

"My friend, you have led a sheltered life."

Pooch, evidently, was a bit more media savvy. He seemed to understand immediately, was none too disappointed. He dropped the Frisbee, went back to his cool patch of dirt under the stream-side willow to lie down.

"What's his name?" Ben asked.

"Pooch."

"And no doubt you were up all night cogitating on that one." It was the red-haired man. He went to the keg and pumped himself a cup of beer. "Sally, my dear, I think I'm done. At least I'm done sitting out there in the hot summer sun. How about you, Ben?"

"Ditto."

"You didn't finish," Sally scolded Ben.

"Just needs a little dab here and there."

"About six thousand dabs," Sally said.

"Everybody's a critic," Ben said. He turned to Owen: "You're an objective observer, new guy. What do *you* think? And don't consider the fact that I invited you over for a beer." He winked broadly at this last.

"Actually," Kelly said, "I'm the one -- "

"Tut-tut," Ben said, silencing her with a raised finger which he then used to direct Owen's attention to his canvas on his easel by the water.

"Ah, well," Owen fidgeted, "I don't really have much of an eye for art."

"Neither does Ben, mister," the red-haired man laughed. "Now, if you want to see some *real* art, check out that one over there," and he pointed to the canvas drying on his easel.

It was Ben's turn to laugh. Loudly. "*Real* art, Red?"

Kelly shook her head. Whatever bubble this Owen fella had been living in, no way he was going to get fucking Red's abstract slashes and blobs of color. Hell, *she* didn't, and she'd aced Art Appreciation.

Owen leaned forward and looked at the painting. "I've...never seen anything...quite like it."

Ben was still laughing. "And, God willing, you never will again!"

"Literalists," Red jeered.

"Don't worry about it, Owen" Kelly said. "Even Red doesn't know what he's doing."

"Unrefined prole," Red declared haughtily.

Kelly watched how Owen gingerly sipped at his beer. I'll bet my ass against a donut that's his first beer. She sat by him. Close. "You don't have to drink it if you don't want to, Owen."

He nodded a thanks, but that he was ok, although it was clear he was still deciding if he liked the taste or not. "You said this was kind of a celebration," he said. "What are you celebrating?"

"Our entry into middle classlessness," the red-haired man pronounced grandly. "Good fellow, those paintings there represent a transmogrification. A metamorphosis."

"That means they're going to turn into cockroaches," Sally said.

"Close," Ben said. "Red and I are heading off for the big bucks. We just graduated from college, got business degrees burning holes in our pockets -- "

"Along with fifty thousand in college loans," Red inserted.

" -- but first we finish up our summer vacation. Our *last* summer vacation."

"Happy trails, to youuuuu…," Red sang.

"We all just finished up at Brown Mackie," Sally explained. "The plan is to party our way down to Galveston, spend a little time on the beach, and then…"

"And then," Ben put in, "it's time to hit the ol' job interview circuit."

"The daily grind," said Red, "the rat race -- " he rolled his r's " -- punchin' the clock, makin' bank."

"Shave and a haircut," said Ben.

"And a three-piece suit," said Red.

"Kelly and I have the honor of doing the shaving," Sally said.

"Actually," Red said, "I don't believe we've been formally introduced. Pardon my lack of couth, and that of my confreres."

Kelly smiled over the puzzled look on Owen's face. "He talks like that all the time. He thinks it makes him sound intelligent instead of like a pompous ass. He's wrong. Any time he says something you don't understand, just assume it's not worth understanding."

"*Tres déclassé, Mademoiselle Kelly.*"

"Case in point," Kelly said. "Gang, this is Owen. Owen, the guy here with the big head and bigger mouth is Red, although we tend to think of him as fucking Red. We call him fucking Red because hardly a day goes by when he doesn't do something that has you shaking your head going, 'Fucking Red, man.'"

Red struck a pose as if he was in the balcony accepting his Kennedy Honors accolades.

"This beer-swilling bozo is Ben," Kelly said. "You met Sally who's that wench over there burning what was once some very nice ground beef."

Sally, back at the barbecue pit, waved her cooking fork at Owen. "*You* call me that and I'll take your eye out with this thing!"

"Nice to meet you all," Owen said. "Thank you for the beer. I should get out of your way and let you get on with your celebrating."

Ben grabbed his sleeve. "Whoa, there, Trigger. You said *you* were celebrating, too. What's the occasion?"

Owen looked to Kelly, Kelly nodded for him to stay.

"Well," said Owen, "Uh, I'm...I'm kind of...I guess I'm a little bit in the same boat as you. Just...you know..." He took a sip of his beer, seemed to like the way it felt going down, said with more certainty: "I'm making a movie."

"A movie?" Red sounded a little skeptical. "What're we talking about? Some little home movie thing?"

"No," Owen said after taking another pull on his beer. "A *real* movie."

Owen looked over at Kelly. She knew he was looking for her to be impressed. She nodded, pretending to be. The beer was putting some needed color in Owen's face, and she knew if he shared any characteristic with the rest of the male species, it was going to be that once he started feeling his booze, the bullshit would flow. But sometimes, she thought, a guy needs that kind of self-promotion...*this* guy.

"Like one of those independent movies?" Ben asked.

"I guess," Owen said. "Actually, it's already been in the local news. I'm pretty sure when it's finished it'll get national coverage."

"Really?" Red still sounded skeptical.

Kelly set her hand on Owen's arm to let him know she wasn't skeptical...although she was. He looked down at her hand on his arm, and it was the first time she'd seen him fully, freely smile.

"Oh, yes," said Owen. "I don't pretend to be an expert. This is the first time I'm doing this. But I've learned one thing so far. You don't need to be some big multi-million dollar blockbuster to get attention. You come up with a story that interests people, and they'll give you all the attention you want."

"It's no different than you guys and your painting," Kelly said to Red and Ben. "It occurs to you that you're running out of time to do the things you always wanted to do, so you just get out there on the road and say, This is my time! This is for me!" She turned to Owen. "Right?"

He smiled, nodding, as much a thanks as an agreement. "That's right!" he said. "This is my time! This is for *me!*" He seemed surprised at how loud it had come out.

"Wow," said Sally, "a movie mogul right here in our presence. And I guess that would be your mobile unit?" She pointed her fork at Owen's Winnebago.

"I guess it is," Owen said, enjoying the idea.

"You ought to have your name on it or something," Ben said.

"Yeah," Red agreed. "It pays to advertise."

Ben nodded in Red's direction. "That's that Brown Mackie business degree at work. You better listen to the man."

"What's the name of your company?" Red asked.

"Hm. I haven't rightly thought of a name." Owen looked into his cup. It was empty. He looked to Kelly, and Kelly handed him hers. He took a deep drink , blinked and wavered. "Oooh, I feel a bit dizzy."

"Go easy, Owen," Kelly said. "Have you eaten today?"

"I don't remember." He turned to Red. "My company; at this point it's kind of generic."

"I love it!" Red said. He stood, holding up his hands to make a frame in the air. "Generic Movie Company! Terrific! 'You pays your money, you takes your chances!' Hey, I've got an idea! We've got all the paints. Let's baptize your mobile unit!"

"What's your movie about, Owen?" Kelly asked.

Owen drained his cup. He held the empty cup toward her, asking without asking. She gave him a cautioning look, but he smiled a little wider, a little dopily, and pushed the cup at her, again. She took the cup and headed for the keg.

"Oh, Kelly," Sally whispered from the barbecue pit.

"Hush."

"You bringing this one home, too? We can't afford to lose another TV."

Kelly topped off the cup. "Again: hush."

"Well," he began after a pull on his fresh beer, "it's about this country preacher, and what happens is he turns over a new leaf. Just like you all are doing; goes on to another stage of life. It's a movie about change." He held up a caveat-indicating finger: "Adults only."

Ben's eyebrows bounced up and down lasciviously. "That could be interesting."

"It's a true story," Owen boasted slightly.

"No kidding."

"No kidding. Definitely a true story." Owen took another deep pull on his beer.

"Did you write it yourself?" Kelly asked.

"I'm kind of writing it as I go."

Sally perked up. "Oh, you mean it's improvisational!"

"Mmm, partly. But I do know how it ends."

"Say, Kel," Red asked, "where'd you put those 'appetizers'?"

"Appetizers?"

"You know." Red put the middle finger and thumb of one hand together and touched them to his lips.

"Ohhhh!" she said, "The *appetizers!*"

"Hey, Owen," Ben said, "why don't you and Pooch join us for our celebration, and you can tell us more about your movie."

"Well, that's very kind of you. We haven't eaten all day. At least I don't think we have. It would be nice to relax for a while." From where she was digging around in one of the picnic baskets, Kelly watched the way Owen looked around at the slow-moving river, the canvases drying in the afternoon sun, the smoking grill, the cool shade under the pines. A Martian marveling at the small, nice things of Earth for the first time. "On behalf of Pooch and myself, we accept."

Kelly finally came up with a sandwich bag filled with grass. She tossed the bag to Red. Red fished a pack of Zig Zag papers out of his hip pocket. He spread one of the little papers on the table, took a pinch from the sandwich bag, then crushed them with a dry rustle between his fingertips, letting them fall along the crease in the paper. He repeated the process until he was satisfied with the amount of material on the paper.

Kelly almost laughed when she saw Owen's eyes widen as he caught a whiff of what was going on the rolling paper. "Is that…?"

Red's eyebrows wagged up and down in a vaguely mischievous way. He carefully picked up the paper in the fingers of one hand, licked the edge, rolled it over, twisted the ends closed, then slid the whole cigarette in and out of his mouth sealing it tight. He ran the cigarette under his nose like a prize cigar.

"Yup. I'd call that marra-ja-wanna, although I don't believe I've heard the proper name used in a few eons."

Owen flushed. "I, uh, I've never, you know…" His voice dropped. "I've never even seen it."

"Ahhh!" Red grinned. "We're deflowering a virgin!"

"I thought everyone in the movies was stoned all the time," Sally said as she moved the cooked burgers to a cool part of the grill.

"Like I said; I'm new to the business," Owen explained.

Kelly came around and sat next to Owen. "Well, then, let me educate you," she said, picking up the baggy. "This," she lectured, "is *grass,* or *dope,* if you will. Smoke, weed."

"Pot," Ben offered. "How do you forget pot?"

"Ganja," Red contributed. "Spliff."

Kelly, Sally, and Ben all looked at Red. "Spliff?" Kelly said dubiously.

"I read it somewhere," Red said. "I read, you know. Some of you should try it sometime. There exists out there in the world these miraculous things with pages called books."

Kelly ignored him and took the cigarette from Red. "This is a *joint.*" She put the joint in her mouth, Red held out a Bic lighter, and she took a deep drag, held it a long moment, then let it out slowly, her eyes blinking against the smoke. "And that," she said hoarsely, "was a *hit.* And a damn good one, too! Where'd you get this stuff, Red?"

"Some pre-law guys I know."

"Pre-law guys get all the good dope," Ben observed. He took the joint from Kelly, took a hit of his own, then held it out to Owen. "G'ahead, give it a try. It'll spark your creative juices. Hey, if you're real lucky, you might even see God." He laughed.

Owen winced.

"Don't force the man," Kelly said. "I've never seen folks be so pushy. If he doesn't want to…"

"I wasn't forcing anybody," Ben protested. "Why are you so damned sensitive today?" His eyes grew in mock alarm. "Hey, Kel, it's not your -- "

"Don't even say it!" Kelly said. "Sometimes you can be such an asshole, Ben!" She turned to Sally. "Any time you get put out with him that's what he always says; you must be on the rag. It never occurs to him that maybe he *is* an asshole."

"The two concepts are not mutually exclusive," Ben said. "I could be an asshole and you could *still* be -- "

Kelly bounced an empty cup off his head.

Owen took the joint awkwardly in his fingers. "Well, I guess it can't hurt. I suppose if you're looking to change your life around…"

"Well, yeah, that's one way to do it," Red grinned.

"What do I do?" Owen asked.

"Just put it in your mouth, you know, like a regular cigarette -- "

"I've never smoked. Even regular cigarettes."

"The virgin's virgin," Red said.

Kelly gave him a fuck off glare.

"Like you saw us do," Ben went on. "And take a big pull, then hold it in your lungs as long as you can."

Owen put the joint between his lips, closed his eyes, inhaled and held it. A weak curl of smoke from the end of the joint tickled at his eyes. He flushed, winced; Kelly knew he was feeling the heat in his lungs, the burning in his throat. He let out his breath and opened his eyes. "Is that it?" he coughed, confused and a little disappointed. "Nothing's happening."

"It's the first time," Ben said. "Sometimes you don't take off right away your first time. Try it again. Aw, look, there's the problem. It's going out." Ben took the joint back and put it in his own mouth. He held his Bic under the other end and puffed until the smoke was coming out in a steady, lulling ribbon. He passed the joint back to Owen. "Try it again. It's good stuff. C'mon, you'll get the hang of it."

Owen tried another drag. "Hmph." He looked down at the joint in his fingers. "So, this is what all the fuss is about. I don't really feel any different. I think. I think I don't really feel any different. I don't think. And I surely don't see God. I don't think."

"Then what're you grinning about?" Ben asked.

"Am I?" Owen reached up and felt his face, his fingertips picking up the upturned corners of his mouth. Kelly knew he was feeling numb.

"Hey, Kel," Red said, "Maybe our friend needs a little shotgun to *really* get going."

"A what?" Owen asked.

Kelly snuggled a little closer to Owen. She took the joint from his hand, put the lit end between her lips. She leaned toward him, almost as if to kiss.

"Open up, Owen," Ben said in a soft, low voice, then, very sing-songy: "Kelly has a sur-prise for youuuu…"

Clyde Thomas followed the ambulance around to the rear of the Boone County General Hospital to the morgue entrance. In the small parking area there sat the now familiar red wedge of Rita Scott's Corvette.

He smiled a little bit, amused at the sight of the car, then put on a stern face as he pulled his patrol car up alongside. Rita gave him a big, teasing smile and a little fingertip wave. Clyde beckoned her over. Then she was leaning in his open door, that big, teasing smile a little bigger and more teasing.

"Fancy meeting you here, Chief!"

"You're lettin' the cool out, Miz Scott, so if you don't mind…"

She slipped in, closed the door, sat with clasped hands in her lap, eyes bright and wide like a kid on her first day of school. "So, here we are, again!"

"I woulda come over to your car but I'm not sure I'd fit in 'at bitty thing. 'N' even if I did manage to get in there, I woulda needed a prybar to get back out. Just didn't want you thinkin' I was bein' rude."

"Never entered my mind. I thought you were just being discreet, worried about how the good people of Boone might start talking if they see us always meeting like this. Especially if they find out you think I'm pretty."

"That was just your nose, Miz Scott."

"You don't think the rest of me is pretty?"

"I'll give you this, Miz Scott; you're somethin' else."

"You don't look surprised to see me."

"I woulda been a bit disappointed in you if you *hadn't* showed up."

More serious, now, as she nodded at the ambulance crew wheeling their covered stretcher through the morgue doors followed by Barney White: "So. Is it Sarah Dawson?"

"Body's in awful bad shape. Can't even make a guess."

"Officer Barnes seems to be of the opinion -- "

"Miz Scott, you don't have to be no Poolitzer Prize-winner to quick pick up on a fact 'at Billy Ray Barnes is somethin' of a low-grade moron."

"Well, I don't know that I'd go *that* far."

"*I* would. Now the victim, we just don't know. Body's in such bad shape we don't even know we got a male or female in there."

"Would you tell me if you *did* know?"

Clyde Thomas looked out the window of his car, shrugged, tried to remember when the last time was he'd had a decent vacation.

"The First Amendment doesn't seem to hold much sway down here," Rita Scott said.

Clyde couldn't have given less of a damn about the First Amendment one way or another. His agenda had been defined by a radio call he'd received on the way back from Wilbur McCoy's place from Mayor Fred C. Reilly who had proclaimed, in no uncertain terms, that the First Amendment or any other gawddamn amendment or the whole gawddamn Consti-fuckin'-tution didn't matter two farts in a gale wind to him. "Clyde, I want that nosy little nigger bitch packin' or come re-election time you're gonna be facin' a mayor on the stump sayin', 'My friends, ever' so often comes time for a change.' Unnerstand?"

"You been around, Miz Scott," Clyde said, "You know it's gonna be *days* for we get an I.D. in a case like this. Maybe even weeks. 'N' I'm hard put to see a big city gal like you wantin' to spend 'at much time in a borin'-ass place like Boone, pardon my French."

"Oh, I don't know," she said, "I'm enjoying the change of pace. Very relaxing. Sometimes you need a change from all that urban hustle and bustle."

"Let me put it another way. Maybe you can stand Boone a couple more days -- "

"But can Boone stand *me* for a couple of days?"

"Now you're gettin' it."

"I was planning to stick around at least long enough to be here when Dawson comes to pick up his shotgun."

"You're a smart cookie, Miz Scott; you really think if he *is* connected in any way to that body, he's comin' back? I'm gonna make you goin' worth your while. I finally got you one a your *quid pro quos.* Thing is, what I got for you will take you on the road, 'n' I suggest at's' where you take it."

"Or?"

Clyde fidgeted uncomfortably. "Elsewise, good chance you're gonna spend some time as a guest a the Boone Municipal Po-lice."

He was impressed: she didn't rattle, just kept up that teasing, little smile. "On what charge, may I ask?"

"Disturbin' the peace, loiterin', *somethin'.* You know it's not so hard to get somebody arrested."

"You wouldn't be presenting much of a case. In fact, we'd probably be talking about false arrest, harassment -- "

"Maybe, but the court system moves a might slow 'roun' these parts, 'n' sometimes it moves even slower for certain kindsa people." He gave her a you-know-what-I-mean glance. "By the time it got worked out, you woulda been coolin' your heels down here a while." He flashed a glance at her shoes. "'N' 'at'd be a shame you havin' such spensive heels 'n' all."

"Wouldn't be my first time, Chief."

"I spect not, but all a time you're keepin' me company to the stationhouse, this story 'at means so much to you'd be gettin' colder 'n' colder 'n' colder." And now, her smile finally faltered. "That's the *real* sore spot, i'n' it?"

She mimed taking an arrow into the heart.

"Miz Scott, I don't want you in my jail, 'n' much as you talk pretty , I spect you don't want to spend any time there. So…"

"*Quid pro quo.*"

Clyde pulled a small sheet of paper neatly folded into quarters from his breast pocket. He held it aloft. "There's this, 'n' an ay-*dios.* You know Owen Dawson left town this mornin'. He coulda lit out down any one a eight roads come through town."

"And you know which one."

"South on 19."

"And you know this because?"

"He gassed up at a Texaco station just outside a town, pulled out, headed south. You don't believe me, check with a guy name Lester workin' a pumps." He handed over the piece of paper. "This here's the make, model, color a Owen Dawson's car, his tag numbers, a physical description of Dawson."

She started to reach for the paper, hesitated, smiled warily. "How do I know this isn't just to get me out of town?"

Clyde Thomas smiled back. "It *is* to get you outta town. But it's also bona-fidey true so's it'll *keep* you outta town."

She took the paper from Clyde, quickly scanned the jotted information. "Any idea where he's going?"

"Nope. But the nice thing 'bout him goin' south is if you don't catch up with him you can just keep goin' in 'at direction'll all a way to Houston where they got a plumb nice airport'll get you anywhere in the country."

"Like back to Los Angeles."

"As a nice for-instance, yeah."

"If I don't catch up to him, I'm going to have to -- "

Clyde held up a hand. "Let's deal with 'at if it comes up. For now, just let me enjoy the idea this is goodbye."

She reached for the door, stopped herself. "Can I ask you something? Not about Dawson."

Suspiciously: "Ok."

"Billy Ray Barnes."

"I knew his daddy back in school."

"Good friends?"

"Not 'specially. But 'at kinda thing counts for somethin' 'roun' here."

She smiled admiringly and reached for the door. "You're something else, too, Chief. I may actually miss you."

"Well, maybe I got a pretty nose, too. Miz Scott, do somethin' for me, wouldja? If you do catch up to Dawson, ask him to call me soon's possible."

She nodded, said, *"Adios*, Chief," closed the door and climbed back into her Corvette.

Clyde sat in his patrol car until he saw the red car disappear down the parking lot exit ramp. "Ay-*dios* 'n' gooooodbye, Miz Scott," he said, then took a breath, climbed out of his car and headed for the entrance to the morgue.

Wednesday evening...

"I don't understand the steps," Owen said.

"There *aren't* any *steps*," Kelly said. "You just *mooove!*"

Owen tried *mooov*ing but it was hard for him to stay balanced on his feet and he wound up toppled over in the dust, laughing.

Kelly laughed with him, continuing to sway to "Take a Picture" coming from the boom box Ben had set by Owen's Winnebago. "I know I said there's no steps, but I think you're at least supposed to stay upright."

"Why?" Owen asked and laughed harder.

Kelly could tell this wasn't just this guy's first beer and first joint. He was *too* giddy, laughing like he'd been stowing up laughs all his life. She felt good she'd done that for him; brought someone a good time who looked like he hadn't had many.

They had pulled the Winnebago down the parking area bank and alongside the river. Ben had brought out his boom box and propped himself on the doorstep, Pooch at his feet, watching Owen and Kelly and Sally move to the music.

"Hey, how's this?" Red called from atop the Winnebago. "I don't read that well upside down."

Red was hanging over the edge of the RV's roof. The letters he had painted along the aluminum hull were bold black edged with bold white, an uneven but generally acceptable representation of the printing that used to be used on generic groceries.

"Wait a second," Owen said as he stumbled past Ben into the Winnebago, returning a few minutes later lugging his camcorder and tripod. He cast a glance at the reddish, lowering sun. "I hope there's enough light left." He switched the camera on. His eyes were teary from marijuana smoke and blurry from the beer and that made it hard to focus, but eventually he got the frame centered on:

GENERIC MOVIE CO.

Mobile Unit

"Beautiful!" Owen exclaimed as he let the camera whir on. "Beauti- ." A burp cut him short.

Which set Red laughing so hard he tumbled off the RV's roof into the sand of the riverbank. He groaned and moaned but the others kept laughing.

"Great!" Owen cried out. "Great stunt! I got it all!"

"Ok, Red," Ben said. "It's almost time for the shaving ceremony. Quit fucking around."

Red painfully pulled himself to his feet. "Well, gee, I'd hate to have my ruptured spleen put a damper on the party." He felt something sticky on his hand. He had pulled himself up along the wall of the Winnebago and in the process had run his hand through the still wet letters on the hull. "Aw, shiiiit…"

Which only made everyone laugh more, including Owen, who, despite laughing so hard he could barely stand upright, managed to capture it all on tape.

Red raised his painted hand solemnly at the lens of Owen's camera, and with equal gravity extended his middle finger. Red wasn't laughing. "Maybe if I ruptured one of *your* spleens…"

Sally, still dancing, wrapped soothing arms around Red. "Now, c'mon, hon, don't be a buzz-killer."

Owen weaved back to the picnic table where he had a cup of beer waiting. "I think this movie business is a lot of fun." He burped, again.

"Careful you don't explode on us, Owen," Ben cautioned.

"Hey," Kelly said, "let's go on with a little toot before it gets too dark for the shaving."

"You mean it about this shaving?" Owen asked.

Red disentangled himself from Sally. "The Ritual Shaving, as it has been proclaimed. You see, my dear sir, it's all part of the entrance into -- " he shuddered " – *adulthood*. It's part of turning over that 'new leaf' you were talking about."

"It's a clean start," Ben said. "A fresh beginning."

Red raised his arms skyward. *"Reee-birth!"* he declared to the red-tinged clouds, his voice echoing along the river.

"Rebirth," Owen said quietly. He looked into his empty cup and his smiles and laughter faded. "'When I was a child, I spake as a child, I understood as a child, I thought as a child: but when I became a man, I put away childish things.'"

"What was that, Owen?" Kelly asked.

Owen shook off the mood and smiled again, but it looked forced to Kelly. He saw her concern and set his hand on hers where it rested on his shoulder, patted it as if to say, "Don't worry, it's ok.

"So," Kelly asked, snuggling closer, "you think you need a shave, too?"

"I think maybe I do."

The morgue at Boone County General Hospital had only two autopsy tables and storage capacity for six corpses. But the human population of Boone County attrited at such a modest rate – even when combining losses due to illness, mishap, and malfeasance -- that this was more than enough space to handle the necessaries, and, in fact, the morgue sometimes stood idle for weeks at a time.

The morgue didn't, however, have enough space to suit Clyde Thomas. He stood as far away from the reeking black figure Barney White had laid out on one of the autopsy tables as he could. Barney White had given him some Vicks VapoRub to smear under his nose, a facemask, and had turned the room blowers up full, but that hadn't helped.

A wall phone rang, and Barney's assistant picked it up, spoke quickly, then waved at Clyde. "It's for you, Chief!"

Clyde, thankfully, found another phone on the opposite wall away from the autopsy tables. "Thomas."

"Clyde, I've been calling all over trying to find you. I tried your office -- "

"Who all is this?"

"It's Henry, Clyde. Henry Gilmore. They told me at your office -- "

"Henry, I really can't talk right now. I'm kinda up to my eyeballs in the cesspool, if you know what I'm sayin'."

"No, I *don't* know what you're saying. What I *know* is it doesn't seem like you're doing much to find Jess Smith."

"Frankly, Henry, I'm not. At least not just now. Doesn't it mean anything to you I'm talkin' from the county morgue? Right now, Jess's not zackly toppin' my to-do list."

"Can't you put one of your men -- "

"I don't have a man to put on it. I'm down a man. You want somebody on this full-time, you're gonna *have* to call the county sheriff's office 'n' get 'em involved."

"Oh, God...," Henry Gilmore groaned.

"Look, Henry, I'll give you a name for somebody over there 'n' he'll see what he can do without makin' too much noise 'bout it. But I'm tellin' you, you're gonna have to face a fact you're gonna have to tell Jess's family."

"Clyde -- "

"Yeah, I know all 'bout Miz June Louise Smith Noonan 'n' what a bitch on wheels she can be, but this isn't gonna get better by you puttin' it off. Her 'n' her sisters find out Jess's been gone 'fore you tell 'em, Henry, 'n' they're gonna be in your hair like a bunch a bats. I'll ask Barney White to put out a call to all the area hospitals -- "

"Oh, *God*..."

"Just in case, Henry, 'at's all, try not to give yourself a hole in your stomach." Clyde gave a quick look across the room to the charred shape on the autopsy table. "You might wanna dig up Jess's dental records 'n' send 'em over to the M.E.'s office."

This time, a wordless moan over the phone.

Barney's assistant was on the other phone, again, waving at Clyde. "Line two, Chief," he called.

"Look, Henry, I gotta go." Clyde picked up the second line to get Waylon Meeks telling him Denny Bemis from the Country Prosecutor's Office had called and would be in his office for just a few more minutes before leaving for the day.

Clyde hung up and called across the room: "Hey, Barney, mind if I use the phone in your office?"

"All this bidness you're conductin' on county premises, I should send a bill to Mayor Fred C. Reilly."

"I wanna be there for that one. 'A's one thrombosis I wanna watch."

Barney White's office was a small, cluttered, windowless room just down the hall from the morgue. Clyde was surprised Barney could get any work done on his desk, it was so crowded with photos of him, his wife, and his troop of kids. He dialed the County Prosecutor's Office and was put through to Dennis Bemis.

"Hey, Ol' Hoss!"

"Denny-burger!"

"Nope, no more Denny-burger," Denny Bemis said. "It's all fresh tossed greens 'n' fruit salad, these days. Once in a while, some veggie meatloaf as a treat."

"Damn!" said Clyde. "Who all's gotcha on a short leash?"

"The missus."

"Well, it's nice she looks after you like 'at."

"Yeah, it'd be nice if she was *bein'* nice, but that's not it. I had this *procedure* last year, some kinda damn blockage, I had to have this bypass thing. 'N' Murline said she'd put a second mortgage on the house 'n' hock her wedding ring if 'at's what it cost to make me better."

"Romantic."

"Like hell. She said there weren't no way I was checkin' out early 'n' leavin' her to raise our three brats by herself."

They laughed.

"It was two boys 'n' a girl, wasn't it, Denny?"

"Yeah, but they're all equally evil. Fact, I think the female is the worst! You didn't have kids, didja, Hoss?"

Clyde looked at the pictures on the desk: Barney White holding up a big-eyed little girl with bangs practically in her eyes and no front teeth; Barney and his wife crouched down around a buzz-cutted five-year-old, wearing a men's white shirt as a gown for graduation from pre-school; Barney and all three of his brood crushing the lap of some poor, luckless store Santa.

"Naw, we managed not to make 'at mistake," Clyde said.

"You think kids're a mistake, Hoss?"

"Nope," Clyde said. "Me 'n' either a my exes bein' parents; *that'd* be a mistake. *I* woulda needed a second mortgage to pay for the therapy we'd a had to put 'at poor kid through."

"So, Ol' Hoss, what can I do ya for?"

"Leroi Jefferson."

A beat, and then, "Ok."

"So you know the name."

"I 'member him bein' in front a the judge more 'n' a few times."

"He got busted 'n' released on a statutory rape beef in Latexo 'bout a year 'n' a half ago, Denny. I'm tryin' to find out 'bout it."

"That file's sealed, Hoss."

"I know. I was hopin' maybe we all could, ya know, have a kinda off-the-record, under-the-table, informal-like talk 'bout it."

Another pause. "Ya know, some ol' boys come up to the house last week' 'n' talked 'bout puttin' me up for State Assembly next term."

"Congratulations."

"I get cow shit on my boots over this bidness 'n' I can pretty much kiss 'at goodbye. Maybe my job, too."

"Look, Denny," Clyde said uncomfortably, "I'm not lookin' to put you in a bad place. I wouldn't ask 'cept I'm kinda feelin' up against it. Here's what it is: I'm just tryin' to find out if this boy's a predator or just plain dumb. I don't care 'bout the girl in the case, I don't need no names. But if there's anything you can tell me..."

A pause, then a sigh. "Don't be takin' no notes. What's Jefferson say 'bout what happened?"

"Well, I haven't talked to him direct, but from what I hear, when anybody brings it up, he won't talk 'n' says it's 'cause he don't wanna muddy up the girl's name."

"That's what he's sayin'?" Denny Bemis sounded surprised.

"So they tell me. Why?"

"I guess maybe he meant it, then," Dennis Bemis said, musing.

"Meant what?"

"Ok, Hoss, it was like this. Jefferson was carryin' on with this girl in high school, knocked her up. She was white, couple years older, 'n' her daddy was what you would call a leadin' member a the community. Her bein' knocked up by some colored boy from crosst the tracks didn't set too well with him. So, Jefferson gets pulled in. He says he's in love with her, says they actually been seein' each other a while. I don't know how, the kid was truant so much I'm surprised he could even *find* the damn high school, but that's what he said. So, then I bring in the girl."

"'N' she says?"

"Same thing; she's just all in *loooove* with her Leroi. To my mind, it was one a those high school crush kinda loves, but, whatever. I think maybe she was just into this whole bad-boy thing. She was Li'l Miss High School -- . 'Member Purdy Watson back in Boone High? Editor a the school paper, cheerleader, class president, stuck-up-tight-assed queen a the whole shee-bang? Same thing with this girl. So, she's on one side -- "

"'N' Leroi's on t'other."

"Then the daddy pulls the girl aside, they have a talk, lotsa hollerin', 'n' now she takes it all back, says she just met Jefferson once at a dance, he got her drunk, 'n' so on."

"I gotcha."

"So, now we bust Jefferson, ;n' when the girl sees Jefferson's lookin' at maybe some juvie time on a sexual rap, she recants *again!* She was just sayin' what her daddy told her to, her lovely Leroi didn't do anything wrong, they're in love... I tell the daddy, first off, I bring this into court with his daughter always changin' her story six ways to Sunday, even a third-rate public defender is gonna poke the case to pieces, 'specially if she buckles on a stand 'n' changes her story a couple *more* times. 'N' then I tell him, in any case, to make it stick, she's gonna have to testify in open court as to what happened. Either way, she says date rape or he's the love a my life, daddy figures it's an embarrassment. He pulls back, I drop the case, next day I get a call from his buddy, a judge who shall also remain nameless, who says to protect all concerned he's orderin' the file sealed. 'N' the girl, she decides in the middle a her senior year she wants to transfer to some private school out in Colorado 'n' then see the sights overseas after graduation."

"In the course a which her li'l problem gets taken care of."

"That's 'bout the size of it. I gotta admit, when Jefferson was goin' on 'bout how much he loved this girl 'n' all like 'at, I just thought he was bullshittin' me to get out from under. If he's still sayin' 'at…well…Some kinda world, isn't it, Hoss?"

"Some kinda."

"You seen his record?"

"Yeah, looks like he's been keepin' his nose clean since he got out a juvie."

"Well, I never bought it. I'm not a big believer in leopards changin' their spots 'n' all. Sooner or later, this kid's gonna fall off the wagon if he hasn't already. But I'll give him this, Ol' Hoss: unless he's graduated, well, I figure him for a habitual, but nothin' sexual. 'Cept for that one time he popped one a the Latexo cops, he never even did anything violent. Any a that help you out, Hoss?"

"*Huge* help, Denny. Tell you what; gimme a couple weeks, 'n' I'm gonna have you up to Boone for some official bidness. 'N' while you're up here where the li'l lady won't know, I'm takin' you to this great little dump I know makes the greasiest, juiciest, most artery-cloggin' charcoal-burnt burger you ever saw."

"Onions 'n' cheese?"

"Swimmin' in 'em."

"'A's a date, Hoss."

As Clyde hung up, an ashy Barney White came through the door, dropped in a chair and sucked in deep pulls of air through his nose. "Gawd*damn!*" he said, "I don't think I'm ever gettin' 'at smell outta my nose." He sniffed at his shirtsleeves. "Great. It's in my clothes. I get to go home 'n' make all *them* sick, too."

"You got anything for me, Barney?"

"I'm not gonna do the full post just now. My department doesn't have the budget for overtime, and unless I miss my guess, Mayor Fred C. Reilly who spends Boone's money like it's his own won't front you the money for it either. But I'll get on it first thing in the mornin'."

Clyde thought about pressing the issue, but then he looked at the pictures of Barney and his family, again. Just because *you* don't have anything better to do, he reprimanded himself. "Go on home, Barney."

"'Sides, we don't have all the teeth. I sent one a my boys back out to Wilbur McCoy's to go through the debris again 'fore we lose the light, make sure we didn't miss 'em. Or they mighta got swallowed if the vic lived through that first hit to the head. I do have *somethin'* for you, Clyde, I gotcha the easy stuff. The vic had O positive blood – 'n' here's your big one – she was a she."

"It's a woman? You sure?"

"Once you get inside, it gets kinda obvious. Female, white, 'bout five-two, maybe 115 pounds. Sound like anybody you had in mind?"

Clyde Thomas nodded grimly. He glanced at his watch. "I gotta go, Barney. Talk to you tomorrow. Look, Henry Gilmore over to Grapeland is sendin' over some dental records tomorrow. If you can, see how they match up with the vic. Maybe we can eliminate a possibility."

"Do my best, Clyde."

Clyde patted Barney on the shoulder as he passed out the door. "I know."

As Clyde walked down the corridor heading for the door to the parking lot, he said to himself, I'm sorry, Henry, but I hope that's *your* missin' lady in there 'n' not *mine*.*

Bubba had his hand in a death grip on Rita's elbow even before she had completely climbed out of her Corvette. "You're obviously a lady of fine and

– I gotta say it – expensive tastes, ma'am. I saw you pull up in 'at eye-catcher 'n' I said to myself, 'Bubba, that li'l gal likes nothin' but the best."

"I do like my creature comforts," Rita admitted, "Mister, uh -- "

"Jus' call me Bubba," Bubba said, "'N' I'll thank you not to laugh *too* hard," after which Bubba laughed too hard. "Family name passed proudly on down through the generations just so's a fine li'l lady like you could say, 'I bought my RV from Bubba!'"

"Actually, I'm not -- "

"I know, I know, I know, you're jus' lookin' 'n' 'at's awright, but jus' allow me to show you what's best to look at," and Bubba steered her gently – but firmly – to one of the largest mountains of aluminum he had on his lot. Bubba's buzzing neon sign and the strings of winking light bulbs hung over the lot, all of which had flickered on with the dusk, splashed sparks of light and color in the windows and gleaming metal hull of the RV. "The best for the best, ma'am, 'n' I guaran-damn-tee you this is the best there is! This jewel's loaded to the gills with every creature comfort you could want or need on the road. 'At damn space station they got up there don't carry as much hardware as this wonderful piece a machinery."

"Bubba, do you mind if I say something? I'm from out of town -- "

"I heard it in 'at lovely voice a yours, ma'am. Out west, if I had to guess. Maybe California? I thought so. Charmin' accent, ma'am."

Rita smiled admiringly. Oh, this one's good, she thought. Obvious…but *good*. "I have to say, no offense to your fellow Texans, but in my short time here in your lovely state you have been the most welcoming soul I've met."

He smiled understandingly, nodded apologetically. "Well, ma'am, there's Texans 'n' there's Texans. I always take the advice a my brother-in-law Virgil, lovely soul runs a funeral home over to Trinity. Virgil says he always looks at each man – and lady – as a potential future customer 'n' treats 'em as such."

"A nice way of saying the only color you see is green."

Bubba ran up a look of mock offense. "Well, ma'am, I don't know's I'd put it such-like!" But then came a mischievous curl of the lips: "But somethin' like 'at."

She laughed and wrapped her arm around Bubba's. "Well, it doesn't get much more democratic than that." It was her turn to steer him through the lot. "Frankly, Bubba, I'm not interested in RVs."

Bubba looked crestfallen, but Rita couldn't tell if it was over the loss of a possible sale or the idea that someone could not be interested in one of his beloved wheeled palaces. But she did get his interest back up when she said, "But there is *something* on this lot I'm interested in."

They were stopped by a tan Plymouth sitting alone in an empty space by the office, as if quarantined.

"You're interested in *that?*" Bubba said, a little surprised.

Rita nodded. "Saw it from the highway and pulled right in."

Bubba dropped quickly back into his high-gear sales persona, snuggling a little closer to Rita. "Well, ma'am, you got a sharp eye. Might not be as flashy as 'at set a wheels you roared in here on, but this li'l jewel makes a fine second car! Steady, reliable, easy to maintain, not too bad on gas which is somethin' you wanna take into account these days. You're lucky. I don't usually handle cars. My brother Elvin's got hisself a lot t'other side a Grapeland 'n' usually anythin' I get on a trade I run up to him, but this is jus' a sweet bit a good fortune for ya! Ain't had time to run 'er up to ol' Elvin, 'n' Elvin, well, he's blood 'n' one a the sweetest, fairest souls I know, but, well, ya know how it is, every time a piece a merchandise changes hands, the mark-up goes up – 'a's just a law a nature – but by you gettin' here kinda cuttin' in line, so to speak --"

"Bubba, I'm not looking to buy."

"No?"

"Afraid not," she said, smiling apologetically. "If I was, trust me, you'd be the man for me to see. Just for the show alone." She fished in her purse for the piece of paper Clyde Thomas had given her. "Did that car come in here with these tag numbers?"

Bubba's face folded in anguish, he let go of her arm and started stomping around in a small anguished circle. "Oh, lordy, don't tell me 'at heap's *hot!* I swear by the good Lord Jesus on his cross, ma'am, 'at fella come in here with all the proper papers -- "

She patted his pillowy shoulder comfortingly. "The car's not stolen, Bubba. Nothing like that at all. I'm just trying to find somebody."

He recomposed himself, grew very serious, cleared his throat and stood with his Stetson in his hands; a very formal announcement: "Well, ma'am, there's what they call confidentiality. I look at every one a my customers as a good neighbor, 'n' I wouldn't be doin' right by my good neighbors handin' out their private information to jus' any ol' body, even a very nice lady like you. You might have perfectly legitimate business with this fella, but for all I know --"

"Bubba, that's a very commendable stand," Rita said somberly. "But confidentiality is for lawyers and doctors and priests. I don't know that it extends to RV salesmen."

"Still, ma'am -- "

"What if I could get that confidentiality rule suspended by presidential order?"

"A what?"

"A presidential order. I mean, I feel bad that you've extended every hospitality to me and then it turns out I'm not here to buy anything, and I know that President Grant would like to compensate you for your time and help ease your conscience about that confidentiality thing."

"Grant?" Bubba slipped his Stetson back on his head, stepped back close to Rita, his voice down to a tone of conspiratorial intimacy. "Well, ya know, as ya might expect, General Grant hasn't been all 'at popular down here since The War of the Northern Aggression as we call it. A presidential order from Mr. Grant ain't gonna cut too much ice, I'm afraid."

"Well, there's Mr. Franklin. He was never president -- "

"Then maybe he needs a li'l reinforcin'. Maybe his twin brother can help 'im out."

"Two Mr. Franklins?"

Bubba big, fleshy face rolled upwards in a pleased smile. "'N' how's ol' Ben been keepin' hisself?" he asked brightly.

"See for yourself." Rita pulled two hundred dollar bills from her purse, but pulled them away as Bubba's thick fingers started floating their way, replaced them with the Clyde Thomas' note. Bubba smiled, one skilled salesperson appreciating the deft work of another, and examined the note.

"Those look like 'em," Bubba said. "I can check in the office. I still got the original tags."

"When you do that, can you write me out a receipt?"

"You want a receipt for -- "

"Your 'service fee.'" It was, she considered, going to be a hell of an expense report she'd be turning into Eric Bird III. "Is this the man who brought the car in?" She pulled her clipping from *The Crockett Courier* with its box on Owen Dawson and his movie from her purse.

Bubba squinted at the photograph. "That's not a great pitcher."

"Newspaper photos usually aren't."

"But, yeah, looks like him."

"He traded the car in?"

"Yeah, on an ol' Winnebago, 20-footer. Got some years on 'er but I tell ya, a good buy, a steal at twice a price. Gray, temporary tags, I got the numbers in my office."

"Which way did he go?"

Bubba took her by the elbow, turned her around, facing back toward the highway, pointing toward where ruby taillights were disappearing over a horizon limned by a blood-streaked sky. "Down that way," he said. "South."

Clyde Thomas pulled his patrol car up to the curb not far from the bus kiosk at the foot of the drive leading to the main gate of the Boone County Juvenile Reformatory. He lowered his sun visor against the late-day glare. When he turned his eyes in just the right direction, there was no reformatory in view, no razor wire-topped fence, just open ground covered with grass turned gold by the lowering sun, then a line of pines silhouetted against a warm, mauve sky, the undersides of the few clouds colored a hearthy red. Gimme a cold beer, he thought, and Waylon Jennings on the radio, and I could spend the night here watching 'til the moon comes up.

Then the gold of the grass grew a shade deeper, the pines became shadows, and he was reminded he had no time for basking in red sunsets.

There was a dozen or so people huddled around the kiosk, most of them Black. Some wore the uniforms of security attendants at the reformatory, others the coveralls of the maintenance crew, and almost all of them were fanning themselves with something: a newspaper, a magazine, a hat. Clyde tooted his horn to get their attention, lowered his window and pointed to one older, gray-templed Black man: the swamper he'd seen in the reformatory front hall that morning. Clyde waved him over.

The old swamper's shoulders sagged as he walked over to the car slowly, trying to make the trip take as long as possible. He opened the door to Clyde's car, took his baseball cap off deferentially. "Yessuh?"

"Whyntcha come in outta the heat," Clyde said. "Take a load off. Bus won't be by for a bit."

With the same reluctance with which he'd walked over from the bus kiosk, the swamper obediently slid onto the front seat, closed the door of the car behind him. He sat with his cap in his lap, his face turned downward. "Thankya, suh."

Break a horse when he's young and he's broke forever, Clyde thought, looking at the humbled figure of the swamper; he's got enough years on him to remember the bad old days, back when you back-sassed a white man, didn't call him sir, didn't tip your hat, and like as not you were going home with a busted nose – providing you went home at all – and nobody to say boo about it. Which, Clyde thought without a lot of pride in himself, is something to use.

"This is better 'n' bakin' out there, isn't it?"

"Yessuh, thankya, suh."

"What's your name?"

"Willits, suh, Clarence Lee Willits."

Clyde reached into his breast pocket for a stick of gum, offered the pack to Clarence Lee Willits.

"No thankya, suh, I don't chews gum. Makes muh teef hurt, suh."

"You know who I am, dontcha, Clarence Lee?"

"Yessuh, Chief Thomas from up to Boone."

Clyde nodded. He pointed to the reformatory beginning to sink into the shadows slipping across the open acreage. "How long you been workin' up there, Clarence Lee?"

"Gonna be 44 years come October, suh."

"Hm, 44 years, no foolin'. Gee, Clarence Lee, just how old are you?"

"Ah's 64, suh.

"Well, damn, Clarence Lee, you should be puttin' in for retirement soon. Forty-four years in; 'a's not a bad pension, 'specially you put 'at together with your Social Security, even if they get 'roun' to messin' with it... Hm, yup, you won't be doin' too bad."

"Ah hopes so, suh."

"I bet you do. Ya know, 44 years is even longer than I been with the police. You got me by, I dunno, 13, 14 years, maybe that 'n' a bit."

Clarence Lee nodded. "Ah know Ah's been seein' you come 'roun' the institution long's I can 'member."

"That practically makes us law enforcement colleagues, Clarence Lee. I catch 'em 'n' you keep 'em."

Clarence Lee fidgeted. "Ah jus' keeps a place up is all, suh."

"Forty-four years in the same place. Damn. I'll bet you know every inch a that place by now."

Clarence Lee shrugged, began running the rim of his hat around and around nervously through his fingers.

"I'll bet you know every place in those halls where a echo carries, which vents'll take a voice from one room t'other."

"Ah don' do nuffin like 'at, suh."

"Like what, Clarence Lee?"

"Ah don't do no listenin' to stuff 's not my bidness."

"I'll bet you don't even have to," Clyde said. "You been there so long you're just part a the furniture, blend right in with the walls. I'll bet people don't even see you, they stand right next to you talkin' private bidness."

Clarence Lee cleared his tightening throat. "Chief Thomas, I'm makin' muh 44 years 'cause I minds muh own bidness."

"Maybe it just comes your way, Clarence Lee. Lotta young kids in there, all mixed up 'n' all, lookin' for what those fancy psychiatrists call a father figure. Ya know, somebody to be daddy for 'em. Some kid like 'at might just come up to you."

"I minds muh own business, suh. I jus' helps keep up a place. The chil'ren, dey ain' my job, suh."

Clyde nodded, sat quiet for a moment. Outside, the other people at the kiosk were looking at the car, talking among themselves, wondering, nodding.

"Maybe I shoulda been more direct up front, Clarence Lee, 'cause I don't think you get what I'm drivin' at. See, if I don't get help from you, if I think you're bullshittin' me, 'at's what they'd call 'obstruction' in a courtroom. 'N' *at* mean's you can kiss 'at pension a yours b'-bye. No pension 'n' you're gonna be just another nigger down in Bucktown sittin' on his front porch wonderin' how he's gonna make it to the first a the month. You unnerstan' me better now, Clarence Lee?"

Clarence Lee's head bobbed up and down tightly.

"I didn't hear you."

"Yessuh."

"Where's Leroi Jefferson?"

For the first time, Clarence Lee looked up, turned to Clyde. Fearful, yes, but imploring, too. But not for himself. "Leroi's a good boy, suh."

"I know, Clarence Lee. People been tellin' me that all day. But for somebody who's supposed to be such a good boy, Leroi's been keepin' a lotta secrets 'n' tellin' a lotta lies. He lied to Miz Gorsham who give him his chance to start over up to the reformatory, he lied to Abner Birney who cut him a break 'n' give him a job in his store, 'n' he lied to that li'l girl he's got over to Latexo he left with his baby girl."

The way Clarence Lee turned away, shame-facedly nibbling on his lower lip, told Clyde he hadn't said anything to the swamper the old man hadn't already been fretting about.

"Listen, Clarence Lee, I don't think Leroi's some big villain or somethin', but he strikes me as not bein' the smartest kid inna world. I'm thinkin' if he's not in big trouble awready, he's *gonna* be. Lessen I find him."

Clarence Lee squirmed in his seat, his weathered face wrinkled in thought, but he remained silent.

Time to squeeze a little, Clyde thought. "I know this one ol' boy, things get pretty thin for him by the end a the month. The way he gets by those last couple days is he eats nothin' but store-brand corn flakes 'n' powdered milk mornin', noon, 'n' night. Ever had powdered milk, Clarence Lee? You can't really *drink* 'at horse piss on its own, but it's not *too* bad when you mix it in with those corn flakes."

"He didn't say, Chief, I swear!" Clarence Lee gasped out, as much a plea for mercy as a response. "He jus' say he had to get away fo' a bit. He got all this *stuff*, like ya said, he got all dese jobs 'n' 'at girl 'n' a baby 'n' ever'thin' else --"

"He needed a break."

"Yessuh, jus' get away for a bit, he say."

"Where?"

"He didn't tell me, Chief, I swear! In front a the Lawd, I'm swearin' he didn' tell me; jus' 'at he was goin' away a bit."

"Calm down, Clarence Lee, I believe you, it's ok." Clyde took a moment, let the other man recompose himself. "Lemme ask you somethin' else. There somethin' goin' on 'tween Leroi Jefferson and Sarah Dawson?"

That same look, again, from Clarence Lee. "Miz Sarah? Miz Sarah, she a good lady."

"I didn't ask you 'bout her character, Clarence Lee."

Clarence Lee's eyes went back down. He was wrestling with the cap in his hands, now, nearly crushing it. "I dunno. He never say nuffin to me direct."

"What did he say to you that *wasn't* direct?"

Clarence Lee shrugged and wriggled and cleared his throat, and when he'd run out of things to do, he spoke sheepishly: "Cuppa weeks ago, he come to me, he as' me…"

"What'd he ask you?"

"He as' me what-all I think'd happen iffen folks find out he's, ya know, been keepin' wit' a white woman."

"G'ahead."

"I say, 'Boy, you don' pay no mind what you see on TV 'n' at a pitcher show; 'at's some other place. 'At ain' Texas. For a lotta folk down here, Texas ain' never gonna change.' I told 'im, 'Ain' you learn nuffin after 'at mess up to Latexo with 'at other girl?' He say dis differen' 'cause dis ain' no young girl, dis ain' no big man's daughter neither. I say it don' matter none. I say people find out you been wit' a white woman, 'n' she a *married* white woman, 'n' she married to a man a the church -- "

"So you knew he was talkin' 'bout Sarah Dawson?"

Clarence Lee shrugged. "Dey spen' lotsa time talkin', jus' a two a dem. You don' never see 'em do nuffin improper-like. But sometime you can tell jus' by da way dey is wit' each other…'n' sometime you see, maybe one slip a hand over, dey touch jus' fingers like ain't nobody gonna see…I jus' had a feelin'."

"He never said, 'No, Clarence Lee, you're wrong.'"

Clarence Lee shook his head.

"You said *they* spent lotsa time talkin'. So, this was back-'n'-forth. This wasn't just maybe Leroi had the hots for this lady, or maybe he was on the hunt."

"It was bof a dem, suh. I try to tell 'im. I tell 'im in Texas, a black boy go to trial he lucky iffen he ain' the only black face inna court. You know 'at's right, Chief."

Clyde said nothing.

"'N' I say lookit dose two ol' boys down in Jasper, wa'nt too long ago when dey tie 'at black man to their truck 'n' drug 'im up 'n' down a dirt road 'n' kilt 'im, jus' drug 'im to pieces. 'N' he wa'nt no Emmett Till. Dey didn' feel like dey even need a *bad* reason. Dey up 'n' kilt 'im jus' 'cause dey felt like killin' a nigger. Like I say; some places in Texas don' never change."

Now it was Clyde who shifted uncomfortably in his seat. "What'd Leroi say?"

"He don' say nuffin but nes time he talk to Miz Sarah, I think he was tryin' to bus' it up."

"You heard what he said?"

"No, suh, but, like I say, you can tell by da way dey is wit' each other. 'N' den it look like she be cryin' 'n' dey talk some more, 'n' den I think Leroi change his mind. Leroi a good boy, suh. But I think, like you say, sometime he don' do da smart thing. He wanna do right, but he don' allus know what it is. 'At boy, he get mix up, he get lost some. I think Miz Sarah, I think she talk 'im into stayin'."

Clyde nodded the old swamper out of the car. "G'ahead, Clarence Lee, your bus'll be here in a minute."

"Yessuh." He opened the door, climbed stiffly out.

"Clarence Lee?"

"Yessuh?"

"Thanks." As soon as he said it, it struck Clyde as a small and empty gesture, like offering a Band-Aid to the man you just beat down with a billy club. He didn't wait or look to see if old Clarence Lee thought the same thing, but, instead, dropped the car into gear and sped away from the curb.

They had built a large fire in the sand close to the river, and as the sun drew lower and the sky grew a darker red and the lattice of shadows from the pines swelled into a single, pervasive shade along the riverbank, the fire took on a warmer shade of yellow.

A beach lounger had been laid out by the fire angled so that whoever sat in the chair would have a view of the sun slipping below the serrated rim of pine crowns. Red was stretched out in the lounger, his head hung back over the top of the backrest, while Sally stood nearby. She had laid a beach towel over Red's chest and drawn it up tight under his chin, while, on another towel spread at her feet, were set out scissors, a safety razor, a can of shaving cream, bottle of aftershave, roll of paper towels, and a pot of water heated over the barbecue grill.

Kelly sat with Owen at one of the picnic tables. She loved this little circle of amber thrown off by the fire, the way it caught the sweat on the young, bronzed bodies and set them glinting as if sprinkled with gold dust. It was hot within the circle, and she could feel the sweat streaming down her body, see it glitter on her bare arms under the firelight, like little diamonds.

She knew this was partly the beer, and more so that good pre-law weed, and that was also probably why she was sitting shoulder to shoulder with Owen, her hand on his. But still, it felt good, she felt good, especially when she compared the quaking little thing that had stumbled out of the RV a couple of hours ago to this guy who looked like he was living a lifetime of good times he'd never had. She was happy for him, and her head found itself on his shoulder.

Sally gave her a look – partly, "Seriously?" and partly, "Here we go, again" -- before she turned to Red.

Earlier, after they had cleared off the table after they'd eaten, while they'd been lugging the trash to the dumpster behind the bathroom, Sally had shaken her head: "What are you doing, Kel?"

"What am I doing?"

"You *know* what you're doing."

"I don't know what you're talking about."

"You *know* what I'm talking about."

"Actually, I'm pretty buzzed; I really *don't* know what you're talking about."

"He's not coming home with us, Kel."

"I wasn't even thinking -- "

"Bullshit."

Which it was. She had been thinking about asking Owen where he was spending the night.

"This little dweeb parks that Godzilla of his in our driveway and I guarantee you he winds up homesteading. That's how we wound up with these other two. We got lucky with them; they're harmless."

"So's he, Sal, trust me."

"Yeah, then a couple of days go by, and the neighbors are wondering what's that funny smell coming from our house, then the cops find our parts in Mason jars in the basement."

"I don't think he's the Mason jar type."

They had looked across the picnic area to where Red was regaling Owen with some of his prime bullshit and Owen's head went back in a laugh.

"Look at him, Sal," Kelly said, proud of her work.

"You were like this with that guy with the alphabet soup name before we lost our TV."

Now, Sally had finished shearing away as much of Red's beard as she could with the scissors and had started working her razor through the lathered patches of tawny growth on his cheeks and neck.

"Damn, Sally! You're gonna draw blood!" griped Red. "This is like getting a shave from Sweeny Todd! Is that an old leg razor of yours?"

"It's not me and it's not the razor," Sally said, unperturbed as she swished the razor clean in the pot of water, then recommenced hacking away at Red's facial hair. "It's your damn beard, it's so tough!"

"You mean *manly!*" corrected Red, hitting the last word with a *basso profundo*.

"No, I don't mean *manly*, not when you scream like a little girl over every last little nick!"

"I do not consider severing the jugular vein a 'little nick'."

"I'd like an anesthetic with mine," Ben called to Sally. He was sitting on the table behind Owen.

"Cry babies, you're all cry babies," Sally said just before she said, "Oops."

Which brought Red's head up erect. "What's 'oops'?"

"It'll stop bleeding in a second," Sally said, pushing Red's head back down.

Only to have it spring back up. "*What'll* stop bleeding in a second?"

Owen's giggles broke into loud, raucous laughter.

"You all right, my friend?" Ben asked.

"Fine, my friend!" Owen gasped out through his laughter. "Fine, Ben. Ben my friend! Friend Ben!"

"He sounds like Dr. Seuss on acid," Red said.

Ben leaned over for a better look into Owen's face, shook his head and grinned. "Owen, my friend, you are *sooooo stoooonnnnned!*"

"*Sooooo stoooooonnnned!*" Owen repeated, loving the sound of it.

"Smoked like a ham," Ben said to Red and Sally.

"You might want to ease off a bit," Kelly cautioned Owen. "This being your first time -- "

"*Sooooo stoooooonnnned!*" Owen giggled.

"I'll bet they had some good dope where you went to school," Red said. "All those cinema *artistes*. Where'd you go? What college? I didn't know there were any good films schools in Texas."

"Oh, I didn't go to film school," Owen said. "I'm kind of learning as I go," which seemed quite funny to him.

"But you went to college, right?" Ben asked.

"Southern Methodist."

Ben ran his fingers nostalgically through his whiskers, then shook his head in resignation over the imminent denuding of his chin. "You study anything there that helped you when you got out?   You know, furthered your professional pursuits, as they say?"

"Not a bit," Owen chuckled.

"What was your major?"

"I was in the Perkins School."

Red pushed Sally's razor-wielding hand aside and sat up. "Perkins? Isn't that a theology school? What were you learning there?"

Owen managed to get his giggling under control, eased back into a broad, wicked grin. "The art of illusion." And at that he reached behind Kelly's ear to produce a quarter.

"Hey, that's pretty good!" Kelly said, impressed, and ruffled Owen's hair. "A regular presti-whatever that word is."

"So besides being your own writer and director and producer and cameraman," said Red, "you do your own special effects, too."

Owen smiled down at the quarter, moved it around his fingers to watch it catch the firelight. "I guess I do."

"You going to have any special effects in your movie, Owen?" Ben asked. "That's the thing these days. CGI and blowing stuff up and all like that."

Owen closed his hand around the quarter, tapped the closed fist with the fingers of his other hand, opened his hand and revealed an empty palm. "Yeah.

For the big finish. A very special effect." Which Owen considered absolutely hysterical.

Red let out a howl as Sally slapped aftershave on his newly-bared face and gave him a small hand mirror. Red held up the mirror, moving it from side to side to see his whole face.

"It'll look better once all the bleeding stops," Sally said sticking little shreds of paper towel here and there on Red's cheeks.

"A little hair gel and my three-piece pinstripe and I'm all set," Red said with not a little ruefulness.

"And a haircut!" guffawed Owen. "Boy, you look ten years younger!"

Red was standing now, brushing whiskers and splattered lather off his shirt, dabbing at the nicks along his jawline. "That would make me look around 12 years old."

"I don't think friend Owen is seeing things too clearly," Ben commented.

"Maybe another addition to his chemical repertoire will clear up his vision." Red said.

"I think he's about as high as he should get," Kelly said protectively.

Owen turned to her, the firelight playing on his sweat-sheened skin, in his wide eyes. He set his head down on her chest, nuzzled in the top of her cleavage. "You're beautiful, Kelly."

"I'd say he sees just fine," Ben said and Red laughed

Sally wasn't laughing. Kelly could see she was unhappily resigning herself to a houseguest for the night...if not longer.

Ben slid off the table, rummaged around in one of the picnic coolers, then he was back behind Kelly and Owen, tapping on the table. "Kiddies, attention here, please." He had Sally's mirror set in the middle of the table and was using a razor blade to dice a little pile of white powder into small, separate lines. "A line apiece; that's all I could afford."

"Those pre-law guys again?" Sally asked.

"Poli sci. See how much prettier Kelly gets with a toot, Owen."

"I'm not so sure he needs a toot," said Kelly.

"What about it, Owen? Do you need a toot?" Ben teased. "Better hurry. I don't want a breeze coming along and blowing this up to the gods."

"Ye gods!" Red bellowed, standing by the stream, legs apart, arms outstretched, head turned toward the blood-streaked sky. "Zeus, my father, desist from inhaling this magical elixir up thine Jovian proboscis!"

"Where does he get this stuff?" Sally said.

"He said something about books," Ben said. "Well, Owen?"

"I don't know if I could get much higher than I am now."

"Never say that," Ben lectured. "You never know 'til you try."

Ben took a dollar bill from his pocket, rolled it into a tight tube, and handed it over to Owen. "One end goes up your nose, the other follows the white line, just like driving down the highway."

"Well, maybe a little better than that," Kelly said, elbowing Owen and Owen giggled.

Owen put one end of the tube in his right nostril while Ben held the glass just below the other end of the tube. "Tell you what; since you're a beginner, I'll make this easy for you. You just inhale, I'll move the mirror. Ready? Pretend you're a Hoover."

Owen inhaled through the tube and a line of powder disappeared. His head rocked, he dropped the bill, wiped furiously at his nose like a child with a bad itch.

"Maybe you'll see God yet," Ben said.

"Go looking for God and you've got a long walk ahead of you," Owen said, still shaking off the snort. "You'd do better to go looking for Truth. God's what they give you to dull the Truth, like the way they give you aspirin to deal with a headache. It deadens the pain, but it doesn't cure anything."

"Take it easy, Owen," Kelly said. Owen's face had twisted, eerie in the firelight.

He took Kelly's hand, squeezing it, not hearing her little yelp. "You boys want to make it out there? Then don't put out the hand of friendship unless you've got a knife in the other hand. You want to make it? You've got to lie and cheat and steal! They just distract you with God, like a magician makes you look at one hand while he's picking your pocket with another."

Kelly freed her hand from his, put it on his neck, gently massaging him. "Relax, Owen, ok? I think maybe we *have* let you overdo it a bit. Look, you go in the chair next, ok?"

"Hm?"

"Your beard, Owen. You're next."

Sally was putting on a smile as she shook the chair towel clean. "Yeah, Owen, c'mon. We'll get you looking human, ok?"

"You'll look ten years younger," Red said.

A thought which had Owen smiling, again: "Ten years younger."

He let Kelly guide him to the chair, and then Sally was tucking the towel up under his chin. "Light around the jugular, right?" Sally said.

Owen nodded, chuckling.

Sally looked up at the setting sun. "I hope there's enough light for this."

"Maybe it'll improve your technique," Red said, balling up one of his little paper towel bandages and flicking it at Sally.

"You need one of those miner's hats," Ben said. "You know; the one's with the light in front."

"*Your* head's lit enough right now," Sally said.

And they were all laughing, again.

Owen laid his head back, and Kelly was happy to see whatever had fired him up ebb. She leaned back against the table, let her head fall back, looking up into the sky framed by the filigree of interlaced pine branches. The sky had gone from streaks of red to a solid orange sheet fringed with crimson along the tree line on one side, and purple at the other end of the sky.

Sally began with a pair of scissors on Owen, shortening his beard.

"Owen, if you don't stop laughing, you're going to wind up with your throat cut," Sally warned. "You need to sit still."

"Yeah, that'll help," Red said dryly.

Kelly grinned up at the open sky, happy that Owen was laughing, again, happy, again. She could hear the quiet whoosh of the aerosol can, the wet slap of lather being spread around Owen's face, then the quiet sandpaper rasp of the blade on his cheeks.

A new man. He seemed like the kind of guy who could do with being a new man. And I'm giving that to him, Kelly thought, wondering why Sally was always getting on her case for being this kind of healing angel.

And considering the pretentious nature of this line of thinking, she giggled to herself and thought, Jesus, I am soooo stooooooned, too!

"Relaxing, Owen?" she called over.

"Niiiiice," Owen sighed. Then: "Hey!" He sat up in the chair, eyes open wide.

"Dammit, Owen, I almost cut you!" Sally said. She came back at him with the razor, but he held up his hand. "Owen, c'mon, let me finish. You look ridiculous. I've only done half your face."

"You don't hear that?" Owen asked.

"What?"

"I thought I heard thunder."

"I hope so," Ben said. "We could use the rain. It's been so damn dry -- "

Owen looked over toward the highway. "There."

And then they could all hear it.

"That's not thunder," Red said.

They all turned toward the highway just as the four Harleys came into view. The bikes continued on past the picnic area, but the helmeted heads turned toward the firelit group by the river. The rider in the lead hand-signaled his troop to follow and the bikes peeled off the highway. They came back along the shoulder and then across the parking area, shadowy in the dimming light and clouds of dust. The bikes pulled up abreast at the edge of the car park, the crackling, popping engines dying one by one until the only sound was the snap of the fire, the gurgle of the stream, the sporadic whoosh of a car passing by on the highway behind them.

"See, boys? Didn't I tell y'all?" The leader threw an ankle across his bike's tear-shaped gas tank, his bearded face split in a grin. "The road's a hospitable place. Everybody's your friend on a road. When you need a little hospitality, your fellow travelers open their hearts – 'n' their camp -- to help you out. Ain't 'at right, friends?" Like his pack, he brushed the car park dust from his bare arms, stretched the kinks out of his back. "Hey, friends, I said ain't 'at right?"

He shook his head over the lack of a response, hung his helmet on his handlebars, slid off his bike and shuffled down the side of the embankment toward the picnic area.

Owen climbed out of the lounger, wiping the lather off his face with the towel. Kelly stood by him, a little in front of him. Down in her gut, where she was feeling a wave of cold working on her colon and her bladder, she knew, somehow, he'd need protecting.

Red, Ben, and Sally clustered together by the fire, very quiet and still, the way people do around a snake, hoping it won't strike. Finally, Red cleared his throat. "Something we can help you with?"

The biker turned toward his pack. "See, fellas? The hospitality a the road."

By the light of the fire, Kelly saw the motorcycle-mounted devil emblazoned on the biker's sleeveless jacket, and the legend, *Lucifer's Children*.

The biker leader stepped forward and threw an arm around Red's shoulder. "Fact, y'all're *soooo* hospitable, I bet y'all were just 'bout to offer us a drink outta that keg I see over there. Ain't 'at right?" He raised one arm – the one with a broken-heart tattoo on the bicep – snapped the fingers of one fingerless-gloved-hand, and two of the other bikers, short, burly types, climbed off their bikes and ran down the embankment so fast they almost tripped over their own boots.

Kelly looked to Owen, wanted to tell him it would be ok, but saw his face hard, his eyes locked on the biker still perched atop his motorcycle, and it was only now, as the rider pulled off his flame-decaled helmet, she saw he was black.

The two, squat bikers had made a beeline for the beer keg.

"Feel free to help yourself," Sally said bitterly.

"You heard the lady, Porky!" one of them said and began working the tap while the other craned underneath the spigot to let the frothy brew pour into his open mouth.

"Hey, Spook!" the leader called back to the Black rider, pointing at Sally. "This one here speaks right up, don't she?" The leader stepped away from Red and toward the girl. "I don't know I like 'em so brassy. I like 'em ol' fashioned. Quiet. What's a word? Demure?"

Now Kelly stepped between him and Sally, standing close enough to the biker to smell his mix of sweat and exhaust. "I don't know that anyone asked how you liked them."

The leader laughed. "Well, 'at's a truth, ma'am!" He turned to the Black rider, again. "She *is* somethin', ain't she, Spook? Spook?"

"What's with you?" the Black rider asked Owen. He came down the embankment, stood in front of Owen. "Lookit this guy, Lenny. Two-Face here is givin' me the stink eye."

Owen must've just then remembered Sally hadn't finished shaving him; Kelly saw him touch his fingertips to the bare side of his face, saw him flush with embarrassment.

That cold sensation in her middle grew heavier, colder, because she knew with fuckers like these, that kind of shame – weakness -- was like blood in the water for sharks.

"Now whatever could he *not* like about *you*," Lenny teased. He wandered over to the two easels still sitting by the water. "Lezzee vat ve haf heah," he said, playing the Viennese art critic. He stood in front of Red's abstract. "Ach, vas is dis presumptuous *c-r-r-r-r-ap!* You call dis *art?* Dis is a *mockery!* A diz-*graze!* I paint better vit da brush in my *toes!*" Then, without the accent: "Someone thinks he's Jackson Pollock. Well, my friends, he ain't," and he casually tipped the easel over onto the sand. Then he stood in front of Ben's painting and his face grew serious. He nodded. "Who did this? I said, who did this?"

Ben slowly raised a hand.

"I like what you did with the ocher. Trying to pick up the creek bottom, right?" Lenny looked from Ben back to the picture, nodded his head appreciatively. "The ocher was a good choice."

An enormous burp from over by the keg. Porky came out from under the spigot, his beard matted with beer. "Damn if '*at* ain't the way to do it!"

The other biker took his place under the spigot, but Porky was walking away.

"Hey, c'mon, Pork," the other biker said, "I did you!"

"Do yourself, Shorty," Porky said. "You're an espert at doin' yerself!" and he laughed.

"One mighty fuckin' fine piece of equipment somebody's got here," Spook said. "Yo, Lenny, you see this? She looks worth a few bucks. And we could definitely use a few bucks."

Kelly turned from the two morons arguing over the beer keg to see the Black rider standing by Owen's camera on its tripod

"Hey, Spook!" Shorty climbed out from under the pump. "How 'bout a shot, Spook, huh? Catch my best side!" He about-faced and dropped his grease-stained denims and holed underwear.

"Hey, Spook!" Porky cackled, "turn a camera sideways 'n' it'll look like he's smilin'!"

Spook smiled at the thought and reached for the camera.

"Don't touch that," Owen said.

Spook turned, looking earnestly surprised. "That li'l noise come outta *you?*"

Kelly was surprised, too. "Owen...," she warned.

Lenny held a finger up to his lips and went, "Shhhhh!" and Kelly stepped back and closed her mouth.

"I said don't touch my camera." Owen's upper lip twitched, and Kelly saw he had that angry, twisted face back, looking even uglier in the rippling light of the fire.

"Now *that* man is *not* hospitable!" Lenny adjudged.

Spook caressed the camera, stroked it the way you'd stroke a woman's hair, smiling at Owen. "Well, seems I *am* touchin' your camera. And, um, you're gonna do *what* if I *keep* touchin' your camera? Like I'm doin'?"

Ben started toward Owen. "Now, Owen, he's just messing around, you know, he's not going to -- " Ben was stopped abruptly by Shorty's beefy arm across his chest.

"That's right, mister," Spook said. He put an arm around the camera, laid his head lovingly alongside it. "Just messin' around."

"Maybe we just wanna borrow it," Porky said. "Like, just for a li'l while. See, our friend Lenny here, he's visitin' his sister. She went off 'n' had herself a bea*uuuu*tiful baby boy 'n' our friend Lenny would just *loooove* to get some home movies a his nephew. Ain't 'at right, Len?"

"Yeah, sure," Lenny smirked, "Ok."

"See, mister?" Spook cooed. "No harm. Tell ya what; you meet us back here in two days 'n' you get your camera back. Same time, same place." Spook reached down and started to fold the legs of the tripod.

"I told you to get your black hands off my camera you nigger bastard," Owen said.

And Spook froze.

They all froze.

Spook's smile twisted in an odd way; Kelly thought he seemed almost pleased. As if somebody had given him an unexpected gift.

"You fucking niggers," Owen said, "You think you can take anything you goddamned want."

"Jesus, Owen!" Kelly hushed.

Spook's smile grew wider.

"Looks like you got a live one there, Spook!" Porky called.

"Maybe not for long," said an entertained Lenny. "Ya know, Spook, I think what you got there is one a those less enlightened types. One a those go-sit-in-a-back-a-the-bus boys. 'N' these seemed like such nice folk, too."

"C'mon, fellas," Kelly said, "leave us alone, ok? Take some beer, take whatever food you want and let it go at that. He didn't mean anything," she said pointing to Owen. "He's had a little too much to drink -- "

"I'm sure he didn't mean nothin', sweet thing," Lenny said, "'n' we *will* be takin' you up on your offer a the goodies." Lenny snapped his fingers again and Porky and Shorty began to root around in the coolers for whatever food was left, wrapping it in the tablecloth they found in the pile of picnic things. "Throw just one more thing in a kitty – just one more li'l thing – 'n' we'll call it even."

"*What* one more thing?" Kelly asked warily.

"Just a li'l itty bitty thing. One a y'all fine ladies gives me a li'l smooch to send me on my way. A li'l good luck kiss, hm? One for the road?" He started toward Kelly. "You might even like it."

"Hey, maybe one for each of us!" Shorty sniggered.

Spook stood in front of Owen a moment, weighing, then sniffed dismissively and turned back to folding up the camera tripod.

"Jesus!"

Kelly was never sure who said it; maybe all of them, but she turned and saw Owen run at Spook, making some kind of animal noise as his hands went up like they were going to grab the Black rider by his throat.

But Owen was filled with beer and weed and coke and his feet weren't working right. Spook easily sidestepped him, stuck out a booted foot which brought Owen down on his knees. Then the blunt, hard toe of the same boot crashed into Owen's side and Owen went over on the sand, gasping.

Kelly wasn't sure what hurt worse; watching Owen go down like that, or the raucous, coarse laughter that went with it.

And then a different, primal noise; an animal snarl.

She turned from Owen to see Pooch with his jaws clamped on Spook's calf, and Spook screaming and kicking at Pooch with his other foot. The other bikers were laughing so hard they looked on the verge of falling over.

Spook's free boot caught the dog solidly in the animal's side. The dog yelped, letting go of the biker's leg, then backed off a few steps and took a stance facing Spook. The dog lowered his head, tucked his ears flat against his skull, pulled his lips back from his teeth as he growled.

"Fuckin' dog, man!" Spook bellowed, the laughter of his three colleagues apparently only infuriating him all the more. Spook limped back up the embankment to his bike and reached for his saddlebags. "Gonna blow this fuckin' little mutt a-*way!*" He came skidding back down the slope with a pistol in his hand; in Kelly's drug-hazed mind, it looked like a cannon with a grip. Spook cocked the pistol and aimed it at the dog.

"Hey, Spook! Let 'im draw first!" Porky cackled. "Then it'll be self-defense!"

"Keep laughin', motherfucker, 'n' you're next!" Spook spat back.

Owen staggered to his feet and pushed himself into a collision with Spook. "Low life bastard nigger," he gasped. That took whatever wind he had, and he slid down Spook's body, grabbing limply at the biker's gun hand until he crumpled to the ground. He grabbed at one of Spook's legs, pulled the cuff of the biker's denims above the top of his boot, and bit into Spook's leg just below the bleeding teeth marks left by Pooch.

"*Crazy motherfucker!*" Spook howled, tripping backward, the pistol flying from his hand.

Kelly saw the first blow, Spook's gloved fist coming down on the side of Owen's head, turned away when she saw it cock for another, heard it drive down again and again, rapid fire, like a piston.

She heard it stop, turned, saw Owen burbling blood onto the sand, still holding on to Spook's leg, the biker standing over him, pistol in hand aimed at Owen's head.

"*You gonna die tonight, you fuck!*" Spook hissed, grimacing against the pain.

"Oh God…" Kelly gasped.

"Spook." It was the leader's voice, very calm. "Spook, man, chill, ok?" He stood behind Spook, leaned forward to whisper in his ear, but she was close enough that Kelly could hear it: "Don't be stupid, bro. Waste 'im 'n' we gotta waste 'em all."

"So where's the problem?" Spook said. "Crazy cocksucker bit me! I'm fuckin' bleedin'! Faggot motherfucker's probably got AIDS."

"Fuck 'im," Lenny soothed. "Take the little prick's camera 'n' leave him to cry himself to sleep. He ain't worth a bullet, Spook, or the cops on our ass."

Kelly saw Spook study Owen over the top of his pistol sights, didn't know why the biker looked so puzzled.

"See?" he heard Lenny say. "Fucker's so wasted he don't even have enough sense to be scared. What's the fun in 'at?"

"Yeah," Spook said, disgusted, disappointed. "Not worth a bullet." He lowered the hammer on his pistol, stuck it in his belt, then turned and grabbed up the camera and tripod.

"My…movie…" Owen managed to get out. He rolled over onto his belly, crawling through the sand. "Let…me…let me keep my movie."

"Keep this," Spook said, and spat on the back of Owen's head.

Then the four bikes' engines coughed and thundered to life.

"You got lucky, mister," Spook called down to him. "You pray I don't ever see you again 'cause if I do, I'll be the *last* thing you see!"

The thunder swelled for a moment, then faded down the highway.

Kelly helped Owen to his feet and led him back to the beach chair. Sally brought over one of the coolers and Kelly soaked a towel in the ice water inside and dabbed at Owen's bruised face.

"You ok?" she asked.

"Those bastards!" Red fumed, looking at the Harleys' taillights streaking off down the highway. *"Bastards!"* he yelled after them.

Ben fulminated alongside him. "I could just -- "

"You could just piss in your pants!" Kelly said.

"Pardon me," Ben said, "but unless my eyes were deceiving me, Kelly sweets, Kelly dearest, they had a *gun* with them. You know; like bang-bang, you're dead."

Pooch was sitting by Owen's feet, whimpering. Owen tried to lean forward but the movement sent pains shooting out from his side where Spook had kicked him, and his hands went to his head, bruises already swelling and mottling his face. Still, he managed to reach out to caress the dog's head. "You all right, boy?" Pooch jumped up, set his front legs on Owen's lap and licked his face.

"You want me to call the cops, Owen?" Red asked.

Owen lay back in the chair with a sigh. "No. No cops." He swung his legs to the side and painfully drew himself upright, pushed past Kelly and Sally. He looked up, saw the blood was almost drained from the sky; night was almost on them. "C'mon, boy," he said, and Pooch followed him across the sand to his Winnebago.

Kelly came after him. "Let me help you."

Owen waved her away, climbed inside the RV with Pooch following, then closed and locked the door. Kelly stood outside the door, heard a thump like Owen had dropped to the floor, heard him sobbing.

Behind her, she could hear Red say, "C'mon, let's pack up and get the hell outta here."

Wednesday night...

"Rita, this connection is worse than the last one. Where are you calling from? Moon Base Alpha? What's the matter with your cell?"

"It's recharging. I ran it down spending all afternoon trying to call you from the road where I couldn't get a signal."

"That's Texas, Rita, not Tierra del Fuego! They have NASA down there! Billions they spend developing space technologies and the phone service is tin cans and string? I don't understand how that can be!"

"Eric, it's been a long day," Rita sighed, "I'm tired. I'm not up on my telecommunications talking points so I really don't feel like a debate about phone service."

"Where are you, Rita? What part of the Texas outback are you calling from tonight?"

Rita was slouched on a single bed, looking around the painted but otherwise bare cinderblock walls of her cold square of a room. There was a hand-lettered sign on the back of the room door that read, 'IF YOU THINK YOU SHOULDN'T – DON'T!!' There were two BB holes in the dresser mirror. The semis that passed by on Route 19 sounded like they were rumbling through her bathroom. The motel's satellite hook-up gave her ten channels. Three were all-sports, one was all-weather, another had something to do with cattle. Thinking it was the best she was going to do, she settled on *Spongebob*

Squarepants. "A perfectly delightful little motor inn in perfectly delightful Lovelady, Texas, population six if you don't count the knuckle-walkers."

"I had no idea you were such an elitist, Rita. Knuckle-walkers. Tch on you, tch I say! Lovelady? What a great name! It has a nice, poetic quality to it."

"Try staying here for a few hours. It'll lose some of that poetry."

"What a story *that* would've been, eh, love?" Eric Bird said with relish. "Perverted *priest* in a town called *Looove-lay-day!* And all we have is a wayward minister in Boone. *Boone!*" She could sense him wrinkling up his nose at the word. "Where's the poetry there?"

"As of now, we don't even have that. Dawson split from Boone this morning. I got a lead on him, tracked him south to a lot where he traded his car for a Winnebago, and then I lost him."

"Define 'lost.'"

The blurt of a passing semi's horn drowned out her reply.

"Was that you, love? I'd stay away from the empanadas from now on. At least say excuse me."

"I said I was hoping to catch up with him before he reached the Lovelady crossroads. I didn't. There's four roads out of Lovelady and I have absolutely no way of knowing which one he took. He's got the better part of a day's head start on me. He's gone, Eric. Eric? Eric, are you still there?"

"Hopefully, no. This is just a dream state," he said ethereally. "I'll wake up and you'll be telling me -- "

"It's over," Rita said curtly.

"That's not what I was hoping you'd be telling me." A pause. Then, hungrily, "What about the gun?"

"What gun?"

"You said Dawson bought a gun, but he had to wait -- "

"I go with the local top cop on that one. He doesn't think Dawson's coming back for it and neither do I."

"But wait, love, wait, wait, wait!" Eric Bird said desperately. "Dawson obviously had something in mind when he bought the gun – your theory was some kind of vendetta thingie – and now just because he doesn't have the gun doesn't mean he's given up his vendetta thingie. He's still out there, Rita, looking to carry out his vendetta thingie! Maybe he'll get another gun somewhere else, maybe he'll go Luddite and resort to clubs and stones -- "

"Eric, he could be anywhere!"

He was firm, now: "The story needs an ending, Rita. Never mind the TV show, I couldn't even put this in the paper the way it is. Not without an ending."

"I can't just pull an ending out of my ass, Eric!"

"Though that does present a delightful picture! I want you to stay out there, Rita, until Dawson plays out his third act. As soon as something breaks, you jump on it. You can't do that from L.A., love."

"And what am I supposed to do in the meantime?"

"Find yourself a nice but modestly-priced place to nestle, enjoy the sights, soak up some of the local culture -- "

"I'm gonna kill you, Eric."

"Yes, love, of course, but *after* the story."

"I'm heading back to Houston tomorrow. If I come up on a lead, if something breaks, I'll move on it. Otherwise, I'm on a plane home tomorrow night. You have a problem with that? Then fuck you and send somebody else out here. Understand?"

"I love when you talk mean to me, baby."

"I *am* gonna kill you, Eric!"

"Sure you are, but now, with all that said, Rita, love, and not meaning to be a piker, but this lovely establishment you happen to be in at the moment..."

"Relax your crack. It's $55.50 a night, the ice machine's broken, the vending machine's empty, and there's no pool. Modest enough, for you?"

"How surprisingly frugal of you!"

"Frugal my ass, it was the best I could find! This is not exactly a major tourist hub."

"Let's touch base before you fly out tomorrow. In the meantime, sleep tight, don't let the bedbugs bite."

Rita hung up, tried to get comfortable amid the ridges and gullies of a mattress long overdue for replacement. She looked around the drab walls, the drawn, faded curtains, listened to the gurgling of the toilet she couldn't get to stop gurgling, and said aloud, "I'll bet I've *got* bedbugs, too."

Clyde Thomas turned his red Chevy pick-up off the highway and between two tall, stone pillars topped with electric lanterns shaped like Victorian gaslights. The bulbs flickered to look like live flames though the more typical impression was that the bulbs were going bad. Clyde followed a long, twirling driveway of crushed gravel running between banks of cypress trees to a parking lot at the far end of which sat The Candlelight Inn, a sleek-looking place with a long, sloping roof and tall windows, and a lot of exposed timbers and open-faced stonework, looking something like a ski lodge which made it come off as a bit out of place since The Candlelight sat a good 800 miles from any decent ski country. The story was the owner's ideas for the design of the place had been inspired by the house at the end of *North by Northwest,* though even *that* house looked a lot more at home among the granite crags of the Black Hills than The Candlelight looked in east Texas.

The attraction of The Candlelight – which was neither a short ride for most patrons nor all that easy to find – was its offer of (according to its ads) "an intimate dining experience." To that end, The Candlelight sat in an alcove in the hills east of Palestine, far from the main highways, with another bank of cypresses shielding the inn from the noise of the road and the flash of headlights. Patrons could look out any window from the cozy little booths wherein they were having their intimate dining experiences and see nothing but stars and the dark humps of the surrounding hills.

Clyde parked and climbed stiffly out of his truck. It'd been an hour drive from Boone and another 20 minutes going up and down this road trying to find the dimly lit entrance to the inn. He went to the passenger side and grabbed his seersucker jacket from where he'd laid it out on the seat, pulled it on, and commenced fidgeting. He hadn't had time to get the suit cleaned or pressed since he'd come back from the county seat two days prior (Clyde wore the suit so rarely there'd been no urgency in getting it refurbished). So, he'd made due with a few quick passes of a steam iron, sprayed pants and jacket liberally with aerosol deodorant, and then held the jacket out his truck window for a good part of the drive in the hopes of airing it out.

Nevertheless, the jacket still felt stale and clammy. He did some more fidgeting, used his vague reflection in one of the truck windows to adjust his string tie, then topped the whole ensemble off with his Stetson before turning for the inn.

The interior of The Candlelight was just as much about intimate dining experiences as the cloistered exterior. Tables and booths were amply spread out and isolated by partitions and folding screens, the windows were covered with semitransparent curtains perforated with lacy patterns. The low-key lighting came from wall sconces and tabletop lamps that looked like candles but weren't. The owner's original plan (so went another story) had been to light The Candlelight entirely by candlelight (hence the name), but when the projected cost of hiked insurance and mandated fire detection and extinguishing paraphernalia had come in, out went the real candles, and in came the electric ones.

Clyde mumbled "Supposed to meet somebody," as he side-stepped the heavily moussed *maitre d'* in his bad tux and peered across the gloomy dining room. He saw who he thought was Kay Gorsham sitting in an especially private corner booth. He walked across the thickly-carpeted floor, tugging at the hem of his jacket and pulling at his collar, feeling as uncomfortable in an intimate dining experience as he did in his clammy seersucker suit. He looked around at the *faux* brass sconces and *faux* crystal chandeliers and *faux* everything else and told himself, Just plant me at a counter eating something greasy and washing it down with a cold can of something alcoholic and *I'm* happy as a pig in shit.

"Kay?"

"My favorite fuzz!" she beamed up at him. "Again!"

He slid in the booth across from her and set his hat down on the bench next to him.

"Isn't that supposed to be unlucky?" she asked, "Cowboy putting his hat on a seat?"

"It's a bed. Putting your hat on a bed."

"How unlucky could it be if you get as far as a lady's bed," she said with a loose, leering grin.

Clyde was smiling, too, but he was thinking, Oh-oh. Kay's words sounded a little thick, and as bad as the light from the flickering table lamp was, it was enough for him to pick up on the unfocused bleariness in her eyes. And she was holding on to her cocktail glass with two hands as if she might fall over sideways if she let it go. "Hope I didn't keep you waitin' too long," he said.

"Not so long," she said and took a hefty sip of her drink. She closed one eye and studied him with the other. "I can't remember the last time I saw you all duded up. You clean up nice!"

"Don't look too close."

"You sell yourself short, Clyde."

"Just a natural sense a Christian humility, I guess."

A waitress was standing at their table asking about drinks.

"I'll do another of these screwdrivers, dearie," Kay said.

"I could do a Pearl," Clyde said. "Frosted mug if y'all got one."

"That's all, Clyde?" Kay asked after the waitress had left, "Just a beer?"

"'N' just a one. It's a long ride, Kay, 'specially in a dark, 'n' 'specially if you don't have a workin' air conditioner which my truck don't."

She took another pull of her drink, emptying it, setting it back heavily on the table with a clunk and rattle of ice cubes. She slouched back in the booth, her face turning soft and musing. "Remember that truck you had back in high school? A Ford, wasn't it?"

Clyde smiled at the memory. "'At was my daddy's truck."

"Had a hood like a cathedral."

"Yup. All a space was under the hood. Wasn't all 'at much room at all in a back."

Kay smiled in a kind of dirty way. "Oh, there was room enough."

Clyde cleared his throat, felt warm in his suit. "Like I said, Kay, 's a long ride. Thirty-three miles by my clock. 'N' I've had a helluva long day. I think I did more po-lice work today 'n' I've done all a rest a the year."

"You didn't used to mind the ride so much," she said. "We used to come out here a lot in the old days. Back when this was just a beer 'n' burger joint. It wasn't set up like this, but I'll bet we sat right here, probably right in this very spot."

"Maybe. One time or 'nother, maybe."

Clyde was happy for the interruption of the waitress back with their drinks. She asked if they'd be ordering dinner and Clyde said he wasn't eating. Kay sent the waitress away.

"I was hoping…" she began sadly.

"Sorry," Clyde said. "I ate 'fore I come. I didn't spect, well…" There was an uncomfortable moment where Clyde wriggled inside his suit and Kay stared emptily into her glass. "Kay, I don't wanna be the grouchy bear 'at got woke up 'fore spring thaw, but… I got home, there's a message on my machine says you got somethin' important to tell me 'bout Leroi Jefferson'n' Sarah Dawson. Says you gotta tell me in person, but it's gotta be all a way out here. I get out my Sunday best, I come ballin' a jack out here, 'n' all we're doin' is goin' over stuff so old it oughta be under glass in a museum."

"You used to be a lot more romantic in those days."

"Maybe under other circumstances."

"Don't you still like me?"

"I always liked you, Kay. You're a great gal."

She made a face. "'A great gal.' Makes me sound like your favorite horse."

"It's just I got a few things on my mind right now."

She took a sip of her drink, then started shaking her head, reprimanding herself. "You're right, Clyde, you're right, you're right, you're right. I'm sorry. God, I'm so sorry. Let me see what else I can do wrong."

Oh-oh, Clyde thought, again. He didn't know how much she'd had to drink before he got there, but he could see she was skating along the rim of that black hole of boozy moroseness. "Hush 'at stuff," Clyde soothed. "Maybe 'nother time we all can sit down for a drink 'n' talk over ol' days, but right now, Kay, right *now*…"

She nodded, understanding, but she seemed on the edge of tears.

"Now, what all is it you got me out here to tell me?"

The state of near-tears suddenly evaporated, replaced by an impish, guilty-but-not-really smile. "I lied."

Oh-oh. "Lied? 'Bout what?"

"I don't have anything to tell you. Not about Leroi or Sarah. I just didn't know any other way to...you know..."

"No, I *don't* know! What's goin' on, Kay? What're we doin' here?"

Now the smile was gone, and her mood swung the other way, again, her eyes growing wet. "Just my entire *life*." Her hand reached out across the table. It was supposed to look random, but it wasn't.

And Clyde knew it, set his own hands safely out of reach in his lap. "Damn, Kay, it's just, ya know, you had a bad day is all," he fumbled around, "you're just tired -- "

"You're damn right I'm tired!" And now anger mixed with the tears. "I have a bad day *every* day, Clyde! I wake up each morning with an ache in my stomach over going into that little office walled in with all that paper! The piles never go down! Stay late, come in early, they're still there, still just as high!"

Clyde waved at her to keep her voice down. The booth partitions and folding screens weren't enough to keep heads from turning.

"There's always *some* damned problem," she went on, "like with that kid today, or Ed Lewis, or that we're short-staffed, underbudgeted, or the sinks in the B-wing won't drain, or the kids stuffed up the toilets on one whole floor, or the kitchen's got a bad load of pinto beans. And then there's the kids, Clyde. You do what you can for them and almost as soon as they're released, they're coming back through the gate. You get a kid like Leroi Jefferson, and for the first time in a long time you let yourself think you're doing some good and now -- "

"Just hold on, Kay," Clyde said, "we don't know anything 'bout what a whole story is on 'at boy."

"But you don't think it's good, do you?"

"Uh -- "

"It's all just so damned...*pointless*. That's how I spend my life, Clyde, doing pointless crap. And it leaves me so damned...*drained!* Every once in a while, it hits you, all those goddamned years of pointless crap! By the time I get home, I have just enough energy left to zap something in the microwave and then crawl into bed."

She was starting to sob now. Clyde saw people looking, faced them back down with a what-the-fuck-are-*y'all*-looking-at stare.

He looked for something positive to throw to her. "I know right now you're not thinkin' too well a him, but you got Thad 'n' he's not 'at bad -- "

"I've got Thad and Thad's got the counter girl at the donut shop on Main," she snapped bitterly.

"Oh."

Sobs, again. "He doesn't even try to hide it anymore."

"Sorry, Kay. I didn't, well… "

"I need something else, Clyde." She said it pointedly, the sobbing over, her eyes fixing on him. "I need a change."

"Well, yeah, I can see -- . Whoa!" Because now he'd caught the targeting look she was giving him. "You better put up 'at booze 'cause it's doin' your mind pretty bad! You're not seein' right, Kay."

"I see fine."

"Naw, you're seein' things 'at haven't been in 30 years. Put your glasses back on 'n' take a good look."

She smiled. "I have."

"Look again! Dammit, Kay, I'm pushin' 50 'n' got jack-squat to show for it! I got this one suit, a gut, more hair on my back 'n' on my head, I'm payin' two alimonies, 'n' I'm livin' out there to Lubner's Trailer Park in an oversized beer can eighty percent owned by the East Texas Farmers 'n' Mechanics Savings 'n' Loan. Frieda divorced me 'cause she couldn't live with me 'n' this damn job, 'n' Valerie didn't cotton to it much better, 'n' 'at was *after* I made *chief!* Fact, Val didn't like it so much, only way Betty Ford's gonna reclaim her is on a five-year plan! I gotta have one a those balloon things to clear an artery, 'n' the Honorable Fred C. Reilly – who won't spend money on law enforcement lessen it's for somethin' to hit people upside a head with – says the insurance I got with the town might not pay for it. I got three boys workin' for me with no hat size among 'em; if brainpower was dynamite, the three of 'em together couldn't blow out a birthday candle! You may need to get out a where you're at, Kay, but you don't need me. I can barely take care a myself! If I could, I'd pin a 'Dear Clyde' note to my pillow 'n' leave my flabby ass flat!"

She chuckled. "You always could make me laugh, Clyde."

Clyde, who'd managed to depress himself with his litany of liabilities, took a deep pull on his beer. "If I wasn't so pathetic, *I'd* laugh!" and he meant it. "Kay, if it's 'at bad with ol' Thad, get out. But don't leave him to go chasin' no ghosts."

"I don't like the idea of not knowing what comes next. Not at this point in the game."

Clyde patted her outstretched arm, soothingly but careful to avoid getting entangled in her fingers. "You got a lotta miles left on you, Kay. Don't you sell *your*self short. But -- " he reached over and extracted her glass from her other hand " -- don't take care a your problems with this. Don't work. Trust me."

She nodded, closed her eyes for a moment, then opened them, gave him a weak smile. "Don't you still like me even a little bit?"

He smiled back. "I like you fine, Kay. Always did. Listen…" He reached for his wallet, drew out a twenty and set it on the table. "In my official capacity as an officer a the law, I am *orderin'* you to take a taxi home. I'll see your car gets took care of. This here's for a cab. That oughta be 'nough to getcha home. 'N' I'll take care a the tab here, ok?" He gave her arm a last pat. "I really gotta go, Kay." He reached for his hat and stood, but he hadn't even cleared the table when she had a hand clamped around one of his wrists.

"Don't leave me, Clyde! Please! I can't go back to that house tonight!"

"Take it easy, Kay. You just had a little too much -- "

"Just this once, Clyde! Just tonight!"

"Kay, don't do this!"

She flashed from pitiful to hateful in an instant. She pushed him away. "To hell with you then! To *hell* with you! You didn't know a good thing thirty years ago and you don't know one now!"

"You're right, Kay," he tried to placate her, at the same time moving away from the table. "Don't have much hat size myself."

She balled up the twenty he'd left on the table and flung it, bouncing it off the back of his head. "Don't go leaving me money like I'm your whore!"

Trying to ignore the stares around him, he scooped up the paper wad and picked up the pace of his withdrawal. He grabbed his waitress on the way out, gave her the crumpled twenty, asked her to get a cab for the lady, and gave her another twenty for the tab, and then almost broke into a run as he headed for the door thinking maybe it *was* bad luck to put your hat on the seat.

"Hey, Clyde!"

He'd been half-way across the parking lot when Billy Ray Barnes' voice froze him mid-stride.

"What brings you out here?" Billy Ray said.

Clyde took a moment to steel himself, then turned. Billy Ray was arm-in-arm with Arva May, both of them wearing moony grins. "What're *ya'll* doin' out here?" Clyde asked.

"It's our anniversary!" Billy Ray announced proudly.

"Seven months!" Arva May said.

"Seven months," Clyde said, trying to sound impressed.

"I figger long's I don't have to get up early in a mornin'," Billy Ray said with a certain edge, "I might as well take advantage. Know what I'm sayin'?"

"I know what you're sayin', Billy Ray," Clyde said, unfazed.

Then Billy Ray and Arva May wished him good night and headed for the door, and Clyde had a picture in his head of the two of them seeing a loud and sloshed Kay Gorsham, and within a day he was sure it'd be a scene being talked about all over Boone. And if that wasn't bad enough, sooner or later somebody was going to say, "Hey, didn't ol' Clyde have a thing for ol' Kay way back when?" and the Boone tongue-waggers would start putting two and two together to come up with five, and ol' Clyde didn't want that for Kay Gorsham who seemed to have enough problems, and he just as surely didn't need to add to his own headaches.

"Hey, there, Billy Ray, hold up a second!" Clyde called, chasing after the two, and feeling a nasty throb above his eyes. Clyde started stumbling his way through some story about how crowded The Candlelight was even though the parking lot was half-empty, and that the kitchen was having problems and how he'd had to wait some ungodly long time for food that wasn't right anyway, and how maybe they should think about going to another place –

And it was about that time a loud and weaving Kay Gorsham appeared in The Candlelight doorway arguing with the *maitre d'* and telling him to get his faggy hands off her.

Billy Ray turned from the melee in the doorway to Clyde with a grin. "Clyde, you ol' sneaky-snake!"

"Shuddup, Billy Ray."

"Whyntcha say y'all just wanted some private time -- "

"Shuddup, Billy Ray."

"Maybe you should hush a bit, sweet Billy," Arva May advised.

Billy Ray probably didn't hear it because Kay Gorsham was yelling pretty loudly at that point, telling the *maitre d'*, "I'm not a goddamned child, Mr. Sissy-Pants, and if you touch me one more time, you'll be pulling back a bloody stump! Clyde! Clyde, where are you? Is that you, Clyde?"

"Oh, Christ," Clyde muttered.

"Jeez, Clyde," Billy Ray said, shaking his head in dismay, "Miz Gorsham there's awful messed up -- "

Clyde bulled by Billy Ray, telling him, again, to shuddup, got an arm around Kay and led her out of the doorway.

"Clyde, they refused to serve me another drink," Kay sobbed, "They won't let me drink in there, Clyde! I want to file charges! You help me get 'em, Clyde! You show me how to do it!"

"Sure, Kay, sure."

She was starting to sag in his arms. "I don't feel good, Clyde. I think I'm gonna be sick."

Billy Ray missed or ignored Arva May's signals to back off. He bent forward peering into Kay Gorsham's paling face. "Boy, Clyde, she's really tied one -- "

Clyde was wondering what one more thing Billy Ray would have to do before he'd grab him by his bony neck, throw him down on the parking lot gravel and throttle him. "Billy Ray, get in your car or get inside, but just *get outta my face!*"

He didn't wait to see where Billy Ray went off to but led Kay into the shadows alongside the parking lot, held his arms around her, patting her back gently, speaking to her in soft, quiet tones as her body started to heave. "It's ok, Kay, it's ok, I gotcha…"

Bob Wheeler and Elwood Poteet stood by Bob Wheeler's car at the curb in front of the parsonage much as they had the night before. Though the parsonage appeared to be empty – more precisely, abandoned – Bob Wheeler felt even *more* reluctant to go down the walk to the front door than he had the previous night.

He looked at the parsonage with its dark, broken windows, and gaping front door looking in on nothing, and the blackened cross on the lawn. Childhood memories of movies and books and supposedly true stories of houses that were taboo, off-limits, haunted, *cursed* came back to him. And that was the word; cursed. The parsonage – this ground – felt *cursed.*

Elwood Poteet, Bob Wheeler thought, must've felt much the same way because he made no move to start down the walk, either.

They stood at the curb a long moment, then, as if on cue, looked at each other, both took a breath, and walked slowly up to the parsonage's open front door. Bob knocked and called inside, heard his voice bounce hollowly around the rooms. He reached in, flicked on the foyer light and they stepped inside.

The memento-strewn living room looked the same. Bob left Elwood in the foyer and went down the corridor to the bedroom. He switched on the light, felt immediately uncomfortable, invasive. He took a brief look in the room's one closet, then withdrew, turning off the light as he left. He turned down toward the kitchen to where he knew Owen kept a spare house key on a key tree. When he returned to the front of the house he saw Elwood Poteet on the living room sofa, his head in his hands.

"It's gone," Elwood said without looking up.

Bob Wheeler needed no further explanation. He crossed to the entry arch to the dining room. The oblong brown paper package from Kirkland's that had been lying across the arms of one of the dining room chairs the night before was no longer there.

They left the house, turning off the lights as they went, and Bob Wheeler closed the front door and locked it with Owen's spare key. They stood a moment, looking at the moon-thrown shadow of the burnt cross on the withered lawn.

"What're we gonna do?" Bob Wheeler asked finally, but it was directed as much to the night as to Elwood Poteet.

"I've done enough to hurt this boy," Elwood said. "Whatever needs doing now is going to hurt him, too. I can't bring myself to hurt him anymore." He started walking away, across the parsonage lawn and down the street.

"Elwood?"

"Do what you have to do, Bob," Elwood called back. "I just can't do it."

"At least let me drive you home."

"I want to walk, Bob," and Elwood disappeared into the shadows at the end of the street.

Bob Wheeler looked back at the parsonage, its broken windows staring back like empty eyes. It was a hot, humid night but Bob felt a shudder just the same. He walked quickly down the walk and climbed in his car, never once looking back at the parsonage, and drove home.

"Ya know you're gonna get busted for pollutin' a water!" Porky chortled.

"Fuck you," Spook said.

"Looks like Jackie fuckin' Chan, don't he?" Shorty said, illustrating the point by dancing around on one boot, kicking his other one out. "Ha! Huh!" He kept at it until he fell over. He laughed, Porky laughed, Lenny laughed.

"Fuck the whole bunch a you," Spook said.

He had his boot off and the leg of his denims pulled up to expose the two sets of bleeding teeth marks in his calf. He was standing on one leg with his punctured calf propped on the basin lip of a water fountain. He was running the fountain, letting the water rain down on his wounds as he swabbed them with his kerchief. He winced at the pain. "Shit…"

But the pain didn't bother him as much as how foolish he looked with his one leg hung up on the water fountain.

Shorty was pretending to do ballet moves. "That's what he looks like, right? One a those fuckin' ballet fags, right? Like one a those fuckin' Russian ballet fags."

"Rudolf Spooksky," Lenny said, and they all laughed some more.

"You guys are gonna get a water fountain enema you keep it up!" Spook said.

He laid all of it – his holed leg, this add-on humiliation – at Lenny's door. They had spent the day cruising toward – according to the road signs -- some nowhere-burg called Boone, but as they neared the town, Lenny had turned them away and headed them south down 19 toward Lovelady. As far as Spook was concerned, Lenny didn't really have a destination in mind.

So, they'd rumbled up and down the highways, getting twitchy because what was left of their collective finances was going the same way as their gas; down to the fumes.

Then Lenny had seen the group camped out by the river.

Not that Spook had had any issue with hassling a group of straights for eats and maybe even some cash, but he wasn't quite sure, at the time, what Lenny's intent had been. Maybe he'd thought it would be a way to score a few bucks, maybe he was just antsy for something to do. Spook ran over the possibilities, finally figuring Lenny had led them in because he *needed* to lead them. Somewhere. Anywhere. As long as he could lead them to *something*, he still had reason to be the leader. At least in Shorty's and Porky's eyes.

And all that would've been just fine with Spook if it hadn't been for that motherfucking mutt and that motherfucking head case with him. You are on my all-time, eternal shit-list, motherfuckers, he kept telling himself, meaning the man *and* his goddamned motherfucking fleabag mutt.

Spook lowered his leg and limped across the parking area of the rest stop. The others had pulled their bikes far into the trees away from the clearing so the cops wouldn't find them and roust them about camping in a No Camping area.

Porky and Shorty were settling down, spreading out their bedrolls. Lenny had popped for a six-pack to wash down the food they'd taken from the group by the river. It wasn't much, but that and a full belly was enough to put the two in a relaxed mood.

Lenny, however, wasn't relaxing. He had his .357 out on his open bedroll in the beam of a flashlight he'd propped on some rocks. He was cleaning out the chambers with a gun rod. It wasn't like Lenny to be so diligent, but Spook didn't think diligence had anything to do with it. Lenny knew the troops were edgy; the gun was out so they could see it.

"How's the leg?" Lenny asked as Spook settled down onto his own blanket.

"Hurts like a motherfucker," Spook grumbled.

"Hey!" Shorty said. "Watch it be the fuckin' *dog* has AIDS 'n' the fuckin' *guy* has rabies!" He and Porky clinked their beer cans in salute and guffawed.

"Pipe down," Lenny said. "I don't want nobody comin' through here hearin' y'all horse-laughin' all night like this is a fuckin' pajama party 'n' then they're callin' in heat." He twitched his wrist and flicked the cylinder of the .357 closed for emphasis.

Spook laid back on his blanket. He pulled the stubby roach from its home in his jacket pocket, lit it, took a deep drag and felt the pain in his leg ease. "I wanna see 'at guy again," he said, more to the sparklingly clear stars above than to Lenny.

"Fuck it," Lenny said. "It's over."

"Fuck you, it wasn't *your* leg. I'm *gonna* see 'at guy again. 'N' I hope you're not there to talk sense to me when I do."

"Owen? Are you ok? We're going, but I want to make sure you're alright before we go?" Kelly knocked on the Winnebago's door, again. "Owen, if you want, you can stay with us tonight. I don't think you should be alone right now. Owen?"

She looked over at Sally standing over by Red's van, an impatient "Well?" on her face.

"Owen, please open up. Let me just see you're ok."

"Give me this; I know how to pick us a good time." It was Red, his easel over his shoulder, heading for his van.

"Not funny."

"Sorry. Look, Kel, if the guy won't answer the door... We're almost loaded up."

"Go wait in the van, give me a minute." She tried knocking and calling out to Owen, again, saw the RV rock like he was moving around, thought the door would open, but then heard a noise, rustling paper, and for a second she flashed on someone unwrapping a gift, like for a birthday or Christmas.

And then a noise that brought that cold feeling back to her middle, startled her so much she stumbled back away from the door.

A harsh, metallic *click-clack*.

Kelly was a Texas girl, raised in a Texas home with a Texas dad who, a little disappointed he'd had a daughter instead of a son, trucked her out with him since she'd been old enough to wear hiking boots when he'd gone hunting for everything from turkey and wild pig to whitetail and puma. After those years, nobody had to explain to her she'd just heard the noise of someone racking the slide on a pump-action shotgun.

Sally was back. "Kelly, we have to -- "

Kelly grabbed Sally by the arm and started pulling her back to the van.

"What about -- "

"Tomorrow you can tell me what a dumbass I am," Kelly said, "but not now. Not *now*. Right now, I just want to get outta here."

THE LAST DAY: Trinity

Thursday morning...

When Rita awoke in her room at the Treasure Chest Motel, she did not wake rested. The bed had sagged and squeaked, the sheets had felt stale, and if the semis thundering by didn't wake her, there had always been the oddly loud whir of the air conditioner and that gurgling toilet to keep her sleep fitful.

So, she lay in her uncomfortable bed, hardly refreshed, scratching at a fresh bump on her arm hoping it was only a mosquito bite. A place to remember, she thought to herself, particularly when it came time to renegotiate her *National Investigator* contract with Eric Bird III.

She showered under a spitting showerhead, dressed, made a few phone calls, then trundled her luggage out to where her Corvette was parked.

"You wasn't gonna forget to settle up now, was ya?"

The manager of the Treasure Chest didn't look much different from the way she'd looked when Rita had signed in the night before. Stout, rubber-faced, bleary-eyed, she was wearing the same ragged-edged bathrobe, had her hair up in the same curlers, had the same newspaper rolled up in one hand, and Rita was almost positive that was the same cigarette sagging from her lips.

"I just wanted to load up my car first," Rita explained.

The manager nodded, not worrying about looking like she considered that a flat-out lie. "Uh-huh. Why don't we settle up first."

Rita produced an agreeable smile and followed the manager into her snug cubby of an office. The manager pulled out a bill book and started writing up Rita's tab. Rita batted at the cigarette smoke from the woman. The woman either didn't notice or didn't care.

"Excuse me," Rita said, "can you tell me where I can get a bite for breakfast?"

The manager didn't look up from her bill book. She nodded at a corner of the office. "You git yer Continental breakfast complimentary with the room."

In the indicated corner was a folding table with a coffee urn, a plate of rolls, and a couple of boxes of Hostess doughnuts. Taped to the table was a hand-lettered sign that said, "Complementary Continental Breakfast – Customers Only!!" Taped to the coffee urn was another sign that said, "One Refill Only!!" Propped against the rolls and doughnuts, another sign read, "Only Take One!!"

"That's very nice of you, thanks," Rita said, "but I'd really like, you know, something more like…well, *more*."

The manager looked up; her eyes narrowed as she studied Rita. She pushed her cigarette from one side of her mouth to the other with her tongue, then pushed Rita's bill across the counter. "Well, there's Flo 'n' Chuck's place. Outside, first left, first right. Be honest with ya; I don't knows it's yer kinda place."

Rita's cheek muscles were hurting from keeping up her polite smile. "Long as they have eggs and coffee."

"Yeah, well, you wanna give it a whirl, 's up to you."

Rita settled the bill and went back out to her car. It was not until she almost had her key in the door that she noticed the crack in the passenger side window and that the door lock was already sprung. "Oh, shit!" She opened the door, tracked the crack in the glass to the rough, scraped edge of the window where a jimmy had been forced into the window seam. "Oh, *shit!*" Now she could see wires hanging from the dashboard where the car radio had been.

"Well, now ain't '*at* a damn shame," the manager said from where she was standing over in the shade of the motel.

"Somebody broke into my car!"

"Mebbe ya left the door open."

Rita shook her head. "You can see where they jimmied the door. Do you want to see for yourself?"

The manager tsk-tsk-tsked unsympathetically, then pointed to a sign on the wall behind her. The sign read, "Park At Your Own Risk!!" "See that?"

"I see it," Rita said.

"Shoulda seen it last night."

"What was I supposed to do? Take the car in the room with me?"

"No need to smart-mouth me, missy!" the manager said.

Rita forced calm on herself. "I don't suppose you heard any noises out here last night?"

"Nope. Had a TV on 'till pretty late. Didn't hear nothin'."

Probably watching the cattle reports, Rita thought. Maybe looking for friends and family in the cow pens.

"Looks to be a might 'spensive-lookin' car, too," the manager said. "Hopes ya got insurance."

Rita threw her luggage in the front seat, climbed behind the wheel, and pulled out of the parking lot giving the engine enough gas to kick up a good-sized cloud of dust. In her rearview mirror she saw the manager's face wrinkle in disgust as she flicked her cigarette after the car.

She followed the two prescribed turns into downtown Lovelady which wasn't quite as cosmopolitan as downtown Boone had been. "Flo & Chuck's Café" was one of only a handful of businesses that didn't have a "Clearance" or "Going Out of Business" or "For Lease" sign in the front window.

There was a parking lot around back but Rita parked in front where she could keep an eye on the car through the front window. Inside, the café was long and narrow, with a counter down one side and a handful of booths along the other. Rita could see clear through to the back screen door and into the parking lot. Except for one mobile home-type thing, it looked like a pick-up truck dealership out back.

The counter was full, and so were the booths except for one in the back. The patrons were all in denims or coveralls, wearing either broad-brimmed straw field hats, or Caterpillar or American Harvester or John Deere caps. They had bare, sinewy, sun-browned forearms, and weather-cracked faces. They were loud and laughed with tobacco-and-liquor hoarseness. Except for the husky, sour-faced woman behind the counter, Rita was the only woman in the place. And also the only Black.

She stood by the door waiting for someone to seat her, ignoring a nearby booth full of burly, rough-hewn types looking in her direction. One of them said something in a low, leering voice that made the others laugh in a dirty way.

Rita smiled, walked over to the table, fixed the man who had started the laughing with an unafraid stare. "Excuse me. Was there something you wanted to say to me?"

He flushed and sank a little into his seat. "Well, uh, as a fact, no, ma'am."

One of the other men wasn't as shy. "Actually, we *was* talkin' boutcha."

Another said, "Noticed how crowded it was." He brushed his mouth with his hand. "I just thought I'd dust off a place for ya to sit."

And they laughed their phlegmy, dirty laugh again.

"Well, you gents are quite the class act!" Rita said, unfazed. "An approach like that, I'll bet you have to beat the women off with a stick. Well, beat *something* off, anyway." When she turned her back to them, she saw the waitress standing over a young fellow now sitting in the once-empty back booth.

"Excuse me," Rita said, stepping up to the waitress. "I think I was here before this gentleman."

The waitress didn't look back at her. "Well, honey, you was talkin' to them boys up front."

"I was being *insulted* by 'them boys' up front."

The waitress sighed. "Chuck!" she called out. "You come on out here! I think we got us a problem!"

"Miss, there's no problem -- "

"*Chuck!*"

Chuck was a beady-eyed, skinny thing who came out of the kitchen wiping his hands on an apron splattered with egg yolk and chili. "What-all's a problem?"

"No problem," Rita said patiently. "I was here before this gentleman, but your waitress -- "

"Flo?" Chuck's eyes were on the dull side, and he seemed to take a while to process information as it came in.

"Flo, I guess, sure," Rita said, "she -- "

"'S no waitress," Chuck said, "'s my *wife!*"

Oh *Christ*... "Oh, well, I'm sorry, I didn't mean to offend anybody, least of all you, Flo. I just came in here for some breakfast -- "

"Well, then, looks like you got some kinda wait."

Rita looked past her to the man who had taken the booth. He was young and the lower parts of his face had the red rash of a fresh shave, but what momentarily took her aback was the way his face was distorted by several ugly, purple bruises. She regained her poise, threw a little sugar into her voice, and asked, "Pardon me, sir, I'm on my way to Houston, I'm hoping to catch an early flight out, and I'm absolutely starving. Would you mind if I sat here? With you?"

His face was blank, and for a moment Rita wondered if he'd heard her. Then, in a flat, lifeless voice: "Yes. I do mind." He turned to Flo. "Miss, I'm ready to order."

Rita's poise was beginning to falter, and she could feel the steam rising up in her. She turned back to Chuck and Flo. "You know, I didn't come in here to make any kind of trouble. All I wanted was a little something to eat -- "

Flo was grinning as she looked past Rita and out the front window. "Well, honey, don't look like ya got much time for no breakfast no how!"

Rita followed Flo's eyes out the front window to the sight of her Corvette hanging from a tow truck's hook and a policeman's talking it over with the tow's driver.

"God*dammit!*" Rita exploded and ran out of the café. It seemed like everyone in the place was having quite a laugh watching her whiz by.

Rita ran up to the policeman. "What the hell's going on?"

This was no Billy Ray Barnes. This policeman was older, sharper, and looked as flexible as an oak tree. He looked her slowly up and down. "This your car, ma'am?"

"Officer, I'm sure your well-trained eye has noted the rental sticker on this car. I *rented* this car."

"Ya don't say? That glass there on the passenger side, looks like she's been jimmied open. Car looks more to be stolen."

"Stolen? Think a minute, Officer. Would I come running up to you if this was a stolen car."

"I've seen dumber things," The policeman said.

The tow truck driver laughed. "'At's true! I 'member this one colored fella -- "

"Shuddup, Harvey," the policeman said.

"I've got the papers right here in the glove compartment," Rita said. She reached into the car, pulled the rental agency folder out and handed it over to the policeman.

He took a minute to study the papers, looked up at Rita, then looked back at the paper, then looked up at Rita, again. "Pardon me, ma'am, but you don't exactly look like an Eric Bird III to me."

Rita gasped in exasperation. "That's my employer, for God's sake!" She rooted through her purse, pulling out her wallet and flashing credit cards, licenses, her work ID. "See? I work for the Eric Bird III Publishing Company in Los Angeles, publishers of *The National Investigator* of which I trust you've heard. I'm a journalist, understand? I flew into Houston Tuesday and rented this car at the airport. I drove to Boone to cover a story. I spent last night at your lovely Treasure Chest Motel. If you want proof, I can show you the bug bites! When I got up this morning, I had the pleasure of finding my car door jimmied and my radio gone and the manager of the Treasure Chest telling me that was just my tough luck!"

The policeman nodded. "'At'd be Nellie."

"Fine, Nellie. I came to Chuck and Flo's here for a little breakfast and wound up with a bellyache instead! Now, I've got you taking my car away and me just a couple of hours out of Houston and a plane back to California which I think we're all unanimous in thinking is a good place for me to be!"

"Hmm," the policeman said, taking it all in. "Ya don't say? Well, ma'am, I'm sorry 'bout ya havin' such a bad day, but it looks like you're gonna have to plan on a late plane. I gotta haul this car – 'n' *you* – down to the station."

Screaming and shouting occurred to Rita as a fair response to the situation, but she skipped right over them to a kind of overwhelmed numbness. "You're *arresting* me?" She didn't disbelieve the policeman; she just wanted confirmation that her bad streak was running *that* bad.

The policeman, who had never lost his businesslike demeanor, continued to be very businesslike as he signed off on some paperwork with the tow truck driver. "I wouldn't call it that zackly, ma'am. Just gotta check your story out is all. This car's got plates 'at expired midnight last night. 'N' y'all got yourself a parking violation."

At which she could only laugh, albeit with an unnerving hysterical edge. "Of *course!* Parking violation? Why not?"

The patrolman – as if he thought it would take the scary tinge out of Rita's laughter – pointed toward the parking meter at the curb. There was a red flag in the meter window that said, "Expired."

Rita laughed harder. "*Naturally! Of course!*" She grabbed hold of the side of the tow truck to hold herself upright as she laughed so hard she could barely breathe.

The policeman and the tow truck driver exchanged worried looks until Rita ratcheted down to a less worrisome chuckle.

"Could I ask you a favor, Officer?"

"What's 'at, ma'am?"

"Shoot me, would you? Please, just shoot me and put me out of my misery!"

Clyde was still so lack-of-sleep groggy when he pulled up in front of the police station he didn't immediately notice the dented Mustang parked in front of him, or Arva May Arlin at the wheel; not until she chirped out a pleasant hello. Clyde mustered a weak smile and a wave but was as happy to get away from chirped pleasant hellos as he was the pounding morning sun and into the air conditioned shade of the station. That is until…

"You're late, Clyde!" Billy Ray Barnes looked at his watch, then the wall clock. "Damn, you're *real* -- "

Clyde froze, he sagged, he hung his head. "Billy Ray. What a hell're you doin' here?"

"You should just be glad I *am* here!"

"I don't know 'bout that." Clyde shuffled past Billy Ray to the coffee machine. "Where's Waylon?"

"On patrol. 'N' this here phone's been goin' like a fire alarm. I got all your messages done up on your desk."

Clyde took his coffee over to his desk where he found message slips arranged in neat spreads on his blotter. He blinked a few times to make sure this wasn't some optical trick arising from his shortage of sleep. "This is awful efficient of you, Billy Ray. Maybe I oughta threaten to fire you more often." Then Clyde put the tidy array on his desk together with Arva May sitting in her car outside. "Who-all helped you with this? Sweet Billy?"

Billy Ray Barnes flushed and busied himself with something on his own desk. "Well, uh, point is, Clyde, well -- "

Clyde flipped through a stack of message slips all from the same caller. "Damn, how many times did the mayor call?"

"For a while it was every five minutes like he was on a schedule or somethin'. Wasn't his office, neither. He was callin' his-*self*, 'n' he sounded plenty pissed. Didn't make him no happier every time he called you still wasn't here."

Clyde dropped heavily into his chair with a sigh. "Hizzoner callin' from City Hall or over to his bidness?"

"His bidness. Says he wanted you over there soon's you come in."

There was a message from Barney White that read, "Clyde'll know"; that one he put aside. Another from Bob Wheeler simply marked "Urgent." Clyde remembered Bob Wheeler as the son of a bitch who'd brokered the health insurance the town held on the police department that wouldn't cover the angioplasty his doctor wanted him to have. Fuck Bob Wheeler and fuck his "urgent," Clyde thought, balled that message up and dropped it in his wastebasket. There was a message from Rita Scott.

"That reporter lady called?" Clyde asked.

"Yeah, I got the info all typed up neat," Billy Ray said and brought over a typed sheet covered with White-Out splotches and type-overs.

"What info?"

"She called, said she thought you'd wanna know Owen Dawson got rid a his car yesterday, traded it in for a camper. A place called Bubba's RVs down on 19 South, headin' toward Lovelady."

"I know the place," Clyde said, slipping on his reading glasses to study the paper.

"I got a description there. Dealer tags; I got the numbers."

"I see 'em, Billy Ray," Clyde said, batting Billy Ray's fingers away.

"She said quid-somethin'. I dunno, it sounded made up to me."

Clyde smiled, then set the paper down, slipped off his glasses, slouched back in his chair, and frowned up at Billy Ray Barnes. "You didn't come in here for extra credit, Billy Ray. You bein' here got anythin' to do with Arva May sittin' outside?"

Billy Ray twitched and shuffled. "Well, uh, Clyde, I was kinda hopin' you'd 'pologize."

"For *what?*"

"Welllll, Clyde, you wasn't zackly polite to Arva May last night. Ya know; out there to The Candlelight."

"Y'all saw I was kinda preoccupied," Clyde said.

"Still, Clyde, last night was supposed to be special for us."

"Oh, yeah, that's right. Y'all's six-month anniversary or somethin'."

"Seven months. Y'all kinda messed up a night for us."

Clyde nodded, beckoned him to bring the girl in. "Awright, Billy Ray."

"'N' maybe you could say somethin' nice 'bout it bein' our anniversary 'n' all."

"Aw*right*, Billy Ray."

Clyde managed to get through a yawn and a sip of his coffee before Billy Ray reappeared with Arva May, depositing her in a chair opposite Clyde's desk.

"Hey, Chief," Arva May giggled.

"Hey, Arva May."

"Arva May, the chief here has somethin' he wants to say to you," brokered Billy Ray. "Right, Clyde?"

"Uh, yeah, 'at's right, Arva May. I just wanted to 'pologize for last night, I didn't mean to be rude to y'all if I was, 'n' I'm just sorry 'bout a whole thing." Clyde winced at Billy Ray standing behind Arva May hand-signaling him that there was more. "Oh, 'n' yeah, right, I wanted to wish you 'n' Sweet Billy there congratulations on this bein' your -- " Billy Ray held up seven prompting fingers " – seven-month anniversary."

Billy Ray beamed and took Arva May by the shoulders, and she beamed, too. "We 'preciate 'at, Clyde," Billy Ray said. "Don't we, Arva May?"

"You're sweet when you aren't mad," Arva May told Clyde.

Clyde made himself smile. "Nice a you to say."

"Maybe you shouldn't be so mad all a time."

"I'd like 'at," Clyde said, still smiling while sending a pointed stare toward Billy Ray. "Wouldn't 'at be nice I wasn't so mad all a time, Sweet Billy?"

"Sweet Billy, I gotta be at Pearl's like ten minutes ago," the girl said. "I'm gettin' myself *coiffed*, ya know."

"I'll run you over in just a sec, Arva May, but I gotta talk to Clyde a bit. Whyntcha wait outside?"

She gave Billy Ray a wave from the door and Billy Ray waved back, and then she gave Clyde a wave and a goodbye and Clyde goodbyed and waved back. When the door closed behind her Clyde sagged in his chair, drained. "What now, Billy Ray?"

"Say, Clyde, I was thinkin', maybe after last night you might put me back on today?"

Clyde closed his eyes and began rubbing his forehead. He'd been willing to apologize to Arva May and even to Billy Ray about what had happened out at The Candlelight. He hadn't been *happy* about it and felt like he'd just about sprained something in his throat trying to sound sincere in the execution, but he was willing to grant he'd been a little out of line the night before. And, by God, he'd done so. But it was just like Billy Ray not to quit while he was ahead.

"What," Clyde said speaking slowly and clearly, "does one got to do with t'other?"

"C'mon, Clyde, ya ruint my special night with Arva May! I figure, maybe, ya know, kinda like a way to make it up to me."

"Make it up to you."

"'N' yeah, I know I messed up, but I learnt my lesson."

"You told me 'at once 'fore," Clyde said.

"Naw, I *mean* it this time!"

"You mean you *didn't* mean it last time?"

Billy Ray flustered. "Naw, 'at's not what -- . I mean -- . You *know* what I mean!"

Clyde thought a moment, then sighed resignedly. "Awright, y'all come on after Waylon, 'n' call Wesley to tell 'im we're back on the usual rotation."

Thanks started to bubble up in Billy Ray but Clyde stifled them with a stare and a jabbing finger. "Hold up! Listen to me: next time there won't be no warnin', or one-more-chances, unnerstand? Next time you fuck up, you're out there on a sidewalk lookin' for a new job."

He sent Billy Ray out the door on that note, washed a couple of aspirin down with his coffee, wished he'd had both the stomach and the time for breakfast, then gave Barney White a call.

"Got somethin' for me, Barney?"

"'Fraid not, Clyde."

"No luck on those missin' teeth?"

"My boys swear they raked those ashes six ways to Sunday, 'n' there's nothin' left up there."

"You said a vic mighta swallowed 'em."

"Well, she mighta."

Clyde could sense a "but" hanging in the air. "Ok."

"Can't do it, Clyde. Can't touch her. First thing this mornin' I got a call from the Honorable Fred C. Reilly -- "

"Aw, hell, shit, 'n' damn."

"Yup. He was pretty het up, did a lotta talkin' 'bout jurisdiction, but readin' 'tween the lines, I figger what's on his mind is financial."

"I didn't even know he knew we'd brought a body in."

"He didn't get to be a four-time mayor sittin' 'round hopin' people think nice 'bout 'im. I'll bet he knows when every yellow dog in town lifts his leg to take a whiz. Anyway, 'cordin' to him, there's no carvin' gonna go on with a vic 'less the sheriff's department calls for it 'n' picks up a tab. 'N' when I called a sheriff's office, well, Walt Bowen put it nice, but a gist was his department had work enough on their own without y'all dumpin' bodies on 'im. I don't think anybody's gonna get to this poor lady on my table any time soon. I guess you should maybe talk it out with Fred C."

Clyde closed his eyes and shook his head. I know things can never be easy, he said to the universe, but do they have to be this damned *hard?* "Those X-rays from Henry Gilmore get there?"

"Waitin' for me this mornin', Clyde, but I can't rightly do a comparison with Fred C. readin' me a riot act like 'at."

"Awright, Barney, I'll get back to you 'n' let you know the score, 'n' if Walt Bowen budges 'n' you come up with somethin', gimme a holler."

Clyde hung up, sat quietly at his desk sipping his coffee for a moment, working up to facing off with Mayor Fred C. Reilly, then went outside where he found a giggling Billy Ray Barnes and a giggling Arva May Arlin jigging this way and that around Arva May's Mustang.

"C'mere ya foxy li'l thing!" Billy Ray said with a big, leery smile, and Arva May just giggled all the more, finally letting Billy Ray scoop her up in his arms and commence to tickle her under the ribs.

At which point they noticed a dead-faced Clyde Thomas standing on the sidewalk watching. Billy Ray and Arva May both went beet red, and Billy Ray let his arms drop to his side. "Hey, Clyde."

Clyde nodded. "I don't mind y'all bein' young 'n' in love, but next time could y'all *not* be young 'n' in love in front a the po-lice station?"

Billy Ray and Arva May mumbled some kind of embarrassed agreement.

"Billy Ray, I need you to do somethin'. Soon's you get back from runnin' your sweetie here over to Pearl's, I need you to get on a phone 'n' find out which dentist handled Sarah Dawson."

"How'm I supposed -- "

"This town don't have but two dentists, Billy Ray. You call Doc Weed 'n' Doc Greenley 'n' *ask* 'em. Whichever says yes, see if you can persuade 'em nice-like to get over to Boone General 'n' have a look at 'at body we brought in yesterday 'n' see if they can tell me if it's Sarah Dawson."

"Gotcha, Clyde. Ya know, you told me I wasn't comin' on 'til after Waylon -- "

"Billy Ray," Clyde said, trying to hold his temper to save himself having to make another insincerely sincere apology to Arva May, "didn't you just ask me not five minutes ago to reinstate you?"

Arva May, always the brighter of the two, gave Billy Ray's arm a supportive squeeze. "I think you should do just like the chief says, Sweet Billy. I'll get myself to Pearl's 'n' we'll meet up later, ok?"

Billy Ray nodded begrudgingly, he and Arva May kissed a little more deeply than Clyde would like to have witnessed, then Arva May drove off in her dinged Mustang.

"Get on in there 'n' go to work, Sweet Billy," Clyde said and shooed Billy Ray into the police station. He watched Arva May's Mustang disappear around a corner. Clyde thought she was a pretty girl, and smarter than she let on. He looked at the door that had just closed behind Billy Ray who maybe wasn't too bad looking but didn't have any more sense than God gave a piss-ant. He shook his head, relegated the communion of those two souls to the category of unexplained mysteries of the universe, and headed out to meet the mayor.

Police Headquarters in Lovelady made Police Headquarters in Boone look like the J. Edgar Hoover Building. The Lovelady P.D. consisted of a white clapboard building about the size of a one-car garage. Inside were a desk, a rifle rack empty except for one Remington shotgun, and a holding cage about the size of a telephone booth.

Rita was standing at a pay phone mounted on the wall. Officer Wheatle – which was the name of the hard and proper patrolman who'd brought Rita in – wouldn't let her use her cell phone because he'd confiscated her personal items, and he wouldn't let her use the departmental phone because it was a toll call. As she heard ringing at the other end of the line, Rita eyed the small holding cage and wondered, if it came to it, how long she could stay in there without going insane.

The phone line clicked open. "Hello -- "

"Eric, it's Rita -- "

" -- you've reached the Eric and Suze Bird House. Neither of us can fly to the phone right now."

Rita groaned.

"We've left the nest and we're out looking for worms. If you'd like us to get back to you, just leave a short message at the sound of the cheep." After which came a bird's tweet-tweet.

"Eric!" Rita shouted into the mouthpiece. "I called the office and they told me you were home! *I know you're there, Eric!* Eric, this is an emergency so please *pick up the goddamned phone!* I'm in jail, Bird! *Bird!*"

Rita went on like that until she'd used up her allotted time and the phone disconnected.

Rita looked over to Officer Wheatle who was sitting at his desk amply enjoying some barbecue on a bun. The closest Rita had been to food all day was a whiff of the Treasure Chest's Continental breakfast and the chili and egg yolk on Chuck's apron. The aroma from Officer Wheatle's barbecue sandwich had the saliva building up in Rita's cheeks.

"No luck?" Officer Wheatle said, dabbing at his mouth with a paper napkin.

"Let me try him again, ok?"

Officer Wheatle shrugged. "Long's the phone bill goes to you or this Mr. Bird."

"Don't worry," she said, reaching for the phone again. "Mr. Bird is gonna *pay!*"

"This time," warned Officer Wheatle and pointed to a placard warning that no smoking, spitting, graffiti-writing, loud music or profanity would be tolerated within the Lovelady police building.

"Hello," the answering machine said, again, "You've reached the Eric and Suze Bird House…"

When it was time for her to talk, again, Rita shouted: *"Eric, goddamn you, pick up the phone! I'm in jail for Chrissakes!"*

Officer Wheatle cleared his throat to get Rita's attention and pointed more emphatically to the warning placard on the wall.

"Eric! Pleaseplease*please* pick up the phone!"

There was a click and a rattle and then a calm, slightly annoyed Eric Bird III came on the line: "I don't know why you have to shout, love. You get so excitable sometimes."

"Oh, I'm sorry, Eric, for some strange reason the threat of imminent incarceration sets me a little on edge. Where the hell were you?"

"Oh, out by the pool. Suze's having one of her afternoon *fetes* today," Eric said tiredly, "and we have to pretend to be a happy couple in front of what passes for the Los Angeles gentry."

"Boo-hoo for you. I have my own problems."

"What's all this noise about trouble with the police?"

"They have some questions about the car rental. It's charged on the company's account. I need someone to vouch for me."

"You mean they don't trust that ever-so-honest face of yours, love?"

"This is not the time to horse around, Eric."

"All right, Rita-love, let me speak with whomever it is I need to speak."

Rita gave up a relieved sigh and turned the phone over to Officer Wheatle who knew how to milk a climactic moment, taking his time setting his sandwich down, wiping his individual fingers clean, clearing his throat with a sip of his sweet tea. He stood, took a pause to adjust his pants, then took the phone.

Eric Bird III liked to hear himself talk and Officer Wheatle seemed to enjoy the fact that someone was talking to him all the way from Los Angeles,

California on official business, the two factors combining to make a long conversation out of what should have been a short call.

Rita took advantage of Officer Wheatle's conversational immersion to pinch off a piece of barbecue from his sandwich and quick pop it into her mouth. Officer Wheatle turned suspiciously in her direction, and Rita hid her chewing by pretending to pore over a county map on the opposite wall.

There was Boone, and the slightly bowed line of 19 South leading to Lovelady. Just out of curiosity – so she told herself – she found Pennington to the east, then just for fun – so she told herself – she mapped out a course along the ranch and farm roads that could, if she'd wanted – and she told herself she didn't – take her from Lovelady to Pennington.

And then she figured, just for fun, not that she really wanted to, that depending on the condition of the roads and holding to the speed limit, she could probably be in Pennington in a half-hour. If she was interested. Which – so she told herself – she wasn't.

Clyde had decided to walk since Fred C. Reilly's place of business was just a few blocks away from the police station. Within a block, under an already roasting morning sun and with his shirt sweat-mottled and sticking to him almost everywhere, he was regretting the choice. Still, he plodded on and soon there it sat ahead of him, an oasis of green awnings and air conditioning:

REILLY & SONS
LAWN & GARDEN

According to a commercial Fred C. Reilly had the local cable company run on TV a few months before, whether you were growing a couple of acres of feed corn or just a few petunias in your front yard, Reilly & Sons had what you needed. The wide apron of the glass-fronted store did, indeed, boast everything from rakes and roto-tillers,ride-along lawn mowers to flatwood trellises and garden gnomes.

Barney White's remark – how Fred C. Reilly didn't get to be mayor etc. -- prompted Clyde to remember the commercial, and that the cable company had to pull it after just a few days because some of Fred C. Reilly's political opponents screamed "Foul!" about Fred C. appearing in the commercial over a chyron that labeled him as Fred C. Reilly, proprietor of Reilly & Sons was fine. But, listing him as *Mayor* Fred C. Reilly, proprietor of Reilly & Sons, well, to them that meant Fred C. was hiding a political ad inside a commercial for garden gnomes.

One of the & Sons was out front showing a gent propane barbecue outfits that were more elaborate than the kitchen Clyde had in his trailer. Fred C. Reilly, Jr. was a good-looking, well-groomed, always-smiling kid in his 20s in a white, short-sleeved business shirt and tie, and when he saw Clyde he gave him a big smile and friendly wave, and Clyde nodded obligatorily in return. He'd never had much use for the boy. Even though Fred Jr. was his daddy's hand-picked successor to the business, his mayoral realm, and all other earthly holdings, Fred Jr. still always had his lips pressed firmly against daddy's ass in case daddy ever entertained second thoughts about this allotment which was a trait Clyde didn't much care for. Clyde didn't see the other son of & Sons, but found Fred, Sr. out under the big, plastic awning alongside the store sweet-talking a man he'd coaxed onto the seat of a huge Toro.

Fred C. Reilly was a tall, fleshy, florid fellow with tortoiseshell glasses that looked too small on his large, shapeless head, and wearing the same workday uniform as his son: short-sleeved business shirt and tie. All that bulk might've been intimidating if Fred Sr. had ever put the littlest bit of work into shaping it, but, as it was, he had the roll-upon-roll shape of a pile of soft-serve ice cream with girlishly slim arms and legs attached.

"I tell ya, friend, if I could get another 30 mile an hour outta this thing, I'd drive 'er 'roun' town 'stead a my Caddie, that's how nice a ride she'll give ya," Fred C. Reilly was telling the man on the Toro.

The Toro rider looked a little balky. "Seems like a lotta machine for what I got. My lawn ain't but -- "

"Friend, this isn't 'bout how big your lawn is. This is 'bout turnin' what used to be a chore into a quick, fun spin 'roun' a yard. You're gonna like drivin' this machine so much you're gonna wind up doin' every lawn on a block just 'cause ya don't wanna get off!"

Fred Sr. noticed a sweaty Clyde Thomas coming across the apron toward him. He excused himself from the potential Toro jockey telling him to take the machine for a trial spin around the store parking lot and headed for the front double doors of his store beckoning Clyde to follow. Clyde trailed across the store floor and past pyramid stacks of weed killer and lawn seed and the like.

Clyde saw the other & Son at the back counter, wearing the pouty face he always wore. He was younger than his brother, had long, unkempt hair with a purple streak in it, a silver stud in one ear, and a black T-shirt stenciled with, "Eat Me." He was leafing through a copy of *Blender*. "Hey, Bert," Clyde called.

Bertram Reilly shrugged in response.

"It's not like I actually spect you to *do* anythin', Bert," Fred Sr. snarled at the boy as they passed, "but could you at least *look* busy!"

To which Bertram Reilly gave a yeah-yeah nod and continued to flip through *Blender*.

Fred Sr. had a small office at the back of the store and Clyde followed him inside, took his place sitting with his hat in his lap across the littered the desk from the mayor. Just above Fred Sr.'s head, where it was hard to miss, hung a picture of the mayor standing with George W. Bush. Fred Sr. had a copy of the same picture hung in the same hard-to-miss place in his mayor's office at City Hall. When people saw the picture and said, suitably impressed, "You had your picture taken with the president?" Fred Sr., with a politician's artfulness, answered along the lines of, "Well, that's me and George W. all right," which neither confirmed nor denied the easy-to-make supposition. Thusly, Fred Sr. could never be accused of lying or even of embellishment; he just declined to advance certain details. Like, for instance, that the president hadn't been the president yet when the picture was taken but had still been just the governor of Texas presiding over a state conference of mayors in Austin when a photographer caught a shot of him standing with a large group of Republican mayors. Fred Sr. had seen the photographer lining up the shot and just before the photographer had taken the picture pushed his way through the crowd and positioned himself close by the governor and in George W.'s eyeline so it looked like he was hobnobbing intimately with the president-to-be, an effect Fred Sr. enhanced by having much of the rest of the group in the picture cropped out.

Fred Sr. blopped his bulk into his chair, unable to find a comfortable position and constantly fidgeting about like a man with piles. On the street where his constituents and/or potential customers could see him, Fred Sr. was always all baby-kissing sweetness and politeness, but behind closed doors... Clyde had once speculated that Fred Sr. was possessed of some sort of psychological *thing* about closed doors because Fred Sr. seemed to automatically get pissed off once he was behind them. Maybe he *did* have piles.

"It's nice you got Bert out there on the floor for the summer," Clyde said. "How long 'fore he goes back to school?"

"Not soon enough!" said Fred Sr., already pissed off. "Ya see 'im out there?"

"I saw 'im."

"I swear people just *see* 'im out there 'n' he scares 'em off! But I'll be damned if I'm gonna let 'im spend the summer sittin' home 'roun' the pool with those chucklehead friends a his. You ever see that bunch?"

"I've seen 'em."

"All in black like a bunch a damn funeral mourners! See 'em all together like 'at 'minds me a cave fulla *bats!* I wisht it was like the ol' days. I went 'round lookin' like 'at, *my* daddy'd put some sense in me with a buckle end a his belt, 'n' nobody was gonna sue 'im over it or call Child Services neither! I swear, they ever bring back the draft I'm gonna run 'at boy's lazy ass down a draft board myself! *Let* the missus cry 'bout it! *Her* fault he's like 'at, babyin' 'im alla time! Maybe some time feelin' bullets whiz by his head in I-raq or whatever shithole we're mixed up in take some the smart-ass outta that boy! Ahh, I don't wanna talk 'bout 'im no more; it just gives me a bellyache. I wanna talk 'bout a bellyache *you* give me. I been callin' you all mornin', Clyde."

"Well, there was this thing last night, somethin' I got into, I got in late so I overslept a li'l, I guess." He yawned, rubbed his itchy eyes. "I haven't had but a couple hours -- "

"'*Somethin'* ya got into?' Ya mean 'at li'l shivaree ya put on with Kay Gorsham out to The Candlelight?"

Clyde frowned. There wasn't a line of gossip, rumor, or over-the-yard-fence story-telling it didn't seem Fred C. Reilly wasn't plugged into. "Well, Fred, she's goin' through some stuff -- "

Fred Sr. shifted around in his chair and the chair groaned. "If she was on my payroll 'stead a the county's I'da had 'er out on 'er ass to*day!* Puttin' on a show like 'at out in public!"

"She's havin' some problems -- "

"Which is none a *your* bidness 'n' which *she* should keep in 'er goddamn house!"

"She's a friend, Fred, 'n' -- "

"*Your* bidness is po-lice problems here in Boone! She wants a make a fool a herself out in front a everybody like 'at, that's *her* bidness, but I'm not havin' *my* chief a po-lice join in 'n' look just as foolish. Understand?"

"I-- "

"I called you at your house, ya know. I didn't even get a goddamn machine!"

"I turned it off when I got in 'cause it was late 'n' I -- "

"You must have balls like a stud bull doin' like 'at, Clyde! You're the goddamn *chief* a the goddamn Boone Po-lice Department, 'n' when a goddamn *mayor* wants to talk to ya on po-lice bidness or any *other* goddamn bidness I shouldn't have no kinda problem gettin' ya on a goddamn phone!"

"You're right, Fred, I shouldn't -- "

"You're goddamn *right* I'm goddamn right! I don't need *you* to tell me I'm goddamn *right!*"

"I'm sorry. I -- "

"Yesterday I'm down to the county seat 'n' 'at smart-ass friend a yours over to the prosecutor's office -- "

"Denny Bemis?"

" – he come up to me 'n' he say, 'Say, hey, Fred, whatcha call a preacher who makes dirty movies?'" Fred glared at Clyde to let him know this was his cue.

"Ok," Clyde said, "what *do* you call a preacher who makes dirty movies?"

"A *lay* minister."

Clyde tried not to, but he smiled. "'A's pretty good."

All that piled soft-serve sticking out of Fred Sr.'s tight collar grew beet red and began to shake. "Don't you dare laugh, Clyde! Don't you goddamn *dare!* This town's a goddamn laughin' stock all over east Texas 'cause a the goddamn Reverend Dawson! *That's* the kinda problem you're *supposed* to deal with!"

Now it was Clyde's turn to get irritated and snap back: "Well, Fred, first off, I'm a chief a po-lice; not your public relations guy! Wasn't much me or anybody else coulda done 'bout 'at once 'at story got in a paper."

"God*damn* Poteet! I swear to Christ I'm gonna string 'at sumbitch up from a lamppost! I'll get 'at goddamn place a his re-zoned, tear it down 'n' put up a dog run! See how he -- ""

"Second off, get holt a yourself! The TV isn't payin' it no mind anymore, neither are the big daily papers. It was a one-day joke for 'em. Only one still makin' a big deal 'bout this is *you!* Owen Dawson left town yesterday mornin' 'n' 'at newspaper lady right after 'im. There! Your two biggest problems are *gone!* Happy?"

Fred Sr. finally found a comfortable spot to settle and went quiet in his seat. "Dawson left town?"

"'A's what I said, Fred."

"'N' 'at lady writes for whatever-the-hell 'at sleazy rag is?"

"As a yesterday. So, all you got left is to put up with some bad jokes 'n' people'll get tired a those soon enough. So they make a few jokes! You don't appoint church ministers, Fred; 's not your fault."

Never one to settle for good news when he could find some bad in it, Fred Sr. started quivering, again. "I'm the goddamn *mayor*, Clyde, don't ya understand? This is *my* town! *Everything* 'at happens in it gets laid at *my* door! Some a those spikey-haired li'l juvenile dicks y'all should be lockin' up spray paint somethin' nasty on a side a the school? Nobody down the county seat's talkin' 'bout their ain't-worth-a-shit *parents!* It's, "Sa matter, Fred? Got kids runnin' wild in a streets up there to Boone? What the hell kinda law enforcement y'all got up there, Fred?' *Now* they're talkin' 'bout how I got all kindsa *perverts* walkin' a streets up here -- "

"Fred, I think you're zaggeratin' this outta -- "

"Next year's election time, Clyde."

"I know," Clyde sighed.

"'N' I got my eye on a state assembly this time 'round. This kinda mess don't zackly make for a great campaign! 'Send Fred C. Reilly to Austin: the man who bought pornography to Boone's churches.'"

"Fred, now you're *really* zaggeratin' -- "

"Lessen 'at don't bother you 'cause 'at smart-ass pal a yers Bemis is gettin' talked up for the same seat?"

"Fred, I didn't even know he -- "

"Where'd Dawson go?"

"South. 'S all I know. Got 'im traced far as Lovelady. After that..." Clyde shrugged.

Fred Sr. gave up on his chair and started pacing around the cramped office. "Shoulda arrested 'im when ya had a chance."

"For *what?*"

"How about 'cause he kilt his damn wife, Clyde! How 'bout *that!* You got 'er body all burnt up sittin' up there to County General!"

"We didn't find the body 'til after he left town, Fred, 'n' we don't even know it *is* his wife."

"That's not a way *I* heard it."

"You been hearin' a lot, Fred, but you haven't been hearin' much of it *right*. We got a body, 's a woman, 'n' 'at's all we got right now. Anythin' else you heard is wild guesses."

"So *you* say."

"Damn right so *I* say!" Clyde said defiantly. "'N' what's this crap I hear Barney White says ya told 'im to hold up the autopsy?"

"Barney White cuts up 'at woman at your request 'n' we're gonna get billed for it. Ya found 'at body over the town line."

"Well, it's pretty close. I'm not sure -- "

"Don't bullshit *me*, Clyde! 'At's Wilbur McCoy's place! I *know* 'bout Wilbur McCoy 'n' I *know* his goddamn *place!* Every goddamn town meetin' 'at sumbitch is down inna front row wavin' his hand 'n' askin' why we don't collect his garbage or send a po-lice up there to chase away those kids he's got neckin' 'n' beerin' in his woods! So I can tell ya down to the goddamn *inch* where the town line is out there, Clyde; down to the goddamn *inch!* 'At's *another* sumbitch I'd like to hang from a lamppost! 'At's the county's corpse; the sheriff's department can pick up the tab. The hell you doin' up there to McCoy's anyhow?"

"It's kind a hard to explain. What if 'at body *is* Sarah Dawson?"

"It's still a county case. I know ya didn't go stupid on me alla sudden, Clyde. Jurisdiction isn't 'bout where a body's *from;* it's 'bout where a body *falls.* 'N' *this* one fell in a county sheriff's lap." Despite the air conditioning in the office, Fred Sr. had worked himself into quite a sweat. He pulled a white handkerchief from a pants pocket, swabbed down his face, then dropped back into his chair, all the ranting and raving having left him spent. He went back to squirming restlessly in his seat. "Look. Your big murder case is gone, Dawson's gone, his wife – if 'at's not her on Barney White's table – is off somewheres screwin' 'roun' so I hear, 'n' 'at nigger reporter's gone. Whatever's goin' on is goin' on..." and Fred Sr. made a vague motion of his girly little hand indicating the world outside the Boone territorial boundaries. "Which means there's no reason this town shouldn't get back to bein' a nice, quiet place, is there?"

"No reason I can think of, Fred. I should let the sheriff's department know what I know, 'bout Dawson 'n' his wife 'n' all. Vehicle identification 'n' all 'at."

"I didn't say don't cooperate. Just 'member: this is *their* case. They wanna work up overtime lookin' into it, 'at's *their* bidness."

Clyde nodded, realized he was dismissed and got to his feet but stopped with his hand on the doorknob. "You're the mayor, Fred, you're the boss. But next time you wanna know what's goin' on, whyntcha try askin' *me* 'stead a goin' by every dirty word comes through your store."

Which was a reprimand that didn't go down too well with Fred C. Reilly, but if he had something to say in response, Clyde didn't wait around to hear it.

Thursday afternoon...

Spook stood at the firing line, legs apart, his .357 held at his side, along his thigh. He tried not to let it show that his weight was resting on his left leg to keep the pressure off his right with its throbbing from the crescents of teeth marks that had still been nasty-looking when he'd woken up that morning. Never let the pain show, he told himself. Never.

He thumbed back the hammer on the pistol. "Ready."

"Go!" Lenny called.

Spook brought the pistol up into his two cupped hands, letting his knees flex at the same time. The sights came up in front of him and he squeezed off the first round, then kept nursing the trigger, sending off round after round, controlling the rise of the pistol as it bucked with each shot.

"Lost a couple there, Spookie," Porky haw-hawed when the sound of the last shot had died away.

Spook's first round had hit the red bull's eye, but the second had only nicked the top of the red zone, and the last four had run up the target in a line. Spook smiled as he popped the cylinder out and emptied his brass into a coffee can sitting on a table in the shooting stand. He smiled because the others didn't know that if the target had been a human silhouette – if it'd been that little fuck from the river – the four "stray" bullets would have stitched a line from heart to head.

"How'd it look?" Shorty asked.

"Like shit," Lenny said. He'd set the camcorder on its tripod and sighted it over Spook's shoulder toward the target. "Too much fuckin' smoke." He peered through the viewfinder. "Can't even see the holes. Too fuckin' small. Even if I zoom all a way in."

Spook brushed past him and took a seat on the bench by the fence, stretching his hurt leg in what he hoped looked like a purely casual motion. "Next time I'll use a cannon. Will that make you happy?"

"I'll betcha one a them Dirty Harry guns woulda give ya some holes ya could see," Shorty said. "Blow 'at whole fuckin' target to confetti I'll bet. Hey, Lenny, c'mon, lemme do the camera for a bit. Ya been hoggin' it all fuckin' day."

"Fuck off," which, coming from Lenny, was enough to end the debate.

Being a weekday and early afternoon at that, there weren't many people at Byrum's Shooting Range. Shooters had spread out through the shooting stands giving themselves a comfortable privacy with several booths between them. Lenny had stationed his troop at the far end of the range. Looking up and down the range Spook saw that whoever had been shooting close by had discretely migrated toward the other wing of the range. That made him smile.

This was bread and circuses, Spook thought, remembering the phrase from God knows where. Another Lenny-sponsored distraction from the fact that Lenny wasn't leading them anywhere. There'd been leftovers from yesterday's riverside raid for breakfast, and now this. Bread and circuses, and there wouldn't be much of either when the money ran out and that, Spook considered with a certain, malicious expectancy, couldn't be far off.

Spook took a cleaning rod from his gun kit on the bench beside him and ran it through the chambers slowly to clear out the powder residue. If he'd learned anything before they'd bounced him out of the Army, it was to take care of your piece and it would take care of you. He looked over at Lenny and wondered when – not if – he would have to test the axiom.

"Hey, Lenny! Get this one!" Porky was in the shooting stand, now. He had a small, cheap .25 automatic between his hands, something only useful for scaring people in a barroom brawl. "Get this!" and he bent over and aimed his pistol between his legs. "Upside down, between my legs while I whistle 'Dixie.'"

"Don't shoot your dick off," Shorty warned.

"He ain't 'at good a shot!" Lenny said and they laughed.

"Yeah!" Shorty said. "He'd need a telescopic sight for that!" And they laughed, again.

There was something Spook remembered about gravity and heavenly bodies. It couldn't've been something he learned in school; all he'd learned in school was he didn't want to be there. Maybe it was something he saw in a *Star Wars* movie or something. Maybe on TV. It was how big things – like the sun, like the planets – attracted little things, like their moons. Things drifted through space and then they passed something bigger and the gravity of the bigger object pulled them in. Sometimes something happened and the smaller thing would pass on through, and other times it would be held in orbit.

Spook looked around at Lenny and Shorty and the bent-over Porky, thought laughing to himself, They're not exactly my idea of heavenly bodies, but things seemed to be working that way. You fall in with a crew, he thought, because it isn't safe out there on the blacktop for a maverick. And they take you in – the Lennys and Porkys and Shortys, all the Lucifer's Children – because that makes more of them and numbers are safe. You don't like each other, you don't know each other, but numbers are safe. Gravity. Heavenly bodies.

Spook raised his pistol to his face and blew the chambers clear and thought it might be coming up on time to drift out of orbit.

"Ok," Porky called to Lenny, "ya on me?"

Lenny turned the focus ring on the camcorder. "Gotcha."

"Ok," Porky said, "Here I go. Ready on the left, ready on the right, ready on the firin' line!" He started whistling 'Dixie' and cocked his .25.

There was a blast, and a startled Porky fell over in a somersault while his target downrange exploded. *"Jesus -- !"*

The detonation had left Spook momentarily dazed, but he quickly shook it off and shot to his feet. God*damn*, he hadn't even seen the son of a bitch come up on them!

It was that little fuck from the river only he had something now he hadn't had then: a pump action shotgun. The man was racking a fresh cartridge into the chamber, the ejecting shell arcing through the air, trailing acrid smoke, clattering across the concrete floor of the stand. Spook heard each sound – the *click-clack* of the shotgun's slide, the plasticky rattle of the spent shell on the floor – with a startling clarity because all other sounds had stopped for him.

"Hey, look who's here!" Lenny said, having gotten past the initial shock, trying to sound unfazed, jaunty, but Spook could hear the strained note in his voice. "Fellas, look! It's our *amigo* from the river! Hey, *amigo!*"

"Be cool, dude," Porky said to the man as he climbed slowly to his feet. "Just be cool. Watch where ya point 'at thing."

"I'm watching," the man from the river said, leveling the shotgun at them, swinging it slowly back and forth along the rank the four bikers made. It hung on Spook for a moment, and Spook thought if he'd had a flashlight he could've seen straight down the barrel to the ass-puckered end of the shell in the breech.

"Look, man," Lenny said soothingly, "So we gave you a hard time. 'At was just messin' 'roun'. Ok, 'at's done. Here's your camera. No harm done."

"No harm done," the man from the river said.

"Hey, c'mon, man -- "

"Shut-up," the man said precisely.

Lenny had misjudged the man, Spook thought, and he could see this was finally sinking in on Lenny, and, with that epiphany, Lenny's face sagged, going white.

Back at the river, the man had been blind angry. This was different. Spook knew *this* look; he'd seen it often enough in the mirror. It was when anger went past the heat into something very cold and clear, where everything you see and hear, the thoughts in your mind have that clarity of the first, chill day of autumn. Beyond the tendrils of smoke twining out of the chamber of the shotgun Spook could see the man behind the shotgun's sights had that cold, clear look, and he seemed to be focusing it mostly on Spook.

Which made Spook feel very naked holding his open, empty pistol.

But then, to Spook's surprise – and no little relief – the man swung the muzzle of the shotgun away and turned it to Lenny, keeping it leveled at Lenny's head.

Lenny mustered up what was supposed to be a defiant grin. "There's four of us, man. You really think you can take us all?"

"No," the man said evenly, "I can't. One. Maybe two," and the man's eyes flicked briefly toward Spook, a flash of a grin. "But certainly one." He bobbed the muzzle of the shotgun a little indicating Lenny: "You."

"I didn't lay a hand on ya!" Lenny protested.

The man nodded toward Spook. "But if I kill *him,* would any of you care?"

"You drop me," Lenny warned, "'n' you'll be a dead man 'fore I hit the ground."

The man shrugged. "I don't think so. Do your friends really love you that much? You *think* someone loves you, but you'd be surprised. Do they love you enough to risk dying for you? Do they love you enough to kill for you? Leave here with a murder hanging over their heads? Do they love you that much?" And then the man smiled. "Even if they do, you'll hit the ground before I do."

Spook hadn't thought much of this little fuck back at the river; back there, he'd just been another straight who'd let anger get in the way of good sense and had gotten the shit kicked out of him – deservedly -- for it. But now Spook had to admit that, like Lenny, he'd misjudged him; the guy was much sharper than he would've guessed. That quick little look and grin he'd given Spook told Spook that, given his druthers, the little fuck's choice would be to empty that pump gun into him. But the little fuck – the *sharp* little fuck – had sized up the situation pretty damned neatly. Threatening to blow Spook away wasn't going to make the other three balky. Like as not, they'd join in, putting a few rounds of their own into poor ol' Spook's wriggling body just for laughs. The nigger is *always* expendable. Spook knew it and so did Mr. Not-Quite-As-Much-A-Dumbfuck-As-I-Thought.

Threatening Lenny, well, now, that was a different story.

The man kept the shotgun on Lenny, but he looked over at Shorty and Porky whose blank faces showed them completely overwhelmed by the tactical complexities of the situation. "Go ahead," he told them quietly. "Show me how much you love this man."

"Don't nobody do nothin' stupid!" Lenny shouted. He looked past the man with the shotgun to the other shooters who were now curiously and cautiously moving in their direction. "Don't *nobody* try nothin'! This fuckin' guy's crazy! He'll waste us all if anybody moves!" Lenny looked to his troops. Porky was frowning his way to a decision, his fingers flexing around the grip of his .25. "Shorty, goddammit -- "

Porky grinned. "This cocksucker's bluffin', Len. He don't have the balls to -- "

Another blast from the shotgun ended the statement and the grin suddenly as dust and splinters from the corrugated plastic roof showered down on his head.

The man pumped a fresh shell into the chamber. "You're right. I'm bluffing. So call me out."

Lenny had ducked and screamed at the shot, understandable in that he thought the blast would be the last thing he was going to hear. He came up out of his crouch more furious at Porky than afraid. For the moment, anyway. "*You fuckhead!*" he screamed hoarsely. "Y'all even *think* 'bout tryin' somethin' else 'n' if *he* don't blow yer ass away, *I* will!"

"Now that we all understand each other," the man with the shotgun said, "let's get on with this. All of you: throw your guns over the fence." He nodded at a pile of prickly pear growing on the other side of the chain link. In there. *Now!*"

To Spook: "You. My camera. Pack it up and bring it over here."

Spook didn't like looking down the barrel of a 12 gauge, but he couldn't help but smile. Sure, he thought, I put you through the hoop back at the river and now you bring it back to me. Sure, but *you* only took shit for a couple of minutes. *I've* been taking it a lifetime. You're dealing with a veteran, cracker. "Fuck you," Spook said.

"For Chrissakes, Spook," Lenny pleaded, "do what the man -- "

"I ain't your nigger," Spook said to Lenny, "or this motherfucker's neither," and he nodded at the man with gun. "You want your camera, you get it."

Lenny was seething. "Shorty! Put up the goddamn camera!"

Shorty deferentially set the camera and tripod at Owen's feet and then took his place back in line.

"Now," the man with the gun said, "everybody lie down. Face down on the floor. Hands out. *Move!*"

Spook lay with his head sideways where he could see the other bikers. He heard shoes moving on the concrete floor and then saw the long, black barrel of the shotgun behind Lenny's head. The muzzle tickled the ends of Lenny's greasy hair and Lenny quivered. The shotgun moved behind Shorty's head and flipped the lobe of his ear.

"C'mon, mister," Shorty said, almost in a sob. "C'mon! We're sorry! *Please!*"

Then the gun was behind Porky's head. "Still think I'm bluffing?" the man said and the muzzle poked Porky in the roll of flesh at the back of his thick neck.

"Non*ono!*" Porky babbled.

Then the muzzle was on Spook's head, resting on the bone just behind his right ear. It wasn't cold steel; it was still warm from the two shots fired, and Spook blinked against the burning smell of powder.

"Beg me not to kill you," the man said quietly.

"Please, mister -- " Shorty began whining.

"*Shuddup!*" A grating scream.

Spook heard the rustle of clothing as the man leaned closer behind him.

"I want to hear *him* say it. I want to hear the nigger say, 'Please, mister, please don't kill me."

Spook closed his eyes. He didn't pray; he wasn't going to be a hypocrite now. Let 'em remember how you went out, he told himself. The fuckers take everything else away from you; they can't take *that.*

"Say it, nigger! *Say it you nigger son of a bitch!*"

The muzzle burrowed into Spook's skull so hard the concrete floor under him rubbed the flesh off his cheek.

"Fuck you!" Spook spat out. "*Fuck* you! G'ahead 'n' kill me ya white trash motherfucker peckerwood! *Do it!*"

Spook didn't know how long he lay there tensed and waiting for the flash and thunder, but then some of the other shooters from the range were standing over them, helping them to their feet.

"Where is he?" Lenny was screaming. *"Where is that prick?"*

"There!" somebody shouted.

They turned and saw the man on the other side of the fence, his shotgun in one hand, the camera and tripod in the other, climbing into a Winnebago in the parking lot.

"Mother*fucker!*" Lenny howled, like a war cry. He grabbed a rifle from one of the other shooters and ran for the gate, Porky and Shorty close behind him.

Spook didn't wait, flew at the fence, clambered to the top and leapt out far enough to clear the nest of prickly pear. His sore leg buckled under him when he landed, and he went down. Then he saw the bikes and sat back in the dust; it was over.

But the others didn't know it, yet.

The kid at the admission gate saw Lenny coming at him with the rifle in his hands and murder in his face and ducked down behind his counter. Lenny tossed off one shot, two, and Porky was beside him throwing stones at the camper, but the Winnebago was already out of the parking lot leaving a wake of spraying gravel and dust.

Porky had gone over to where their guns lay in the cactus. He tried to pick his pistol out from the flat, round stems, howled, pulling back a paw full of needles instead.

Lenny ran for his bike.

This, Spook thought, is gonna be good.

Lenny jumped on his kickstarter and wrenched the throttle to full. The Harley leapt ahead a few feet before it wobbled on its flat front tire and tumbled over.

"Fuckin' guy!" Porky was hollering. He was standing over the bikes looking down at their slashed front tires. *"Fuckin' guy!"*

Lenny was limping toward the highway, and Porky and Shorty followed. "You are a *dead man*, you fuckin' cock*suckin'* mother*fuckin'* -- " Lenny couldn't find an epithet that would quite do the job and fell back on a bear-like roar he let loose at the dwindling shape of the Winnebago.

Spook got to his feet and dusted off his jeans. You're right about that, Lenny, he thought. You're just wrong about who's going to do it.

The Corvette sat idling on the shoulder, just shy of the dusty drive that led from the road up to the house.

House. As a descriptive, the word was a joke, Rita thought. The gray, weathered planks came together in a sagging heap, a shack, the kind of place where people lived who had little, never had much, and never expected much more. Out front were a few rusting car hulks sitting on cinderblocks. An ancient pick-up truck sat near another sway-backed building; a small barn. On the other side of the house, wash hung limply in the still heat. On the porch was a refrigerator plugged into the house's only outlet mounted on the outside wall, alongside the old-fashioned kind of washing machine that had a wringer on top.

Sharecroppers, Rita said to herself. Lincoln hadn't freed the slaves; he'd just created the circumstances to disguise the arrangement.

There was a Black woman sitting on the porch; small, white-haired, tipping back and forth in her rocker, the afternoon sun glinting on her spectacles. The old woman gave no sign she was aware of the car; her rocker continued tilting back and forth with no break in its rhythm, like a flywheel, a regular, autonomic marker of time.

Rita fed a little gas into the engine and turned the Corvette up the drive, pulling to a stop in front of the shack. She let the dust kicked up by her tires pass before she climbed out of the car.

There was a low, pointless fence around the shack, made from the same kind of weather-beaten slats as the house. Rita walked to the fence, swung open the creaking gate and stood in the dry dirt of the front yard.

"Ah's wonderin' when you's gonna get 'roun' to it," the old woman said. Her face was crisscrossed with deep cracks, like sun-baked clay. "Coulda told ya no need a you a-comin' up here tryin' to sell me nuffin'. Ah ain't gots nuffin to buy nuffin *wit'*."

Rita wanted to move but the steps didn't come. She hadn't expected to freeze like that, or the tightness in her throat, the welling up in her chest, the sting in her eyes.

The old woman stopped rocking and leaned forward in her chair, the cracked face folding in concern. "Y'awright, honey?" she asked.

"Aunt Lizzy?"

The old woman squinted through the thick lenses of her glasses. "Wha's 'at ya say?"

"Aunt Lizzy. It's me." Then it came with a sob: "It's Rita Fay."

The old woman stood on her twiggish, bowed legs, put one of her thin, frail hands on the rotting banister. "*Who* ya say?"

"It's *me*, Aunt Lizzy. Rita Fay."

"Oh, Lawd…" The old woman wavered on her skinny legs, one hand reaching to touch her cheek, then she started moving toward the stairs, her legs stiff, but Rita was there first, her arms shooting around the bony little figure.

They held each other a long moment before the old woman pushed Rita away and put a finger to her smiling lips. "Willy?" she called out. "Hey, Willy? Better c'mon out heah!"

"What is it this time, woman?" came a deep, gravelly voice. "A man cain't have no peace lessen he -- " Then he was standing frozen in the shack's doorway. He was small and snow-topped, like his wife, and his shoulders were hunched from decades of planting and picking, but his arms were thick, sinewy. His small, dark eyes saw Rita and went wide. With a shocked slowness he stepped out onto the porch. "Rita Fay Scott?" His face slid into a smile. "Oh…" came a quiet, awed gasp. He stepped alongside his wife. "Ma, I thinks Ah sees a ghos'!"

Rita stepped forward. "Hello, Uncle Willy. How've you been?" and she held out a hand. The old man grabbed her hand in his two, calloused paws and pulled her toward him, lifting her in a crushing bear hug.

"Hello, Unka Willy she say like she jus' went off yesterday!" He planted a hard kiss on her cheek, his unshaved bristle burrowing deep into her soft skin.

"Careful, Willy!" Aunt Lizzy scolded. "Ya gonna break 'at li'l girl!"

"You don't break no Rita Fay Scott!" Uncle Willy declared. He finally let Rita down and chuckled watching her try to get her breath back. "See? She ready to go 'nother roun'!"

"Not quite yet," Rita gasped, smiling, and they all laughed.

They sat Rita down on the porch stairs. Aunt Lizzy had a jug of sun tea setting on the rail and poured them each a glass over ice from the fridge on the porch, and then they all sat together.

"Gettin' so we tooks ya fo' dead, chil'," Aunt Lizzy said. "Tweren't no word 'bout ya never. Figger sumpin' musta happen' to ya."

"Well, Ma, she don' look so dead to me!" Uncle Willy said. He pointed to the red Corvette. "Fack, she look like she done hit it right rich!"

Rita shook her head. "It's a rental, Uncle Willy. It's not mine."

He winked. "I bet ya got one like 'at at home, right, chil'? Where ya been, Rita Fay? After your mama pass, ya just disappear. We thought ya's gonna move in wif us. Ain't 'at right, Ma?"

"Leastways 'at was what we was hopin'," Aunt Lizzy said, ruefully. The nostalgic sadness of what hadn't happened passed quickly. "Ya stand up 'n' lemme see ya, Rita Fay! My, chil', ya is a sight for sore eyes! Willy, don' she look like she done step out dat ol' Montgomery Ward book?"

Uncle Willy smiled proudly. "Rita Fay, ya done come a long ways from 'at li'l pickaninny wif fourteen pigtail 'n' rag ribbons! Ya done finally fill out, too!"

Rita self-consciously ran a hand across her stomach. "Not too much, I hope."

"Ahh!" Aunt Lizzy said, dismissing Rita's concern. "Ah never seen no purtier girl 'roun' here. You, Willy?"

"Ya done good by yaself, chil'," Uncle Willy said. "Ya mama woulda been real proud."

"Ya stay 'n' eat wif us, right?" Aunt Lizzy asked.

Rita started to shake her head. "I don't know, Aunt Lizzy. I've got so much I need -- "

"I don' wanna hear no such thing from ya, chil'. Ya up''n' present yaself outta nowheres, y'ain't gonna tell me ya gotta disappear wifout sittin' down wit' us a bit."

"She ain't goin' nowhere," Uncle Willy said firmly. He stood up and dusted off the seat of his coveralls. "Ma, ya start fixin' some 'at good food like this girl ain't had since she left." He took Rita by the arm, heading around the back of the house. "Meantime, we's gonna pick us some fresh mint for 'at tea. C'mon, chil'."

Rita didn't resist. She felt giddy holding the old man's hard hand, her smile feeling permanent. "Whatever you say, Uncle Willy."

"We gonna go down 'at place down to 'at swimmin' hole where all y'all young uns usta play."

"Oh, Uncle Willy, is that still there?"

"Still there?" Uncle Willy's laugh rolled across the cotton rows stretching out in back of the house. "Honey, i's still got some a da same turtles in it!"

Hearing the voices on the other end of the phone, Billy Ray Barnes grimaced like a little boy in the waiting room of a dentist who hears a scream from the dentist's chair in the other room. Which was a singularly apt feeling, considering.

"Who?" he could hear a faint voice demand.

"Somebody from the Boone po-lice," a voice closer to the phone said.

"God*dammit!*" the other voice said. "Don't those knotheads know what a *vacation* is? It's not like I'm some goddamn heart surgeon or something! They have to bother *me?* Why don't they hound that senile old coot Weed?"

"I don't know, Horace. Why don't ya ask 'im. He's still on the line."

"They can stay on that goddamn line from now until fucking *doomsday!* I manage to unload Della and the brood on her mother-in-law so I can have a few days peace and quiet -- "

"Horace, why don't you just talk to the fella and see what he wants? Maybe it's nothing."

"Those assholes wouldn't be bothering me if it was nothing!"

"Horace, talk to the man, goddammit, elsewise they're just gonna keep calling and calling and -- "

"All right all *right!* Give me the goddamn thing!"

While Billy Ray was waiting on the phone, the office door swung open and there was a depleted-looking Clyde Thomas, his red face streaming sweat. Billy Ray waved, Clyde barely nodded an acknowledgment. Clyde cocked his head, listening in, and Billy Ray clarified the matter by covering up the mouthpiece and whispering, "Greenley." Clyde nodded approvingly. Billy Ray nodded back, gave an A-OK sign followed by an emphatic thumbs-up to assure Clyde that operations were well in hand and that this was the new, efficient, and obedient Billy Ray Barnes on the job. To which Clyde rolled his eyes and went into the bathroom to throw cold water on his face.

The phone rattled and Dr. Horace Greenley, D.D.S. came on the phone. He didn't say, "Hello." What he said was, "Who the hell is this? How'd y'all find me? Ya know, I just *got* here and -- "

"Well, sir, your message service -- "

"Goddamn *morons*..." Greenley seethed.

" -- told me where ya could be reached in a emergency, so -- "

"This goddamn well *better* be an emergency. Did you say who the hell you are?"

"Officer Billy Ray Barnes with the Boone Po-lice."

"Big woo."

"Doctor -- "

"Barnes? Which one are you? You that skinny fella makes me always waste stamps telling you it's time for your check-up and you never come?"

"Um -- "

"C'mon, Officer Barnes, what the hell do you *want?* You're using up my valuable vacation time!"

"Well, Doc, it's about Sarah Dawson."

"The minister's wife?"

"Yessir. Were you her dentist?"

There was a pause, and Billy Ray was sure he heard a pained sigh. "You didn't call me all the way up here to take a goddamn census, did you, Barnes?"

"Mrs. Dawson's missin', Doc. Maybe kilt."

The line went silent. Another sigh. "Sorry," though he sounded more impatient than sorry. "What do you want from me?"

"Well, Doc, we need a positive ID on a body. See, we got a body might be hers, 'n' it was in a fire 'n' -- "

"You've gotta be kidding."

"No, Doc, I found the body myself -- "

"Not about *that*, ya moron! You know how long I've been planning this trip?"

"Doc -- "

"Nine months! *Nine goddamn months!* You know what I had to go through to get my wife to agree *not* to come with me? She thinks when you're married, you're joined at the hip! This is gonna cost me a new Lincoln for that woman, you know that?"

"I'm sorry, Doc, but -- "

"Look, the poor lady's dead, right? I'm sorry 'n' all that, but she's certainly not going anywhere! This can wait'll I get back next week. It's going to *have* to wait'll I get back because I'm not going *anywhere* until I bag me a wild pig! You understand, Barnes?"

Clyde Thomas was back at his desk, his head in his hands, and Billy Ray thought he looked awfully tired. Then Clyde humphed, pulled the phone close and punched in a number. Billy Ray overheard him say, "Yeah, darlin', is Sheriff Bowen there?...Yeah, hey, Walt, it's Clyde Thomas over to Boone..."

"I said do you read me, Barnes?"

Billy Ray sat up in his chair. Dr. Horace Greenley was allowed all the disrespect in the world for the dead he wanted to show; it was a free country. But you couldn't just tell off The Badge that way. No, sir! "Dr. Greenley," Billy Ray said, forcing his voice down into what he thought was a more authoritarian range, "we maybe got us a *murder* here! If I gotta get Judge Ellis to issue me a search warrant so I can root 'roun' in your office myself, by golly I'm gonna do it! 'N' *you're* gonna be the one picks up after!" A pause. Billy Ray pushed more gently: "Look, Doc, it'll only take you five minutes."

"Yeah," Greenley said, "five minutes and a two-hour drive each way! Look, Barnes, let's call it first thing Monday morning, ok? Give me just a few days -- "

Billy Ray smirked; he had Greenley on the run. "Sorry, Doc, no can do. I need to see ya back here A.S.A.P. or we go into your office without ya soon's I get 'at warrant."

The phone was silent, again. Billy Ray heard the other voice go, "What's the matter, Horace?"

"This jackass is jerking me around by my nuts is what's the matter."

While Greenley mulled it over, Billy Ray caught bits and pieces of Clyde's conversation with the Boone County sheriff, heard him say something about the body at Boone General, some unkind words about His Honor Mayor Fred C. Reilly, then, "So I guess she's all yours, pard," followed by chatter about Dawson, a physical description, and then information about Dawson's newly acquired Winnebago.

"Ok, Barnes," Greenley finally said, "I'm on my way."

"Thanks, Doc."

Bowen must've said something of great interest to Clyde because Clyde sat up, and his tired face suddenly grew very sharp. "Where's that, again?" Clyde asked, then, with phone in hand, he went over to the Boone County map on the wall. "Byrum's, a few miles south of Lovelady? But nobody got the tag numbers on the vehicle? Might be him, Walt, sure *sounds* like 'im, but I'll be damned if I could tell you what he's up to or where he's goin'. Lemme know if you get anythin' else, ok?" Then Clyde hung up his phone and stood staring at the map.

"Barnes? *Barnes!*"

Billy Ray re-focused on Greenley. "Yeah, Doc?"

"You better pray to God you never wind up in my chair after this."

"It looks like it got smaller."

Uncle Willy laughed. "More's like *you* gots *bigger!*"

The creek curled along the edge of the cotton field, at the bottom of a deep cut in the red clay, supporting a line of cypress trees on either bank keeping the water in sun-dappled shade. Rita and her Uncle Willy stood at the top of the bank over a spot where the creek widened into a shallow pool of clear water.

"I remember not being able to touch the bottom," Rita said, "of being scared to death I could drown out there. I could probably walk right across it now."

"Mos' likely," Uncle Willy said. He found himself a comfortable tuft of grass against a chair back-sized rock and sat down.

Rita kicked off her shoes and walked down the cool clay to the water. She stuck her toes in. "Mmmmm, warm."

"She never did run too deep or too fas', but a day like today, she feel good."

"She feels good," Rita said.

"You 'member when your mama would bring ya here 'n' ya'd go swimmin' wif 'at Randy boy? Li'l bit a hellfire 'at one. Never walk nowhere. Run here, run there. He had a sof' heart for ya, child."

Rita's toes flicked at the water. "Uncle Willy, we were twelve years old."

"How ol' y'all gots to be? Married your Aunt Lizzy when we wa'n't much older! Been wif her this whole time."

Rita started back up the cut. "Oh, my God…" Smiling, she ran to a tree halfway up the bank. An old tire hung from a branch by a frayed length of rope. She gave the tire a push and it arced out over the water. She remembered a twelve-year-old girl with fourteen pigtails and rag ribbons in her hair swinging out over the swimming hole and letting herself slip out of the tire, a moment of joyous, screaming flight, and then the roar of splashing water in her ears.

She walked up to the trunk of the tree. There was a crudely carved heart in the bark, and inside the bark the rough-hewn letters: RETA + RANDE.

She wandered back to her uncle. He slid over, making room for her to sit alongside him against the rock. There was a hollow in the stone that perfectly fit the back of her head, and she lay back and closed her eyes, nestled close against the old man.

"Ya know," Uncle Willy said quietly, "I t'ought ya's auntie's heart gonna bus' when she saw ya. Gots to admit; t'ought mine's gonna bus', too."

"I have to admit something, too, Uncle Willy. I wasn't going to come here. I had to come out to Texas for my job, but… Every time I looked at a map to find out where I had to go, there was Pennington poking me in the eye. But I didn't want to come."

"But ya did."

Rita chuckled wryly. "Yep, I did. I don't know why. I thought that part of my life was all over and done with. I wanted it to be."

"Don' work like 'at, child," Uncle Willy said. "All a time, ya is everythin' ya allus was. Ya got nuffiin' to be 'shame' of. Lookit ya!"

"Yeah. Look at me."

"Oh, your mama be proud if she was here! I knows Ma's proud. *I'm* proud! We wanted ya to stay wif us when your mama pass, but nuffin' wrong wif goin' off 'n' makin' sumpin' a yaself. Believe me, chil', lots better things to be 'n' a nigger sharecropper spendin' ya life scratchin' 'roun' inna dirt. Just lookit ya! Look what ya done for yourself!"

"Yeah, look what I've done for myself," she said heavily. "Oh, Uncle Willy." She opened her eyes, smiled, but it was a wry, self-mocking smile. "Look at me. What do you see? Aunt Lizzy's right; I'm right out of a Montgomery Ward catalogue. If there was still a Montgomery Ward catalogue and it covered Rodeo Drive and The Galleria. I've got the nice clothes, and a nice place to live, I know the good restaurants and the right wine to order when I'm in them, and when I'm home, I have a trainer who helps me keep all the parts in the right places. But you know what? I'm still just a nigger digging in the dirt."

. He studied the pain in her face, and his eyes narrowed in study. "Whatcha come back to see, chil'?"

She shook her head, not knowing. "I guess I was afraid to come back because then I'd find out I really haven't come so far. Then once I *did* come out…I had to know. So I came. Now I know."

"C'mon." Uncle Willy stood and held out one of his calloused hands to her, easily pulled her to her feet. He put an arm around her shoulders and kissed her on the cheek. "Ya go get them fine shoes a yours, 'n' let's go get 'at mint. Your Aunt Lizzy skin me a-live iffen I forget it."

She picked up her shoes and followed him along the bank until she could smell the mint in the air.

"You 'member what it look like?" Uncle Willy asked. "Think ya can still find it yaself?"

Rita smiled at the challenge. She wandered through the brush along the bank until she saw the familiar white petals. For a brief moment, she was twelve, again, sent out for mint by her aunt to grace jelly glasses filled with sun tea, and she felt a happy lightness.

She walked with her uncle back across the fields, between the cotton rows toward the shack, her shoes under one arm and her face buried in a bouquet of mint she carried in her other hand.

"Where ya livin' now?" the old man asked.

"Los Angeles."

"'A's in California, right?"

"Right."

"They grow any mint there?"

She shrugged. "I don't know."

They cleared the stalks of cotton and Willy took her by the hand as they walked across the clear ground toward the house. "Maybe ya do yaself some good growin' some."

The street was narrow and quiet and cool under the canopy offered by the elms along either curb. The noises of the day were rarely more than those of children playing on front lawns, the hum of air conditioners and fans, the *fit-fit-fit* of lawn sprinklers, the burble of daytime TV heard through window screens. The houses were small and neat, painted in soft pastels like faded pink and powder blue and sea green. The lawns were well-watered, well-edged squares.

Every time Billy Ray Barnes drove down that street, he hoped for the day when he could live there, or at least on a street like it. He would like one of those small, neat houses, maybe something with that powder blue vinyl siding he could just powerwash clean. Maybe on the lawn he'd have one of those little lampposts with the name "Barnes" in gothic script hanging from it on a shingle. Maybe he'd live in the house with somebody like Arva May, and she'd be waiting for him every night with a cool can of Coors in one hand and a frosty mug in the other, and the TV would already be tuned to *Wheel of Fortune*.

There'd be a boat parked in the driveway, a nice 14-footer he could take down to Lake Livingston on Saturdays, and next to the boat would be a fire engine red SUV, or maybe a new pick-up, or maybe, well, a fire engine red *anything,* just so it wouldn't make him feel stupid and out of place the way he felt in his patrol car with its wake of blue smoke and knocking engine and body rot. Every time Billy Ray rolled down that street in his patrol car, he felt like eyes were peeping around the edges of curtains at him, that people were pointing at him and laughing.

Billy Ray almost kept going past Arva May's house when he saw Arva May's mother sitting out on her front porch. She was a frog-faced woman, eyes huge behind thick-lensed glasses, a wide mouth with thin lips always pursed. She was wearing a flowered housecoat, and her gray-streaked hair was tucked up in curlers under a hairnet. She was sitting on a lawn chair shelling peas over a large pot. Every time Billy Ray came down that street, he hoped Mrs. Arlin would be off somewhere in the back of the house, in the backyard, captured by UFOs...any place but *there*.

Billy Ray took a deep, firming breath and turned into the driveway of Arva May's house. He turned the ignition off and reddened as the engine clunked along for a few more cycles before it died with a gasp and a final, ugly puff of blue smoke out the exhaust. He forced on a polite smile and climbed out.

"Howdy, Miz Arlin."

"Hope 'at heap don't drip no oil," she said in an inhospitable flat drone. "Just had the driveway redone 'n' sealed 'n' ya drip oil on it 's gonna mess it up all over agin." She looked up briefly, just enough to get a glimpse of him in his wrinkled uniform and made no attempt to hide a disappointed sigh as she went back to her peas. "You could go into the fumigatin' business with 'at pile a scrap."

"Yes'm, I believe I rightly could." He stood at the bottom of the front stairs passing the brim of his Stetson through his hands. "Is Arva May -- "

"Gonna have to rinse these peas extra good just to get all 'at oil smoke off 'em."

"Sorry about that, Miz Arlin. I was wonderin' -- "

"Whatcha doin' in uniform?"

"'Scuse me, ma'am?"

"I heard Clyde Thomas bounced your patootie outta there yesterday."

Billy Ray's red face grew a little redder. "Well, 'at was just a li'l misunderstandin'. I'm back on duty -- "

"If you're on duty, whatcha doin' here 'steada off catchin' criminals 'n' savin' lives 'n' such?"

"I don't go on 'til four today, ma'am. Factually, I was just on my way over to the station 'n' thought I'd stop -- "

"Stop by 'n' flirt with my li'l girl."

Billy Ray was flushing so hotly he thought he'd melt into his khakis. They oughta send this ol' cow down to that Guantanamo, he thought. She'd break down those A-rab terrorists in about five minutes if she grilled them the way she always grilled him when he came by.

"Sure wisht ya'd put as much energy into findin' my Jesse as ya do in comin' over here to get all moony over my li'l girl."

Billy Ray swallowed hard. "Findin' your...?"

Arva May's mother put down her peas, sat back in her chair, and fixed him with gray eyes so light it often looked like she barely had eyes at all. "How come it is I gotta find out from my daughter 'at Jess's missin' from 'at zoo Henry Gilmore runs over to Grapeland?"

"Uh -- "

"Ya can tell Clyde Thomas to tell his friend Henry Gilmore that when my sister June Louise's done with 'im, his mama won't be able to identify the remains! 'N' when her *lawyer's* done with 'im, Henry Gilmore won't have a pair a BVDs left to call his own! 'N' if somethin' *happens* to Jess? I don't even wanna *think* 'bout what's gonna happen to Henry Gilmore! Give ya nightmares just *talkin'* 'bout it." And she shuddered to emphasize the point.

Not knowing what to say – or even if he was supposed to say anything – Billy Ray fidgeted at the bottom of the stairs. "Uh, Miz Arlin, speakin' a Arva May -- "

"It's not like I speck much better when y'all can't even figger out Sarah Dawson's murder."

Billy Ray cleared his throat authoritatively and drew himself up straight. "Well, now, ma'am, seein' 's we don't have a positive identification on those remains, we have to list the body as a Jane Doe -- . Say, how'd ya know 'bout us findin' a -- "

Arva May's mother shook her head, as if Billy Ray never ceased to amaze her, and not in a positive way. She turned those pale, goggle eyes on him and Billy Ray felt like he was being studied under a microscope. His straight posture wilted as those big, blurry orbs looked him up and down the way they did on his every visit, then she sighed and went back to her peas. "Everybody 'n' their dog knows ya got 'at burnt-up body up there to Boone General, an everybody 'n' their dog knows who it is 'n' who done it. 'Ceptin' maybe you 'n' Clyde Thomas for God knows what-all reason. Land, no wonder there's mass murderers walkin' a streets -- "

"Momma, you tormentin' Billy Ray, again?" Arva May said as she pranced out onto the porch, much to Billy Ray's relief. She was wearing a pink dress cut low and high in the right places. Billy Ray gulped at the sight and thought, Yep, I wouldn't mind seeing that standing in the doorway every night with my frosty mug and a can of Coors.

"Ain't tormentin' nobody," Mrs. Arlin said. "Just makin' conversation with Sherlock Holmes here. Ain't 'at right, Sherlock?"

"Uh -- "

Mrs. Arlin looked up at her daughter, tsk-tsked over her dress, and shook her head over her new hairstyle, a wild tangle of tendrils. "Don't know why ya'd go off 'n' do somethin' like 'at. This ain't Paris, France, ya know. Billy Ray, I'm surprised at you lettin' her do her head up like 'at."

"I didn't -- "

"C'mon, Sweet Billy," Arva May said, bouncing down the stairs and looping her arm in his. "You got time for a walk 'fore you have to go off to work, dontcha?"

"Hold on a minute, li'l girl," Mrs. Arlin called. "I'll probably be in back cookin' when ya gets back 'n' I know ya'll be off with them dizzy girlfriends a yours, so come gimme a kiss now case I don't see ya later."

Billy Ray turned to watch Arva May trot back to her mother not because he had a sentimental spot for mother-daughter moments but because the rear view on Arva May was just as good as the front view. Arva May stood at the bottom of the stairs as her mother leaned over to receive a peck on the cheek. When Arva May turned she was surprised to find Billy Ray right beside her and a bit disturbed to see that he was staring slack-jawed at the little bit of cleavage peeping out of her mother's housedress.

"Billy Ray, what're you gawkin' at?"

Billy Ray passed a sleeve across his damp forehead and leaned in closer.

"Someday, li'l girl, me 'n' you gotta have a talk 'bout some a these boyfriends ya bring over," Mrs. Arlin said.

"Billy Ray!" Arva May said, tugging at Billy Ray's sleeve. "Would you stop that!"

But Billy Ray didn't stop. His hand came up, slowly folded leaving the index finger extended pointing at the gold chain around Mrs. Arlin's neck that had slipped out of her collar when she'd leaned over to take her daughter's kiss. At the end of that chain, sitting in the wrinkled gully between Mrs. Arlin's two flaccid breasts, was a small, gold cross.

"Ya like whatcha see?" Mrs. Arlin said dryly.

"It's just this *cross*…"

"I'll bet," said Mrs. Arlin.

"'At cross… Where'd ya get that cross?" He turned to Arva May. "Where'd she get that cross?"

"I bought it for her," Arva May said.

"You?…Where…?"

"Gypsy Spurlock."

"Who?"

"'Member I told you all 'bout 'at sweet ol' crazy person comes by Mr. Gilmore's every week to sell things to the ol' folks? Gypsy Spurlock? Well, Miz Gypsy had a whole slew a these necklaces 'n' -- "

"Whole slew?"

"Miz Gypsy says it's one a her most popular items."

Billy Ray started feeling woozy and reached out for the stair railing. "It looks like the one we found on Sarah Dawson," he said feebly.

"Don'tcha mean Miz Jane Doe?" Mrs. Arlin jibed.

"'That's what I was thinkin' when I bought it," Arva May bubbled on. "I thought, well, don't they just look like 'at pretty li'l cross mama 'n' a church ladies bought for Miz Sarah when she 'n' a reverend first come to town? I always thought that was a prettiest li'l thing, but I could never afford one like 'at, what with real gold 'n' all -- "

Billy Ray sat down on the stairs.

"I don't usually go in for this kinda cheap jewelry," Mrs. Arlin said. "I only wear it 'cause my li'l girl bought it."

"Oh, Mama!" Arva May frowned. "Can't you ever say anything nice?"

"I like ya got it for me, li'l girl, but a truth is the truth. I wear it, don't I?"

Arva May ignored her mother in the easy way of one well-practiced in so doing and turned to a peaked-looking Billy Ray. "You ok, Sweet Billy?"

Billy Ray groaned.

"You don't look so good, sweetie," Arva May said, concerned.

"Ya done lookin' at my titties now?" Mrs. Arlin said. "It's not as flatterin' as y'all might think."

Somehow, Billy Ray found the strength to pull himself up by the railing to his feet and turned to Mrs. Arlin.

"Ya come back for a second peek?" Mrs. Arlin said. "We're closed," and she tucked her cross back inside her housedress.

"I gotta use your phone, Mrs. Arlin. Please, ma'am."

"Ya know where it is," Mrs. Arlin said, unimpressed by the look of urgency on Billy Ray's face. As Billy Ray passed to the back of the house, he could still hear Mrs. Arlin: "It's bad enough, Arva May, I gotta sit here 'n' watch some a these goobers get all big-eyed when ya come switchin' out here showin' all your bidness, but when they start pracally jumpin' down a front a *my* dress -- "

"Mama!"

Billy Ray went to the kitchen at the back of the Arlin house, as far away as he could from what he assumed would be the eavesdropping ears of Arva May's mother. There was a cordless wall phone in the kitchen which Billy Ray took out onto the back porch for even more privacy. It took Billy Ray a while to get Barney White on the phone because the medical examiner's office didn't answer, and when Billy Ray tried Barney White at home, Barney White didn't want to come to the phone because, according to his wife, he was standing over a barbecue with a set of flank steaks and once Barney White had set himself at the barbecue nothing short of the North Koreans landing in Galveston Bay could pull him away. But then Mrs. White got peeved ferrying messages between Billy Ray on the phone and her husband out on the patio and finally Billy Ray heard Mrs. White saying, "Barney, you take this damn phone *now* before I stick you you-know-where with that barbecue fork!"

Barney White took the phone with obvious displeasure. "Goddammit, Billy Ray, you better have a damn good reason to be botherin' people in their homes! I got myself home early just so I could enjoy watchin' them steaks brown up -- "

"I got a damn good reason awright, Barney," Billy Ray said. "That cross y'all got off the Jane Doe..."

"Yeah? What 'bout it?"

"Is it real gold?"

"What?"

"Is it real gold?"

"How the hell do I know? I'm just the ME, Billy Ray. You want a jeweler, you're gonna have to -- "

"Where is it, Barney?"

"Where's *what?*"

"The *cross!*"

"It's -- . Hold on a sec, Billy Ray." Then Billy Ray could hear Barney's voice away from the phone: "Hey, Hon? You want to flip those over now?

No, no, no, that's how they're *supposed* to look! Would you just turn 'em over like I ask?" He came back on the phone. "Lemme give you some advice, Billy Ray. You ever want to ruin a barbecue, let a woman poke 'round the grill. They got absolutely *no* aptitude! If it's not a stove with an electric timer -- "

"Barney, the cross! The one from the Jane Doe! Where -- "

"Oh, yeah, well, it's with all the rest a her effects down to my office."

"Could you tell if it was made a real gold?"

"Sure, easy. If Clyde had asked when we brought the body in -- "

"I'm askin' *now*, Barney!"

"Jesus, Billy Ray, I'm not goin' back to the office! Not *now!* When I close those doors, those doors are *closed*, understand?"

"Well then ya better open 'em up, Barney, or I'm gonna come on over to your house 'n' drag ya on back to the hospital!"

"Your mayor told me to keep my hands off -- "

"I don't care *what* a mayor told you, Barney! *I'm* tellin' ya I want ya back up to the hospital to tell me if 'at cross is real gold or not!"

There was a pause and Billy Ray could practically hear Barney seething on the other end of the phone, then, "All *right!* But *after* dinner!"

"Barney -- "

"I'm gonna finish grillin' up my steaks 'n' bakin' my potatoes 'n' what-all, I'm gonna *have* my dinner, 'n' *then* I'll meet you at my office, 'n' be happy you got *that* much compromise outta me! Now; you mind tellin' me what's got you so fired up 'bout this you gotta pester me after hours?"

"What it is, Barney, is I got a dentist comin' down as we speak to look at the teeth in 'at body, 'n' 'tween what he says 'n' you tellin' me if 'at's a gold cross or not, I'm gonna have a name on 'at body by tonight!"

The filling station sat off the highway on a flat, baking bed of black tar. The only shade outside the garage was a small canopy over the pumps and a crooked cottonwood sheltering the two-dollars-a-blast air pump.

Spook and Porky had parked their bikes under the cottonwood tree, Porky having found a way to arrange his bulk in a precariously balanced reclining position along the spine of his bike. Spook, on the other hand, was not relaxing.

Spook looked through the wavering heat coming off the blacktop to the service bays where Porky was rifling through his pockets to come up with enough crumpled bills to pay the garage man. Porky nodded a sour thanks at the grinning mechanic, then walked his Harley across the blacktop on its new front tire into the little scrap of shade.

"Wha's 'at leave you with?" Spook asked Porky.

"I don't think I got enough to buy any a this fuckin' air," Porky grumbled, nodding at the air pump.

"You 'n' me both," Shorty said. He sat up on his bike, his face opening with enlightenment as he stared at the air pump. "Jeez, now *there's* one smart fucker, boy! Guy who thought *'at* fuckin' thing up? Sellin' air? *Air?* What kinda dude thinks *'at* stuff up?" He pondered the thought a moment, then said, "Don't seem right, though, does it? Y'all gotta pay for fuckin' *air?* Fuckin' country's fucked up, man. I mean, what's this country comin' to y'all gotta pay for air?"

Porky didn't care what the country was coming to. He was more worried about what his personal finances were coming to. "Fuckin' tires, man," he said, "they just 'bout tapped me out. I ever find 'at fuckin' guy..."

"Get in line," Spook said. He turned to sit sidesaddle on his bike. Even in the shade the tar felt soft under the heels of his boots. He pointed toward the men's room at the back of the garage building. "You know what's gonna happen when he comes outta there?"

Porky and Shorty looked at each other for clues. They didn't have any.

"He's gonna have his dick in his hands?" Porky tried with a snorting laugh.

"He's gonna come outta there 'n' he's gonna go for his bike 'n' he's gonna look at us 'n' he's gonna say, 'Pay the man.' He's gonna say, '*Pay*-thee-man.' He *always* tells *us* to pay the man."

Abstract reasoning not being a strong suit for Porky and Shorty, they missed Spook's point. "And?" Porky prompted.

Spook sighed. It's your own fault, he said. Should've known better than to try to be subtle with these guys. "He's fuckin' with us, man. He's *been* fuckin' with us all along."

Porky and Shorty frowned, not so much because they thought Spook might be telling them the truth, but because if he *was* telling the truth, they now had to consider options, and that was more brainwork than they were used to.

"We been shellin' out for his eats, his booze, his dope, even his broads, 'n' now his fuckin' tires!" Spook said.

"He sprung for the gun range," Shorty said.

"Let's not bring 'at up," Porky said. "Look how that turned out!"

"'S what I'm sayin'," Spook said. "'S all his big ideas got us sittin' here with slashed tires! 'N' now we're bust, right?"

"Or close to it," Porky said.

"So," Shorty said, "you're sayin'…" Spook could tell Shorty wanted Spook to finish the thought because that would, in some bizarre Shorty-stupid kind of way, take the culpability away from Shorty.

"I'm sayin' let's cut outta here *now* while we still got a few bucks for gas to get outta here *with!* Maybe hit a couple those stores down the highway for grocery money. I grew up 'round here, it don't look like much's changed. You don't have to go far to find easy pickin's on this road."

Shorty and Porky frowned again.

Spook slid his one leg over the top of his bike and jumped down on the kickstarter. The Harley growled and vibrated to life. "The time to go is *now!*" he said with an urgent look back at the men's room. Then the bathroom door opened, and Lenny came out, still tugging at his pants' zipper. "Shit…" Spook sighed.

Lenny saw Spook on his bike, the engine running, and paused. Then he smiled that peculiarly threatening smile of his. He knows, Spook thought.

"Hey, bros, what's comin' down? My bike ready? Hey, Porky!"

Porky studied his boots. "Still workin' on it."

Lenny slapped Porky on the back and Porky winced. Lenny walked over to Shorty and slapped *him* on the back and Shorty winced. "Y'all look like y'all got a little powwow goin'." Lenny looked to Spook. "You leadin' the powwow, li'l chief?"

Spook didn't turn away, but stared back and goosed the throttle of his bike, revving the engine to a low roar.

Lenny put an arm around Shorty's shoulder in a friendly way that was anything but friendly. "'S goin' on, Short-man?"

"W-well, Lenny, uh, Spook here was jus' sayin', well, ya know, jus' talkin'…"

"That's right!" Porky said in enthusiastic confirmation. "Jus' talkin'! Ya know, bullshittin' 'roun'! No harm done."

"Well, nothin' wrong with 'at," Lenny said. "Right, Spook? Nothin' wrong with a li'l conversation 'tween my buds, right? My *amigos?*"

Spook didn't flinch. He'd known that when it came down to any kind of face-off, he'd be facing Lenny alone. "Tired payin' all a bills, Len."

Lenny turned to Shorty whom he was still holding tight and close and gave his shoulders a squeeze. "That so, Shorty? Y'all think the same thing?"

Shorty twitched his head, shrugged his shoulders, and mumbled something unintelligible.

"It's just, uh, well," Porky stumbled, "ya know, Len, we're pretty low, all of us, 'n', well, we keep goin' in our pockets 'n' now there's almos' nothin' left."

"Yeah," Shorty squeaked, "'s all we're sayin', man. We're broke. This tire money killed us."

Lenny nodded in agreement. He clapped his hands together, as if that proclaimed the end of the emergency, then went and leaned against the trunk of the tree where he could face the three of them.

"Hey, bros, I understand. Shit, I'd feel a same way I was in y'all's boots. Hey," and he laughed, "I *am* in y'all's boots! I'm tapped, too! But now, if any y'all're gettin' antsy, y'all wanna split, fine, I'm cool with 'at. 'S a free country. I can always find me more partners. Jus' lemme know where y'all're at, ok?"

The reasonableness of his tone left Porky and Shorty feeling guilty. "Well, it ain't 'at, Lenny," Porky said shamefacedly.

"We don't want to break up or nothin'," Shorty said. "We're family, man, right? Ain't 'at what y'always tellin' us?"

Lenny turned to Spook. "'S right, ain't it, bro? We're all family, right?"

Spook told himself the sensible thing to do, right then, right *now,* would be to drop the bike into gear and scream out of the station. That would have been the smart move.

Which he didn't take.

He rationalized it telling himself Lenny would've led the other two after him, riding him down, just to prove the boss was still the boss and you didn't cross the boss.

But the truth of it, which he didn't like to face, was he didn't want to be a nigger alone on a bike deep in Texas. He'd grown up here, knew that was a bucket of shit he didn't want to be in. No, they weren't family, but they were all he had. Heavenly bodies.

He killed his engine, gave an acceding shrug.

Lenny gave him a pat on the shoulder that said Welcome Home, but the look in his eye was more like, One day you and I are going to get down to it, bro.

"Say, uh, Lenny," Porky said, "Spook had this idea."

"Yeah? Spook, bro, you had an *idea?*"

"I get 'em once in a while."

"You shouldn't get so many. Some of 'em can get you into trouble. What was this one?"

"Well," Porky began, "Spook says he knows this road, 'n' he thought maybe we could hit a couple these convenience places. Ya know; for a li'l cash money."

"Hm."

"Says're kinda easy to hit," Shorty said.

"Hm."

"I mean, like, I don't think I got 'nough money to coat a bottom a my tank, Len," Porky said.

Lenny smiled, put his arm around Spook's shoulders. "Now *that* particular idea is a *good* one! Not like some a those other ones y'all might be havin'." Lenny stepped into the middle of them, his hands raised out, his face beaming. "We do it together, right, bros? The whole family?" He turned to Spook. "Right?"

Spook looked down at the ground, a little sick with himself. "Yeah, Len. One for all. The whole fucking family."

Lenny laughed. "Good."

The garage man whistled from the door of one of the service bays. "Hey, chief!" he called. "This last bike's ready to roll!"

Lenny slapped Spook on the back and started cheerfully across the blacktop toward the garage. "Wind 'em up, boys!" he called back over his shoulder. "Y'all heard the man! Ready to roll! Hey, somebody dig down deep 'n' pay this fella!"

When Bob Wheeler had signed off on Smitty McKee's plans for the office addition he was going to hang off the side of his garage, it had certainly seemed roomy enough laid out on blueprint paper. And Smitty had sure made "one hundred and fifty square feet" *sound* like a lot of room, especially when he said, "square feet" in an excited verbal italic. But after Bob had got his desk in there, and a few file cabinets and a few chairs, his office started feeling like something out of a submarine movie. Especially when he had clients. Like now.

Squeezed into the narrow space across from him, their knees practically touching each other's as well as the front of his desk, was a young couple. The "he" was maybe a little short of being halfway through his twenties, self-conscious about sitting there in grease-stained coveralls, trying to dig the grime out from under his fingernails when he thought Bob wasn't looking. The "she" was a few years younger, wearing a faded, flowered smock kind of thing that didn't quite cover all of her very, very pregnant belly. Bob was shuffling forms and copies of forms back and forth between them to get their signatures.

"I know it's a kinda thing I'm supposed to say," Bob Wheeler said with practiced sincerity, "but I mean it; y'all won't come up on a better investment for a future family member."

Young Daddy-To-Be shrugged, uncomfortable. "Maybe, yeah, but it feels funny buyin' insurance for a baby. 'Specially one ain't come yet."

"I know," Bob said.

"Almost makes me 'fraid a jinxin' the baby."

"Hush, Vern!" Mama-To-Be admonished. "Talkin' like *'at'*ll jinx the baby!" and she put an arm protectively around her tummy.

"Everybody says a same thing," Bob said assuringly. "But when 'at li'l fella -- " and here he smiled respectfully at Mama-To-Be " – or li'l gal is ready to go to Texas U. -- "

"Austin," Mama-To-Be said, hugging her baby-to-be with both arms.

Bob smiled and nodded in concession, " – or Austin, 'at policy's gonna be comin' up on maturity and it'll pay his – or her – way. Leastways a good bit of it. That'll be a right big load off your mind for the next twenty – whoops! Excuse me."

He picked up his ringing phone. Mrs. Bob Wheeler was on the other end of the line. Bob could peek over the top of the air conditioner mounted in the window behind him and see Mrs. Wheeler waving and smiling at him from the house's kitchen window. He waved and smiled back.

"Dinner's almost ready, Bob," she said into the phone. "Is that your last appointment?"

"You start settin' a table," he said. "I won't be but a few more minutes." He made a kissing face at her through the window and hung up.

"Sorry, Mr. Wheeler," Mama-To-Be said. "We all didn't mean to keep you."

"No problem," Bob said.

"This was a only time we could both get over here," Daddy-To-Be said. "Eunice goes on at the mill for second shift 'n' I don't get off at the shop 'til -- "

Bob held up his hands. "Never y'all mind 'bout 'at. Folks, y'all need to understand; I'm here to help *y'all! I* work for *y'all!* If y'all ever have a need to ask a question, or y'all got some worries, I don't want y'all thinking, 'Well, gee, maybe we better not disturb ol' Mr. Wheeler.' 'S my job. 'Sides," and he smiled with a warmth as well-practiced and polished as his sincerity, "I feel good when I get a chance to help young folks like y'all just startin' out. To me, 'at's worth me spendin' a time. All 'at call was was my li'l lady lookin' after my welfare. Twenty years from now, if y'all still got 'at kinda lookin' out for t'other 'tween y'all, well, 's the best y'all can ask for."

Mama-To-Be and Daddy-To-Be held hands for a moment. "I guess," Daddy-To-Be said and Mama-To-Be blushed in agreement.

Bob took the signed papers back, gave them a quick look-over, and started his countersigning. "So, you still workin'?" he asked Mama-To-Be.

"Oh, yeah," she sighed.

"I told her to stay home," Daddy-To-Be said defensively.

"But we need the money," Mama-To-Be said, "'specially now. All a things ya gotta get for a baby! You have children, Mr. Wheeler?"

"We were never blessed, sad to say."

"'S ok, though. I knew this woman up to the mill? She worked right up 'til a week 'fore she dropped 'n' it didn't seem to bother her too much. Fact, she said it made her good 'n' strong for the delivery!"

Bob finished his signing and handed the couple their copies. "Well, like I said, an investment like this takes care a some a those worries. 'Bout money 'n' your future 'n' the future a the li'l one. Congratulations, folks, 'n' good luck."

They all smiled and shook hands and Bob walked them out to a nearly-new Ford pick-up that Daddy-To-Be had probably spent more on than he should've. Bob stood by the curb waving goodbye until the pick-up disappeared around the corner.

He went back to his office and left the door open to clear out the smell of garage oil and sweat the young man had left behind, then filed away his copy of the contract, turned off the air conditioner and office light, and turned back to the open door…

And didn't move.

He glanced quickly at his watch: some time after 4:30.

He closed the door, sat back in his chair, turned on his desk lamp, reached for his phone and dialed the Boone Police Department. He told the officer who answered who he was, said that this was the fourth time he was calling that day, and wanted to know if the chief had gotten his other messages and had he noticed they'd all been marked "urgent"? To which the officer answered "yes" and "yes," nevertheless the chief had gone home for the day, but he would certainly take another message for him and see that the chief got it first thing in the morning.

Bob Wheeler hung up without leaving another message, and sat at his desk for a while, pulling thoughtfully at his chin. With the air conditioner off it soon began to grow stuffy in his cramped office and Bob felt beads of sweat blossom on his forehead. He eased up out of his chair to look out over the air conditioner, could see his wife through the kitchen window puttering around the stove. He smiled. Twenty-one years and I still like looking at her, he thought, and then he thought about Owen Dawson and realized how lucky he was.

And thinking of Owen Dawson made him sad, and then made him frown, sit back down, and reach into a desk drawer for his Boone residential phone book.

Along the west edge of Boone, where the houses began to thin out, sat a few acres of one-time cattle pasture now host to a couple dozen mobile homes surrounded by a rail fence. Bob Wheeler could remember not so long ago when it had been called, in comfortably plain-faced, self-explanatory fashion, "Lubner's Mobile Home and Trailer Park." Somewhere along the line, Mr. Lubner (prop.) got tired of hearing jokes about trailer parks and trailer park white trash, and, more to the point, *his* trailer park and *his* trailer trash. In the search for something that might instill a more upscale image, he went through, in rapid succession, the re-christenings "Lubner Village," "Lubner Estates," "Lubner Square," and "Lubner Gardens," all of which – instead of elevating the image of the place – only got people laughing with their presumptuousness and irrelevancy i.e., *"What* gardens?" and "Estates my ass!" Mr. Lubner had finally settled on "Lubner Park Garden" which managed to escape similar mockery and derision only through its complete encryptability; as phraseology, "Park Garden" made no sense at all.

Bob Wheeler slowly rolled along the narrow drives of Lubner Park Garden. There were mobile homes that were immaculate, and there were some in such rusting, banged-up bad shape that Bob thought they were derelict until he saw figures moving past the windows or heard the sounds of a TV or a radio through the screen windows. He stopped at the lot number he'd gotten from the office at the entrance.

It was an old Fleetwood, showing a few rust streaks but otherwise well kept. The end facing the drive was demarcated by white metal garden fencing, and there was a flagstone walk across what passed for a front lawn; a pinched few feet between neighboring trailers just wide enough for a small porch and almost filled by a beach lounger and a kettle-top barbecue. Bob Wheeler took a moment, then climbed out of his car and immediately had to hug his fender to miss getting bowled over by some kid with moussed hair flying along the drive on a skateboard. He went up the flagstones and the few steps to the porch. The porch was under an awning of corrugated green plastic, and there were flowerpots filled with marigolds along the steps, and more pots hanging from the awning overflowing with Virginia creeper and ivy. Bob Wheeler looked at the marigolds and the overhead pots in macramé slings and went back to the drive to check the lot number and make sure he had the right place. The number was right, but he was nonetheless more tentative as he went back up the flagstones and practically tiptoed up the porch stairs. He rang the doorbell, then deferentially backed down the stairs to the walk and waited.

He waited quite some time, and when there was no answer, he went back up the stairs and – rudely, he was ashamed to admit to himself – put his ear to the door. If he wasn't mistaken, he was sure he could hear *All My Children*'s Erica Kane tell some "little wench" that if she didn't clear out of town, Erica would make sure she couldn't hold her trampy head up in Pine Valley ever again. Bob tried the doorbell again, a bit more insistently this time, then stepped back down to the walk.

He waited, again, was almost on the verge of arguing with himself over a third try or going home when he heard the inside door open and saw Clyde Thomas' shadowy, slumped bulk on the other side of the outside screen door wearing rumpled uniform slacks and a T-shirt.

"Can I help you?" Clyde Thomas mumbled irritably.

"Bob Wheeler, Chief."

"Ok."

"I hate to bother you at home -- "

"Good, because I hate you botherin' me at home."

"I'm sorry, Chief, but I've been callin' you at the station all day -- "

"Been a busy day, Mr. Wheeler," Clyde Thomas said through a yawn.

"I had 'em mark my messages 'urgent.'"

"*All* my messages are marked 'urgent,' Mr. Wheeler. Old lady calls 'bout her cat stuck up in a tree 'n' *she* leaves me a message marked 'urgent.' So, what's so all-fired urgent with *you* 'at you gotta come bother me here in my private situation?"

Bob took a step closer and dropped his voice. "Owen Dawson."

Even through the bug screen, Bob could make out Clyde Thomas closing his eyes in a pained sort of way, then the chief sighed and opened the door. "I guess you'd best come on in."

Bob stepped into a living room not all that much bigger than his office; big enough for a settee, an E-Z Boy lounger, a few occasional tables and a TV. On a lamp table by the E-Z Boy were two empty cans of beer and a half-finished bowl of chili. On the TV there was, indeed, Erica Kane, this time spitting venom at some blow-dried male mannequin whom she told could follow the aforementioned trampy wench out of town for all she cared.

Clyde nodded Bob to the settee, then turned off the TV.

"I didn't think 'at show was on anymore," Bob said, nodding at the TV.

"Some cable channel runs a old ones. I tape 'em so I can see 'em when I get home."

Bob looked from the TV to Clyde whom, he guessed from his mussed hair and bleary eyes, must've been asleep in front of the set. He couldn't quite put Clyde together with *All My Children* any more than he matched him with the potted marigolds but let those go as points to ponder another time as there were more important matters at hand.

"Can I getcha a beer or somethin'?" Clyde Thomas asked. Bob shook his head no, and the chief dropped heavily into his E-Z Boy, levered up the footrest, and sat back. "Ok," the chief said. "Now that you've disturbed my after-work hours, you have my full attention. Owen Dawson."

"He's missin'."

"Well, he left town. Doesn't really qualify as missin'."

"You know?"

Clyde Thomas nodded. "Left yesterday mornin' headin' south on 19. I'm not completely oblivious, Mr. Wheeler. I just look it."

"I didn't mean to make it look like I thought you...well..." Bob Wheeler waited for Clyde Thomas to tell him what he was doing about the situation, but the chief just looked at him with a, "So what?" look. "Aren't you worried?" Bob asked.

"Why should I be worried?"

"Sarah's missin', too. His wife."

"Well, technically no. She told people she was goin' visitin' people down to Galveston 'n' off she went. 'Til somebody files a missin' person report says different, that does not constitute 'missin'. Unless you're here to file such a report. Which you coulda done down to the station. Without comin' here. To bother me."

Bob shrank a little in his seat. "It's just I heard..." Bob had trouble saying it because he didn't want to hear the words aloud. "I heard...there was a body found yesterday...I heard it was..."

"Unidentified is what it is, Mr. Wheeler."

"But I heard -- "

"I know what-all people're sayin', but the body is unidentified."

"I heard they found Sarah's car -- "

"The body is unidentified, Mr. Wheeler." Clyde Thomas put his head back and studied his ceiling for a few moments before he turned back to Bob. "Owen Dawson a friend a yours?"

"Owen and Sarah are both friends," Bob said. "Good friends."

Clyde Thomas nodded. "Here's a thing, Mr. Wheeler. There's no law 'gainst some fella throwin' a bag in his car 'n' lightin' out from a town 'at hasn't been showin' him all 'at much love lately. It may make you scratch your head 'n' fret 'bout 'im, but 's got nothin' to do with a po-lice. Same way, no law 'gainst a lady up 'n' takin' off on a vacation where nobody can find 'er. As for that body, it got found outside a town line, which means if you got some concerns 'bout it, you need to take 'em down to the county sheriff's office. 'N' as for the good reverend, once his car passed over the town line, he's not my problem neither." The chief put down his footrest, passed his fingers through the thinning mess atop his head, then set his elbows on his knees and turned back to Bob. "It's not just 'at you don't know where they went, is it?"

Bob shook his head.

"Whyntcha try tellin' me what-all's got you so rattled?"

"Owen bought a gun t'other day."

Clyde Thomas nodded his head. "Winchester pump. At Kirkland's. Got a paperwork on my desk. Still a day left on a waitin' period."

Bob shook his head. "He has it with him. The gun."

Clyde Thomas became very still and stayed that way for a long time. Bob stared at the wall-to-wall, fidgeting and twisting his hands around each other as he felt the chief's eyes on him.

"You're sure?" Clyde Thomas finally asked.

Bob nodded. "I saw it. Elwood Poteet an' I both saw it t'other night when we were over to his house. It's gone, now. I think he took it with him."

Clyde Thomas' head hung down on his chest. "Ol' Kirkland just lost his dealer's license," he said with an irritated heaviness. Then, with a sigh, "Mr. Wheeler, I do wisht you'd a said somethin' 'bout this in one a your messages."

"I didn't want...I was afraid if I mentioned Owen's name...The way things get around in this town..." Bob shrugged helplessly.

Clyde nodded; he understood. "He's your friend. 'N' he hasn't zackly been havin' an all-time best week."

"There's more," Bob said and Clyde Thomas winced. "You should come over to the parsonage with me. Somethin' there you should see."

Clyde nodded unhappily, grunted to his feet, and began shuffling toward the bedroom at the other end of the trailer. "I need to stop by the station on the way over first. Gimme a couple minutes to get a shirt 'n' somethin' on my feet."

Bob Wheeler's hands had stopped their squirming and clutched together, fingers interlaced. The way he held them when he was praying. Only now they were clasped so tightly together they began to hurt.

They were on the porch of the shack where they could catch the late day cool rolling in, watching the lowering sun pass into a shade of orange. They saw the first fireflies flare, and other insects rise up out of the grass and flit among the blades for their evening feed. They sat around a metal-trimmed linoleum-topped table in creaky wooden chairs that also made the porch floor creak.

Aunt Lizzy waddled back and forth from kitchen to porch and back again on her stiff legs, toting out plates of hamhocks and beans, peas and greens, and fried okra. She set a plate of fresh-sliced tomatoes from the vegetable garden back of the house on the table along with a wicker basket of biscuits warm from the oven, a bowl of red-eye gravy for biscuit-dipping, and a slab of cornbread still in the pan. They washed the food down with sun tea flavored with the mint Rita and Uncle Willy had picked that afternoon.

Rita kept offering to help truck out the victuals, but Aunt Lizzy scolded her, saying such behavior was unbecoming a guest, and when Rita looked to Uncle Willy for support, he gave her the understanding smile of someone who had long ago learned not to argue with the little splint of an old woman who ran the house.

Aunt Lizzy and Uncle Willy asked about Los Angeles and California and her job over supper, and they were impressed with the people she'd met and the places she'd been. And Rita asked about people from long ago, from a Pennington she'd known as a child, people who had drifted through her reminiscing dreams, who were often little more than shadows of memories.

There was Cleotus Jones, the farmer she remembered as a huge gentle giant who always carried butterscotch candies in his pocket for any child he passed on the road or in town. Cleotus had got the cancer, Uncle Willy told her, and it had eaten away at him for months until the morning he woke up just long enough to tell his wife it was time for him to sleep and then he never woke up.

And there was Ol' Lady Winslow, who'd been a little crazy even when Rita had lived there, crazy ever since her man had died, a wild-eyed Cajun who had taught her voodoo. She'd gone crazier and crazier year by year, living in a shack full of wild cats until one night she went dancing off across the cotton fields in her nightgown under the full moon and nobody'd ever seen her again and her place had been full of cats ever since.

Alvin Watson, his lady and their passel of kids went off to California to see if life was better there. The Rollins boy, who'd always had a little rabbit in his blood, left his common law wife and six kids to find work in the car factories of Detroit. Told her he'd send her money to come up as soon as he got himself fixed but never sent even a word. Then there was Della Glover who lost her hand to a loom at the mill but got herself a hook she could open a can of peaches with.

There were people who'd gone off looking for something else, and people who'd run off just because that's the way they were. And, there were people who'd stayed, had their families, lived through good times and bad, worked the land, worked in the mills and fields and machine shops, fell sick, got better, died and were mourned.

Rita Scott sat back in her squeaking chair, rubbed her stomach in sated, purring contentment. "That was *goooood*," she moaned ecstatically. She told her aunt and her uncle about women back at her office, the constant dieters and health food fascists who would have screamed over that plate of hamhocks; and the undernourished-looking types anorexizing themselves into skeletal non-beauty who couldn't've choked as much as one of Aunt Lizzy's little fat, juicy peas down their pinched gullets.

She pulled herself lethargically out of her chair and sat on the porch stairs, leaned against the railing and closed her eyes to enjoy a wisp of cooling afternoon breeze, a brief little puff that kissed her across the eyes and passed on. She opened her eyes, looked across the field toward the woods where the old creek lay. She thought back to the name carved next to hers on the tree by the swimming hole. "What about that boy Randy?"

Uncle Willy chuckled and slapped his knee. "I *knew* you was sweet on 'at one!"

Rita's face grew warm. "We were kids, Uncle Willy."

Uncle Willy pulled himself out of his chair, grabbed Aunt Lizzy around the waist while she was trying to clear dishes off the table. "I told 'er how old *we* was, Ma! How old ya gotta be?"

Aunt Lizzy batted at Willy's arms around her. "You make me drop any a these dishes, you ain't gonna get no older!"

Uncle Willy laughed and let her go.

"I was just curious," Rita said unconvincingly.

Uncle Willy sat down next to her on the porch and shrugged. "Went off, long time ago. Army I heard. Hey, Ma? Whatever happen' wif 'at Randy Jackson boy? Didn't he go off inna Army or sumpin'?"

"I do believe," Aunt Lizzy called from inside the shack. They could hear the clatter of dishes in a metal washtub, and then the wheezing of a hand pump and the slosh of pumped water. "But I recollect he got hisself throwed out for some reason or t'other. Roamin' all over the place on one a them motorcycles, his mama say. She say sometime he come by ever' great oncet in a while. Not up to much good, she say."

Uncle Willy shrugged philosophically as he reached into his coveralls pockets for a small, cloth sack of tobacco and a rolling paper. "Most all 'em go off," he said deftly sprinkling flakes of tobacco along the creased paper. "If Ah'd had a brains when I was a young un, I woulda run off, too."

Rita was about to say that maybe running off from Pennington wouldn't've necessarily been the smart move, but Uncle Willy seemed to anticipate it, held up a hand to stop her. He licked the paper closed, struck a wooden match on the porch stairs and lit his cigarette. "All day you been moonin' 'bout what ya think was 'em 'good ol' days.' Chil', they only good ol' days when ya look *back* on 'em." He put one of his gnarled hands over hers. "Ya did a right thing goin' off, Rita Fay, if 'at's what-all's botherin' ya. Maybe it ain't all ya want it to be... Well, sometimes it get like 'at. But it ain't over yet, chil', right?"

She smiled. "Right."

But Uncle Willy sensed the truth of her unconviction. "Ya changed oncet. Ya don' like a way things is, ya can change 'em again."

They sat hand in hand until Aunt Lizzy came out on the porch. "Them dishes gotta soak," she said, and then to Rita, "'n' 'fore ya open your mouth, no, I don't want ya helpin' me with a washin'! I don' want ya goin' back to 'at Los Angeleeze California sayin', 'I went half-way 'crosst a country to see mah fambly 'n' 'ey make me wash a dishes!'"

The sun had reached the crest of the trees across the field, had gone from orange to red, a warning light telling Rita to look at her watch.

"Ya gots to go," Aunt Lizzy said sorrowfully.

Rita shrugged. "I'm booked on a flight out of Houston tonight."

"Then ya best be gettin' 'long. 'At Houston's a long way from here."

Rita stood and hugged her aunt tightly until Aunt Lizzy pushed away, one of her hands fluttering around her mouth, her eyes blinking and growing red. "I gots 'em dishes to take care of," she said weakly. "You take care 'n' get there safe 'n' all," and she went inside the shack.

Uncle Willy smiled and shook his head. He took Rita by the arm and walked her to her car. "She don' like nobody to see 'er cry or nuffin'," Uncle Willy said, nodding back at the shack. "She plenty glad ya come see us, chil'."

"I'm glad I came."

Uncle Willy held the fence gate open for her, but he did not follow her out to her car. He closed the gate after her.

Rita stopped and turned. "I don't know when I'll be able to get back -- "

Uncle Willy waved it away. "Don' matter none. Ya got a life out there. 'S fine. If ya jus' send one a them pitcher cards oncet in a while, 'at'd make the ol' girl right happy. Fact, make *me* right happy, too!" Then, "Listen to me, Rita Fay. We never had no chilren. You was as close to bein' one a our own we was ever gonna have. No matter what ya thinks a yaself, we're proud a our li'l girl, our li'l Rita Fay. Y'always 'member 'at."

She reached over the fence, hugging her uncle tightly as she'd hugged her aunt, so tight it pressed on her lungs, and it was hard to draw a breath. She buried her face in his coveralls, and her strained breaths took in the commingled smells of denim hand-washed in the same metal tub her aunt was now using to wash the dishes, of late-in-the-day sweat, of the tobacco tucked in her uncle's breast pocket. Her eyes began to sting. And, as his wife had done, Uncle Willy slowly, gently pushed Rita away.

"Ya gots to go," he said.

She nodded, turned, and slid behind the wheel of the Corvette.

"'Member what I said," Uncle Willy said.

"I'll remember." She started the engine.

"Ya know how to get back?" Uncle Willy called over the noise of the engine. "Ya just follow this road back to the highway, head west 'n' look for signs for Trinity. 'At'll take ya where ya wanna go."

He waved, and Rita waved back, then slipped the car into gear and headed down the drive, careful not to kick up any dust.

Thursday evening...

The four Harleys had fallen into a formation that, by accident more than intelligent design, had a dramatically unsettling effect on the straights which, any other time, Spook would have loved no end. Lenny was in the lead, planted center lane, while Porky and Shorty were back a few yards on either edge of the lane. Spook was in the rear, filling in the bottom point of the diamond.

The straights, sealed up in their air conditioned sedans and minivans and SUVs, heard the rumble of the Harleys even through their raised windows. They flicked looks over their shoulders and at their rearviews, saw the formation of bikes sailing along the blacktop like a spearhead of Cossacks, and they shrunk down behind their steering wheels. Sometimes the quadrangle of bikes would pull up alongside and Lenny would have them pace the car, enjoy watching the driver sweat as he – or she – hoped not to be the featured party in a next-morning headline beginning, "Driver Assaulted..." The bikers watched the straights trying not to get caught nervously staring and they laughed.

Except for Spook. As pleasant a pastime as rattling the straights was, Spook was not in a laughing mood.

Lenny had said he liked the convenience store idea, but since then they had passed an appetizingly lonely 7-Eleven, and then a ripe Quik Chek, and then an Exxon Tiger Mart. It always played out the same: either Porky or Shorty would goose the throttle, pull up next to Lenny, there'd be some head nodding and pointing toward the store, but then Lenny would shake his head, making a big show that something about the set-up wasn't quite right, or the target wasn't juicy enough to warrant his attention, and they'd drive by.

But there was nothing wrong with the set-ups, and, as near broke as they were, a blind grandma selling pencils would've qualified as a ripe and fat score. The problem was something else. Pushing dweeb motel clerks around was one thing; drawing down on a store clerk took a different kind of nerve.

Chickenshit, Spook pronounced to himself. He said it out loud: "Chickenshit." He shouted at the back of Lenny's flame-garnished helmet: "Chickenshit!" And the engines and the wind carried the words away.

Not that Spook didn't think Lenny had it in him to drop the hammer on someone. In fact, he didn't think Lenny'd give it any more thought than breaking wind to bust a cap on any of the three guys riding behind him. But then if somebody found Porky or Shorty or – *especially* – Spook laying in a roadside ditch with a quarter-sized hole in the back of his head, it was more than likely people wouldn't be so much incensed as asking the local law enforcement if it was really necessary to invest any hard-earned taxpayer dollars in chasing down someone who'd obviously done Christian civilization a favor.

Drilling a straight; that was different. Heavyweight. In Spook's mind, way out of Lenny's class.

Spook held up a hand, made a pistol of his gloved fingers and aimed it at the back of Lenny's helmet. "Bang," he said.

He could see the lit sign of a Quickie Stop up ahead. Watch, he told himself, shaking his head, watch this chickenshit peckerwood pull another chickenshit drive-by. This time it was Porky who eased up alongside Lenny and pointed at the store. Yup, thought Spook, here we go. "Chickenshit," he said aloud.

This time Porky wasn't taking a shrug-off as an answer. He was shouting something, debating Lenny's wave-off as much as the yammering four-stroker and wind would allow, but Lenny kept shaking his head and shouting something negative back.

"Chickenshit, chickenshit, chickenshit..."

The place was ripe, too, Spook noted. No stores – no *nothing* – for miles in either direction, the parking lot was empty, the evening drive-by traffic just about zip.

"Fuckin' *ripe,*" he muttered, and cast a last, rueful look in his rearview as the Quikie Stop fell behind.

Which was when he saw the familiar hulking shape parked behind the store, where he hadn't seen it on the drive-by.

"Fuck..."

He didn't signal the others, didn't even think to do it, his moves were too quick, instinctive. He heeled his bike over so hard he almost dumped it, the rear wheel fishtailing wide. He wrestled with the handlebars, brought her back and roared across the opposite lanes oblivious to any oncoming traffic.

He pulled up alongside the Winnebago, pushed himself along by one foot, rolling from window to window. He didn't see that little fuck inside, but there was that goddamn dog, following him from window to window, jumping up on seats and tables, barking and snarling.

Spook killed his engine, dropped his kickstand, then leaned back and pulled his .357 out of his saddlebag. He grinned at the barking dog as he thumbed the hammer back on his pistol. "I can bark, too," he told the dog.

The other bikes thundered up behind him. It had taken them a while. Lenny must've pretended he hadn't heard him peel off, and then Porky or Shorty or both had moved up to let him know about Spook and the Winnebago. Lenny would've gone into some act about them already being too far past or some other bullshit, but, in the end, he would've *had* to turn around. The fuck in the Winnebago had humiliated them, and Lenny himself had stood out there in the parking lot of the firing range vowing revenge. Like it or not, want it or not, Lenny was committed.

Spook turned his smile toward Lenny. Even with Lenny's face half-hidden by his helmet and dark glasses, Spook could see Lenny wishing this dumb fuck in the Winnebago had taken another road.

"Whatcha up to there, Spook?" Lenny asked.

"I'm gonna do this fuckin' little hairbag mutt, 'n' then I'm goin' inside 'n' I'm gonna fuckin' do *him!*"

Lenny nodded. "But you do the dog now, he knows we're here, right?"

Spook lowered the hammer on his pistol. "Ok." He pointed a gloved finger at the barking dog. "Later, shit-eater."

"What we oughta do," Lenny said, trying to sound like the voice of wisdom, "is dog this sumbitch 'til it gets dark 'n' then off 'im somewheres where nobody's gonna -- "

"Fuck that," Spook said, "I'm not gonna lose this asshole again."

"Fuckin' A!" Porky said.

"Let's do the fucker *now!*" Shorty said.

"I'm just thinkin' do this smart," Lenny said. "What 'bout witnesses?"

"I don't see no other cars here, Len, do you?" Spook said.

"There's gonna be somebody on the counter," Lenny said.

"We could cover our faces or somethin'," Porky said.

"Wear Halloween masks, I don't give a fuck," Spook said. "I could wear a Cher wig 'n' a Sanny Claus beard 'n' I'm *still* gonna get made as a nigger on a bike. How hard you think it's gonna be for the heat to make me in this part a the world? You worried 'bout witnesses, Lenny? You leave 'em to me. I'm goin' down for one, no difference me goin' down for two."

"Don't matter who does it, bro," Lenny said. "It's still heat for all of us. Doin' a double, that's gonna bring a *lotta* heat."

For the first time, Porky and Shorty started to frown with uncertainty.

"I know this country," Spook said. "I can backroad us into Louisiana 'fore the heat's got time to drop their doughnuts. Better, I got family less 'n' an hour from here. We can hole up there 'til it cools off enough to get over the state line. Or Mexico, even."

Which, to the limited mental faculties Shorty and Porky could bring to bear on the situation, seemed more like a vacation plan than an escape plan. They were back to nodding in support.

Lenny looked around the parking lot, and then up and down the empty stretch of highway. Keep looking, Spook thought, but no one is coming down the road. You're either down for this or you give up the crown.

Lenny shrugged as if it was no big deal and went into his saddlebag for his own piece.

"Ya really got fambly 'roun' here?" Porky asked Spook.

"What else'd bring my black ass *here?*"

They lined up at the corner of the store out of sight of the front windows. Lenny pointed to three banana-seated bicycles parked in front of the store.

"Gonna off the kids, too, Spookie?" Lenny taunted. "They don't give ya the needle for that; they fuckin' burn ya at a fuckin' stake."

Which was a dilemma that solved itself when three kids came exploding out the front doors scrambling for the bikes. Spook and the others flattened themselves against the wall, out of sight, heard some old guy yelling, "Gosh darn y'all! Ronnie Ben King, you bring 'at back to me or see I don't call yer momma onna phone this minute! I know who *all* y'all's mommas is, so don't see if I don't sic 'em all on y'all! Gimme no end a pleasure see 'em take a switch to all y'all's backsides!"

The threats didn't seem to carry much weight. The three kids were doing skidding donuts in front of the store, taunting the old man.

Spook ventured a peek around the corner. Apparently, the object of discussion was a magazine held aloft by one of the gloating kids: brown paper band covering most of the cover except for a woman's head, an open-mouthed blonde with just-been-humped tousled hair, and over her head, in big, yellow letters, *Juggs.*

Lenny'd seen the magazine, too, and he and Spook traded grins. "Kids' got potential," Lenny said.

"I get holt a y'all 'n' never mind yer mommas!" the old guy kept on. "I'll be callin' a po-lice!"

One of the kids gave the old man the finger, the one with the magazine used it to pat his ass, and then the three pedaled off down the road.

"They got style," Lenny said.

Then they heard a second voice, one they'd heard before. At the shooting range earlier that day.

"Why do you have that filth for the children to see?"

"Look, mister, iffen this was my place, I wouldn't stock none 'at stuff, but I'm just a man onna counter, know what I mean?"

They heard the younger man huff and turn back; the doors whoosh a second time as the old guy followed him still apologizing for what he claimed wasn't his fault.

"Tsk-tsk," Lenny said. "Tight-ass got no respect for the First Amendment." He told Porky and Shorty to come in behind him and fan out as soon as they came through the door, sweep the store, corral any customers, cover the back door. He told Spook to follow in last. "This dude at the counter sees me 'n' these two comin' up to the door, he's awready gonna be givin' us the stink eye," Lenny said. "You go in first, even if you got a three-piece suit 'n' a seein' eye dog, this redneck'll awready be reachin' under the counter."

They stayed by the corner of the store while Lenny let a few sporadic cars go past on the highway.

"We wait any longer 'n' he'll be dead a ol' age," Shorty cracked.

"*I'll* be dead a ol' age," Porky said.

"How 'bout it, Len?" Spook prodded.

Lenny took a deep breath. "Ok, fellas. Showtime."

They held their pistols at their sides, behind their legs, so no one inside could see them through the windows. Spook lagged behind, didn't make his move until the three disappeared through the door and he heard Lenny shout, "Nobody fuckin' moves!"

Spook came through the door, saw Porky and Shorty still moving around the aisles, Lenny standing at the counter with his pistol in the face of the old fart at the register, a shriveled little guy wearing one of those stupid-ass store smocks and an equally stupid-ass little paper hat.

All this Spook saw in just a quick eye-sweep of the store. Then his eyes settled and fixed on the man standing in front of the counter. Spook pushed past Lenny, stuck the muzzle of his .357 in the little fuck's face and said, "Hello, asshole. How ya been keepin'?" Spook felt so giddy watching the fuck's eyes go wide he almost laughed. Then he did something that felt even better; he put the .357's muzzle against the man's forehead and pushed him back and back until he fell against a rack of snack cakes. "'Member *me*, fuckhead?" Spook gloated, still burrowing the muzzle into the skin on the man's forehead. "'*Member me*, you li'l cocksucker?"

"Business first!" Lenny cautioned. "We're doin' this smart, right?"

"Fuck business," Spook said. "Fuck smart." He flexed his trigger finger so the man under his gun would see his time was close to an end.

"Hey!" Spook turned at Lenny's alarm. The old fart at the register looked like he'd been making a move for something under the counter, but Lenny had stepped in, got his gun in the man's face. "I wouldn't, old dude!" Lenny warned. "Sit tight, behave, let us go 'bout our bidness."

Spook turned back to the man sitting among the spilled snack cakes. Spook – as he'd already succinctly represented his position to Lenny – could have given less of a shit about business. He didn't care about the old fart or what might be in the register or if Porky and Shorty had found anyone else in the store. He only cared about the man pinned under his gun. "You wanna make movies, mister? I got a great ending for ya."

"Yeah!" Shorty said enthusiastically. He had checked the aisles and was now standing at Spook's elbow, cheerleading. "Blow him 'nother asshole, Spook!"

Spook's finger started to squeeze the trigger, the pistol's cylinder began to revolve. "Maybe if you beg me, huh?" Spook taunted. *"Beg me!* Say, '*Please* don't kill me!' Say it you motherfuckin' cracker asshole! *Say it!"*

The man under the gun closed his eyes. Spook paused; the man's face was strangely, unexpectedly, frustratingly at peace. You are *not* gonna take the fun out of this! Spook told the man in his mind. If I have to flesh-strip you one square inch at a time with a dull butter knife, I'll have you begging me to either spare you or finish you, but I *will* break you!

"Yo, Spook, hold up!" It was Porky, standing watch by the front windows, silhouetted by a flare of headlights blazing up outside against the green sunshades over the front windows. He had his pistol in one hand, an open can of Coors picked up in his sweep of the store in the other.

"What is it?" Lenny asked.

"Car pullin' in," Porky said.

"Fuck," Lenny said.

"'S a right word!" Porky said wolfishly. "Hey, Spook, this bitch is a 'sister' 'n' she *got* it, dude!"

Spook stepped back from the man lying across squashed Twinkies and little cellophane-wrapped squares of crumb cake. "If he's right, fucker, 'a's 'bout a only thing's gonna buy you five more minutes on this earth. Maybe I'll let you have a treat 'fore you go; maybe I'll let you watch."

Rita turned off the Corvette's air conditioning and rolled down her window, hoping the rush of wind would take some of the heaviness out of her eyelids. Too many damned hamhocks back at Aunt Lizzy's, she told herself, too much of that damned cornbread and gravy.

Well, maybe, she said to herself in rebuttal, but it all felt *soooo* damned good in her belly, and she felt full and satisfied in a way that sitting alone in her glass-and-chrome apartment dining on a plate of precisely portioned carbs and calories and protein didn't manage.

The wind fluttering through the open window had an evening's cool to it, carried the smell and taste of grassland and cattle and horses and there was something satiating – surprisingly so, she reflected -- about that as well. The sky had gone purple, and there was little of the sun left other than a charcoal glow along the western horizon. She flicked on her headlights and started looking for a place where she could get something to keep her awake until she made it to the airport.

She saw a glowing sign coming up on the northbound side of the highway, then the blocky form of a convenience store. Some coffee that's been sitting in the pot all day might not taste good going down, Rita thought, but would probably be just the right thing to get her to Houston.

She hit her blinker and crossed the empty highway, her tires crackling across the gravel parking lot. Despite the lit sign she thought the place might be closed, but then she realized that the windows were dark because of the sunshades someone hadn't bothered to raise. Looking more closely, she could see the inside was bright with light, and even see figures moving around.

She climbed out of the Corvette and stretched, lightly rubbed her taut, full belly with her fingernails. A little more of that and you'll fall asleep right here in the parking lot, she warned herself. She heard a dog bark, sounding not too far off, and the idea of ending her perfectly less than perfect sojourn in rural Texas with a dog bite hurried her to the door.

Before the door even closed behind her, she was getting a look from the old gent behind the counter, as if he was willing her to turn around and scram, and she wondered if, before she climbed on her plane home, she'd ever manage to walk up to a counter in Texas without one of these crackers giving her a hard time.

It took her about a half-second to realize she'd read the storekeep's look right – he had, indeed, wanted her to turn around and scram – but she'd gotten the motive wrong.

Inside the door, a heavy, leather-gloved hand grabbed her by the collar and pushed her forward, down to the floor.

"Ok, Porky, bolt that door!" she heard a voice behind her. "Flip 'at 'Closed' sign over, 'n' then see if you can kill a lights in this place."

Rita rolled over and held herself up on her elbows. The one who must've been Porky was trying to figure out how to bolt the door without setting down the small automatic he had in one hand or the can of Coors he had in the other. By the counter was a tall, lean one; the one giving the orders. And near him, another short, fat one, one hand in the collar of a small, weedy man, twisting the collar into a choking tightness, while his other hand held a pistol against the back of the man's head.

Rita saw them only quickly, turning now to a fourth man, a Black man, his dark face splitting into a hungry smile.

"You's right, Pork," the Black man said in a deep, throaty voice. "She definitely *got* it!"

Rita started to pull herself to her feet, but the Black man put the sole of one of his thick-soled boots against her breast and pushed her back down. He raised his pistol and aimed it at the center of her face.

"Don't bother, mama," he said. "Right there's just fine."

Porky must've found the lights; they flickered, and the store went dark. The ebony skin of the man standing over her shone in the faint gleam of light from the glass-faced beverage and ice cream coolers.

"Brown sugar by candlelight, huh, Spook?" Porky cackled.

"Let 'im entertain hisself," the lean one said. "Shorty, get asshole here --" meaning the slim man Shorty was choking with his own collar " – to load us up some groceries. Porky, get Grandpa Ol'-Fart to open a register."

"How come Spooky gets all a fun?" Shorty balked.

The lean one was over at the pay phone on the wall. He yanked the receiver cord out of the phone panel. "You want sloppy seconds, fine," he said, sounding impatient. "Hey, Pork, see if he's got a phone under the counter 'n' make sure he ain't carryin' no cell."

Rita heard Porky pull the counter phone free, then a crash and jangle as he threw it down one of the aisles.

"Whyanchall leave 'er alone," the counterman said. "I'll git yer money for y'all."

Porky laughed wickedly. "Ol' man, ain't no question ya gonna get the money, whether we poke this bitch or not! Maybe y'all'd like a shot at 'er yourself, huh? Huh, Ol'-Fart?"

The old man muttered something under his breath that Porky didn't like. Porky clamped one of his pudgy hands around the old man's thin neck and jabbed the old man's face into the keys of the register. "'Stead a openin' your mouth like ya shouldn't, just open a fuckin' register like you been told!"

The Black one, the one they called Spook, was kneeling by Rita now. He ran the muzzle of his pistol along her body, over the swell of her breasts, then lower, across the flat of her belly, her groin, down to the hem of her skirt. The muzzle sneaked under the hem, catching it on the blade sight, then began tugging it upward.

Rita lay still, her eyes burning into the shadowy face of the man over her. She was afraid, but not terrified. Terror is paralyzing, blinding, eclipses all reasoned thinking. Rita was afraid, but she never stopped thinking, *Give me* one opening, you pig, and I'll kick you in the balls so hard they'll pop out your ears.

Spook saw the unflinching, raging look and chuckled, which only infuriated Rita more. "Damn, y'ain't a shy one, are ya?" Spook said. "Well, 'at's good. You won't mind an audience."

"Go to hell," she spat at him.

"Eventually, momma, eventually." The gun pulled her skirt higher. She reached for it, but he held up a forbidding hand. "Uh-unh," he warned. "Momma, you can either lie back 'n' enjoy or spend a rest a your life goin' to plastic surgeons. It's up to -- "

"FUCKIN' GUY!"

Spook stood, turning to the tussle going on at the register. There was the sickening dull thud of metal on flesh as Porky brought his gun down on the old counterman's head. The counterman slumped forward across the counter, then slid to the floor.

"What a hell's *at* all about?" the lean one asked.

"Lookit this!" Porky said. He reached under the register then dropped a small caliber revolver on the counter. "Ol'-Fart here was reachin' for *this!* Y'all believe it? *This* ol' bastid! Grandpa fuckin' Earp!"

With the Black man's attention diverted for the moment, Rita quickly got to her feet. She hurried around behind the counter and knelt over the old man. It was too dark to see anything clear, but she reached out tentatively to the dark shape on the floor, found the old man's head and a sticky wetness. She moved her hand down, trying to find his chest to see if he was still breathing.

"You *bastards!*" Shorty had been in one of the food aisles, holding his gun on his prisoner while the man stuffed a plastic grocery bag with food from the shelves. They had both turned at the sound of the struggle at the register. Now the man dropped the groceries and started behind the counter to kneel by Rita over the old man. "Cold blooded *bastards!*"

"Jesus, Porky, did ya *kill* a ol' fucker?" the lean one asked.

Porky shrugged.

Headlights again flashed along the store's front windows. Shorty ran to peep around a sunshade. "Holy shit, it's a car fulla kids pullin' in!"

"That's *it!*" the lean one said, exasperated. "Get the money 'n' let's shine on this fuckin' place!"

Rita was just starting to think she might get through this more or less intact when once again a hand grabbed her by the collar and began to pull at her. She fought and struggled, but then heard Spook calling out, "What a *fuck…?*" and realized it wasn't Spook who had her. She let the hand take her, guide her through the dark. A door opened, heavy, creaking on hinges, a gust of icy air. She stumbled over a sill into the cold, fell onto the floor, then the door closed with a heavy clank and then the rattle of a latch sliding into place. Shouts, muted by the thick door, the dull pop of gunshots and the metallic thunk of bullets pounding at the lock.

"Jesus…," she gasped.

And then it was quiet. Except for her own heavy breathing.

She held her breath, listening. Someone else was in the dark, cold room with her, shuffling around. She could hear him breathing…

Spook had heard the shuffle behind the counter, saw the two shadows stumbling toward the back of the store. "What a *fuck…?*" Spook took off into the dark after them, bumping into aisle shelves, toppling over display racks.

From the front of the store, Lenny hissing: "Spook! Knock it off!"

Front door rattling, someone outside shaking the handle, a young voice: "They *can't* be closed! How the hell can they be closed?"

Another voice: "I thought I saw somebody movin' 'round in there."

And another voice: "*Some*body's parked here!"

Spook felt a wave of cold air, heard a heavy, metal door clang shut. He reached out with his free hand, feeling around; he was in some sort of alcove. He ran his fingers along the walls until he found a light switch; a single, bare bulb above him.

"Spook!" Lenny whispered. "What a fuck're you doin' with 'at light?"

"Hey!" said one of the voices from outside. "See? I *told* y'all somebody was in there!"

Spook was standing in front of the vault-like door of the store's main storage refrigerator. He tried the handle. Locked. He raised his pistol.

This time, Lenny didn't bother to whisper: *"Spook!"*

Spook fired once, twice into the plate around the handle, but the door wouldn't give.

Then Lenny was in his face. "You dumb shit! What a fuck's a matter with you?"

"Jesus, Lenny, whatta we do?" Porky and Shorty were standing by the front door, watching the kids outside scramble back into their car and peal across the gravel lot and fishtail out onto the highway. "If one a those li'l twerps got a cell phone there's gonna be heat on us 'fore you can spit!"

Lenny stormed back and forth in the small alcove, seething because Spook had blown it for them, and also because he *didn't* know what to do. "Fuckin' *asshole*, man!" Lenny fumed. "What kinda shit you got for brains, dude? What a *fuck* kinda *brain damage --*"

"Bullshit to *this!*" Shorty said and he was out the door with Porky only a step behind them. Spook heard their bike engines crank up.

Lenny stopped his pacing and faced Spook. "Bro, you *really --* "

"Shuddup," Spook said calmly.

"*Excuse* me," Lenny said, "but even Porky's got more smarts! He's right! One a them kids is on his cell right now, Mr. Big-Talk-I'll-Take-Care-A-The-Witnesses, 'n' when a pigs show up they're gonna find 'at stiff 'hind a counter 'n' two witnesses safe in this here icebox. Sorry if 'at makes me nervous."

"That's not what they're gonna find," Spook said. He had been looking around the alcove for something that might get him through the door. Instead, he found something that made getting through the door academic: the thermostat for the storage fridge. "What they're gonna find is *three* stiffs." Spook turned the thermostat to its lowest setting. He took the storage fridge's locking pin from a hook near the thermostat and pin-locked the door. "We can go now."

But Lenny was already halfway to the door.

Spook switched off the alcove light. He walked across the store, picking up the dropped bag of groceries. He stopped at the counter, leaned over and scooped a fistful of bills from the open register drawer.

By the time he stepped outside, his was the only bike left. He dumped the groceries into one of his saddle bags, then looked up at the Winnebago. He didn't see or hear the dog. You *better* keep your ass hid, he thought.

He slipped his .357 into the other saddlebag, mounted up, kicked the starter, and was soon off down the road. The others had lit out so fast he couldn't even see their taillights ahead.

"Chickenshit!" he called after them and laughed into the wind.

The storage fridge's single light flickered before it settled into a dull glow. Rita looked up from where she'd fallen on the floor to the man standing by the light switch at the door. He was breathing like her, harsh and ragged, making long plumes of vapor in the icy air. In the harsh shadows from the one bulb, she at first thought he'd been beaten; she could see bruises all about his face. But as she stood and came closer, got a better look, she could see the bruises were not fresh.

There was something about the face, though. If only the light was better.

She wrapped her arms around herself, shivering. She studied the storage fridge: barefaced metal walls rimed with frost, blocked by stacks of refrigeration-necessary drinks and food. She turned back to the man at the door. He was leaning against the metal door, listening. "Well?" she asked.

"I think they left." He tried the handle, but the door wouldn't open. He tugged harder.

"Maybe it's stuck," Rita said, hoping more than knowing. She went to the door and set her hands on the handle by his. The metal was so cold it burned, but she kept them there and tugged. Her hands brushed against his and he pulled his hands back, as if he'd taken an electric shock. He walked away, stood in a far corner of the room.

"Pardon me," Rita said caustically. She tugged on the handle again. "They must've locked it from the outside." She turned back to the man, found him glaring at her from his corner. "I was going to thank you for saving my life," she said, "but you're looking at me like it's my fault."

His eyes flicked self-consciously away.

"Hey," and she stepped closer. "I know you from somewhere."

He turned his face to the wall.

She stepped up to him, finally got her good look, then shook her head at her incredibly consistent bad fortune. "Damn…" she sighed. "You're that jerk from that greasy spoon this morning, back up the road. You took my seat. Well, if you think this makes us even…" She stepped around so that he had to look at her. "That last part was a joke," she said.

He walked away, finding another corner far from her.

"Hm," she said, "You *are* a cool one, aren't you? That was another joke."

He sat on a packing case of orange juice, staring at the floor.

There was still something else about his face… Not just that she'd remembered him from the morning, but something *else*… Something…familiar…

Her sudden silence made him curious, and he looked up to see what she was doing. He found her holding out her hand, her thumb and index finger upraised in a U that framed his jaw line. Like a beard.

Rita smiled. *"Damn…"*

Billy Ray Barnes was sitting by himself in Barney White's office. He was gnawing his way through his fingernails and restlessly bouncing back and forth and swinging left and right in Barney White's desk chair. As nervous as he was, he was also bored. He wondered why Barney White didn't have a TV in his office; that guy couldn't be carving up bodies *all* the time. He'd said the same thing to Clyde Thomas once about getting a TV for the station to help pass the slow hours of which, in Boone, there were quite a few. Clyde's answer had been, "If bidness is so slow, maybe we just need fewer po-licemen," and that was the end of the TV discussion.

Then, finally, thankfully, Barney White was standing there saying, "Well, it is and it isn't."

Billy Ray stopped swinging and bouncing in Barney White's chair. "Is and isn't *what?*"

"There's gold there," the ME reported, "but it's just electroplate."

"And?" And then Barney White gave Billy Ray a look that irritated the hell out of Billy Ray because Clyde Thomas was always giving him that same look like he was talking to a child that wasn't going to understand everything without someone having to draw pictures. Which, Billy Ray thought, was their own damn fault for making everything more complicated than it needed to be. Like now with a simple question: "C'mon, Barney, is it a gold cross or isn't it a gold cross?"

There was that irritating look again, but then Barney White sighed a surrendering kind of sigh and said, "Ok, Billy Ray, it is *not* a gold cross. It's something you could get for a couple of bucks up in the hospital gift shop."

Was *that* so hard?

Then the door flew open almost clipping Barney White and there stood the balding scowl of Horace Greenley, D.D.S., his face almost the same nasty red that was in his plaid huntsman's shirt. He didn't say hello or introduce himself or apologize for almost clipping Barney White with the door. He took one look at Billy Ray in his uniform behind the desk and his scowl twisted a little nastier. "It *is* you." He flapped a manila X-ray envelope at Billy Ray and said, "Let's get this over with."

Barney White peeped from around the door. "Barney White. I'm the ME."

"Good for you," Greenley said.

Barney White led them to the morgue, flipped on the lights, headed for the bank of corpse storage drawers. As soon as his hand went for the handle, Billy Ray moved to a far end of the room and Horace Greenley to another.

"I'm just a dentist, ya know," Greenley said. "I don't usually see this kind a thing. I'm not going to have to stick my nose in there, am I?"

Barney White nodded Greenley toward a row of light boxes on the opposite wall. "I'll just call 'em out to you, I guess. We're not working with a full set. A burning shack collapsed on top a her. Her head took a couple good shots and I'm figuring the impact cost her some teeth. The four upper incisors are gone, and the two lower central incisors."

"Forget the incisors," Greenley said clipping his X-rays to the light boxes. "We can make this real quick. Her third molars -- " Greenley turned to Billy Ray " – her wisdom teeth," he explained. "She got 'em?"

Billy Ray turned away as Barney White pulled on a set of rubber gloves, got his head in the storage drawer and started poking around with a Mag light. "Let's see…doesn't appear to."

"Any of 'em?"

"Uh, nope."

Greenley flicked off the light box and started taking down his X-rays. "That's not Sarah Dawson."

"You sure?" Billy Ray asked.

"Sarah Dawson had all four of her third molars. I've been telling her she should have 'em pulled since she started coming to me. She's gonna wind up looking like a chipmunk if she doesn't. But nobody listens to their dentist." He looked sharply at Billy Ray: "But at least *she* comes in for *her* check-ups. Fellas, it's been fun." Greenley jammed his X-rays back in their envelope and headed for the door, but Billy Ray stepped in front of him.

"Hold on a sec, Doc. Hey, Barney, ya got those other X-rays come over from up to Grapeland?"

As Barney White went back to his office to retrieve the other films, Greenley again tried to push past Billy Ray.

"Y'all wanted me to tell y'all if this is Sarah Dawson, I looked, it isn't, goodbye."

"C'mon, Doc, y'awready drove all a way here, it'll take ya just a second. One quick look."

"All right, a quick look. But I'm not sticking my nose in there!" Greenley warned, jerking a thumb over his shoulder at the open storage drawer.

Barney White was back, Greenley clipped the new set of X-ray films to the light boxes while Barney White returned to the body.

"Jesus," Greenley said, "these snags belong to Grandma Moses. Hey, Doc What's-Yer-Name, what'd you say about those incisors?"

"Missing all four from the top and the lower centrals."

"The rest a her teeth; they all angle toward the front? Those lower centrals leaning toward each other? They should all be pushing toward the gaps in front."

Billy Ray saw the Mag light flash around inside the drawer again. "Yeah, 's how it looks."

Greenley flicked off the light box. "She's missing those front teeth 'cause she never had 'em. At least she hasn't had 'em for a while." Greenley tucked the X-rays back in their envelope and shoved it toward Billy Ray. "Your teeth are kept in place by the teeth on either side. You lose one – or a couple – and if you don't put anything in there to fill the space, like a bridge or an implant, over time the rest a the teeth start to cave in-like toward the open space." Greenley nodded at the drawer Barney White was now closing. "She's missing a same six teeth as that one -- " he nodded at the X-rays Billy Ray was holding to his chest " – plus a match on missing all four third molars, and her teeth are all caving in toward the front because she's probably somebody *else* who didn't take her dentist's advice and get herself a bridge."

"So you're tellin' me *this* -- " Billy Ray meant the X-ray envelope " – is *her?*" and he nodded at the closed door.

Horace Greeley gave Billy Ray that same look Barney White had given him a little while ago. Greeley looked over to Barney White, Barney White shrugged with a look of, You don't have to tell *me*, and then Greeley looked back to Billy Ray. "Looks like." Greeley started to walk past, then stopped. "Just so you know, Barnes, I'm billing the town an hour for this visit, plus my travel time and mileage. Bother me again on my vacation and I'm coming back with my ought-six."

The morgue doors swung closed behind him, then Barney White was there turning off the room lights. "This is o.t. for me, Billy Ray," he said as he ushered Billy Ray out the door. "I would like to be a fly on a wall when Fred C. calls you in to ask you what all these invoices are for on a body 's not even in y'all's jurisdiction."

Billy Ray caught up to Barney White in the hall as the ME was heading back to his office. "I'm glad ya pointed out this isn't my jurisdiction," Billy Ray said, pushing the X-ray envelope into Barney White's hands. "'At means *you* gotta make a call to Henry Gilmore."

And before Barney White could say anything in objection, Billy Ray was off down the hall. "Where the hell do you think *you're* goin'?" Barney White called, but the only answer he got was the hush of the automatic doors that led to the parking lot.

"Mr. Gilmore! I don't see why it is I'm finding out from my niece – my *niece* whoifshedidn'tworkinthisrattrapIwouldn'tknow*anythin'* – that my aunt is wanderin' 'round out *there* somewheres, probably buck *naked*, catchin' her death a cold -- "

"Well," Henry Gilmore squeaked, but didn't get much further.

" -- my *husband* pays this goddamn rattrap a yours some six thousand, four hundred 'n' thirty-two dollars each 'n' ever' month – sixthousandfourhundred'n' thirtytwodollarsnot*countin'*pre*scrip*tions 'n' such – 'n' I would *think* for *that* kinda money we wouldn't *have* to worry 'bout my aunt traipsin' 'round wheresomever buck naked!"

Henry Gilmore looked down at his blotter, fiddled with papers and pens, anything providing an excuse not to look up from his desk at Mrs. June Louise Smith Noonan. She offered an intimidating personage under the best of circumstances, being very much a torchbearer of the hardy pioneer stock that had come West to annihilate the Indians, subjugate the Spanish and Mexicans, and beat the life out of the land through overfarming, overgrazing, and overbuilding. She was tall and broad and thick without being fat, with sharp and aggressive features, and a tendency to make herself come off even bigger and more aggressive with broad-brimmed flowered hats and wildly flowered dresses.

This, however, was not the best of circumstances, and when she had a head of steam up – as she now did – her air raid siren of a voice wailed up and down, and she started stomping this way and that, her pleated, floral skirt swirling around like a hurricane rustling up the bougainvillea.

Which, for a man like Henry Gilmore who flinched at thunderstorms and the Fourth of July, was enough to make him consider crawling under his desk. It was only his high sense of decorum and devotion to duty that kept him in his chair, albeit busying himself with the clutter on his desk.

"Mrs. Noonan, she probably just got a little lonely -- "

"Jesse Smith is *damn* lonely, Mr. Gilmore, 'cause her friends all dropped *dead* years ago! Y'all sold us on *security*, Mr. Gilmore! *Security!* If y'all's idea a *safe* is lettin' senile ol' folks wander off any which ways, I'd *hate* to think what y'all would consider *dangerous!* What would *that* be, Mr. Gilmore; land mines on the shuffleboard court?"

"Mrs. Noonan, we have the best security short of a locked facility," Henry Gilmore rushed out, trying to get a word in while June Louise Smith Noonan took a rare pause to lean against a chair and catch her breath. "This is not a jail, nor is it a maximum security mental hospital. We've got full-time attendants --"

"I've *seen* those boys!" she gasped. "*None* a 'em could find his own *butt* with both hands 'n' a road map!"

"Mrs. Noonan, whatever your opinion of the staff, they can hardly be held accountable for your aunt's propensity for disrobing whenever she feels like it. As she did, may I remind you, at the last Christmas pageant. With children in attendance. Nor would it be fair to hold us responsible for your aunt's late-in-life affinity for lighting matches."

"You know something, Mr. Gilmore? Whether my aunt likes to air it out now 'n' then or any *other* stuff is besides the point. Tell me, Mr. Gilmore -- " and now she stood looming over his desk, the thick index finger of one hand tapping heavily on his desk emphasizing each word " -- how *long* has my Aunt Jesse been gone?"

Mr. Gilmore cleared his throat, scratched his head, studied the floor. "I'd have to check with my head nurse for a specific -- "

"How *long?*" Tap tap.

"Since Monday."

Mrs. June Louise Smith Noonan's eyes went wide, and she began hurricaning around the office again. "Monday? *Monday?* Good *God!*" She grabbed on to the back of a chair, gasping again, and for a moment Henry Gilmore thought she might pass out.

"But the authorities were notified immediately! Mrs. Noonan, you have every right to be upset -- "

A statement which, much to Mr. Gilmore's dismay, seemed to rejuvenate her. "You're damn *right* I have every right to be *upset* 'n'Idon'tneedthelikesayoutellin'meI havearighttobe*upset!* 'N' even if you *don't* think I should be upset, I'm *still* gonna be damn *upset!*" She dropped into a chair and began fanning herself with one hand. Mr. Gilmore offered her a glass of water from the pitcher on his desk which she pushed away. "When a *hell* were you gonna *tell* us my aunt's gone?"

"Uh, well -- "

Mrs. June Louise Smith Noonan pushed herself back to her feet, rummaged around in her deep floral-printed pocketbook and produced a business card which she slapped down on the middle of Henry Gilmore's blotter. Mr. Gilmore caught "Esquire" at the end of the name on the card and his vision began to blur. Oh my, he thought.

"Mr. Elroy J. Quinlan, Esquire, of Quinlan, Quinlan, Coburn 'n' Bix 'n' me don't *care* what *y'all* think 'bout my aunt's *'propensities'* 'n' *'affinities'* 'n' such, 'cause a bottom line, Mr. Gilmore, is y'all *had* 'er 'n' y'all *lost* er! 'N' this isn't the *first* time, 'n' it's not even the *second* time! Y'all *lost* 'er 'n' if anythin' happens to my aunt, Mr. Quinlan will see I *own* this rattrap 'n' every *other* thing y'all have's worth more 'n' two cents! You're gonna be lucky you leave court with your damn *socks* 'n' *drawers!*"

My my my, Mr. Gilmore thought, rubbing at his throbbing temples.

The intercom line on his phone rang and that only sharpened the pain in his head. Mr. Gilmore held up a pleading finger to Mrs. June Louise Smith Noonan begging for a moment and picked up the phone with one hand while his other hand fished around in his desk drawer for his stash of generic aspirin. "Miss Frye, I told you I wasn't to be disturbed while I was in with Mrs. -- "

"You have a call, Mr. Gilmore, and I think you better take it. It's from Boone General."

Mr. Gilmore apologized to Mrs. June Louise Smith Noonan, begged her forbearance for just one more moment, downed two aspirin dry, and had the call put through.

"Mr. Gilmore, this is Dr. White over to Boone General. I'm chief of the county Medical Examiner's office."

At which Henry Gilmore's head pains were joined by a feeling in his bowels and he couldn't tell if he was on the verge of throwing up or soiling his pants. He managed to gulp out a, "Yes?" into the phone.

"I'm trying to check the identification on a body we recovered from a fire scene yesterday…"

Fire scene? Oh *my!*

"…Elderly Caucasian woman," Barney White continued, "seventies or eighties, slight build, maybe five-two or so, 100-110 pounds, missing front teeth top 'n' bottom. Y'all got anybody go missin' up to the home 'at fits 'at description?"

Henry Gilmore looked up at Mrs. June Louise Smith Noonan glaring down at him. His head began to swim, he felt convulsions deep in his middle, wanted to run for the men's room but couldn't get his rubbery legs to move, and then he felt his bowels let go and his stomach twist as he soiled his pants *and* threw up, his two just-downed aspirin landing amidst a splat of vomitus square on Mr. Elroy J. Quinlan, Esquire's business card.

Rita pealed open the plastic wrap on a case of beer.

"I would think you'd want something hot to drink," Owen Dawson said from where he was sitting on milk crate in a corner.

"Ah! It speaks!" Rita declared grandly.

Owen turned away.

"I was beginning to think your jaws had frozen," Rita said. She took out a can of beer, popped the lid and took a sip. "I'm hoping the alcohol'll keep me warm. Failing that, I don't think I'd mind drinking until I pass out so I don't feel myself freeze to death. Or does that kind of comportment in the face of imminent doom offend your ministerial principles?"

The man seemed not to have heard, continued to stare blankly into his corner.

Rita poked among the boxes in the storage fridge, pried into a box of Baby Watson cheesecakes. "Maybe I can pack on enough lard to keep me warm. Like a walrus." His sulking annoyed her. She set down the beer and cheesecake, bellowed like a walrus and beat the back of her hands together like flippers.

At last, he turned back to her, his face at first showing surprise, then settling into studying curiosity. "You don't seem to have much of an appreciation for us dying in here."

"Well," she said, raising her beer in a toast, "pardon the bad English, but we ain't dead yet." Though as her shivering felt worse, she wondered for how much longer. She started pacing back and forth, rubbing her arms, anything to keep her blood moving.

"You know who I am," the man said.

She nodded.

"How?"

"I'm a reporter, Reverend Dawson. For a national news weekly." No need to mention which one, she thought. "Out from Los Angeles. We pulled your story off one of the wire services. That means you're national news, Reverend. Small a story as it was, you're coast-to-coast famous."

"Don't call me that."

"What?"

"Reverend. Don't call me that."

She bowed her head in mock apology. "I get it. You're not in uniform. No salutes."

He frowned at her flippancy and turned back into his corner.

She smiled at his obstinacy because it was not nearly the armor she knew he thought it was. He'd left his key in plain sight. "It must be important to you that people know what you're doing. That photo in your story; you posed for that. You wanted that story out."

He shrugged.

"Owen – do you mind if I call you Owen? – like I said, we got your story off one of the wires. That means it went to the press around the country. But people don't read, Owen. You know that. If it's important to you that people know what you're doing – I mean, if it's *really* that important to you – you need television. And I think I can help you out with that."

"It *would* have been on TV," he said into his corner. "Everyone *would* have known." And now he raised his head, looking around at the frost-laced steel walls and blank ceiling. "No one's going to know now."

"You're quite a pessimist for a religious fellow."

For the first time, he smiled, though it was a wry, bitter smile.

She was shivering so hard now she had to set down her beer can. She could see that Owen Dawson was shivering, too; that the color had retreated even from his bruises.

"You ski, Owen?"

"Ski?" He shook his head.

"I do. Took a First Aid class for skiers. Sooner or later, somebody's going to come around. The trick is to last until then. Now, in this First Aid class they said that if you're with another person and you're cut off by an avalanche or storm or something..." There was a sheet of cardboard on the floor, a disassembled box. "This should work."

He turned to her, curious.

She held up the cardboard. "They call it 'body wrapping.' We use this and wrap our bodies together to keep each other -- "

"No."

"It works."

He turned away. "No."

"Then maybe we *will* die before somebody gets here."

"Then we die."

"I see! You'd rather freeze to death than wrap yourself up with a nigger!" She laughed. She remembered that giddiness was a symptom of hypothermia which, all in all, made it not such a bad way to go. "Boy, Reverend -- "

"I said don't call me that."

She ignored him, kept laughing. "Boy, *Reverend*, that must've been some church of yours! What'd you do in your spare time? Minister to the troubled souls of the local Klan chapter? Part-time chaplain for the Aryan Nations? Is that your little spin on The Good Book? Jesus only loves the *white* sheep in his flock?" Which she thought was particularly hilarious. "Say, tell me, Reverend, was this a nice, ecumenical, traditional kind of bigotry? No niggers, kikes, spics, chinks, fags? Or was this a more progressive kind of racism. 'Well, we'll live with the spics because they do such a nice job cutting the grass, and the chinks have great food. But the niggers, sorry, they're still on the shit-list.'"

Owen Dawson turned to her and there was a sense of stillness about him, of study, that quieted her. "'For ye are all the children of God -- '" he leaned forward "' – *all* the children of God by faith in Christ Jesus.'" He closed his eyes, hung his head, like he was concentrating on a problem that refused to solve out. When he looked back up to Rita, the look on his face was one of befuddlement, helplessness: I don't know why it went wrong. "I never saw color. I welcomed all to my church. The only ones unwelcome were those who wouldn't welcome others."

"You *never* saw color?" she asked skeptically.

"We didn't have much. It was a small ranch up in the panhandle. More dust than pasture. My daddy ran it with a colored boy and three Mexicans. They were a part of my raising. I didn't think anything of it. He was a good Christian, my daddy. He didn't see color. He thanked Jesus every day for what we had, even thanked him for what we *didn't* have.

"We were coming back from visiting family in Oklahoma. Got lost on a back road in the dark. I don't know how old I was. Six, seven. Young. I fell asleep on the back seat. My parents' talking woke me up. We were on a small road in some woods, and the sides of the road were lined with cars. And up around a turn I could see a light, like a bonfire. I thought it was some kind of big picnic, a barbecue. Then we came around the turn and there was a clearing. It was some kind of gathering of the local klavern. There was a big, burning cross in the middle of the clearing, and all around I could see Klansmen in their white robes and hoods. Against the woods and the firelight, they looked like ghosts. My mama told me to lay back down but my daddy said, 'No. Let the boy see.' He told me to look out there and he said, 'Boy, they may have a cross and they may call on God but there's nothing about them that's Godly. That's evil out there, boy. Remember that.'

"One of them saw us, then, and he turned, started walking toward us. With the fire behind him you couldn't see his eyes; just two black holes in his hood. My daddy hit the gas and we left. When I grew older, when I took up

The Word, I looked back on that night and I believed – I really *believed* – that *God* had been speaking to me through my daddy, showing me the right way. I didn't think any more of the color of somebody's skin than the color of their hair."

"But you see color now, don't you, Reverend Dawson? You see it so bright you'd rather freeze your cracker ass off than cozy up with a -- "

"With a nigger!" It was an explosion that brought him to his feet. "With a nigger!" he hissed. "If I touched a nigger, I'd cut off my hand! If I rubbed against a nigger, I'd burn off my flesh! I held out the hand of welcome and it came back bitten! *By a nigger!"*

And then Rita understood, shook her head sadly. "This isn't about niggers, is it, Owen? This is *personal*. This is about *one* nigger. Your wife is sleeping with a Black kid. You can't hate him; he's not here. So you hate us all. Very sophisticated."

He started walking toward her, and she found herself stepping back, for the first time feeling she had more to worry about than dying of the cold as he pressed her toward the wall.

"I was going to kill them both tonight!" he said. "I was going to kill them both while that nigger was…was…" His lips twisted, disgusted at the word he couldn't speak. "I was going to kill them both and record it all! Every second of it! Do you think that would make the six o'clock news, Miss Big Smart Los Angeles Reporter? Do you really think I would need *your* help getting *that* on the television?" He had his face inches from hers now: "The world would've lined up to watch the whore and her nigger die! Now…Nothing! *Nothing!"*

The words had come out in a spitting rush. He started to stagger backward, gasping for breath. Rita saw his chest heaving, the frantic look in his face. She started to move toward him, but he stumbled back from her, his arms blindly waving to fend her off.

"You're hyperventilating," she said calmly. "Sit down. Concentrate on breathing deeply. Slowly."

He made his way back to his milk crate, closed his eyes and began to breathe deeply. After a while, the breaths came regularly and easily.

Despite the vehemence of his tirade, Rita pitied him. It sounded like hatred and racism but now she saw it for what it really was; a wound, gaping and open, painful and still bleeding. She knelt near him. "I guess you should know, Owen…it's about your wife."

He seemed not to hear.

"Owen…I don't know a good way to say this…They found her body yesterday morning."

His eyes fluttered, then opened, confused. "Body…?"

She nodded.

He sat erect. "Body? You mean…"

"Your wife is dead, Owen."

He still didn't seem to grasp it, not for a few moments, then it sank in, and he stood, walked past her. She saw his bony shoulders sag. "No. No! She *can't* be dead!" He turned and Rita saw what her years working for Eric Bird III had taught her; no matter how good a handle you thought you had on somebody, they could always manage to surprise you. Owen Dawson, who a few minutes before had been ranting about recording his wife's murder at his own hands, had tears in his eyes.

"Owen…I'm sorry."

"It *can't* be," he sobbed. "This was our anniversary. Five years ago, I lay with her for the first time. It was the first time for both of us. And she was going to mark that day by being with *him* tonight. That was how she was going to celebrate: with *him*. At the Shady Tree Motel. That's where I was going to kill them." He said it with a sad, wistful smile that chilled Rita beyond what the refrigeration system was managing. He began to sob, again, and his knees buckled and he collapsed into a heaving ball on the floor.

Rita wasn't sure whether to feel sorry for him or fear him, but her shivering made it academic. She picked up the sheet of cardboard, crouched down by him, and wrapped it around them both.

Owen Dawson did not pull away.

"What a hell's *this*?" asked a dazed Clyde Thomas.

"It's Owen's movie," Bob Wheeler said.

They were standing in the foyer of the parsonage, Clyde Thomas rooted where he stood by the scene in Owen Dawson's living room Bob Wheeler had revealed to him when he'd flicked on the room lights.

"He was tapin' all this stuff," Bob Wheeler said as he threaded his way through the mess and past the easel at the far end of the room. "He said he was makin' a movie 'bout his life. This is Owen's life." He was in the arch leading to the dining room, pointing toward the dining chairs. "'S where he had the gun. 'S gone now."

"You looked 'roun' a house when you were over here with Mr. Poteet?" Clyde was slowly picking his way through the living room.

"Li'l bit. I didn't see it anywhere. It didn't look like Owen'd took much else with him far as I could tell."

Clyde found a loose-leaf photo album on the sofa. There was a hand-knitted wool jacket on the album, with a space in front for a photo taped to the front cover of a smiling Owen Dawson and his wife standing arm in arm on the front step of the parsonage. Over the top of the photo somebody had used some press-on gold letters to spell out:

OWEN & SARAH

OUR ALBUM

bracketed with press-on golden hearts.

Clyde sat on the sofa, pulled the album over on his lap, slipped on his reading glasses. He'd only known Sarah Dawson enough to wave hey to on the street, and up until a few days ago hadn't known her husband much better. Now, he studied the photo on the cover of *Our Album* to get his first good look at them: Owen Dawson's gangly frame, his patchy beard; short and petite Sarah Dawson, with a smile almost cartoonishly wide, soft-featured, small-breasted, still carrying a bit of baby fat around her cheeks and neck, around her hips.

Bob Wheeler nodded at the cover photo. "'At was a day they moved in."

Clyde smiled. "Just a couple kids." He opened the album. There were more press-on letters and hearts on the first page:

OUR EARLY DAYS

Bob Wheeler propped himself on the arm of the sofa, looking over Clyde's shoulder. "Those are from before they were married."

Clyde flipped through the photos: a beardless Owen Dawson bent over a desk littered with open books, taking notes; Owen and Sarah walking across what Clyde guessed was some kind of campus; Sarah trying to block the camera from taking a picture of her in a food server's smock and bonnet, standing behind a line of steam trays. Clyde peered more closely at food-serving Sarah, saw a squiggled pattern across her teeth.

"Did you know her, Chief?" Bob Wheeler asked.

"Not really. Those braces on her teeth? She looks mighty young there."

"She's a couple years younger than Owen. She was still in high school when they got engaged. Owen says they went straight from her high school graduation to the city hall to get their marriage license. She was workin' part-time at a cafeteria on campus where Owen was taking his divinity classes. 'S where they met."

"Where was this?"

"Southern Methodist in Dallas."

"She from Dallas?"

"Actually, she's a small town kid, family had a turkey farm out in the country 'round Abilene somewheres, but her parents up 'n' died when she was still a kid, didn't leave much, she wound up livin' with an aunt in Dallas. Neither one of 'em is city kids. Fact, when it got time for Owen to take on a church a his own, he asked for a small-town church. He'd pretty much had it with a big city after Dallas."

Clyde flipped a few more pages. Another chapter heading:

OUR WEDDING

And underneath it a date.

"Where was this?" Clyde asked.

"They went back to Owen's hometown for the wedding, up in the panhandle."

From the pictures, it looked to have been a typical small-town church wedding: Owen in front of the altar in a bad-fitting dark suit, Sarah in a simple wedding dress Clyde was willing to bet had come down through the family generations, then afterward down to the church basement for some punch and coffee, cake and pie, some family pictures in front of a humble collection of weathered white clapboard under a steeple surrounded by dusty prairie.

"Funny," Clyde observed, "young couple like 'at 'n' no kids."

"They tried. Saw some doctors. Looked like Sarah couldn't…ya know."

Clyde nodded. "You musta been pretty good friends with a Dawsons, Mr. Wheeler. You seem to know a lot 'bout 'em."

"I'd say we were good friends, close friends. And the Poteets. It was usually the three of us. The three couples I mean."

"Spent a lotta time with 'em, then, didja?"

"Well, Owen's ministry kept him pretty busy."

Clyde took a last look at the newlyweds, feeding each other a piece of cake, smiling faces full of food playfully shoved in. Just kids, he thought again, and closed the album. "But when they all had some social time, like as not they'd spend it with y'all 'n' the Poteets."

"Yes."

Clyde slipped off his glasses and grunted to his feet. "'S nice. I mean they come to a new town, make some nice friends."

Bob Wheeler looked around the cluttered living room and shook his head. "But I never saw anything to get me thinkin' they might be havin' trouble."

"Yeah, well…" Clyde looked for something soothing to say, couldn't think of anything. "Where's their room?"

"You mean their bedroom?"

Clyde nodded.

"Just there off the hall. You really need to go in there?"

Clyde nodded. "'N' probably best you don't come in there with me."

Clyde closed the bedroom door behind him. He stood at the door a long moment, thinking to himself, If it makes you feel better, Mr. Wheeler, I'm not too keen on doing this either.

Like the rest of the house, the furnishings were simple: a bare wood floor, a bureau and mirror, an unmade bed, two night tables, one closet. He looked through the closet first, then the night table drawers, putting the bureau off until last because he suspected if he was going to find anything of note, that's where it'd be. The left-hand bank of drawers belonged to the reverend: men's underwear, socks, T-shirts, pajamas, so on. He pulled out each drawer, poked around for anything tucked at the back or underneath.

The right-hand drawers were Sarah's. He just then noticed her bottom drawer sticking out about a half-inch. He didn't rush himself; Clyde went through the upper drawers first, picking through pullovers, sweaters, socks and pantyhose, denims, pajamas and some modest nightgowns.

He pushed at the bottom drawer, but something kept it from sliding in flush, though it pulled open easily enough. It was Sarah Dawson's underwear drawer: panties, brassieres, a package of Tampons. Clyde reached into his pocket and pulled out the plastic bag containing the pair of panties Billy Ray Barnes had found out by Abner Birney's store not far from Sarah Dawson's car. He took the panties out of the bag and spread them out on the bureau top. He sifted through the panties in the drawer: nothing fancy, most of them plain white cottons, but all trim, snug fits. Clyde set one pair next to the baggy, shapeless pair Billy Ray had recovered.

Clyde dropped to his knees, pulled the drawer as far out as it would come, then jiggled it off its runners and set it on the floor. He reached into the opening, felt along the back of the bureau, and found a paper bag. He pulled out the bag, took an unhappily expectant breath, and emptied its contents on the floor.

There was a pair of red fishnet hose, and a pair of black mesh hose. There was a lacy red garter belt, a pair of black lace crotchless panties, several different colored thongs. A black lace bra without cups, and a silky red teddy with lace-rimmed holes in the vicinity of the wearer's breasts. Some lipsticks: bright red, a deep maroon, black. Some deep blue eyeshadow and black mascara. And there were some foil-wrapped condoms.

There was a book, narrow and short, like a – appropriately enough – guidebook, entitled *Little Book of Sex*. Clyde flipped through the heavily illustrated pages. The book was a quick-reference kind of thing, with thumbnail definitions, explanations and how-to's on foreplay, intercourse positions, and the whole rest of the variety of sexual practices from the traditional to the gymnastic. Clyde paged through the book a second time, more slowly. You have led a sheltered life, he said to himself with not a little envy.

There was also a plain, white envelope and when he looked inside, he saw, at a guess, maybe two dozen photographs. They featured Sarah Dawson endeavoring to enact the poses and practices demonstrated in the little *Little Book*. She was not always engaged with the same male partner. Some were faces he recognized from around town.

None of them was Owen Dawson.

One of them was Black. Very young, teenage young. Clyde guessed it to be Leroi Jefferson.

Clyde set one of the thongs and the crotchless panties on the dresser on the other side of Billy Ray's find. Clyde looked from Sarah Dawson's daily wear to the baggy drawers to the items he'd taken from the paper bag. He picked up the baggy drawers and shook his head. "Maybe your grammaw, but not you."

He replaced the bureau drawer, stuffed the paper bag's contents back in the bag along with the panties from Abner Birney's store. He sat on the edge of the bed, felt a sad cloud pass over him because it was now clear – all too clear – to him what had happened, and how things had come to this point.

And also where they were going.

From her skiing days, Rita remembered being told that freezing to death was not unlike falling asleep. But how the hell were you supposed to fall asleep when you were shivering so hard you felt like your bones were going to fly apart?

The door latch of the storage fridge rattled.

"Owen! Somebody's here! I told you somebody would come!"

The door swung open, and Rita no longer saw anything to smile about.

"Surprise!" In his leather biker regalia, Spook looked big enough to fill the storage fridge doorway. Hanging at his side was his pistol. "Well, well, well," he said, grinning down at her and Owen Dawson bundled together in their cardboard tent. "Ain't 'at cozy! Ya won't make it with a brother, but this li'l cracker's lily-white ass is fine with you, hm? Well, I'm just gonna have to break you a that habit, girl."

"You must be out of your mind coming back here!" Rita said. "How long do you think it'll be before the cops -- "

"Long enough," Spook said confidently. "Plenty a time to warm up a li'l brown sugar if ya know what I mean." His smile went cold as his eyes flicked to Owen and he thumbed back the hammer on his pistol. "'N' plenty a time to take care a some other unfinished business. In fact -- " and he raised his pistol toward Owen " – let's take care a business first."

Owen closed his eyes, bowed his head, and waited.

And then there came a solid-sounding *thud*, like someone thumping a full, ripe watermelon. Spook went rigid, his eyes fluttered, and he wavered on his feet a moment before his joints gave way and he collapsed to the floor.

Through the now clear doorway, in the light of the alcove outside, Rita could see the old counterman. His little paper cap was gone, and an ugly gash ran halfway across his barely-covered pate, tendrils of blood radiating in a web across the pale skin. Though it looked like a lot of blood, it didn't seem to have left him weakened much. No pain showed on the old man's face; just a hostile triumph, and his hands looked quite strong and firm around the grip of the fungo bat he was holding.

The counterman reached down and took Spook's gun from his limp hand and stuck it in his belt. He looked down at Spook, then to Rita. "I woulda shot 'im 'ceptin' one of 'em took my gun."

Rita stood and helped Owen to his feet. "Under the circumstances," she said, "I think you did just fine."

Thursday night...

Clyde turned off the bedroom light and quietly closed the door behind him as he stepped back out into the parsonage hallway. Bob Wheeler didn't seem to notice him; he was still sitting on the sofa, the photo album now on his lap, lost in pictures of better times. Behind the man on the sofa, around the edges of the drawn shades, Clyde could see it was full on dark outside, recognized the soft iridescence of the rising moon.

Clyde followed the hallway. At the back of the house was a small room that could've been used as a second bedroom, but which Dawson had, apparently, set up as some kind of study. There was a scuffed little desk, a sagging couch, and a self-assembled set of bookshelves thinly populated with what Clyde guessed were religious texts from Dawson's Southern Methodist days. Clyde sat at the desk, turned on the desk lamp and started rummaging through the desk drawers.

He called out to Bob Wheeler who found Clyde at the desk, his reading glasses parked on his nose as he thumbed through an address book. "Why dontcha have a seat, Mr. Wheeler," Clyde said and nodded toward the couch. He offered Bob Wheeler a stick of gum, which the other man refused. "I guess this was the reverend's office, huh?" Clyde asked, popping a stick of gum in his own mouth.

"Yep. What's 'at?" He meant the address book.

344

"This? This here appears to be the reverend's address book."

"Do you need to go through his personals like 'at?"

"'Fraid so, Mr. Wheeler. You said you never saw any sign there was some kinda trouble 'tween Dawson 'n' his wife."

"Nothing I could see. They always seemed happy enough when we saw 'em."

Clyde looked over the top of the address book, over the rim of his glasses, and could see something still nagged at Bob Wheeler. "C'mon, Mr. Wheeler, share it with a class."

Bob Wheeler fidgeted uncomfortably on the couch. "Well, I didn't think much on it 'til now 'cause I thought it was 'bout *us.*"

"What was *what* 'bout *who?*"

"The last few times…well, tell you the truth, it's been goin' on some months now."

"What's 'at, Mr. Wheeler?"

"We weren't really seeing much of 'em…together. It come to where most a time, whenever we'd get together, it'd be just Owen. Sarah'd find some reason not to be there. She had things to do, maybe she wasn't feelin' well; you know. 'N' then she started spendin' a lot a time with a cousin a hers down to Galveston way."

"That's what she said? She had a cousin in Galveston?"

"Yeah. I just thought it was *us* she had a problem with. That maybe she was gettin' bored with us."

"She say somethin' to make y'all think 'at?"

"Well, ya know, Chief, the Poteets 'n' us, we're – let's face it – we're not kids. We're practically old enough to be those kids' parents. Ya get to a point where y'all just like doin' a same kinda things all a time. Ya know; fall into a habit. We all'd get together, have somethin' to eat, maybe just sit 'n' talk, watch a li'l TV, or maybe out'd come the board games. Ya know how it is."

Clyde smiled and nodded. "Yeah, me 'n' my ex were real Parchesi fiends there for a while. My grammaw, lord, her 'n' her mah jong…"

"Owen seemed to enjoy 'at kinda thing well enough. We used to joke he always seemed so...I dunno, like he was older, like he'd never been a kid. But Sarah, after a while..."

"Wasn't so much fun for her."

"She didn't say anything, but leastways I got to feelin' maybe 'at's how it was. I guess her being young 'n' all...Well, she got to be, 'Why don't we do somethin' else for a change? Why don't we go out?' But, ya know, Boone's night life isn't so much, 'n' even less if you're a church fella."

"You 'n' a reverend, y'all spend much time together? I mean, just a two a y'all?"

"Some. He'd come by the office sometimes, just to sit 'n' chat. Sometimes I'd stop by." Bob Wheeler looked sadly around the shabby little study. "We'd sit in here, sometimes, have a couple Cokes or some lemonade or sweet tea. Talk church business, or maybe just pass some time."

Clyde nodded. "Mr. Wheeler, I gotta ask a couple things, 'n' I'm not rightly sure I know how to ask 'em. Kinda delicate. 'N' I can't think of no nice way to put 'em."

Bob Wheeler seemed to take a moment to prepare himself, then nodded for Clyde to go ahead.

Clyde already felt his face growing red. "Dawson, he, ah, ever mention him 'n' the missus were, maybe, havin' any problems, uh, ya know, in the boo-dwah so to speak?"

"Scuse me?"

"Difficulties of a -- " Clyde winced " -- sexual nature, let's say."

Now it was Bob Wheeler's turn to flush and wince. "Oh! Well, uh, lord no! I think even if Owen was havin' those kindsa problems I don't, uh, no, I don't think he'd a said anything. I don't know it was in 'im to talk like 'at. Sometimes I'd give Bea – my wife – you know, a li'l pat on a bee-hind, just to be cute, 'n' 'at was enough to get Owen red as a beet."

"Think maybe Mrs. Dawson mighta said somethin' a such a nature to your wife?"

"I dunno. I don't recollect 'em spendin' all 'at much time together, just a two of 'em."

"Think the reverend mighta confided somethin' to Elwood Poteet he wouldn't say to you?"

"You'd have to ask Elwood. I thought we were *all* pretty close friends. Owen mighta had problems talkin' 'bout 'at kinda thing, but if he had *some* kinda problem, I think he woulda, ya know, said *somethin'*."

"Yeah, you'd think so. But any bartender'll tell ya people'd rather tell their deepest secrets to a total stranger than to their best friend, 'cause you tell the bartender 'n' a next day you can just go to another bar 'n' another bartender. You tell your friend 'n' you're lookin' 'im in a eye every day seein' him judge ya."

"I wouldn't judge Owen like that."

"Maybe, but he'd *think* you might. 'N' this bein' a small town like it is... You gotta live every day waitin' for the secret to slip. 'N' a town this small, sooner or later they *do* slip. People got nothin' much better to do than stick their nose in other people's business. Best way to keep a secret is never tell it. I think whatever was goin' on in this house, both of 'em kept here.

"Now, I'm lookin' through this here phone book. The reverend, he was a pretty thorough fella. Like here's your name, Mr. Wheeler, gotcher number there, your address, your wife's name, says what-all you do for a livin', gotcher weddin' anniversary, you 'n' your wife's birthdays, says here you handle 'insurance matters for the church'... Like 'at all a way through. There's Miz Reilly, says she's head a the Ladies Church Auxiliary, the mayor's wife, birthdays 'n' such, whose on a Church Finance Committee... See here, he's got his momma 'n' daddy up north, I guess this here is Sarah Dawson's aunt in Dallas with all her information, too..."

"Owen was good like 'at," Bob Wheeler said. "He never let a birthday go by, 'membered when loved ones had passed, he even knew the names a their dogs 'n' cats 'n' such."

Clyde nodded, impressed. "'S nice. But you know what I *don't* see? All this information he's got on everybody, but I don't see a single phone number with a 409 area code; 'a's Galveston. I don't see no Galveston addresses for no cousins or anybody else."

"Well, they were *her* family," Bob Wheeler offered feebly. "Maybe she keeps all that in her own phone book."

"Maybe, but he seems to got all a rest a her people in here. Look here, Mr. Wheeler, if every couple weeks *your* wife was spendin' time outta town with an acquaintance, wouldn't you wanna be able to get a-holt a her? Like for an emergency? Tell 'er 'er momma suddenly took sick, ask her she fed a dog 'fore she left, tell her you forgot how to use a microwave 'n' you don't 'member if you're supposed to wash your whites in hot water or cold? Maybe just tell 'er you miss 'er?"

Clyde Thomas closed the address book, dropped it on the desk and his reading glasses on top of it. He rubbed his eyes, let out a long, tired breath. "You know there's stories goin' 'roun' town 'bout Mrs. Dawson."

"There's always stories goin' 'round a small town like this, Chief," Bob Wheeler said dismissively. "You *know* that. Like you said; people got nothin' better to do. I don't pay that kinda thing much mind."

"I don't pay it much mind, either, Mr. Wheeler. But then I find somethin'…"

Then Bob Wheeler noticed the paper bag sitting on the desk at Clyde Thomas' elbow. He didn't ask the question, but it was on his face.

Clyde glumly nodded. "She was. 'N' I think the reverend got a handle on it, or some of it leastways, 'n' 'at's what got this whole ball rollin'."

"I heard…" Bob Wheeler took a moment, afraid to ask, finally forced it out: "I heard…y'all found a woman's body… They say -- "

"I'm pretty sure 's not Sarah Dawson, Mr. Wheeler."

"But they say y'all found her car -- "

"Fact, I think she's off with somebody right now, 'n' I think Owen Dawson knows where 'n' 'at's where he's headin'. Can't be too far. I figure she left her car 'cause wherever she's gone it's close 'nough she was afraid somebody who knows her might come crosst it 'n' recognize it 'n' wonder why it wasn't down to Galveston like it was supposed to be."

Bob Wheeler leaned forward, put his arms across his knees, his head hanging forward, shaking side to side. "I…can't see it. I *can't.*"

"Why? 'Cause she's a nice kid just got her braces off, preacher's wife 'n' all? Married to a nice fella like Owen Dawson?"

"Somethin' like 'at."

Clyde nodded sympathetically. "Young girl goin' from her momma's lap to that auntie in Dallas 'n' straight to her husband's house. Never really had time to grow up. 'N' in a beginnin', musta seemed like a big thing, goin' off married, goin' to a new place, first home a your own 'n' all. 'N' then some time goes by, 'n' you start thinkin', you start askin' 'at nasty ol' question: is this *it?* Starts sinkin' in 'at yeah, this *is* it, this is all it's ever gonna be, 'n' there you are, havin' one a those midlife crisis things ceptin' you're only twenty, twenty-one. Start wonderin' how you're gonna survive fifty more years a this.

"'N' it's tougher 'cause you *are* the preacher's wife 'n' everybody's eyes're *always* on ya. You got no babies to take your mind off things, your job's just showin' up to bake sales 'n' all, 'n' sittin' in a front pew on Sundays keepin' a smile on your face all a time. 'S gotta be a tough row to hoe after a while, Mr. Wheeler, 'n' in a town like this where bein' nosy 'n' gossipin' 'bout every li'l thing is a favorite pastime? Gotta be like livin' under a microscope.

"Ya know, you 'n' *your* wife have a fight, 's just another kitchen table spat. But your *minister* 'n' *his* wife have a thing, well, they don't *get* to. Leastways, they're not *supposed* to. They're not supposed to have a same problems the rest a us got 'cause they're in good with God. *They* have a problem 'n' it's a big religious crisis 'n' everybody figures 'at makes it everybody's bidness. 'N' if the problem's got to do with sex? Man, thinkin' 'bout your preacher 'n' his wife 'n' sex, 's like thinkin' 'bout your momma 'n' daddy doin' it; ya *don't!*

"'N' you gotta look at it from *their* side, too. Preacher's marriage goes on a rocks, maybe he figgers he's failin' his flock, ya know? What kinda example is he settin'?

"'S a lotta pressure, Mr. Wheeler, a *lotta* pressure on two people who look to me weren't nothin' but a couple kids. Put all 'at on their heads, 'n' if somethin' wasn't square in this house? Somebody…maybe everybody…was gonna break."

Bob Wheeler sat back on the couch and seemed to collapse much like the tired springs in the cushions had. "'S a hell of an insight you got into the human condition, Chief. 'At go with bein' a po-liceman?"

"Bein' a cop don't have much to do with it," Clyde said with a rueful smile. "I don't know much 'bout a human condition, Mr. Wheeler, but I am personally acquainted with disappointment. I got a job everybody tells me how to do, two divorces, 'n' a home in a trailer park. I am an *expert* on life's disappointments." Clyde switched off the desk lamp. "County sheriff's got an APB out on Dawson," he said. "Maybe they'll pick 'im up 'fore he gets where he's goin', but if they don't…" A mournful sigh. "I don't see no happy endin's here."

Bob Wheeler sat upright on the couch as if he'd shifted over onto a burr. "This is the day."

"Whatcha mean?"

But Bob Wheeler was already out the room door. Clyde followed him down the hallway back to the living room. Bob Wheeler pointed him toward the photo album on the sofa as he headed for the easel at the far end of the living room. "Look at the part 'bout the wedding. Look at the date."

Clyde quickly flipped through the pages, found OUR WEDDING and felt a ball of ice in the pit of his stomach. "'S today."

"It's their fifth anniversary. *Today is their fifth anniversary!* Lookit this." Bob Wheeler was pointing to a corkboard propped on the easel, and tacked to the corkboard was a matchbook emblazoned with, "The Shady Tree Motel." "Owen was taping this Tuesday night," Bob Wheeler said. "It musta been one a the last things he recorded here 'fore he left. I know Owen Dawson since he come to Boone. He told me 'bout his weddin' 'n' his honeymoon, 'n' where him 'n' Sarah would stay when they wanted to get away for a couple days, where he liked to go off by himself outside a town sometimes to just think. But I don't recollect 'im *ever* mentionin' *this* place."

Clyde detached the matchbook from the corkboard, squinted through his reading glasses at the fine print under the name: directions to the Shady Tree's location. "That's down 'roun' Trinity," Clyde said. "You lock up. We'll take my car; I got a scanner."

While Bob Wheeler turned off the house lights and tended to the front door, Clyde Thomas hustled out to his patrol car, popped the trunk and dropped the paper bag he'd taken from Sarah Dawson's bottom drawer inside. He slammed the trunk closed, looked for the other man, saw the house dark and Bob Wheeler kicking at the charred wooden cross still standing on the parsonage lawn. At first, Clyde thought he heard Bob Wheeler gasping with the effort, but as he stepped close and saw the glistening trails on the other man's face in the moonlight, he realized the man was sobbing.

Bob Wheeler stopped his kicking, stood there helpless, his chest heaving, only having managed to jar the cross into a slight angle. Clyde stood next to him and set a hand on the blackened wood. He looked to Bob Wheeler, nodded, and Bob Wheeler set his hand next to Clyde's, and they pushed together until the cross toppled over and shattered in black fragments on the moon-washed grass.

Rita eased back in the lawn chair the counterman had pulled out of a sales rack and snuggled warmly under the pile of two-for-one-sale beach towels he'd thrown across her and around her shoulders. He handed her a cardboard cup of black coffee. She took a deep slurp and nodded appreciatively. "That's a lot better. Thank you."

The old man smiled and pointed to the square of gauze she'd taped across the gash on his head. "Thank *you*, ma'am. Sorry the coffee's not hotter. Ever since 'at lady sued McDonald's for a kajillion dollars, we're not supposed to --"

"It's just fine," she said graciously. Certainly a lot more warming than cold beer and chilled cheesecake. "Does it hurt?" She nodded at his head.

"More 'n' politeness'll let me say." He smiled. "But he only clonked me onna head, ma'am. Nothin' too vital up there. You warmin' up some?"

"Better every minute. What'd you do with that gorilla?"

"Don'tcha get to worryin' 'bout him, ma'am. Got 'im locked in the cooler. Oh, don't worry. I turned up a thermostat. Well, some anyways. I rate 'im for at least a *li'l* bit a discomfort. If those kids who come by did make a call, sheriff's officers oughta be here soon." The counterman looked to the back of the store where the storage fridge was and patted Spook's heavy pistol where it was sticking out of his belt. "Ya know, every time my head gets to throbbin', I almost hope 'at fella finds a way outta there 'fore the po-lice get here."

Rita laughed. God bless him, the old man had style. Perhaps it was the effects of the cold, or the psychological trauma of the whole affair, but now that she was warming up under Spongebob and Avengers beach towels, and her insides were starting to thaw, she realized that she and the old counterman were the only two people in the store.

She sat upright in the chair. "Where's the reverend?"

"The who?"

"That guy who was in the icebox with me!"

The counterman looked around the store surprised. "Gone, I guess. Ya know, I didn't even see him leave."

Rita drained her coffee cup, thrust it at the old man, shrugged off the towels and started running for the door.

"Hey, where you goin'?" the old man called after her.

At which Rita suddenly realized she wasn't quite sure. She spun around, started pacing about frantically, ready to move but not knowing where to. "You ever hear of a place called the Shady Tree Motel or Hotel or Inn or something?"

"Uh -- "

"Phone book!" she demanded.

The counterman blinked his eyes, puzzled.

"Do you-have-a-phone-book?" Rita tried.

He pointed to the counter but before he could give further details Rita had hopped the counter – earning an admonishing "Hey!" from the old man – found the phone book on a shelf underneath, viciously whipped through the book until she found a thankfully unmissable quarter-page ad for the Shady Tree Motel and ripped the page out.

"Hey! That's my -- ! *Hey!*"

Rita had hopped back over the counter and was heading for the door again.

"Where ya goin'?"

Which gave Rita pause to actually look at the torn phone book page. She stormed back to the counterman and thrust the ragged paper in his face. "Do you know where this is?"

"Uh -- "

"Maps! Maps!"

"Got road atlases inna rack by the door. Ya want Boone County."

She pulled the Boone County book from its pocket in a revolving rack so violently she almost pulled the rack over. She turned for the door.

"Hey, ma'am, 'at's a $19.95 item plus tax!"

Rita spun around in the doorway, quickly rummaged through her shoulder bag and threw a business card in the general direction of the counter. "Bill me at that address! *Double* bill me if you want!" and she was out the door.

The counterman, dazed and shaking his head, followed her out to the parking lot. "Hey!"

"Thanks for everything!" Rita called from her car as the Corvette's engine turned over with a high rev roar. "I mean it!"

"What 'bout a po-lice? They're gonna wanna talk to you!"

"I have a phone!" Rita yelled whipping the front of the Corvette around in a spray of gravel that had the old counterman flinching and dodging flying stones. "I'll call 'em from the road!" The rear tires of the Corvette spun, more gravel flew, then the car lurched back out onto the highway, tires chirping and smoking when they hit the asphalt.

She flicked on her overhead light and threw a quick glance at the ad for the Shady Tree. The ad contained a simple map showing the location of the motel. It was some place further south, just beyond a place called Trinity.

Clyde Thomas and Bob Wheeler sat quietly in Clyde's patrol car as it shot down 19 South at a good 80 miles an hour or so. Clyde looked over at the other man who stared out into the night, his brooding face illuminated by the brief flash of a lone car heading the other way, or a roadside island of light that was a filling station or convenience store quickly flashing by.

"You're thinkin' it don't make sense," Clyde said.

"I never felt…" Bob Wheeler kept running it around and around in his head. "I *never* felt she didn't, ya know, love him. Even all this time, lately, when she was goin' off…"

"Maybe she still does. But what she wants is somethin' he can't give 'er. Or won't. Listen, Mr. Wheeler, you were their friend; I'll tell you somethin' won't be goin' in a o-fficial report. Sarah Dawson had some stuff hid away, some of it was a kinda underthings you usually only see in certain kindsa men's magazines; know what I mean? There's no kids in 'at house. They got a cleanin' lady?"

Bob Wheeler shook his head glumly. "Sarah preferred to keep her own house."

"So then who's she hidin' it from? Who's left in 'at house?"

"'At doesn't make any sense to me either," Bob Wheeler said, sounding lost. "I can't think of Sarah…"

"Yeah, 'at sweet li'l girl raised up on a turkey farm. You know 'at ol' sayin', 'Y'all can't keep 'em on a farm once they been to Paree'?"

"Neither of 'em's ever been outta the state! I don't think they've even been outta east Texas 'cept on their honeymoon 'n' 'at was to a religious retreat!"

"Here's a thing, Mr. Wheeler. Today, you don't have to actually *go* to Paree to see it. You gotcher cable box or your satellite dish 'n' 200 channels showin' there's some serious partyin' goin' on out there. Or you get on your computer, 'n' if you don't have one you can go down to the liberry 'n' use theirs 'n' you can see stuff on there puts any teenaged dirty dream I ever had to shame. Way I see it, you get an eyeful a that 'n' you're either gonna be disgusted or you're gonna be curious."

"'N' you think Sarah got curious, 'n' Owen got…disgusted."

Clyde shrugged. "Or maybe she was afraid he would. Maybe she didn't have to say anythin', she just knew it wasn't gonna go over too well. She's his wife, she'd have an idea a what he'd take 'n' what he wouldn't."

"So she went with another man," Bob Wheeler said bitterly.

Clyde glanced over at Bob Wheeler and even in the minimal glow of the dashboard lights he could see that along with puzzlement and sadness, Bob Wheeler was also dealing with disappointment.

Clyde clucked his tongue. "It's not just about a bedroom, Mr. Wheeler, leastways not far as I can see. I think she found somebody felt like she did 'bout a *lotta* stuff. This don't have nothin' to do with anybody bein' a bad person. What I got 'bout these two people, neither one of 'em's whatcha'd call a bad person. The way I'm seein' this, this is 'bout two people needin' more reasons then they got to get up in a mornin'."

Bob Wheeler was quiet for a long time, then he sighed in a way that said even if he disagreed, he maybe understood. But, "Then there's Owen."

"Your friend a preacher's the easy one to figger, Mr. Wheeler," Clyde said unhappily. "Him I got a read on even 'fore I got the rest."

"How so?"

"He bet everythin' on God. He's a preacher, Mr. Wheeler; God's a biggest thing in his life. 'N' now God's let 'im down. What's 'at leave 'im with?"

Billy Ray Barnes had a lot on his mind, and was having a hell of a time trying to get it all in any kind of arrangement where he could understand what it was he was in the middle of and what he should do about it. It was still pretty much a mish-mash in his head when he got back to the station and it didn't help his thinking any that Waylon Meeks was on him like a cloud of gnats as soon as he came through the door.

"Where the hell you *been*, Billy Ray?" Waylon Meeks said. "I'm four hours past my shift, Dottie's all pissed at me bein' so late home, 'n' don't *think* I ain't puttin' in for 'at time! You can do the splainin' to the chief what-all I'm doin' with all this overtime!"

Waylon had come up on Billy Ray so fast Billy Ray wondered if Waylon hadn't been lurking right by the station house door waiting to pounce as soon as Billy Ray showed his face. Billy Ray batted his hands up at Waylon, trying to keep him off while he went to his desk and dropped heavily into his seat, threw his hat on his desk. All this brainwork was tiring him out.

And Waylon wasn't letting up. "You didn't tell me I's gonna wind up here half the night, Billy Ray! Dottie's got dinner waitin' 'n' she's callin' me every ten minutes to tell me how cold it's gettin' 'n' it's not like she's no gore-

may cook to begin with! 'N' if it ain't her callin', it's somebody else! Phone's been goin' like I don't know what-all! 'N' a chief was by, Billy Ray -- "

Which finally roused Billy Ray from all his cogitating. "The chief was here?"

"Damn straight he was here, 'n' don't think he wasn't royally pissed when he didn't see *you* here 'stead a me!"

Which was now something *else* Billy Ray unhappily had to throw into the mental mix. "Wha'd he say?"

"What-all do ya *think* he said? He said, 'Where the hell's Billy Ray?'"

"Wha'd *you* say?"

"I told 'im I didn't know 'cause I *didn't* know! Then he got somethin' outta his desk 'n' lit out."

"Ya know where he went?"

"He didn't say, 'n' frankly, Billy Ray, the way he was lookin', I didn't feel like askin'."

"He say anythin' else?"

"Yeah, 'fore he left he said, 'New 'n' efficient my ass' is what he said. I tell ya, I don't wanna be you when he catches up with ya, Billy Ray."

Billy Ray moaned.

''N' then Sheriff Bowren called sayin' they got another sightin' on Owen Dawson."

"Dawson? Where?"

"A convenience store robbery a few miles north a Trinity."

Billy Ray went over to the county road map on the wall. "Trinity, huh? Dawson robbed a convenience store?"

"No, he was one a the victims looks like."

Billy Ray traced a line down Route 19 from Boone: first Bubba's RV lot south of Boone, then the incident at the shooting range this morning south of Lovelady, now this business with the convenience store north of Trinity. Moving south, but to where? Sarah Dawson's car out to Abner Birney's store, Sarah Dawson missing since last week, Owen Dawson and his damn movie... What's this jasper up to? he kept asking himself as he stared at the map.

"'N' 'at color girl, 'at reporter lady ya blabbed to, she's been callin' -- "

"Rita Scott?"

"Yeah, she's been callin' -- "

"For me?"

"For the *chief*, Billy Ray. Called couple times."

"Ya don't know where he is?"

"I tried everythin'. I tried 'im on a radio but either he don't have his on or he's outta range, 'n' I tried callin' 'im at home but I only get his machine, 'n' his cel comes up 'No Service'. Can I go home now, Billy Ray?"

While there was still a lot whirling and whizzing going on in Billy Ray's head, certain bits and pieces were beginning to fall into a rough kind of order. "Hold on for now, Waylon. 'At Scott lady, she leave a number?"

"On a chief's desk."

Billy Ray sat in the chief's chair which, by the look that brought on Waylon Meeks' face, you would've thought was a blasphemy sure to bring down thunder and lightning. It's just a damn *chair*, Waylon, Billy Ray wanted to lecture. Billy Ray picked up the chief's phone and dialed the number Waylon had left on a slip of paper on the blotter.

"Rita Scott."

"Miz Scott, this is Officer Barnes up to Boone."

"Billy Ray! I've been trying to reach your chief! Where is he?"

"We haven't been able to locate 'im, Miz Scott. He's out on a road somewheres."

"Billy Ray, this is an emergency! It's very important I get through to him immediately! Is there any way you can reach him?"

"He hasn't been respondin' to radio calls, Miz Scott, 'n' I ain't got no idea where he is or when he might be back or get in touch. Miz Scott, if this really is an emergency, you should maybe tell *me*."

The line was quiet for so long that Billy Ray called her name to make sure she was still on the line.

"I'm here," she said, sounding like she'd made a decision and was none too happy with it. But still she said nothing more.

Billy Ray tried prodding her a little: "Like I said, Miz Scott, no tellin' how long 's gonna be 'fore the chief shows up. 'N' even if he calls in, well, he's not zackly your biggest fan. Lessen I can give 'im some idea what you're callin' 'bout, I don't know how bad he's gonna wanna get back to ya. Wouldn't ya say a's right?"

Another pause. Then, a sighed, "Ok. Listen. Take this down. I know where Owen Dawson's going. He's heading for the Shady Tree Motel which is off Route 19 somewhere south of Trinity." She started to give him the address.

Billy Ray's pen ran out of ink. He tossed the pen away, reached for a cup of pencils on the chief's desk but moved so hastily he knocked the cup off the desk. He did manage to snag one pencil but was trying too hard to catch up with Rita Scott's dictation and snapped off the point. He tossed the pencil away, beckoned Waylon Meeks over, then grabbed the pen in Waylon's breast pocket so hard he almost tore the pocket.

"Hey!" Waylon barked, retreating as he checked his pocket for damage.

Billy Ray copied down the address for the Shady Tree.

"Now listen to me Billy Ray," Rita Scott went on, "I was going to call 911, but if the local cops hear this – unbalanced, armed and dangerous – they're going to come down hard with a SWAT team or whatever you people have down here, and then somebody's going to get hurt. I don't want that, I don't think your chief wants that either. I'm sure your chief knows the local cops. If he can get in touch with them, he can explain things to them, maybe they can figure out a way to take Dawson without trouble. If you don't think you can get the chief, *you've* got to make those calls, Billy Ray. Do you understand?"

"Yes'm." He was polite but he was thinking, Don't be talking to me like I'm a damn child, lady. I get enough of that from everybody else.

"If you do get the chief, tell him I'm on my way to the Shady Tree now. I don't think Dawson's that far ahead of me. If you call the local cops now and they hurry, maybe they can be waiting for him when he gets there."

"Where are ya, Miz Scott?"

"I'm not exactly sure, but I just started seeing exit signs for Trinity." A pause, then, "Billy Ray, if you get the chief, tell him I said *quid pro quo.*"

"Awright, Miz Scott, I better get to it," and Billy Ray hung up. He turned up his nose at *quid pro quo* and the chief and this colored gal being so smart-assy throwing that back and forth. Then he bowed his head and closed his eyes for a few seconds and a few more of the pieces buzzing around in his head fell into place. He scooped up the piece of paper with Rita Scott's cell phone number, reached for his hat and headed for the door.

"*Don'tcha* think you're leavin' me here *again!*" Waylon Meeks warned.

"Ya gotta stay, Waylon, I'm sorry," Billy Ray said.

"Gaw*dammit,* Billy Ray, I been here all a damn day! I ain't stayin' here all a damn -- "

"Waylon!" Billy Ray turned on Waylon with fire so uncharacteristic it shocked Waylon into frozen silence. "I got more service time in 'n you 'n' right now 'at makes me senior officer on duty! 'At makes me in *charge* if the chief is indisposed! *I* don't know where he is, *you* don't know where he is; 'at makes 'im in-dee-*sposed!* This is an emergency situation, Waylon, 'n' ya gotta stay here to cover the office. That's all there is to it. That's an *order!*"

"What do I tell the chief if he calls in?"

"Tell 'im 'bout the sheriff's call 'bout Dawson, tell 'im 'at Scott lady called, I talked to her, 'n' I took off to take care a it."

"Take care a *what?* Where ya *goin'*, Billy Ray?"

"If I don't tell ya, it won't be no lie when ya say ya don't know, Waylon," Billy Ray said, shoving Rita Scott's number deep in his pocket.

"Man, Billy Ray, I hope you know what you're doin'," Waylon Meeks said with a cautioning shake of his head as Billy Ray headed out the door.

You and me both, Billy Ray thought.

It was not long after they had passed the Quikie Stop – its parking apron filled with the flashing lights of an ambulance and police cars from the sheriff's office and nearby Trinity – that Clyde's scanner fixed on a county-wide bulletin saying a witness who had left the convenience store scene fit the description of Owen Dawson, subject of an APB issued in connection with a shooting incident at Byrum's range earlier that day.

Clyde started to reach for his radio mic. Bob Wheeler made a noise that stopped him. Clyde looked over, saw Bob Wheeler, a ghostly image in the green glow of the dash lights, his face twisted in that way that happens when no matter how hard a person thinks, they still can't come up with the right thing to do.

After a bit, Bob Wheeler quietly asked, "What would they do?"

Clyde shrugged not because he didn't know, but because he didn't want to say. "What time you got?"

Bob Wheeler held his watch up to the dash lights and squinted. "Looks like nine-thirty almost."

"He should already be there," Clyde said. "Too late to get somebody there 'head of 'im."

"Maybe," Bob Wheeler began, his voice tight, "maybe he already...ya know...did whatever --"

"It'd be on a po-lice band by now," Clyde said. "He's there 'n' he's waitin' on somethin'. I call it in 'n' they'll go down there 'n' beat a bushes lookin' for 'im." Clyde frowned. "I'd tell 'im to go in easy. Sheriff Bowen's a good fella, got good people under 'im. He'd unnerstand what I'm sayin'. But he's also gonna tell his people not to take no chances. Your friend a preacher makes a fuss..." Clyde cocked his head, shrugged, sighed.

Bob Wheeler turned away, looking out at dark shapes slipping by in the night, his shoulders melting into a defeated hump. He looked for little bits of hope. "I don't think Owen'd make trouble."

"You didn't think your preacher friend'd go off huntin' down his wife with a Winchester pump 'n' a movie camera, neither, didja? He's snapped, Mr. Wheeler; he's gone off the rails. I'm not 'fraid a him makin' a fuss with po-lice. I'm thinkin' it won't get to that. The minute – the *second* – he sees po-lice 'n' figgers 'at's the end a his movie-makin', like as not he's gonna stick the muzzle a that gun in his mouth. I'd like to be wrong 'bout 'at, Mr. Wheeler, I surely would, but people get theyselves in a box like 'at, seems to be what they-all do." Clyde, again, reached for the mic. He found Bob Wheeler's hand in the way.

"If we can get there before...before Owen does what he went there to do... I can talk to 'im, Chief. Wouldn't you rather end this with a conversation 'stead a shoot-out?"

"You're takin' a hell of a chance with Mrs. Dawson."

"Please."

Clyde waved a hand as if to say, Fine, but this is on your head, but even as he agreed to Bob Wheeler's request, Clyde was kicking himself, telling himself this was a bad idea, a damn *lousy* idea, telling himself, Man, you should know better.

The entrepreneurial thinking behind the Shady Tree Motel wasn't too unlike the thinking behind the Candlelight Inn which was that anywhere you went there were going to be people looking for the kind of quiet hideaways where they could do the kind of things people could only do in quiet hideaways. The Candelight was a quiet hideaway for people who wanted to pitch a little woo over an electric candle-lit dinner; the Shady Tree was for what people had in mind for *after* dinner. Or, who didn't want to bother with dinner at all and skip right to dessert.

So, like the Candelight, the Shady Tree sat isolated, a few miles down a small, twisty, side road off Route 19 among the pine forests southeast of Trinity. At night, with the lights of Trinity and the traffic on 19 hidden by low hills and curtains of pines, the Shady Tree was an oasis of soft glows in a black void.

Despite a common intent, unlike the Candlelight, the Shady Tree hadn't been built with much in mind about creating a romantic atmosphere, the idea being the guests would bring all the romance they needed with them, and all the Shady Tree needed to do was supply a comfortable bed and a modicum of privacy. The place looked like a million other roadside motels; a cinderblock L of a dozen rooms, a coffee shop at the end of one arm, an office at the other, and a kidney-shaped swimming pool enfolded in between. By each door was a small, unobtrusive yellow lamp providing just enough light to walk by, and at the end of each arm's walkway blue bug lights hummed and crackled sporadically, and between the haloes of door lamp yellow and bug light blue rippled a soothing aqua cast by the pool lights.

Unsurprisingly, the Shady Tree did most of its business on weekends, so, this being a weeknight, the motel was exceptionally quiet and exceptionally dark. Three cars were scattered about the gravel parking lot, two rooms showed amber lamplight around drawn curtains, the third the pale flickering blue of a television, the rest were dark. At one end of the motel the coffee shop was closed until morning, and at the other end, only a nightlight glowed in the office.

Across the road from the Shady Tree was a shaded picnic area overlooking a shallow stream, and tucked among the trees was Owen Dawson's Winnebago, buried deep enough in shadows that even someone standing on the road shoulder and peering closely into the blackness might, at best, only catch the barest glint of a reflection from one of the Shady Tree door lamps on its windshield, or perhaps the slimmest streak of moonlight on its aluminum hull.

But they would not have been able to see into the unlit interior, and see Owen Dawson sitting at the wheel, his shotgun across his lap, his eyes on the motel.

Pooch lay curled by Owen's feet. Owen heard the dog sigh in that resigned, sleepy way dogs do. Owen let his right hand fall from the butt of the shotgun to absently run along the animal's spine. Pooch shifted receptively under Owen's fingers.

Owen had his window open. The night was warm, filled with the little, sleepy-time chirps of crickets and the buzzing of mosquitoes, the bubbling of the stream and the belches of frogs. From across the road came the smooth hum of air conditioners, the occasional quick, quiet little *bzzt-crack* of the bug lights at work.

Owen gave up his own sigh, one that sounded as resigned and sleepy as the one from the dog. The nigger woman at the Quikie Stop had told him Sarah was dead, but he had come anyway. It was always possible she had lied because niggers lied, and niggers stuck together, and maybe she was protecting the nigger who had dirtied his wife. It was always possible she was wrong or confused, because the body had been found in a fire and niggers were always wrong or confused. And even if Sarah was dead, maybe her nigger boy didn't know -- just as Owen hadn't known -- because niggers were stupid, and that meant maybe, hopefully, the nigger boy would still come.

And whether or not the nigger woman had been lying or was wrong, whether or not Sarah was already dead or still off in the Trinity night somewhere, whether the nigger boy was still coming or not, or coming with Sarah or not...none of that mattered. Not anymore. His movie needed an ending and one way or another, in one form or another, this would be the place and the time was nigh.

If the last few days had taught him anything, it was acceptance of imperfection. Desires live to be frustrated, hopes to be destroyed. All bad things – all mishaps, bad circumstances, wrongdoings, miscalculations, malevolence, short-sightedness, error, injustice, all sins intentional and inadvertent, of commission and omission – were possible. Probable.

And this was the truth – The Truth – that had, at long last, after years of believing and preaching The Lie, grabbed Owen Dawson by the throat and thrown him down on the ground with one hand, and with the other punched him in the heart.

The Lie – that great, lulling, hypnotic narcotizing Lie – was this: there is a plan. It is God's will. Everything is a part of his masterful design. All things happen for a reason.

You stand by a graveside as someone buries their two-year-old who died of leukemia and tell her parents God has a purpose for everything, a reason.

A man goes out for a pack of cigarettes, decides to stop off and get his family some ice cream and gets side-swiped by a semi, and you tell his widow and three children God must have needed him, and it is not for us to question God's plan. There is a reason for everything, you tell them. God needed him, you say.

Their house burns down or gets spread across a pasture by a tornado, they get diagnosed with lung cancer, a business partner guts the company account and leaves his them stranded in bankruptcy court, a government man shows up in his little white sedan telling them their herd has to be put down and buried in quicklime because of a bad blood test, their dog dies spitting up blood because someone – probably that sonofabitch down the block always complaining about his barking, they say – threw a pound of chopped meat laced with broken glass over the yard fence.

No matter how inexplicable, how tragic, how pointlessly painful, you tell them to trust, to have faith, to believe.

God has His reasons.

He has a purpose.

There is a plan.

All lies.

All lies making The Great Lie.

And Owen felt the shame of a dupe, of a gullible hick conned out of every penny in his pocket by a sidewalk Three Card Monte master.

And now he knew The Truth.

And The Truth had come to him in a night of beseeching prayer. He had lived his life pledged to God, lived his life by His Word, carried out His work on Earth. *Trust in the Lord with all thine heart*, went His Word, *and lean not unto thine own understanding*, and thus had Owen lived…he had obeyed and abided and the reward for his life of piety and devotion and purity and faith was to lose his wife to a nigger. To a nigger and to the filth she hid behind her dresser drawers.

And he had dropped to his knees on the hard wood floor of the parsonage and asked – begged – God for help. To understand. To at least provide him solace.

And none came. Only the The Truth came.

And the Truth was this:

People suffered.

They were maimed and died.

They went without food, they went without water. They went without homes, without clothing. They suffered in heat, in cold.

They suffered in wars, in violence in the streets, from unsafe machines and homes built on poisoned land. Terrorists came into schools and killed their children. *Other* children came into schools and killed their children.

They were pulled off streets in the dead of night and disappeared. They stood in squares and demanded freedom and were crushed by tanks. They sold themselves for money and died riddled with disease. They sold their children for money and *they* died beaten, abused, and diseased.

They bled in torture chambers, wallowed in their own filth forgotten in rest homes, died of despair and dope in ghettos.

Tidal waves and floods, forest fires and earthquakes took their homes because nobody told them their homes sat in the most dangerous places on earth, and when they were left stranded and hungry and thirsty afterward the world watched them on the nightly news and saw them die waiting for help that came late if at all. And if their deaths were unspectacular, if they came from famine, from backwater wars that ground on for years, for decades, then their deaths went unwitnessed, unknown.

And so The Truth was this: that the just, the fair, the incorruptible, the brave, the loving, the generous, the innocent all suffered. They grew ill, they were robbed, deprived, brutalized, disenfranchised, forgotten. Betrayed.

And The Truth was also that others did not suffer. The avaricious and ruthless, the self-aggrandizing and selfish lived in palaces and castles and towers of gleaming steel and glass, and they lived lives as removed and indifferent to the suffering and deprivation they caused and from which they profited as that of an astronaut to an ant.

And The Truth was that if there was a God, He was in His Heaven looking down on a panoply of pain and anguish, of bloodshed and victimization, of exploitation and destruction, of neglect and apathy, of hunger and poverty and illness. And he did nothing.

He did nothing.

Perhaps He *chose* not to raise His hand, feeling Man's doings were Man's business, which made Him an insensitive God, an uncaring God, incapable of feeling the heartache and suffering of the beings He had created.

Or, perhaps, He fostered the agonies of the world, He *allowed* them because He derived some sort of amusement, of pleasure from watching what Man did to his own, and how energetically and imaginatively he did it.

And these were all options which made it preferable to believe there was no God at all.

And this is what Owen Dawson had come to believe to be The Truth, for when he found his pious life had been paid back with shame and humiliation, and had fallen to his knees and prayed until his flesh grew raw and split and bled, and he had lifted his face Heavenward and called on God, all he had heard was his own, pained sobbing and the creaking of an empty house.

Heaven, The Truth told him, was a place above the shingles of his roof that consisted of empty, cold space, barren planets, and the mindless burning of distant starts. You can pray until your raw knees bleed you dry, until your legs wear down to nubs, and you won't hear any more of a response than you're hearing now.

And The Truth was that Man was on his own, and there was no grand plan, no intelligent design. Man had what he took, kept what he could defend, and took it from the weak and vulnerable. Right and wrong were determined by capabilities, not the mandate of God or the temptations of Lucifer. "God" was only another taming myth, like the boogieman, something to frighten the children and the ignorant and feeble, and all that talk of a plan and a purpose was just a spiritual nightlight to keep lost souls from being frightened in the dark.

And at first it had pained Owen Dawson deep in his heart to discover that he – like any man, like *Man* – stood on the earth alone. But then...

Then, in his night of prayer and pain, he had found peace in that knowledge, in that Truth. It was not a satisfying or warm answer, but it was *an* answer, *the* answer; definitive. The world was now resolved in his eyes in a way that God and His Word – The Lie – had never been able to put it to rest, to make sense of it.

"Intelligent design"; any day's headlines made a mockery of the idea. Any day's catalogue of catastrophe told all but the blinded and deluded that there was no intelligence at work, no design. No heart. Rather, each day was a frank, incontrovertible declaration that Man was alone, each person fending for himself amidst the chaos, fighting for no greater reward than survival.

It was a truth that was plain as day. As any day. Plain as any day's news.

And so the peace he had once found in the lulling poetry of The Bible, in the warm cocoon of meditation and prayer, in the once pure embrace of his wife and the absoluteness of his faith, he now found in the wooden stock, rubber grips, and cold steel of the mechanism lying across his lap. And he found peace in the knowledge that all questions were finally answered, and that all things of meaning to him would this night find their resolution.

Sound carried far in the quiet of the night and Owen heard the murmur of tires on asphalt long before headlights swept through the woods and turned into the unlit parking lot of the Shady Tree. He could not make the car out well in the gloom, but it was a small, boxy sedan; he guessed a rental car. It crackled across the gravel lot leaving a small wake of dust, then pulled up to a stop by one of the rooms. The car's lights died, the engine stopped. Owen could barely see inside the car, vague silhouettes backlit by the walkway lights of the motel; heads tilting toward each other, nuzzling, then moving in the way heads move in a deep kiss.

Owen's right hand came back from stroking the dog and settled on the black crescent moon of his gun's trigger.

The two figures sat in the car for a long minute, then climbed out opposite sides. The man was not much bigger than his woman, but he had a deep, rich voice, and Owen could hear him chuckling and teasing as he pretended to run after her, deliberately giving her time to dodge him and weave away.

She giggled back in a voice that came through the night to him; light like glass chimes.

After a bit, she stopped dodging, let the man close and wrap her in his strong arms, picking her off the ground. She bent her head down toward his and they kissed. Then, he set her down gently, took her hand in his and they walked toward one of the motel room doors. He was holding her left hand with his right, but the room key was in his right pocket, and he would not let go of her hand as he clumsily tried to fish for the key with his left hand.

She murmured something in a low, intimate tone, and stuck her free right hand down inside his pocket, digging deep. Her hand moved to the front of his pants. He pulled her close and kissed her, this time without affection or tenderness. This time the kiss was hard and lustful.

They finished, there was the clatter of a key in the lock, the door opened, then shut behind them.

Owen drew an arm across his forehead. It was warm in the Winnebago, and his body was sticky with sweat. He climbed out of the driver's seat, drew the curtains hung behind the RV's front seats, and went to the camper's closet-sized bathroom. He closed the door behind him so there'd be no chance of anyone spying a light, flicked on the lamp over the sink mirror. He stoppered the drain and filled the sink with water from the jug he'd taken from the Quickie Stop, then opened his shaving kit for his razor and cream. He shaved away a day's worth of bristle, then washed his face.

A shred of Scripture came to him, but they were no longer His words; they were words Owen had taken for his own:

I go to prepare a place for you...

His ablutions done, he sat at the dining table with the shotgun. Working by the moonlight coming through the window behind him, he emptied the magazine and wiped the receiver clean with his gun rag. He was sorry he did not have a cleaning rod to swab the barrel clean; this night the pellets should have been able to come down a clean path. But then, it was an imperfect world.

And if I go and prepare a place for you,

I will come again, and receive you unto myself...

He took a fresh box of shells from his travel bag and set it on the table. From this he took five shells and slipped them into the magazine, then racked the first one into the chamber.

He slid out from the dining nook and slipped out of his clothes. He unzipped the suit bag he'd taken with him when he'd left the parsonage and took out his dark minister's suit, and a bright, white clergyman's collar, and dressed.

He took the remaining shells from their box and dropped half in his right pocket, the other half in his left. He fixed his camcorder to its tripod, put the tripod over one shoulder, and picked up the shotgun with his other hand.

He opened the door of the camper and the dog stirred and rose from where he'd been laying up front, coming toward the door. Owen blocked him and kept shooing him inside until he'd managed to step outside and get the door closed behind him. Pooch scratched at the door a few times, then the camper was quiet. Owen set the tripod and gun down on one of the picnic tables, sat himself on the bench, and waited.

He needed to give them time. It had to be just the right moment. With all the imperfections, this one thing had to be perfect.

...that where I am, there ye may be also.

And this would be how Owen Dawson would gain retribution from all those years of believing The Lie, and atone for all those years of preaching it. Retribution and atonement would come with his revelation of The Truth, the doctrine of a new church, *his* new church, for which he would preach this night his first and final evangel, captured for all time on a memory chip, and ordained in blood.

Billy Ray Barnes didn't see any need for discretion which wasn't surprising since Billy Ray Barnes rarely saw the need for discretion, and, besides, it was the rare day when he got the chance to fire up all the emergency accoutrements on his patrol unit. So, when he hit Route 19, he lit up the roof lights and kicked in the siren although there was hardly enough traffic on the road at night to even justify an occasional horn honk. He fed the engine as much gas as he thought it could take without blowing something, and with the car rattling and shaking and shimmying, he highballed his way south.

But all that rattling and shaking and the wailing of the siren and even the occasional car or semi he passed didn't hold his attention for much more than a few seconds at a time. Billy Ray Barnes was trying to work through a lot in his head.

Whatever Billy Ray Barnes' intellectual limitations may have been, it was painfully evident to him he'd been digging himself into a deep-getting-deeper hole. He'd shot off his mouth in front of that colored girl reporter about that overcooked body out at Wilbur McCoy's being Sarah Dawson, and it only made it worse that he'd been wrong -- *way* wrong – about whose body had gotten dragged out of Wilbur's burned-down shed. On the good side, he'd gotten the body ID'd and, in the process, found out what had happened to poor ol' Jesse Smith (that should count as *two* good things, shouldn't it?). But then, in trying clean that mess up he'd run up the city's tab on an investigation His Royal Highness Fred C. Reilly wanted closed by calling Barney White back in as well as that smart-mouthed hot-headed dentist Greenley, and now that little fart Waylon Meeks was pissing and moaning about OT pay, and, according to Waylon, Clyde Thomas had been pretty pissed when he'd come by earlier that evening and found Billy Ray not being where Billy Ray was supposed to be...

Yep, he thought, that was a pretty damn deep hole. Good work, Billy Ray, he told himself. Real good. First rate. Top drawer. You done put together such a masterpiece fuck-up you should sign it and hang it in the Houston Museum of Fine Arts. At this rate, by the time the sun comes up tomorrow, ol' Clyde's going to want your sorry ass put against a wall and shot …if His Majesty Fred C. Reilly doesn't do it first. And once ol' Clyde finds out you took that colored girl reporter's call and lit out on your own, that's pretty much what he's going to do.

Unless…

By Billy Ray's calculation, he had one shot at evening it all out, and if he screwed that up, well, he was already knocking on the Devil's roof as it was; he couldn't dig himself much deeper in a hole.

In the perfect blackness on either side of Route 19, it was easy to pick out the distant fluorescent glow of the Quickie Stop from far up the highway along with the flashing of red and blue police and ambulance flashers. Which also meant it wasn't hard for the county cops at the Quickie Stop to pick up on Billy Ray's flashers and siren as he streaked by.

Billy Ray heard his erratic radio crackle: "…County Unit One-Five…emergency vehicle on Highway One-Nine South, please identify…"

Billy Ray picked up his radio mic. "Ah, 10-4 that. This is Officer Barnes out of Boone on a Code 3, no assistance required."

The voice came back and even with half the words dropping out Billy Ray could tell the county cop was angry: "…the hell doin'…a Code 3…no jurisdiction…Pull over and…"

"Uh, this is Officer Barnes," Billy Ray responded. "You, uh, you're breakin' up there, County, sorry, unable to receive. I'll get back with y'all later."

Billy Ray's radio crackled and snapped again: "…the *fuck* you *mean* -- "

Billy Ray turned off his radio. He gave a friendly wave at the police cars in front of the Quickie Stop and at the burly man he could see standing by one of the cars, screaming into his radio mic as he frantically waved at Billy Ray's car.

Billy Ray sunk a little deeper into his seat, gave the car a little more gas, felt the car buck and rattle a bit more and thought if the car did blow itself up it might not be the worst thing that could happen to him the way things were going.

And with that in mind he kept speeding toward Trinity.

Of all the people barreling toward the Shady Tree Motel that night, by rights Rita Scott should've been the first one there behind Owen Dawson. In point of fact, considering the differences in performance between her Corvette and Owen's antiquated and less-than-aerodynamic Winnebago, and even allowing for Owen's head-start, Rita should've made it to the Shady Tree *before* Owen Dawson. Instead, long after she *should've* been skidding into the parking lot of the Shady Tree, she was still bouncing along a pitch-black dirt road winding through God knows where, and that seriously abused the underside of the low-slung Corvette.

The oil pan of the 'vette clanged against the pitted and rutted road for the umpteenth time and Rita pulled to a stop. She didn't bother pulling over to the shoulder. She hadn't seen another set of headlights – in fact *any* kind of lights – since she'd pulled onto the road, so she wasn't worried about getting back-ended. Besides, it was so dark outside she couldn't even see if there was a shoulder. Beyond the wedge her headlights cut into the night in front of her there was nothing.

Back on 19 there'd been a billboard reading:

Shady Tree Motel

Campus Country, Texas

Next Exit and 5 miles down the road.

See y'all soon, hear?

And then in smaller print at the bottom: "Just follow the signs, pardner!"

Rita had come to the opinion that whoever had put up that billboard and thought up those instructions must have done so in the daytime when you could actually *see* signs. But either the billboard had lied, or the supposed signs had been swallowed up by the overgrown brush on either side of the road, or – Rita's preferred opinion – it was just too goddamned *dark* to see signs, landmarks, or any other indication of terrestrial life, because, in fact, she *hadn't* seen any goddamned signs…or much else for that matter. No houses, outbuildings, property markings, no other cars, nothing. And when the macadam road she'd turned off on had become a roller coaster ride of dirt and rocks, she thought, You know, girl, this just *might* be time to panic.

She flicked on the dome light and reached for the road atlas she'd appropriated at the Quikie Stop, but it didn't take her long to realize the study was pointless. To use the map, she had to be able to pick out some kind of reference point…which she couldn't. From what she could figure, she could be on any number of ranch roads crisscrossing the open country below Trinity. She tried Google Maps on her phone but it kept glitching; she must be in another of those poor cell service areas that'd been dogging her since she'd set foot in Texas.

She stepped out of the car and stood on the rocker panel, hoping maybe the extra few inches of altitude might broaden her scope of vision enough to pick out some guiding sight. And far off to her right, she did manage to see…*something*. A soft, barely perceptible glow.

She kicked off her shoes because she was already going to have to answer to the car rental agency for the jimmied door lock, missing car radio, and probably a dented oil pan, and didn't need any additional grief from them about ruining the 'vette's paint job. She stepped onto the car's front hood and then onto the roof which made some unsettling buckling sounds under her.

But now she could see better: some kind of lights, a building maybe just a half-mile or so off to her right and behind her. It *had* to be the Shady Tree because there wasn't anything else out there. She slid back down the roof, climbed back into the car and pulled the road atlas across her lap. Assuming the lights were the Shady Tree, she figured out her own probable position and quickly mapped out a course back to 19 and then to the correct turn-off for the motel.

She wrestled the car through a hurried five-point turn-around; it was a narrow road and she didn't want to stray onto a shoulder that might not be there. And then she was banging her oil pan off the road again as she roared back down the way she'd come.

She'd lost time, but she took heart that the Shady Tree had appeared peaceful. No screams coming across through the night air, no angry police flashers disturbing the mellow glow of the motel.

With luck – of which, she'd had to admit, she hadn't seen much lately – she might just be in time.

Owen Dawson sat among the dark shadows across from the Shady Tree, his camcorder and shotgun on the table in front of him, listening to the trickling of the creek behind him, the night sounds of mosquitoes and frogs. His eyes began to slip closed, his head bob down toward his chest. He shook himself awake, reprimanding himself. Wouldn't *that* be a fine way for it all to end; him found sound asleep in the picnic area the next morning!

But he was tired, so tired, as if he'd toted the camera and shotgun a million miles, and it seemed like that, like it had been a million miles from the parsonage to Trinity. And it was hard to remember what things had been like a few days ago, other than as a half-remembered dream. Unreal. Never real.

And he did not know how long he sat there, waiting, did not look at his watch, but he wanted them to have time together, because for all the imperfections he was willing to tolerate, the one thing he needed to be perfect was their shame and abasement, for this was not revenge; this was retribution.

And after a while, when he felt the time was right, he stood with the sigh of a man who's worked a long day only to find there's one more chore left to do. He picked up his camera and put the tripod across his left shoulder, then picked up his shotgun in his right hand, and couldn't remember them ever feeling this heavy before. He looked skyward, toward the stars half-hidden by the latticework of branches overhead, and he said aloud, "If you're there and you've got something to say, this is the time." There was only a slight breeze which rustled the leaves, made the branches moan. He smiled ruefully. "Amen," and he walked out of the shadows, crossed the narrow road and then the unlit parking lot.

Owen stopped at their car and saw the decal of a car rental agency on the back window. He stopped for a moment, and he thought of the rented car and the room at the Shady Tree. He knew how little he and Sarah had to spare, and he knew the nigger had less. He thought of how long and how hard they must have worked to put aside a few dollars here and there, to lie and cheat a few dollars out of a week, week after week, so they could have these few days together. And as he considered this, his weariness dropped away, burned off with a building, consuming anger that set him trembling, and the camera and shotgun no longer seemed heavy.

He strode to the door of their room and set the camera and tripod nearby against the wall, making sure it stood steady and wouldn't fall. He put his ear to the door, but it was a heavy, metal door; he could hear nothing. He took the Winchester in both hands and stepped back from the door.

And he stood there a long moment confused by the abruptness of it, thinking there must be something else before it began, that this was like vaulting into the abyss rather than a slow walk down the canyon wall. And he realized the only way was simply to take a breath and leap. And so he took a deep breath and put the shotgun to his shoulder where it nestled snug and natural, pointed the barrel at the plate around the doorknob, and squeezed the trigger.

And a million things ran through his mind at once with the detonation, like how the incident at the shooting range with those four Neanderthals had been a blessing preparing him for the thunder and the bruising kick in his shoulder, but since there'd been no walls at the range he hadn't expected the concussion wave which rebounded off the motel door all hot and acrid-reeking of cordite, smelling and tasting of Old Testament hellfire, and how even before the smoke cleared he could see that the round had destroyed the hammer mechanism but something else still held the door and he raised the barrel to where he thought the dead bolt would be, telling himself to hurry, not to give them time inside to react, and pumped a second round into the chamber and fired again, surprised that the double-0 buckshot didn't completely sunder the door which still somehow some way still hung closed until Owen delivered a kick near the knob and wood cracked and gunfire-tortured metal snapped loose and the door sprang open...

The only light came from a night table lamp and next to the lamp was a screw-top bottle of wine and two half-filled paper cups. His Sarah sat on the bed. She was wearing a bustier of black lace, with garters attached to black fishnet stockings, and though she was in bed she wore patent leather stiletto heels. Between the swell of her small breasts, exaggerated by the push-up underwire of the bustier, lay a small, gold cross hanging from a chain that went around her neck, the gold glinting in the lamplight. Her face was heavily painted with crimson lipstick and blue mascara and almost fluorescent rouge.

Standing over her was a Black man naked but for a pair of satiny bikini briefs. He was small-statured, not much bigger than Sarah, and Owen couldn't see his face well in the dim lamplight, but his small, compact body was taught with muscles; a man's body. He was standing over Sarah holding a pair of fur-lined handcuffs.

Sarah looked at Owen, her arms crossed over her breasts, her face a collection of little surprised "o"'s; wide eyes, an open mouth.

The nigger looked at him, his face frozen, but his eyes full of confusion and fear, his hands held away from his body in some vague, supplicating plea.

Owen stood in the doorway, wreathed in cordite vapor, not quite sure exactly what should come next, what he should say and do, what *they* should say and do. It came to him, with an icy clarity, as it had come to him quickly, easily, clearly back at the firing range, and he pumped a fresh shell into the shotgun's chamber with an exquisite feeling of power knowing that none of the nigger boy's muscles could stand against the power and lightning of the old gods. He, Owen, held that great, rending power in his hands, could tap it with a firm squeeze of one finger.

Owen smiled and stepped casually into the room. As he stood at the base of the bed, deeply inhaling the cordite smell, he turned his sick little smile toward his wife and said, "Happy anniversary, Sarah."

At which, she could no longer face him and turned away to the wall.

"Hello, Leroi," Owen said to the nigger boy. "Sorry to interrupt your enjoyment of my wife."

The boy stepped back until he bumped against a wall. "Look, Preacher, I'm I'm I'm -- "

"Shhh," Owen said quietly, and waved Leroi Jefferson quiet with a wave of the shotgun's muzzle which left arcs of smoke in the room. "On the bed."

A frightened Leroi exchanged a look with a frightened Sarah. "What?" he asked Owen.

"I said get on the bed. Snuggle close."

"Please, Preacher, let me -- "

"*Do it!*" Owen exploded.

Leroi did and that brought Owen back to his icy cool and little smile. "Closer," Owen told Leroi. "Put your arm around her. Like you love her." He kept the shotgun on them while he reached outside the door and brought the camera in.

"Owen!" Sarah begged, "Please -- "

"*Shut up, whore!*" Another explosion. "Don't dirty my name with your mouth!"

Leroi and Sarah held each other close, but not in an embrace of intimacy for she was sobbing, now, shaking, and holding on out of fear...as was the boy.

Owen set the camera up at the foot of the bed and sighted it at the couple. In the viewfinder they were just gray shadows. "Hmm." There was another bedside lamp, and another lamp on the dresser, but they wouldn't do. Too many crisscrossing shadows, the light falling all wrong. People had to be able to see them clearly. "Stand up," Owen told them.

"Whaddaya gonna -- " Leroi Jefferson began.

"You don't talk, nigger," Owen said flatly. "You do what a good nigger should. Do what you're told and keep your mouth shut. Now, stand up, both of you. You, boy, take those handcuffs and cuff yourself to her. C'mon, boy, what's the big problem? It's a little late to pretend you're shy about this sort of thing."

Leroi Jefferson slapped one cuff on his left wrist, then gently put the other around Sarah's right.

"Why so gentle all of a sudden, boy?" Owen asked. "I thought it was the rough stuff you *both* liked. Isn't that what you like?" He stepped forward, holding the shotgun in front of Jefferson's face. "Isn't that what you like, boy? You like it rough, right? Dirty? Isn't that why she's here, because you'll do it rough and dirty for her?"

"Owen," Sarah heaved out between sobs, "won't you...won't you please listen?"

"To *what?*" Owen laughed. "'Ohhh, Owen, I'm so *soooorrrryyy!*' 'Owen, I didn't mean it!' 'Owen, it's not what it looks like!'" And the laughter stopped as his face twisted into a disgusted sneer. "What could you *possibly* have to say, whore? What could the whore tell me?" He turned back to Leroi Jefferson. "How about it, nigger? What do you think your whore could tell me that would make a difference? Could she tell me you're just good friends? Hm? Is that what the whore could tell me? Hm, nigger?"

Up close, now, he could see Leroi Jefferson's face, a boy's face, still with black smudges of acne along his neck. And Owen felt his face twist in repugnance because it was not enough that his Sarah had made herself a whore and an adulteress, it was not enough that she had done so to indulge her perversities, but she had done it with this nigger *boy*. As if in so doing she was saying that even this nigger *child* was more man than her husband.

The boy was terrified, which Owen liked, Owen thought it was good, but for all his fear the boy didn't look away. Instead, he turned his eyes – soft, dark orbs shining with tears – directly into Owen's. "Maybe," Leroi Jefferson said in a strained voice mustering some small shred of defiance, "maybe she could tell you *you're* why she's here."

Owen's laugh turned caustic. "*I'm* why she's here? Because I didn't want to go along with her *sickness?* Because I didn't think my wife should act like the dirty bitch street whore she *is? That's* why she's here? Is that what you're trying to tell me, nigger?"

"If we could've talked," Sarah said wiping at the tears that were running down her cheeks, black with mascara. "There's things...things I want, Owen."

Owen's face wrinkled in disgust. "I see what you want."

"No," and she shook her head tiredly, knowing making him understand was hopeless. "You don't see. That's what I mean, Owen. I knew you'd believe even *thinking* some things was sick and dirty...It's just...*play*, Owen. Just -- "

"*Enough!*" It was not he who was here to be judged, and he was through hearing it. "Outside."

Leroi Jefferson swallowed, and pulled his hard little body erect. "Reverend, I don't blame ya for feelin' like this. But leave 'er be. Me 'n' you take care a this, jus' 'tween us -- "

"Man to man?" Owen taunted. "I don't think so. With a nigger, we'd be one man short. *Outside!*"

"Least let us put some clothes on. Her, anyway."

Owen grinned. "I thought the two of you were proud of your wares! That's why you took pictures of yourselves, right? Because you're so proud – *so goddamned proud* – of yourselves? That's good, that's very good, because that's how you're going to be remembered."

"Owen, it's me you want to punish," Sarah pleaded. "Let him go."

"That's a thought, my dear." Owen lowered the shotgun and pointed it at the bulge in Leroi Jefferson's briefs. "Maybe I'll do that. On the condition I separate Mr. Stud here from his equipment so he won't be much of a buck anymore. Would you like that, nigger? Tell me; between that and dying, what's your preference? I still believe in mercy, nigger, I'll give you that choice. Consider it a holdover from my Christian days."

Leroi Jefferson brought his one free hand around to cover his genitals. His ebony skin shone with sweat. "Oh, sweet Jesus, Preacher, please, you're a man a *God*, how can you do this?"

"Well, I'm afraid God and I have come to a parting of the ways." Owen frowned in contemplation. "Maybe I'll be *truly* merciful and make it sudden." He raised the muzzle of his shotgun and set it against Leroi Jefferson's lips. "I'll bet you've given my wife a lot of pleasure with that mouth, hm, nigger? Whispered sweet nothings in her ear? Used that tongue on her, stuck it in that filth of hers and made her scream with delight, hm, nigger? Maybe if you said you were sorry. Are you sorry, nigger? You coveted a man's wife; are you sorry? Maybe if you said it, maybe if you *begged* me and said you were sorry - -."

"Sorry for *what?*" Scared as he was, Leroi Jefferson was growing angry. "I didn't covet *nothin'!*" the boy declared. "She *came* to me, man! You *lost* 'er! Now you're gonna waste us 'cause you're so tight-assed -- "

"Shut your filthy mouth!" Owen commanded, silencing Leroi Jefferson by spearing him in the diaphragm with the muzzle of the shotgun. He liked the nigger better when he was just scared…and quiet. Better for the movie. "We're going outside. Just the way you are. Both of you. *Now!*"

Owen put the tripod under his arm and followed Sarah and Leroi Jefferson outside. They walked slowly, Leroi Jefferson's bare feet flinching on the sharp-edged gravel of the parking lot, Sarah tottering on the stones on her tall, spindly heels. The boy and the girl drew closer together out in the open, and the boy's cuffed hand took hold of Sarah's, their fingers intertwining.

For Owen, that was perhaps the most painful thing; that this was not just carnality and lustful appetite, but that his wife, his Sarah, had given to this boy something more than just her body.

It was all he could do not to kill them both right then. But let's not cheat the audience, he told himself.

The other Shady Tree guests had heard the shots and naturally had come to their doors in curiosity, had heard the exchange in the room and craned their necks to gawk and ogle. But then they saw the man with the shotgun and Owen heard doors around the motel slam closed. He felt a new and strange invigoration at the idea that these people were afraid…of *him*.

Across the parking lot, the lights were on in the motel office and a short, round figure stood in the open doorway. "Hey!" the rotund silhouette called out. "You better throw that thing down! The po-lice is awready -- "

Owen raised his Winchester and sent another of his thunderbolts across the lot, shattering one of the office windows, setting off a burglar alarm. The round man scurried back inside the office and a second later the windows went dark.

Owen positioned Sarah and the boy in the middle of the parking lot, then set the camera on its tripod in front of them. "Kneel."

They looked at each other, then Leroi Jefferson turned to Owen. "Preacher, I got a baby chil' 'n' I got his momma -- "

"I'll be sure to send them a copy," Owen said coldly, "to make sure they know how much they meant to you. *Kneel!*"

Still they hesitated. Owen walked around behind them and kicked Leroi Jefferson behind one of his knees. The boy's leg buckled and he dropped to the gravel, and Sarah, shackled to his wrist, was dragged down beside him. The boy and girl shifted painfully trying to find some little movement that would keep the stones from digging into their flesh.

"These rocks hurt," Leroi Jefferson said.

"You won't have to worry about it much longer," Owen said as he went behind the camera and began fiddling with the angle and focus. The image was still dark and shadowy, but he could see Sarah had stopped her crying. Her head hung low, resigned, her cloud of yellow hair falling forward concealing her face. And there was a small sparkle on her chest, something catching the moonlight. Owen came out from behind the camera, went over to her, reached down and grabbed Sarah's cross, pulled it sharply snapping the chain. "Not right for the part," he said and threw the chain and cross into the blackness across the road. He turned back to them. "Still not enough light. But I have in mind something spectacular. What we in the movie business call a 'special effect.' I hope you like it."

He reached for the shells in his pocket and topped off the Winchester's magazine. He took a stance a few yards from the tail of their rental car, leveled the gun at the rear and fired. Once, twice, and he stopped himself, realizing that energizing shock that ran through him with each blast of fire and smoke was so intoxicating that he could pump his way through the magazine before he knew what he was doing.

The smell of gasoline wafted to him from the punctured gas tank, and he could hear it trickle onto the stones, see its spreading stain beneath the car. Owen fired again, then a fourth time. The pellets from the fourth shot sparked on the metal of the car and the pool of gas ignited, fire dancing up the little cascades falling from the holes in the tank. Owen stepped back and the gas tank exploded, lifting the car off its back tires. The car crashed down on creaking springs, engulfed in the base of a column of dirty flame and oily smoke.

"Every premier needs a special event," Owen proclaimed, feeding fresh shells into the magazine. "Just like the spotlights they use in Hollywood. This is a first-class production all the way! Ahhhhh," he purred satisfied as he looked through the viewfinder and set the camera running. The clamor of the burglar alarm, Sarah and Leroi Jefferson clad in their grotesqueries, lit by the flickering red and yellow of the pyre, with only impenetrable blackness beyond…it was a perfect picture of Hell. Perfect.

Leaving the camera running he stood in front of Sarah and Leroi Jefferson. "Why so glum? You should be flattered at all the effort I've gone to make sure you look your best."

"Oh, God, Owen," Sarah sighed, drained, "just finish it, will you?"

And he came around and stood behind them. He leaned toward the boy. "This is your big finish, nigger. The world doesn't end in a whimper; but with a bang." He turned to Sarah. "'I will deliver thee…and thou shalt glorify me.'" He straightened, tucked the stock of the shotgun back in its home at his shoulder, and put his finger around the crescent of the trigger…and hesitated.

He would pull the trigger twice and it would be over and then there would be nothing. Everything had built to this, but afterward…emptiness. Purposelessness, again.

Or was he feeling…mercy? Were all those old weaknesses – all those products of The Lie – rationalizing themselves back into his heart? No, he wouldn't allow himself to be fooled, not again. No more of The Lie. For once Sarah was right; it was time to finish.

He hugged the stock of the shotgun closer, his finger grew tighter on the trigger. He believed there was no reason to fear the nothingness that would come after for he had nothing now.

The siren stopped him. He hadn't expected it so soon. But that would make it better. Police escort, flashing lights, the many luminaries are arriving for the world premiere of Owen Dawson's *magnum opus.* This was turning into a regular Hollywood event.

Clyde Thomas had lit up his roof lights, kicked in the siren and floored the gas when he'd heard a *whump* and seen an explosive flash against the night sky beyond the treetops maybe just a mile ahead. He was still calling in a report on the county sheriff's frequency when he pulled his car to a skidding halt in the gravel lot of the Shady Tree. Clyde wasn't ready for the bizarre scene he found there – a Black man and white woman in vulgar underthings kneeling in the middle of the lot with Owen Dawson standing behind them, his shotgun pointed at their heads, all of it lit up by a burning car – but he took some consolation from seeing that he'd made it to the motel before anybody had been hurt.

Bob Wheeler had his door open even before the car pulled to a stop. Clyde reached over and grabbed him by the belt.

"Hold up, Mr. Wheeler," but the other man kept trying to struggle loose. "Mr. Wheeler! You spark 'im wrong 'n' we're gonna have a massacre on our hands!"

"So what do we do?" asked a frantic Bob Wheeler. "Just sit here 'n' watch this…this…"

"Do what we-all came here to do. Don't judge 'im. You're his friend. Talk to 'im like one. He's hurtin', Mr. Wheeler. As long as you keep him talkin', he won't be shootin'."

They climbed slowly out of the car. As Bob Wheeler took a few steps toward Owen, Clyde let Owen see that he was unhitching his holster and leaving it in the car.

"Hi, Bob!" Owen called cheerily, his face flashing blue in the police car's roof lights. "Hello, Chief! Welcome to the premier of an Owen Dawson presentation of a film by Owen Dawson. Uh, that's close enough, Bob, if you don't mind."

"Sarah?" Bob Wheeler called to the woman kneeling in the dirt. "Sarah, is 'at you?"

The woman kept her face turned down, shamed.

"Who else would it be, Bob?" Owen asked. "Typecasting. A whore to play a whore."

"Owen, I know you, I know Sarah. Whatever you think -- "

"Pardon my interrupting, Bob, but you don't know a damn thing," Owen said flatly.

"Owen," and Bob Wheeler took another step forward.

Owen fired.

The man and woman kneeling before Owen pulled into themselves, thinking they'd just heard their last sound on earth, but the blast wasn't for them, pellets kicking up a splash of dust near Bob Wheeler's feet, freezing him in place.

"I said that was close enough, Bob."

It took Bob Wheeler a moment or two to get over the fact that his good friend the Reverend Owen Dawson had come pretty close to intentionally blowing his foot off. He tried, again, but this time his voice quavered, unsure. "Owen, it's not too late to stop this craziness before you hurt someone! You don't want to hurt anybody!"

"Oh, that's where you're wrong, Bob. I *do* want to hurt someone. These two, as a matter of fact. You have no idea how *much* I want to hurt them."

This doesn't seem to be going as well as I'd hoped, Clyde thought, and began eyeing his pistol sitting on the front seat of his car.

Owen saw him looking.

"Chief, I'd appreciate your saving yourself a temptation that will provoke me into blowing your head off. Why don't you step over here by my friend Bob."

Clyde smiled good-naturedly, like an impish little boy caught sneaking into a cookie jar, and moved up to stand by Bob Wheeler. "Look, Reverend --"

"There are no reverends in my church, Chief!" Owen barked. "There is nothing *reverent* in my church!"

Great, Clyde thought, he's pissed off *and* nuts. But at least the preacher was still talking and as long as he was, there was a chance of getting everybody out of the situation in one piece. Including Owen Dawson.

"So, uh, Reverend – I mean, *Mister* Dawson, what happens after?" Clyde asked. "What-all you think is gonna happen when this is done?"

Owen smiled condescendingly, as at a child who didn't understand the most elemental of things. "There's not going to be an after."

Clyde nodded gravely. "I see."

"Nobody's hurt yet, Owen," Bob Wheeler said.

Owen shrugged. "That'll change soon, Bob. I'm glad you're here for my world premiere. It's good to have a friend close by at such an auspicious moment."

"Owen, we've always talked. We could always tell each other what was goin' on. I don't know how many times 'at kinda talk from you helped me. Let me do the same for you now. You might think this is how you want things, but if you could just stop 'n' talk it out, you'd see this isn't what you want."

That condescending smile from Owen Dawson, again. "Bob, my good friend, you are such a child."

Bob Wheeler looked to Clyde, looking for some clue, some suggestion as to what the verbal key might be to turning off the horrible mechanism working away in front of them, but Clyde had nothing to offer.

They looked up at the sound of another siren, then several more still further off.

"Sounds like it's going to be getting a little too crowded here, soon," Owen Dawson said. His face grew soft, contemplative, then resolute. "I think...I think it's time."

But the nearest siren wasn't the first car to pull into the lot.

Prayer did not come easily to Rita Scott. She had stopped praying the day her father died, and certainly there'd been nothing she'd witnessed in her years working for Eric Bird III to prompt her to reconsider her position. But she prayed now.

She prayed her meeting up with Owen Dawson had not been an incident of random chance or capricious fate but of a purpose, and she prayed she would reach the Shady Tree in time, and she prayed that for once in her life she'd be given the opportunity to do something useful and good.

But then she'd heard the explosion somewhere ahead of her, saw its bright flash behind the knolls and trees hidden until then in the dark, and saw the dull, amber glow of the flames that followed, and heard a siren in front of her and more behind her.

Oh, God Jesus no, no, *no*...

Rita pulled to a stop in the Shady Tree parking lot where yellow flames mixed with the blue flashers of a police car sitting ahead of her. She saw Clyde Thomas and Bob Wheeler and past them, in the headlights of the police car, a white woman and Black man kneeling, handcuffed together, and standing behind them was Owen Dawson.

She heard sirens closing behind her. More cops meant more of a chance of somebody getting trigger-happy. She still had time but not much. She quickly climbed out of her car and started toward Owen, didn't slow or flinch when his shotgun swung her way, didn't stop until she saw him take aim.

"That'll do fine, Miz Scott," Owen warned. "Glad you could make it. You can cover the climax of my movie for your paper. Maybe they'll even let you do the review."

She looked over at Clyde Thomas and Bob Wheeler. The chief gave her a skeptical look as if he expected no good to come from her presence. God, she prayed, let me say the right things...

Rita took a small step closer to Owen. Then a second one. "Owen," she said as quietly as the office's clanging burglar alarm and crackling of flames would allow, "you know this is wrong. You headed a church -- "

"Past tense, Miz Scott."

"You can't believe in this!"

Owen shook his head and chuckled. "No one seems to understand my character's motivation. Maybe it can be cleared up in the editing. Would you look after that for me, Miz Scott?"

"Owen, I can prove to you that inside you somewhere you still know this is wrong!"

"Wrong, Miz Scott? *This* is the way of the world."

"You might be right about that, Owen. But you believe in something better."

Owen lowered his head, thinking. "Maybe. Once."

"Still. That's why you saved my life back there! The man who does that, that's not a man who's ready to write off the good in the world. I understand you're hurting. Badly! Anybody would! I'm not asking you to turn the other cheek, to forgive and forget. I'm asking you to be what I've seen you be: more than *they* are. You did it once before, tonight, back there on the highway. It's still in you. Bring it out again."

She had, small step by small step, slowly closed the distance to Owen and now stood just a few yards away. She looked down at the man and woman kneeling in front of Owen. "Leave them to Hell, Owen. To *Hell* with 'em. Throw your collar away, throw *her* away, and go off and start over. Build yourself a new Owen Dawson. Make yourself happy, Owen. You want revenge on these two? That's the best kind. Coming out of this better than you went in. *They'll* be the ones who suffer."

He looked up, for the first time noticed how close she'd come, and the shotgun came up in her direction and she froze.

He shook his head. "For there to be a Hell there has to be a Heaven, Miz Scott, and for there to be a Heaven there has to be a God. The bad never suffer, Miz Scott." He looked down on the two people kneeling before him. "You have to have a conscience to suffer. But this time…this time they'll -- "

"It's the *good* who suffer, Owen, when they sin. You'll know that if you pull that trigger. In your church, it was never bad people that came to you for help. It was the good who misstepped. You *saw* how they suffered."

"And I gave them God like aspirin. Say two prayers and call me in the morning."

"That's right, Owen. Maybe it was a sham, maybe it was useless -- "

"A lie."

" -- maybe it *was* a lie. But you understand their pain now, and how they suffered, because now you've suffered like them. Owen, you can do something here you were never able to do as a preacher. You turn away from this and you show all those people that *they* can turn away from it, too. Everything you always meant to do as a preacher you can do now. Tonight. There's good out there still; you proved that tonight when you saved my life. You want to help people? Make people believe in good? *Be* the proof, Owen. *Now!*"

She couldn't read the look on his face, too much was battling back and forth there: confusion and fear and all those feelings that infuse when clarity and certainty disappear. He shook his head, but not in conviction: he was trying to fend off the complication.

And in that, she took hope.

"To what end?" he asked. "The world'll still be -- "

"A shithole," Rita Scott said, "full of shitty people doing shitty things. You don't save the world, Owen. You save people and you save them one at a time. If you're right, if there is no God, then they need people like you showing them the right thing more than ever."

He still fought it over in his head, weighing it all, and while he did the shotgun lowered, its muzzle pointing to an empty patch of dirt.

And this was good because the flock of sirens Rita had heard behind her on the road sounded terribly close, and there were so many of them, as if every police car in the world was coming down on them.

You'd be working a long day trying to find somebody in Boone who'd ever been impressed by what passed for smarts in Billy Ray Barnes, and it'd be just as pointless an exercise trying to get someone to confess to ever having judged Billy Ray Barnes to have done much that smacked of prudence and practicality. But in the days to follow, one and all would begrudgingly have to admit that that night, as he closed with the Shady Tree, Billy Ray Barnes had acted – shockingly, so, considering his past record – with great prudence and practicality. At least on some counts.

Billy Ray had been barreling along the dark road to the Shady Tree when he'd heard the explosion not far ahead. He had no doubt it had something to do with an unpleasant crossing of paths between Owen Dawson and Sarah Dawson, although how exactly those components had come together in a big boom was a puzzle. Still, it was a nasty enough sound to spur Billy Ray to do his first prudent and practical thing that night. Whatever the explosion meant it probably wasn't going to be a good idea to just crash on into the scene lights and siren going like a carnival, so Billy Ray turned off the lights and silenced the siren and eased up some on the gas.

And then he was one curve in the road away from the Shady Tree, able to see the splash of blue police flashers and the glow of flames on the road ahead, and that's when Billy Ray made his next prudent and practical calculation. Maybe cops already on the scene meant things were over, but maybe not, and, again, it didn't pay to go barging into the middle of things without knowing the whole score. Besides, if things *were* over, as mad as the county cops seemed to now be with him, it wouldn't hurt to go about this in a way where, if he had to, Billy Ray could just sneak off without anybody knowing he'd ever been there. So, still around the curve and out of sight of the Shady Tree, Billy Ray pulled his car off the road, parking it deep in the shadows of the trees there. Then he climbed out, drew his .357 and started loping toward the motel.

After which nothing Billy Ray did was so much as prudent and practical as it was skilled stalking. Even Billy Ray's most ardent detractors gave him this; that those hours he'd spent with his daddy chasing white-tail around the public lands had left Billy Ray one of the best trackers, stalkers, and shooters you were likely to meet in that part of east Texas, and now those few – but exquisitely refined – talents of his came into play.

It looked to Billy Ray like the police flashers were parked close to the entrance of the Shady Tree's parking lot, so he decided to flank whatever was in the lot by creeping along the outside of the L made by the two wings of the building. At the junction of the two wings was a breezeway where the management had installed a bank of vending machines and an ice maker.

Billy Ray stopped at the entrance to the breezeway. He could hear voices from the parking lot, but they were echoing off the cinderblock walls of the motel and he couldn't quite make out what anybody was saying. One was a woman, sounding pleading and frantic. The other was a man's voice, quieter, calm. Billy Ray tiptoed along the bank of machines and their displays of Cokes and Lorna Doones and Cheetos, and made a mental note to get himself a soft drink and a bag of those Cheetos later because he couldn't remember when he last ate and he was starved. He stopped where the breezeway opened onto the swimming pool area, and peeked around the corner of the entryway, and said, "I'll be damned."

The good news, by his figuring, was that the police car out there was not a county sheriff's or Trinity unit. The bad news was that it belonged to Clyde Thomas who he saw standing not far from it alongside Bob Wheeler.

Off to the side was that colored reporter lady from Los Angeles, Rita Scott; hers was the woman's voice.

Which Billy Ray thought to be *more* bad news for him once she got around to telling Clyde – if she hadn't already -- how she'd called in to the office and got Billy Ray on the phone and so on and so forth.

All of which Billy Ray put out of his mind, as a good hunter should, then he went up high on his toes to see over the tops of the lounge chairs scattered around the pool. He could see the backs of two people kneeling in the parking lot. The man was Black, the woman was white, and neither one looked like they were wearing much of anything. Billy Ray guessed them to be Sarah Dawson and companion. Billy Ray studied the woman for a moment, trying to figure out what it was she was wearing, and once he did, shook his head and thought it was no wonder the preacher had gotten so all fired up about her running off.

And then there was the preacher himself, standing behind the two kneeling people. He was in his dark minister's suit which made a good match for the black metal of the Winchester pump in his hands. The preacher's back was to Billy Ray, which kept Billy Ray from being able to clearly hear what he was saying to Rita Scott.

Doesn't matter, he told himself as he cocked his pistol, long as she keeps his attention.

He could hear a flood of closing sirens. Those would definitely be from Trinity and/or the county sheriff. He didn't have much time to make his move.

He bent into a crouch and walked quietly on deft, light feet away from the walkway lamps and bug lights, moving toward the pool, dropping down behind one of the wooden sun loungers. He waited a moment, listening. Good, he thought, nobody'd seen him, their attention was all on Owen Dawson.

He chanced another quick, quiet move to another sun lounger further up, but that was as close as he dared get. He wasn't worried about drawing Dawson's attention so much as maybe catching the eye of the colored lady or Clyde and Bob Wheeler, and their reaction tipping off the preacher. Billy Ray set the wrist of his gun hand on the rim of the lounger's seat back and, like Daddy had taught him, brought the muzzle down letting the blade sight fall on his target. Aim center-mass, Daddy had taught him, widest part of the target so even if you're a little off or if he jumps, you'll still catch a piece.

The parking lot went quiet; the talking had stopped. Billy Ray could see Owen Dawson seem to sag, his shotgun lowering and pointing away from the two people kneeling in front of him.

Oh, man, *perfect!* thought Billy Ray. Even if Dawson twitched at the impact and his gun went off, nobody else'd be hurt.

Quite pleased with the circumstances, Billy Ray did like his Daddy had taught him, took a breath, let half of it out, then firmly squeezed the trigger.

Rita Scott had covered wars and riots and police shootouts, and working for Eric Bird III, she had also covered any number of grotesque and macabre incidents which had also left her well-acquainted with the sound of a gunshot. But, as a rule, she had been somewhere *behind* the gun in action, and its sound had typically been a surprisingly dull *pop.* She had never been almost directly in front of one, and the experience was quite different; a knifing crack and a vague, quickly passing pressure on her face – like a gust of breath – as the shock wave passed by her.

And there was something else; a fine, warm spray on her face.

She wasn't sure where the shot came from, but she knew immediately where it was going. She saw Owen Dawson shudder, and his face turned mildly surprised.

Rita touched at her face, at the spray, and saw her fingertips come away dark. The bullet must have passed clear through Owen Dawson. She was wearing his blood.

Owen Dawson stood for a moment, a long moment, so long the two people kneeling in front of him braved the shotgun to turn around to see what was going to happen next and what was, hopefully, *not* going to happen.

Still, Owen Dawson stood unmoving, and then another moment passed, and his body began to quiver, as if he had a chill. His arms began to droop as he began to lose the strength to hold them up, and the shotgun finally slipped from his fingers and clattered to the gravel.

Leroi Jefferson did not wait for further clarification of his fate. He scrambled to his feet and pulled Sarah Dawson along with him so quickly she stumbled out of one of her spiked heels.

Owen's legs began to waver. Slowly, he settled down on one knee, then the other knee came down to the ground alongside.

"I get 'im? Clyde, did I get 'im?"

She looked across the pool and saw an excited Billy Ray Barnes standing behind one of the loungers, his smoking pistol still trained on Owen Dawson.

"I got 'im, didn't I?" He was sure, now, and elated. "God*damn!*"

"Leroi! No!"

It was Sarah Dawson, and Rita turned to see her trying to hold back Leroi Jefferson who was dragging her along as he charged back toward Owen Dawson. The boy reached for the shotgun lying on the ground, and his fingers were just short of it when Clyde Thomas' boot came down on the Winchester.

"Haven't we had enough, Leroi?" Clyde said. He picked up the shotgun and tossed it back to Bob Wheeler. "Keep an eye on 'at, Bob." Then, to Leroi Jefferson and Sarah Dawson: "I suggest y'all get on back to your room 'n' stay there, maybe get some clothes on. Miz Dawson?" He tossed her her stray stiletto heel. He turned to Billy Ray.

"Hey, Clyde!" Billy Ray bubbled. "You don't know how lucky this all -- "

Clyde grabbed the pistol out of Billy Ray's hand and backhanded him across the face so hard Billy Ray staggered back a few steps until he fell on his rear.

"Jesus Christ, Clyde! What a hell's -- "

"Just haul your ass over to my car 'n' radio for an ambalance!" Clyde ordered.

Billy Ray didn't move, sat there on the ground with one hand cupped over the glowing red mark on his face, his eyes blinking with confusion.

Clyde's hand flexed around Billy Ray's pistol like he was considering using it, so when Clyde barked *"Now!"* Billy Ray didn't waste any time scrambling to obey.

The shotgun hit the ground again.

Rita Scott turned. Bob Wheeler had let the Winchester go. He walked to Owen Dawson and knelt by his side, put his arm around the younger man's shoulders. "Owen?"

Owen was beginning to hunch over.

"I'm here, Owen."

Rita knelt at Owen's other side. She saw he was coughing up blood.

The sirens were there, now, filling the grounds of the Shady Tree with flashing lights as she heard cars skid to a halt behind her.

There were tears running down Rita Scott's face, as they mixed with the blood on her cheeks and left little round stains down the front of her blouse. From somewhere across the road Rita heard a dog howling.

Owen looked up at the sound of the dog, then he turned to Rita with a sad smile framed by rivulets of blood. "Way of the world," he said in a whisper.

And then Owen Dawson faded, his body going slack, slumping forward until his face touched the dirt and stones, but still on his knees under a heartless sky and mindless stars.

EPITAPH

"I don't know what all this crap is," Hank Fletcher said to Smitty McKee. Hank was looking over several sketches Smitty had set out on the bar of the Horseshoe while his hands signaled W.D. for another strike at old center target.

"It's a bathroom, Hank. Ya wanted to upgrade a bathroom, *that's* a bathroom. I know I ain't DaVinci, but can't ya tell a toilet?" Smitty said. "'N' this here -- "

"I *got* that," Hank said, a little peeved. "But I mean all this other...*stuff*. I was just spectin' a plain ol' crapper where ya go to read the sports section 'n' take a dump. *This* -- " and here he made an ornate flourish of his hands above the sketches, " -- is like somethin' outta them *Star Wars* pitchers. I'm just lookin' to boost the askin' price on this shack a couple grand, Smitty. I'm not tryin' to get some goddamn A-rab *sheik* in there."

"Look, Hank, ya wanna go low, I'll build ya a shithouse out back."

"Now don't go gettin' all sore," Hank said. "I'm just sayin', well, maybe can we trim some a this stuff down? I mean like what-all is this light here in a shower stall for?"

"You gotta see that dirt, Hank."

Cecil Tredway broke up the debate with a shrieking whistle. "It's on!" he called and that superseded all other barroom activities and distractions. "Hey, W.D.! Turn it up!"

W.D. turned up the sound on the TV over the bar so they could better hear the reportage on Owen Dawson and his bizarre last few days including his sojourn down Route 19 and his dramatic *coups de grace* at the Shady Tree. It was a top story on all stations, including the national cable news networks. This extensive coverage was not due to any great impact Dawson's death had on the national consciousness at large, or because the story was felt to have any major social or cultural significance or impact on the debate of police use of excessive force, or even because anyone thought it to be exceptionally tragic. The decision derived from the simple fact that broadcast news editors had gotten their hands on dupes of the recording in Owen Dawson's camera, and watching a man get shot down on TV after threatening his lingerie-clad wife and her lover was thought to be a sure ratings-booster.

The particular newscast on W.D.'s television ran the sequence of Dawson's shooting a number of times: twice at normal speed, and then in slow motion, and then again in *super* slow motion with the off-screen reporter commenting on the action.

"It's like the damn Super Bowl," W.D. said disgustedly.

"Shame they only got the one angle," Cecil Tredway said. "Alls y'all gets to see a ol' Billy Ray is that flash over to the side."

"Sorry, Cecil, maybe next time someone'll let ESPN in on it so y'all can get a dee-luxe coverage," W.D. said.

"Whatchall gettin' so sore 'bout, W.D.? I'm just sayin' -- ..." In a rare attack of common sense, Cecil shut himself up before making things worse.

"Hey, that *was* a helluva shot, W.D., ya gotta admit," Hank Fletcher said. "Whadya figger, Smitty? Twenty, twenty-five yards? In the dark?"

"Maybe close to thirty," Smitty said with respect.

"Didn't think Billy Ray was that good at *nothin'*," Cecil Tredway said.

"He shoulda said somethin'," Smitty McKee said ruminatively.

"Who? Billy Ray?" W.D. asked.

"Naw, the preacher. That day he was in here, he shoulda said somethin'. Told us what-all he was up to. Maybe nobody woulda give 'im such a hard time he told us what he was up to." Smitty McKee leaned forward, sharing a secret: "Tell y'all the truth, I could name y'all 'bout two dozen ol' boys woulda *helped* 'im iffen they knowed he was after some nigger puttin' it to his wife."

"Hey, his *wife* shoulda told us what *she* was up to!" Cecil Tredway leered. "I know *three* dozen guys woulda helped *her* out! 'N' she wouldna had to do no coon huntin' for it neither!"

"Hell, Cecil," Hank said, "she see *you* in the buff 'n' she woulda started thinkin' she mighta been better off with somebody a the bull dike persuasion!"

They all laughed liquory laughs.

"Now *that'd* be somethin' I'd like to see on TV!" Smitty McKee said and they all laughed their boozey laughs again.

The newscast was running videotape of Mr. Kirkland. The camera crew had caught him locking up his store and without looking up at the camera Mr.

Kirkland was mumbling something along the lines of, "I don't tell people what to do with them; I just sell them."

Cecil Tredway started doing an imitation of Mr. Kirkland selling someone a flamethrower and saying, "Well, what you do with it is your business. I just sell 'em."

W.D. watched them make jokes and laugh and thought – not for the first time – he should go into another line of business. Something that didn't deal with people so much.

He took a bottle of good stuff from the rack behind the bar, grabbed himself a shot glass and walked to the back booth where Thelma Plover was buried in an especially deep mope over her own glass. She didn't even look up when W.D. topped off her glass, then poured himself a shot and sat across from her. "Y'ok there, Thelma?" he asked.

"I thought he was gonna make a love story," she slurred. "I thought he was gonna make a love story with a happy endin'." She studied her drink the way long-time drinkers do much of the time, like she was briefly considering pushing it aside, drying out, cleaning up, and changing her entire life. But then she picked up the glass and took a deep swig. She focused her red-rimmed eyes on W.D. "How come they-all don't make no love stories with happy endin's no more?"

W.D. topped off her glass again and took a sip of his own drink. "They just don't."

The day after Owen Dawson's death, Randolph Archibald "Spook" Jackson, county prisoner number 05144, awaiting arraignment on multiple felony charges ranging from armed robbery to attempted rape, was sharing a cell designed for two in the county lock-up with three other black guys.

After evening chow, Spook and his three cellmates were returned to their cramped cell and bumped and scuffled around each other until they managed to get into their bunks and out of each other's way. From somewhere far down the cellblock, they could hear watery echoes from the radio the block guard kept on his desk. Spook heard the story of Owen Dawson on the radio. As the newscaster traced Dawson's path down Route 19, the incidents at Byrum's shooting range, and the Quikie Mart, Spook propped himself up on an elbow on his lower bunk, surprised with recognition. He rolled over in his bunk to hear the radio better.

When the story was over, Spook lay back on his bunk, chuckling. "What goes around comes around."

One of his cellmates leaned over. "Whazzat? You say sumpin', bra?"

Spook shook his head. "Nothin'."

It was well into evening when Clyde Thomas went into the little space between his trailer home and the next one and fired up his barbecue grill. Clyde was never one just to throw some charcoal into the bowl, douse it with lighter fluid and set it off. He always built a neat pyramid of briquettes sure that this channeled the heat better, and used the lighter fluid sparingly, just enough to get the coals going but not enough to get the taste of the fluid onto the bars of the grill and from there into the meat.

But this time Clyde wasn't cooking and he wasn't so careful. He filled the bowl with briquettes and sprayed them heavily with lighter fluid. And then in the middle he set the paper bag he'd taken from behind Sarah Dawson's dresser drawer, and soaked that heavily with lighter fluid as well. He tossed in a match, the fluid lit off with a soft *whuff* and flame jumped up a good few feet.

Clyde opened a can of beer and sat nearby in a lawn chair, and every time the flame started to lower he gave it another squirt of lighter fluid. It didn't take long before the air was heavy not only with the smells of charcoal and lighter fluid, but also with the particularly unpleasant stink of burning plastic and nylon and polyester.

"Kind a hot for a barbecue, ain't it, Clyde?" one of Clyde's neighbors called.

"Never too hot for a barbecue," Clyde said.

But then the neighbor got a whiff of the smoke coming off the coals. "Jesus, Clyde! Wazzat stink? You cookin' with turpentine or somethin'?"

"Not cookin' nothin'," Clyde said. He gave the fire another squirt of lighter fluid, then settled deep in his chair and took a sip of his beer. "Just burnin' some trash."

His Honor Mayor Fred C. Reilly called up a friend with connections to the Dallas Police Department to see if he could get a copy of one of the Dallas P.D.'s commendations for bravery. There had never been a police citation for bravery issued in Boone, at least not within the living memory of Fred C. Reilly or anybody in his administration, and he wanted to see what one looked like.

The mayor awarded the aforementioned citation for bravery to Patrol Officer William Ray Barnes out on the front steps of the town hall two days after Owen Dawson's death, with Elwood Poteet and some out-of-town press people in attendance, taking photographs, shooting video snippets for the local TV news. Mayor Reilly tried to hand the roll of paper tied with a red ribbon to Billy Ray with one hand and shake his free hand with the other, but neither of them could seem to figure out which hand was supposed to go where and their hands darted in and out amongst each other like a bunch of dueling snakes.

After they finally got the handshake business sorted out and after the mayor handed the citation over, Fred C. Reilly made some generous comments to the press people about P.O. Barnes' courage and commitment to duty, and his going above and beyond and so on and so forth. Out of the corner of his eye, the mayor saw Billy Ray starting to untie the red ribbon. Never letting his professional mayoral smile droop in the slightest, His Honor leaned over and whispered in Billy Ray's ear to leave the goddamn ribbon alone because all Billy Ray was holding was a rolled up sheet of blank paper. "We don't have the citation proper printed up yet," he explained, "but we'll hustle that over to ya soon's we get it from the printer."

The photographers took a few more pictures and the TV crews another video clip or two, and then Fred C. Reilly thanked them all for coming and guided Billy Ray into his office to "extend my own, *personal* congratulations."

The mayor's town hall office was more magisterial than the office Fred C. Reilly's kept at his "bidness," what with its shiny oak desk and a lot less clutter, but Boone was a small town and the town hall a small town hall, so not by much. Fred C. Reilly offered a cushy chair across from his desk to Billy Ray and took his own seat in a padded leather throne behind the desk.

Billy Ray gaped at the photo just over Fred C. Reilly's head showing him and George W. Bush. "Ya had your pitcher taken with the *president?*"

Fred C. Reilly gave a shrug calibrated to look like a modest it's-no-big-deal gesture which was a neat way of letting the photo lie for him. "Got somethin' here for ya, son." Fred C. Reilly reached into a desk drawer and set a box of Robustos on his desk. He opened the box and handed Billy Ray one of the aluminum tubes and took another for himself.

"I thought nobody could get these," Billy Ray said trying to figure out how to get into the aluminum tube. "Isn't it against the law or somethin'?"

The mayor opened his own tube, ahem-ing to get Billy Ray's attention so he could see how it was done. "Nah, 's ok, now, ya know, we're all suppose' to be buddies again, us 'n' our Cubano amigos. I used to still get 'em back when you wa'n' suppose' to. Had a friend worked the port down to Houston," the mayor said. "'N' he' had a friend who's got a friend… ya know how it is." Again, all very nonchalant; that's just how things run for we the powerful.

Billy Ray had finally managed to get the tube open and was running the thick body of the cigar under his nose. "Mmmm. That ain't zackly no White Owl cherry flavor!"

"Know your cigars, son?"

"Not really, sir."

"But you know what you like."

"I guess." Billy Ray bit off the tip, wasn't sure what to do with it so he unobtrusively slipped it into his pocket. The mayor tossed him a box of wood matches and the two of them lit up and soon filled the office with a rich, blue smoke that made Billy Ray think of a sunny afternoon on the beach at Galveston with a fishing pole stuck in the sand, a cold can of Pearl in one hand, his Robusto in the other, and a bikinied Arva May bouncing around in the low waves.

The two of them sat quietly for a second, basking in the aroma.

"How's that cigar?" Fred C. Reilly finally asked.

"Damn fine, Mayor, thanks. Ya know, I woulda thought the chief shoulda been there today. Official ceremony 'n' all. I mean, I know Clyde 'n' me don't zackly see eye-to-eye on what-all happened out there -- "

"Don't you fret none 'bout 'at, son."

"I mean, where I was, I couldn't hear nothin'. Clyde says he was gonna give up but *I* couldn't tell nothin' like that! All I saw was a mental subject with a gun threatenin' harm -- "

"Son, I'm with *you*," calmed Fred C. Reilly. "That's why ya were out there today."

"'N' I seen where some a the news on TV is makin' out like it's the Wild West or somethin' out here -- "

Fred C. Reilly dismissed those cavils with a lazy wave of his arm. "That's those fellas think the way ya deal with a nut with a gun is to get a po-lice psychologist to talk to 'im for a couple days 'til ya bore 'em to death. Listen, son, I said don't fret, so don't fret. Way I see it, this town's been takin' it on the chin last couple days ever since that big mouth Poteet let the story out 'bout Dawson 'n' his damn movie. Well, now the people a this town – 'n' that's all who counts, son, don't forget that; the people who live *here* – know we got law 'n' order here, 'n' there's only so much nonsense we're gonna take. Even from a church preacher."

"I 'ppreciate that, Mayor."

The mayor rolled his cigar to the center of his mouth, leaned back in his chair and placed his arms atop the bulge of his belly. He took a few meditative puffs. "Fact is," he said around his cigar, "I didn't want Clyde there today. No disrespect meant." He offered Billy Ray a drink of cold water or a soft drink or a glass of sweet tea or even something stronger if he was of a mind, but Billy Ray said No, thank you, officially he was still on duty. Mayor Fred C. Reilly smiled proudly. "See, *that's* why ya were out there today, son. Ya got a sense a duty. 'N' initiative. 'N' ya aren't 'fraid to take decisive action when it comes down to it."

Billy Ray sat up a little straighter in his chair. "I try my best, Mayor."

"I know ya do, son, I know ya do." The mayor put his head back, sent puffs of blue smoke toward the ceiling. "Clyde Thomas is tired, son. He's been chief here a long time. Done a right good job, too. I wouldna left 'im in there all these years otherwise. But he's had his time, know what I mean? There's an election comin' up next year, 'n' I don't mind tellin' ya it wouldn't hurt me to get some new blood in that chief's spot. Somebody the people a this town got a new respect for."

Billy Ray was still a thought or two behind the mayor. "I didn't know Clyde's been thinkin' a retirin'."

Fred C. Reilly looked at Billy Ray with a small, sly smile. "Welllll, he's not thinkin' 'bout it just yet. But he will."

The mayor waited patiently for the enlightened look to show up in Billy Ray Barnes' face. He had a long wait.

But finally, Billy Ray smiled, too. He lounged back in his chair and put a booted ankle casually across the top of the opposite knee. "Ya know, Mayor, I *am* a might thirsty. I'll take that drink now iffen you don't mind."

On account of the exceptional heat of the afternoon, Mrs. Dailey, Mrs. Hanratty and Mrs. Ledbetter had opted to lunch indoors. They were at Mrs. Hanratty's house, all three lined up on Mrs. Hanratty's floral sofa watching the news on television. Actually, Mrs. Dailey and Mrs. Ledbetter were doing most of the watching while Mrs. Hanratty fiddled with the lace antimacassar on her sofa arm wondering why her tatting always came out lopsided.

The newscast was dishing up yet another recap of Owen Dawson's video, but now with the addendum of Billy Ray Barnes' getting his gift-wrapped blank piece of paper in front of city hall that morning.

"I don't know why they have to show that on television," Mrs. Hanratty said, trying to re-arrange the antimacassar so nobody could tell how off the pattern was.

"Well, I'm no fan of that Billy Ray Barnes, neither," Mrs. Dailey said. "Fella don't have 'nough sense to come in out the rain."

"No, I don't mean that," Mrs. Hanratty said. "The *other* thing. I don't know why they have to show it. 'N' *keep* showin' it. We all *know* what happened."

"No one's holding a gun to your head 'n' making you look," Mrs. Dailey said.

"I *didn't* look," Mrs. Hanratty said. "I looked away."

"It's hard not to look," Mrs. Ledbetter said apologetically.

"*I* didn't look," Mrs. Hanratty reiterated.

"Oh, they have things like this on the TV every day," Mrs. Dailey pooh-poohed them both. "The only difference is we knew *this* fella."

"I still don't think it's right they show it," Mrs. Hanratty said.

"Such a shame," Mrs. Ledbetter said. "He was one a the best preachers St. Mark's ever had. I think he was the youngest one, too." She turned to Mrs. Hanratty. "He *was* the youngest, wasn't he?"

"Of course he was," Mrs. Dailey said, annoyed. "You don't 'member anything right."

"That's not true!" Mrs. Ledbetter said. "I do so 'member!"

"I didn't say you didn't 'member," Mrs. Dailey corrected, "I said you didn't 'member *right!*"

"I do so!" Mrs. Ledbetter protested. "Reverend Dawson was the youngest preacher we ever had here! 'N' everybody loved 'im!"

"Everybody *didn't* love 'im," Mrs. Dailey said. "Most people *liked* 'im. They didn't *love* 'im."

"He always seemed a decent 'nough fella," Mrs. Ledbetter said.

"Yeah," Mrs. Dailey said, "'Til we all found out what a *loon* he was!"

"People *did* love him," Mrs. Hanratty put in. "If he heard you were sick, he was there. Christmas, he always did 'at special service up to Grapeland to let the seniors know they weren't forgotten on a holiday. He was good with the young people, too. Those magic shows at Christmas -- "

"How long has he been here?" Mrs. Ledbetter wondered.

"See?" Mrs. Dailey said. "You *don't* 'member!"

"Three years?" Mrs. Ledbetter guessed. "Four years? Does that sound right?"

"It was the summer Charlotte Aubrey broke her hip," Mrs. Hanratty said. "Are you sure?"

"He stood up there in that pulpit 'n' asked everybody to pray for her 'cause she broke her hip."

"I don't 'member 'at."

Mrs. Dailey gave Mrs. Ledbetter a this-is-what-I'm-talking-about look. "It was three years ago!" she stated emphatically. "Charlotte broke her hip, her son couldn't wait to ship her off to Grapeland, put her house up for sale, 'n' use the money to buy one a those drywall monstrosities Hank Fletcher is always trying to pawn off. That was three years ago! Keep up like this 'n' *you're* gonna wind up up to Grapeland sittin' there with yer oatmeal 'n' medications!" The Owen Dawson story finished, and Billy Ray Barnes smiled at the cameras brandishing his ribbon-tied scroll. "They'll be givin' badges to monkeys next," Mrs. Dailey groused at the images of Billy Ray. "What I'd *really* like 'em to show is that tramp wife a his."

"They *did*," Mrs. Ledbetter said. "But they had her face all fogged up. Her 'n' that colored boy."

"They shoulda showed her face," Mrs. Dailey said sternly. "Like in the old days. Like in the Bible days. Stone the harlot."

"I don't think it's nice to talk 'bout her like that," Mrs. Hanratty said. "Leastways not right now with her loss 'n' all."

Mrs. Dailey looked irritated. "Why not? It's in every paper in the country by now, I'm sure! It's all over the TV! It's no secret. The woman was a tramp, plain 'n' simple! That's what everybody's thinkin' 'bout Boone! Place is full a tramps 'n' loons! The fair thing woulda been if he'd killt her 'n' 'at nigger 'fore they got 'im! *That* woulda been fair!"

"What a horrible thing to say!" Mrs. Ledbetter said.

"I'm sorry, I have somethin' on my mind 'n' I say it!" said Mrs. Dailey.

"Well, I'm sorry, but I liked her," Mrs. Hanratty said with just a touch of defiance. "I mean, I don't know 'bout all this thing on the news, but I always thought she was nice. I know *you* never liked her -- "

"*Nobody* liked her," Mrs. Dailey snarled.

"*I* liked her."

"*You* like *everyone*," Mrs. Daily said. "I 'member you even liked that fella replaced Pat Sajack on *Wheel a Fortune*."

"When did they replace Pat?" Mrs. Ledbetter asked, alarmed.

"It was on the daytime show," Mrs. Dailey said, shaking her head over Mrs. Ledbetter. "*Years* ago. *I* 'member! *You* never 'member *anything* right."

"I do so!" Mrs. Hanratty protested. "He was some athlete. He was good-lookin'."

"He was *awful,*" Mrs. Dailey said.

"Oh!" Mrs. Hanratty said, sitting up suddenly. "That 'minds me!" She stood, went over to the TV and turned the channel to *Wheel of Fortune.* "No more a this talk 'bout the reverend 'n' all that misfortune. Times're sad 'nough. Now; who would like some more sweet tea?"

"I can't print it, love," Eric Bird III said and tapped the sheets of paper neatly stacked and sitting square and alone in the middle of the polished top of his desk. His lips were pursed, his face possessed of a gravity Rita Scott had not thought him to have at his disposal.

She nodded, unsurprised.

"No juice."

"No juice," she said.

"All squeezed out, love."

"Too small a body count?" she asked. "One man dying doesn't quite come up to our journalistic standards?"

He smiled tolerantly. "It's that video."

"Ahh."

"It's everywhere. How'd *that* happen?"

She shrugged tiredly. "It was on the internet by the next day, then everybody and his brother was downloading it, and after that it was everywhere. Like the flu."

"That doesn't leave us much to give the readership that they haven't already seen, then, does it, love?"

"Nope. I guess we lose our TV scoop, too."

"So it would seem. You look tired, love."

"I *am* tired, Eric." She turned to lazily look out the windows of Eric Bird III's office. The city's night lights were starting to come up, soft, suffused glows in the smog. The night always made the clean, uncluttered lines of Eric Bird's office feel cold, tomblike. "*Very* tired. I haven't been home yet, Eric. I need a bath. I need something to eat. I need to climb into bed for about a year." She pulled herself stiffly out of the plush chair and headed for the door.

"Rita, love? This -- " and he tapped the copy on his desk " – is very good. *We* couldn't run it; you *know* that. Insightful, personal observation, social commentary…not exactly our shtick, is it?"

"No." She reached for the doorknob.

"I do have connections in what is euphemistically referred to as the 'legit' press. They like to keep in touch with me." He smiled wryly. "It's good for their sense of integrity. Makes them feel better about themselves. If you don't mind, I'd like to show it to some of them. I think it might make a good fit for one of their rags. As I say; only if you don't mind."

"I don't mind."

"Of course, a placement in something like *Time* or *Mother Jones* will forever compromise your reputation with the tabloid community. If you can live with that."

"I can live with that."

"I owe you some vacation time, too, don't I? I'll see you next Monday."

"Thank you, Eric."

She opened the door.

"Something out there got to you, love."

"Yes, Eric."

"Him? The story? Texas?"

"All of it."

He nodded. He stared down into the gleaming black top of his desk at his own, ghostly reflection. "'For now we see through a glass, darkly," he intoned, "'but then face to face. Now I know in part; but then shall I know even as also I am known.'" Then, in answer to her curious look, he replied, "I never told you I was an altar boy when I was young?"

She shook her head.

He saw another unasked question in her face. "Nothing's worse than a fallen angel, love."

"Yeah," she said, and went home.

No one wanted Owen Dawson's body. Dawson's corpse sat two days in a morgue drawer at Boone County General while the county, Trinity, and Boone powers-that-be fought over who was going to have to pay to put it in the ground.

The Shady Tree's address put it in Trinity, but the Trinity P.D. claimed the motel actually sat outside the town limits which made custody of Dawson's body a county problem. But when Barney White got the body at Boone General, he said that Billy Ray Barnes' poking into that body they all thought might've been Sarah Dawson but had turned out to be Jesse Smith meant Boone had exerted jurisdiction in the case which made Owen Dawson's remains *their* problem, and that if they didn't willingly take possession of the body, Barney White swore to God he'd commandeer himself a Boone General ambulance and leave Dawson's corpse on the front steps of the Boone town hall.

Fred C. Reilly approached the board at St. Mark's, who said there was no way they were putting up the money to bury Owen Dawson after the way he'd disgraced the church, and then the mayor tried Dawson's superior, Reverend Harper, who told him no way was the Methodist Church going to take responsibility for burying a madman like Owen Dawson for pretty much the same reasons, and phone calls to Dawson's kin up north went unanswered, and Sarah Dawson seemed to have disappeared.

Clyde Thomas finally convinced His Honor to authorize a small amount of money for a cheap, quick burial. Clyde pointed out that Boone had already received plenty of negative attention in the national media. The marital oddities of the Dawsons and the spectacular bringing-down of the reverend had been elevated to national prominence thanks to Owen Dawson's widely-distributed video. Owen Dawson's persistence in remaining aboveground only threatened to give the press a reason to extend the story with an even more unflattering denouement.

"This is like a dead fish," Clyde advised the mayor. "The longer you leave it up in the sun, the more it's gonna stink. Do yourself a favor, Fred, 'n' get the poor bastard inna ground."

So, Mayor Fred C. Reilly had the check cut and the arrangements made, although he continued to fulminate to all and any about the outside pressures forcing him to do so. "They're all makin' us sound like a bunch a two-bit lynchin' redneck yahoos," he would say. "But see which a them woulda let 'im baptize *their* kids!"

Mr. And Mrs. Bob Wheeler stood at Owen Dawson's graveside along with Mr. and Mrs. Elwood Poteet. Standing a discreet distance away were two gravediggers and a backhoe driver propped against his rig. There was no minister, no one spoke over the grave. Elwood Poteet kept looking at the clouds thickening overhead and hoped he would beat the rain home.

The casket was of plain wood, and the grave was in a part of the cemetery where gravestones were small, plain markers laid flush in the ground. Dawson's marker stated his name, the year of his birth, the year of his death, and nothing more.

After the casket was lowered into the ground, Mrs. Wheeler and Mrs. Poteet went back to their cars, and Bob Wheeler and Elwood Poteet stood by while the backhoe driver pulled his rig up and began pulling dirt into the grave. The backhoe was still at work when Clyde Thomas pulled up in his patrol car. He climbed out of his car and walked toward the grave. He was wearing his seersucker suit.

Clyde stood with Bob Wheeler and Elwood Poteet, his hat in his hands. "Anybody else come?" Clyde asked, and the other two men shook their heads.

"It was good you come," Bob Wheeler said.

Clyde shrugged.

The backhoe was finished. The two gravediggers stepped forward with rakes and shovels. They raked out the rocks and evened off the top of the grave making small puffs of dust in the dry earth.

"I keep wonderin'," Bob Wheeler said, "if maybe we could a done something different."

"Stop wonderin'," Clyde said. "Wouldna made no difference. I'm just sorry I didn't have 'nough sense to grab that camera right then 'n' there." Clyde shook his head at himself.

Bob rested a forgiving hand on the chief's shoulder.

Clyde swabbed the sweatband of his hat with his kerchief and put his Stetson back on his head. He looked up at the clouds getting darker. He sniffed at the breeze, at the damp scent coming in. "Feels like rain."

"'Bout time," Bob Wheeler said. "Cool things off."

"He'll have fresh grass, then," Elwood Poteet said.

Bob Wheeler took Clyde aside. "That stuff a Sarah's…"

"Gone," Clyde said.

"Gone?"

"A lotta people're hurt bad enough, dontcha think?"

Clyde and Bob Wheeler and Elwood Poteet said goodbye to each other, then headed back to their cars and drove off their separate ways.

And then the rain started to fall.

Bill Mesce, Jr. is an award-winning author and playwright as well as a screenwriter. He is an adjunct instructor at several colleges in his native New Jersey.